SeaBEAN
the trilogy

To Destiny
You can do whatever
you want when you
grow up!

Published by
Medina Publishing Ltd
310 Ewell Road
Surbiton
Surrey KT6 7AL
United Kingdom
medinapublishing.com

ISBN: 978-1-911487-07-4

Printed and bound in Great Britain by Clays Ltd, Elcograf S.p.A.

Map illustrations by Louis Holding

CIP Data: A catalogue record for this book is available
from the British Library

Sarah Holding asserts her moral right to be identified
as the author of this book

Cover designed by Taslima Begum

SeaBEAN
the trilogy

SARAH HOLDING

Medina Publishing

Reviews of SeaBEAN

"... griping, capturing, unputdownable ... an exciting and imaginative book."
The Guardian

"I am giving SeaBEAN to my 8-year-old twin grandchildren to read...they are going to be captivated by the hero of the story, 11-year-old Alice."
Huffington Post

"Flawlessly written, the language is simple and straightforward but not condescending for young readers ... the pace romps along with constant changes of venue and lots of adventure."
Best Book Review

"An absorbing and intelligent tale with a strong environmental angle."
The Swallow's Nest

"There's no feeling that you are reading a children's book, as the language is clear and intelligent ... Highly recommended."
GoodReads

"... a different way of introducing children to environmental issues."
Dame Jacqueline Wilson DBE FRSL

"Think Secret Island meets Doctor Who's Tardis and Greenpeace Junior. This non-stop adventure will excite imagionations and stimulate eco-debates."
The Rt Hon Sir Edward Davey , MP

"Sarah Holding has very cleverly woven contemporary issues and concerns affecting St Kilda, Scotland and the world into a great kids' adventure story."
Susan Bain, Western Isles Manager, National Trust for Scotland

Reviews of SeaWAR

"The book is really fast paced and packed full of adventure, it's definitely a good book for older children"
Compelling Reads

"SeaWAR is a great book that covers a lot of different aspects, like time travel, ghost stories, friendship, ecology and family history. This might seem too much for only 164 pages, but Holding has done a fantastic job knitting them all together in a marvellous story."
DJ, Edinburgh Book Review

"...entertaining and eminently readable... SeaWAR will engage the interest of readers aged 9 and over who enjoy intelligent adventure stories."
Safie Maken Finlay, The Swallows Nest

Reviews of SeaRISE

"SeaRISE is the latest installment in the SeaBEAN trilogy... Sarah Holding does a great job."
The Guardian

"The author has done a great job to try and teach children about the environment and how easily it can be destroyed, but also show how to care for it, and how to think about the effects their actions have."
GoodReads

"An unputdownable, exciting and surprisingly serious book, SeaRISE was a book that was so interesting it kept me glued to the sofa reading it... I thought it was brilliant and captivating and is a must-read for kids over 8."
The Guardian

Amazon reviews for The SeaBEAN Trilogy

***** *Inspiring read*
"My daughter loves this book. She read it because we were going to Costa Rica and then found some sea beans on the beach while we were there. She was so happy. Very inspirational."
K. Stritton, 21 February 2018

***** *Five stars*
"Great book looking forward to reading the rest of the trilogy."
Pete 51, 3 April 2015

***** *An excellent read!*
"A great book! I would recommend this to anybody without hesitation! It's an excellent book full of thrilling adventures with the C Bean, a Portuguese speaking parrot, a dog, and some adventurous children! I am thoroughly looking forward to the next one!"
ollyon, 18 November 2013

**** *An educational adventure fantasy with depth*
"... good, evocative writing, a strong narrative, engaging characters, an environmental message, and creative energy to burn. What a nice find."
Ancient Marineron, 7 April 2015

***** *An exciting children's adventure story*
"I thoroughly enjoyed this book. It is an exciting classic children's adventure story ... It is beautifully written, brings in current environmental issues and I particularly liked the portrayal of the main character, Alice, who is so very believable."
Susan Peterson, 23 October 2013

***** *A great mix of fact and fiction that should appeal widely*
"Thoroughly readable second episode in the series. A great mix of fact and fiction that should appeal widely to young and not-so-young readers."
martinr, 2 December 2014

To Louis, Ray and Nina

my reasons for being and my inspiration to write,
this trilogy is for you.

Contents

SeaBEAN

Book I

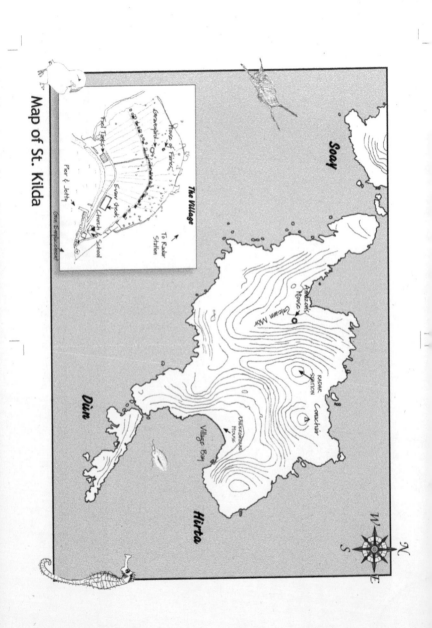

Map of St. Kilda

The Village

House of Fairies
Graveyard
Owen Gods
Post Office
Pier & Jetty
Church & School
To Radar Station
Gun Emplacement

Soay

Dùn

Hirta

Amazonic House
Oiseval Mòr
RADAR STATION
Conachair
Storehouse House
Village Bay

N W S E

Contents

No one noticed it at first; a strange black object bobbing in the steely grey water, drifting up the Mersey somewhere before daybreak. It was not until it appeared alongside a cruise ship returning from the Caribbean that it attracted any attention.

As the ship docked in Liverpool that dull November morning, the captain reported sighting an 'unexpected navigation buoy' that was not marked on his nautical charts and somehow seemed to be affecting his ship's navigation systems. The Port Authority sent an officer down to investigate, and by lunchtime a curious black cube measuring three metres on all sides was hoisted from the water and deposited on the dockside. It appeared to be not the slightest bit wet and had no identifying marks or features, except that when it was touched by human hands it temporarily changed colour from a dense black to an electric blue.

Tests showed that it failed to transmit a signal either via radar or GPS. The bomb disposal team was called in to carry out a thorough check. The cube-like object was reported as being of unknown origin, constructed of unknown but strangely magnetic materials, probably a foreign buoy that had drifted free from its original mooring. It was scheduled for removal to a landfill site.

Just before midnight, the dockside CCTV cameras picked up some unusual activity. A door opened on one side of the black cube, and a man with white hair stepped out, carrying a battered leather briefcase. The Port Authority failed to locate him with their thermal camera, but when security alerted Merseyside police on suspicion that a man with no staff pass or security clearance had just left the passenger terminal, they took him in for questioning.

Approximately two hours later, the man was released; no charges were made. He walked out of the police station and, stopping in front of the first postbox he encountered, took a large brown envelope from his briefcase, posted it and walked on.

Alice's Blog

1st January 2018

My name is Alice. I am ten years old and I live on a really small island called St Kilda, surrounded by weather, waves, and the rest of the world. My new year's resolution is to write a blog about everything that happens here, so people all over the world will be able to read about our life on St Kilda.

Until we came to live here five years ago, no one had lived on our island for eighty-three years. Well, there were some army people stationed here, but that doesn't really count. They were only here to look after the missile detector station on the top of the mountain. It must have been awful in the olden days because it takes hours to come across from the mainland by sea, mainly because the waves are so huge and powerful. But then someone realised they could get energy out of these waves. So now, my Dad, Charlie's dad and some other engineers are going to put wave machines out in the Atlantic near St Kilda, to make electricity for Scotland.

The first thing they did when we got here was build the Evaw shed down by the harbour (that's wave spelt backwards). Next, they are making and testing the wave machines inside it before they put them out in the actual sea.

So nowadays there are exactly ninety-nine people who live on my island, if you include old Jim and the army people. When my baby brother arrives in a few weeks, he will make it a hundred. One, two, skip and few, ninety-nine, a hundred. My Mum and Dad are thinking of calling him Ceud or Kiot, because it means a hundred in Gaelic. They're not Gaelic, and they don't even speak it, but on St Kilda that's what they all used to speak for centuries. Old Jim's the only one here who speaks Gaelic now.

Every hundred hours – well roughly every four days - the ferry comes from the mainland and unloads stuff onto the harbour. The weather is different every day here, so it's often a bit late or not at all, and Mrs Butterfield our shopkeeper goes mad because she's got customers waiting for toothpaste or toilet rolls. Last week they ran out of ketchup, which was a disaster, but Mum says not as much of a disaster as if they run out of nappies when my brother arrives.

My school is also exactly one hundred steps from my house, if you stretch your legs out properly when you walk and you only go in straight lines and do right angles when you go round corners. I usually count it every day, and for the last few weeks it's always been a hundred. When it's raining, I don't count because:

a) I am running in my wellingtons and

b) there are too many puddles to walk in straight lines.

I can't wait for my brother to arrive, because there just aren't enough children on my island. There are only six of us in my class, and my teacher, Mrs Robertson, who is also my Mum, says when we get up to ten she will see about getting us a class pet. Hannah, Edie and I want to get a dog, but the boys, Sam Fitzpatrick (he's the tall one), Sam Jackson (he's the adventurous one), and Charlie Cheung, who is nearly twelve, keep saying they want a fish tank. I think keeping fish in a tank is cruel. Anyway if you want to see fish you just need to go down to the harbour and ask one of the fishermen and they'll open up their polystyrene boxes and show you what they've caught.

7th January 2018

Yesterday we put all our Christmas decorations away. I don't like it much because the house is all bare now. Dad says next year we'll get a real tree with roots from the mainland so that after Christmas we can plant it in the garden and watch it grow. There aren't any trees on our island, so it will be nice to see it blowing in the wind and making a little shadow in our back yard. Mum and Dad say that in the old days the people who lived here didn't even have a word for tree because they'd never ever seen one.

Hogmanay was a lot of fun. That's what we call New Year's Eve in Scotland. There was a big announcement at the party: the people who own our island are giving us the chance to buy it, but they've said we've only got until May 1st to get enough money together — one million pounds — otherwise they're going to let it be sold to this Russian company that wants to set up an oil rig here and drill for oil. Dad says he's not going to let that happen — they're so close to making the wave energy project work, and an oil-rig would totally spoil St Kilda.

We have already saved four hundred thousand pounds from all the fund-raising we've done, and then just before Christmas Mr McLintock (the sort of mayor of our island) got a big cheque in the post for five hundred thousand pounds. He doesn't know who it came from, which is a shame because you should really write a nice thank-you letter when someone is as generous as that. Anyway, just to say, if anyone out there has a spare hundred thousand pounds, please let us know, because that's how much we still need, and then we can make our island safe and sound forever!

8th January 2018

It was our first day back at school today. Mum – I mean Mrs Robertson - let us bring in something we got for Christmas for show and tell. I was going to bring the thing I got in the toe of my stocking. At first I thought it was a walnut or an orange, but it's a sort of smooth brown stone that looks like a miniature hot cross bun. Mum and Dad both asked to have a proper look at it on Christmas Day morning, and they looked really puzzled and said they had no idea where it had come from. That makes it even more special. I have put it in the box beside my bed where I keep my favourite things.

Instead I took in my new watch that's a glow-in-the-dark stopwatch as well as a telling-the-time watch. Edie brought in her new compass, and her little sister Hannah, who's very artistic, brought in some drawings she'd done in her new sketchbook. Sam J got a toy fire engine. It's as red as his hair and is actually an American one because it has a stars-and-stripes flag on the side and says 'Fire Department New York' in big letters, but he insists it's a Scottish one. I suppose he wouldn't know because he's never seen a real fire engine. If there is a fire on our island, Mr McLintock gets in his truck with the hosepipe on the back. Last year, Davie Killigan had a fire in his woodshed, but he'd put it out himself before Mr McLintock got there.

Charlie is still in Hong Kong at his grandpa's while his Dad does some tests on the wave energy equipment there, so we don't know what he got for Christmas. He said he wanted a mobile phone, but I don't see why he needs one when you only need to stand outside your front door and shout if you want to get a message to anyone else around here. He sent me an email today to say it's still hot in Hong Kong, which is funny because it's been snowing a bit on St Kilda.

Mum made a special announcement at the end of the day. I knew she was going to say it because she was talking to Dad last night about how she'd got a letter from the Department of Education or something. She had a sort of sad-but-glad face when she told us she would only be our teacher for another few weeks. The people in charge of Scottish schools are sending over someone called Dr Foster to be our teacher while she is at home looking after my little brother. Mum said Dr Foster was from New York, just like Sam's fire engine.

Dad says that when my brother is born, Granny and Gramps and my big sister Lorina (Lori for short) will come and visit us by helicopter. Dad said he would pay even though it's really expensive, so that they could get here quickly without having to be seasick on the boat for hours and hours. He said as his parents are now both well past seventy it's only right. But it's not fair that Lori gets to go in the helicopter too because she is nowhere near seventy. Lori is going to be fifteen this month. She's at boarding school in Glasgow on the mainland, and so Granny and Gramps are going to meet Lori there and get in a helicopter and fly here.

My brother is due to arrive in between my birthday and Lori's birthday. Lucky Lori was born on 01/02/03 – that's onetwothree. Un Deux Trois, Lori likes to say in a funny accent. I was born on 20/01/07, which is a lot less interesting. Apart from the fact that, if you look on the Internet, it's the day that Barack Obama became president of America in 2009, and it's also the day that someone discovered Adelie Island in Antarctica in 1840. But that's nearly two hundred years ago. Even Granny and Gramps can't remember that.

Anyway, that's the end of my first blog. This is definitely the most I have ever written. Ever.

It was a cold, wet Tuesday afternoon. Alice trailed home from school up the grassy road, dragging her bag along behind her. She felt too tired to count her steps or even care that the bag was getting muddy. On the far side of Village Bay storm clouds gathered, and there was an ominous kind of mood, like something strange was going to happen. All along the top of the cliffs beyond the village she could see flocks of fulmars and other seabirds circling round and round, squawking and diving, unable to settle. In the olden days people had dangled barefoot on ropes off the cliffs to catch them and collect their eggs and even the bird droppings. Alice could hardly believe people would dare to do such a dangerous thing.

Mr McLintock passed in his truck and tooted his horn at Alice. She waved. He leaned out of the window as he drove slowly past up the grassy road.

'You better get home quick lovie, I think your Mum needs you.' He was about to say something else, but then he rolled up the window and stared straight ahead as he moved off down the slope.

Alice hitched her school bag over her shoulder and started walking a little faster. Her Mum always went home early on Tuesdays for an Internet meeting with the teachers from the other Hebridean Islands. The vicar, Reverend Sinclair, who was also the pharmacist, taught them history, 'thinking' and Religious Education on Tuesday afternoons. Alice liked doing 'thinking'. The vicar said things like: 'Walruses have moustaches. I have a moustache, therefore I am a walrus.' It made her laugh, even though the vicar was very serious. But she didn't find the history lessons quite so funny.

The vicar told them stories about the past on St Kilda – like the story about how a whole group of islanders decided to leave in 1852 because they were finding life too difficult, so they sailed on a boat called the Priscilla all the way to Australia. He told them there was a place by the sea there, in the city of Melbourne that was also called St Kilda, in memory of the few passengers from the island who survived the terrible journey.

Today the vicar had told them another awful story. The children listened with wide eyes:

'You know, children, for two hundred years most of the babies born on St Kilda died in the first week after they were born, but no one knew why. They think it was because they used to put oil on the babies from fulmars' feathers to keep them healthy, only the oil had got infected and it made them very sick and they died.'

The vicar said that lots of these babies were buried in the village graveyard. After he'd told them the sad story, the children all looked very upset. Alice felt sorry for the vicar, because he couldn't think logically how to cheer them up. But most of all she felt sorry for all the lost babies.

'So children,' the vicar concluded, and he sounded more like the pharmacist talking now, 'The good thing is, that was all a very long time ago, and we have lots of brilliant medicines now to fight all these diseases that babies used to get. Medicines that I have in the pharmacy right here on the island. In the last five years, apart from when young Samuel Jackson here broke his arm, no-one has had to leave the island by air ambulance to go to hospital, which is quite something.'

He looked around. Sam J and Sam F were poking each other with coloured pencils, and Edie was plaiting Hannah's hair. Alice looked at the clock. The vicar followed her gaze, and clapping his hands together said, 'Right then, off you go.'

Alice reached the back door of her house and shoved it open with her shoulder. She dropped her bag by the door and hung up her coat. Her dad was in his slippers pacing round the kitchen on the phone.

'Yes, well, I'd come right away if I were you. No, she's fine, thanks. Don't tell Lorina yet.'

'Don't tell Lori what, Dad?' Alice asked.

'Ah, poppet, you're home. Good. Put the kettle on, will you?' Her Dad looked flustered. 'Right, got to go now Gramps. I'll call you later.'

Alice moved slowly around the kitchen finding mugs and swilling out the teapot. Her dad wasn't usually home at this time. She had the feeling that maybe her parents had been arguing, and she hated it when they did. Her mum always said, 'It's being on the island, the long winters, and the never-ending wind, and the being cooped up, it's not natural. Sometimes you just have to let off steam. I still love your Daddy, of course,' she would add, and smile weakly.

'Dad, I need a hug. The vicar told us this horrible story today, and it's made me feel funny…' Alice stopped. Her dad bundled his arms around her and they stood still for a moment in the middle of the kitchen.

'Alice, Mum thinks the baby is coming.'

Silence.

'But it's too early yet, she said so.'

'I know, but you can't choose these things. A baby just comes when it comes.'

'Where is Mum?'

'In bed.'

'Can I go and see her?'

Alice's dad nodded and she went into her parents' room. Her mother was sitting up in bed, still wearing the clothes she'd worn at school.

'Hi Mum. Are you OK?'

'Yes, sweetie. Don't look so worried, it's going to be fine. Jim McLintock has just gone to organise the helicopter for Granny and Gramps and Lori to fly over tomorrow, and Edie's mum is going to come round a bit later to see how I'm getting on. She's delivered lots of babies. Come over here love, you look tired.'

Alice sat beside her mum on the pillows.

'Mum, you've got to promise me something.'

'What's that, love?'

'Wait here.'

Alice ran off to her room and came back with something.

'Close your eyes and hold out your hands.'

Alice placed something in her mother's palm and then folded her fingers around it.

'Right, you've got to absolutely promise me that when my brother is born you won't put fulmar oil on him. Promise?'

Alice's mother opened her eyes wide and looked at her daughter.

'I promise. No fulmar oil. What's all this about?'

'It's not a joke Mum, I'm deadly serious.'

'OK. And what's this? Ah.' Her mother opened her hands and saw a small smooth brown object, shaped like a miniature hot cross bun.

'It's that special stone I got in my stocking at Christmas, remember? It's to bring you good luck. With having the baby and everything.' Alice's mum smiled.

'Thank you Alice, that's very special. You know, I think I know what this is. It's not actually a stone; it's a seabean. I think this kind is called a Mary's Bean. You find them sometimes washed up on beaches here. Some people look for years hoping to find one.'

That night Alice went to stay over at Edie Burney's house, while Edie's mum, who was a nurse, went to take care of Alice's mum. Normally the two girls chatted non-stop, but both girls were very quiet while they ate tea with Edie's little sister Hannah and Edie's dad. They watched a DVD about tropical rainforests, and then all got in their pyjamas and went to bed.

In the darkness Alice whispered, 'I hope my mum's going to be all right'.

After a while Edie said, 'Just think, by the morning, you'll have a baby brother, you lucky thing'. But by then Alice was already snoring.

The last few hours had been a complete blur: she remembered being woken at eight, and eating half a bowl of corn flakes at Edie's house before running back in her dressing gown and flowery wellies up the grassy slope to her own house. Alice's dad picked her up and swung her round the kitchen so fast he nearly dropped her, and then he laughed, put her down and said, 'Would you like to meet your brother now?'

Alice nodded eagerly. Her dad held the camera above their heads, filming as they walked into the bedroom. Alice's mum was in bed, just like the night before, only now she was wearing Dad's old blue dressing gown, and in her arms was a tight little bundle.

'Alice, come and meet Kit.'

Her brother was all wrinkly and scrunched up, and Alice thought he looked like a caterpillar poking out of its chrysalis. Or should that be a moth? Maybe a bat. He had a soft furry head and little squirrel hands. She hadn't realised he was going to be so small, and was too scared to hold him at first, so she said, 'I want to wait until Lori gets here. She should hold him first, because she's the oldest.'

And now, in a daze, Alice was watching the patterns in the long grass caused by the helicopter's rotating blades. Mr McLintock stood on the shoreline and waved to the helicopter pilot who was trying to land. Alice's dad squeezed her hand as the door opened, and they could see Alice's grandparents inside. Alice jumped up and down and waved in excitement.

Lori ran towards them, bending over to keep out of the way of the helicopter's blades. Granny and Gramps followed, dragging their suitcases across the grass to where Alice and her dad were standing. They all shouted hello to each other but no one could hear anything because it was so noisy. The pilot collected some crates from Mr McLintock and loaded them into the helicopter and then lurched it away.

Back at the house, they had all taken turns to hold the baby, first

Lori, then Alice, then Granny and Gramps. Alice couldn't believe how light Kit was, just like the time when she held a baby fulmar chick that had injured its wing. (She was trying her best to put the fulmar oil story out of her mind, but it kept coming back to her.)

Then they all went back into the kitchen to leave Mum in peace to feed Kit. Alice stood next to her sister. They didn't look very alike: Alice had dark hair, pale skin and green eyes, and Lori was much taller with blonde hair, a freckly face and brown eyes. Alice was sure she had got taller even since Christmas, because now she reached up to Lori's shoulder. But she didn't dare say so, in case Lori bit her head off. Well not literally, but Lori often got mad with her. Lori was wearing silver eye make up and pink jeans. She told the story again and again about how she'd tried all night to ring Dad's mobile but the connections were down.

The neighbours came round one by one, the Butterfields, the Burneys, the McLintocks, the Jacksons, the Fitzpatricks, the Killigans, Mrs Cheung and Reverend Sinclair. Granny showed them all the clothes she'd been knitting for her grandson and Dad made them all mugs of tea and handed out leftover Christmas cake. So, thought Alice, this is the day we've all been waiting for in the Robertson family. Wednesday 17th January 2018. She looked on the calendar on the back of the kitchen door. In the square for the 17th was a tiny black circle.

'Daddy, what does that circle mean in the corner of today's square on the calendar?' Alice's father went to have a closer look.

'Ah, that's interesting, it means your brother arrived at new moon, sensible lad.' He thrust his mug of tea in the air like he was about to say cheers and clink glasses with someone, and tea slopped over the side of his mug onto the floor. He didn't even notice, because he was too busy proclaiming a toast.

'To a new baby, a new moon, and a new beginning.' Everyone cheered. Now Alice knew what her mum meant about the cooped up feeling. She needed to get some air all of a sudden.

'I'm going out to see if I can see the new moon,' she said, pulling her coat on.

Outside it was going dark already. The air was very still, and the frost was just starting to turn the grass stiff and sparkly. Alice made her way up past the row of houses to the graveyard and climbed over the stone wall. She sat down on one of the gravestones and looked up. There was no sign of the new moon in the sky, but there were a few stars visible. Alice imagined that each star was the soul of one of the dead babies.

'Poor things,' she whispered, shivering slightly.

After a while she saw colours start to shimmer in the sky, first green, then red and pink, folding and billowing like huge curtains drawn across the sky. It was something Alice had only seen a few times, but she knew for certain what it was.

'The northern lights! It's the northern lights to welcome Kit!' she shouted into the darkness, and ran back to the house to tell her family.

On the day of her birthday, Alice overslept and her dad had to wake her. She felt a bit cross that she hadn't woken up by herself – usually if something exciting was happening, she would wake before it was even light, even on a Saturday, like today, and rush into her parents' bedroom. Her mum and dad would groan a little, especially if Alice had cold feet, but they would make room for her in the middle so Alice could snuggle down and chatter to them until one of them got up to make the porridge. But today it didn't even feel like an exciting day, let alone her birthday. And she couldn't snuggle into their bed any more really, because by morning the baby was asleep in between her parents.

Alice's dad sat on her bed and handed her a small stack of birthday cards to open – including one from Charlie Cheung sent all the way from Hong Kong. Her dad cleared his throat apologetically.

'Alice, we've got a confession to make: Mum and I haven't got your present yet. I'm sorry love.'

'Uh-huh,' Alice said, trying to keep the disappointment out of her voice until her dad went out of her room. She sighed and then slowly got dressed in her favourite jeans and stripy long-sleeved fleece. Then she opened her birthday cards and took them to show her mum, who was feeding Kit in bed.

'Happy birthday, sweetie,' she said. 'Sorry about your present. Can you wait?' She smiled but looked a bit tired.

'That's OK Mum, don't worry.' Alice perched on the edge of the bed beside her mother and stroked the reddish hair on her brother's soft little head for a minute.

'I'm really hungry now. I'm going to have breakfast with Dad.'

The Robertson's kitchen had an old-fashioned range instead of a cooker and was always lovely and warm. Alice sat at the table where she could see sun shining on the wild sheep in the field in front of their cottage.

'How about some pancakes, birthday girl?' her father asked brightly.

'Yes please! With maple syrup?'

'Don't see why not.' Alice's dad whisked up the eggs, milk and flour. 'Well, poppet, what would you like to do? Shall we go for a walk? The ferry is due in today, you know, with a load of stuff on for my wave energy project, so I'll be down there later. And Mum says Edie is coming over for your birthday tea this afternoon – is that right?'

'Mmm.' Alice mumbled. She was in one of those daydreams where you are staring but not looking, and everything is fuzzy.

'I think I want to go for a walk by myself,' she announced after a while. She had a plan to go and see Jim, the old man who lived in the underground house at the end of the village. Everyone said they thought he'd been living there before anyone came back to St Kilda, but it was probably just a story. They also said that Jim was mad as a hatter, but Alice thought he was kind and wise, even though she couldn't understand him because he only spoke Gaelic.

With the last pancake wrapped in a napkin, Alice pulled on her flowery wellingtons and her winter coat and trudged outside. The air was very fresh and the wind was not as noisy as usual. First she walked from her house up the slope past the seven other single-storey houses that had been rebuilt, and then past the seventeen houses that were still ruins. She walked in and out of the empty rooms with no roofs any more and tried to imagine who used to live there. The old crofters' cottages felt lonely and lost. She watched as a little St Kilda wren appeared and started to hop from one stone wall to another, and followed the bird up the hill as far as the old Earth House. She'd heard some people call this the House of the Fairies. There was a thick stone on top of an entrance like a big rabbit hole with some smaller stones surrounding it. Old Jim lived inside.

'Jim,' she called, stepping through the entrance into the earthy interior. 'Are you there? It's me, Alice.'

She could hear Jim shuffling towards her in his worn-out shoes. His beard came down to his waist because he never shaved, and his clothes wrapped round his body like ragged black bandages. She held out the napkin.

'I've brought you a pancake. It's my birthday today. I'm eleven now.'

Jim took the napkin and started eating hungrily. He nodded at her when he'd finished and brushed the sugar from his beard. Then he shuffled off and came back with a tatty red notebook and a pencil. He flicked through the notebook full of what looked like complicated maths and strange diagrams until he found an empty page. There he scrawled a long number – 500,000 – and then pointed at himself with a dirty thumb and nodded vigorously.

Alice giggled and said, 'Oh Jim, you're not that old.'

She said goodbye and went back outside. In the distance she could see the ferry was coming into Village Bay. She checked her watch: ten thirty-two. She tried to work out how long it would take her to run down to the harbour: she wanted to time it just right so she would arrive at the same time as the ferry. Marks, get set, go, Alice whispered, as she pressed the button on her stopwatch and then sped down the hill, jumping over the tussocks of grass. As she whizzed back past the houses, people called out 'Happy Birthday Alice! In a hurry love?' But Alice just carried on running, keeping her eye on how far the ferry had got as her legs jumbled on.

The St Kilda ferry was a smelly old thing that people on the island are always saying might not get through another winter, but then it turned up again and they all relieved, because although it was unreliable it was full of all the things they needed, and they looked forward to it arriving. Most families on the island had their own chicken coops, and when they first arrived they brought six cows with them. The cows were kept in a stone enclosure to stop them trampling over all the vegetables, which they also grew in little stone enclosures, to keep the wind off. So apart from milk and eggs, everything else had to come on the ferry.

When Alice got down to the harbour they were already unloading. Ten thirty-eight. It had taken six minutes. She felt disappointed because she had run really fast and now had a stitch. There were the usual shouts from the ferrymen as containers full of things were dragged off the boat along the metal gangway, while the dog that always came with them tried to round everything up. There were no cars on the island, apart from Mr McLintock's truck, so things had to be wheeled off on carts and trolleys. But today there was a new noise to be heard above the constant chugging of the ferry's engine. Alice could hear it grinding and beeping before she could see it: a forklift truck.

Alice's dad was down by the ferry beckoning to the driver of the forklift truck. It was lifting big wooden crates containing the hydraulic wave energy parts, and some other long orange components that her Dad called floats. Alice stood and watched as they brought them up the harbour road and unloaded them outside the Evaw shed. It took five trips to get all the pieces of machinery brought up, and when the crates were all inside, Alice's father rolled the huge doors shut.

Someone shouted, 'There's one more thing, Mr Robertson!'

'No, that's everything.' He pulled a sheet of paper out of his jeans back pocket and checked down a list. But as he was checking it, Alice could see the men lifting another large item with the forklift from right at the back of the ferry's hull. It came out backwards, slowly emerging into the sunshine. The forklift deposited a large and rather peculiar black box on the beach.

'What the dickens is that?' asked her dad.

'Is it OK to leave it here, Mr Robertson?' shouted the forklift truck man, 'only we've had a rough weather warning and we need to get going now.'

'Sure. Leave it there,' Alice's dad called back, scratching his head. 'I'll ask around in the pub this evening – we'll find out whose it is and get it moved.' He shrugged his shoulders, gave Alice's ponytail a friendly tug, and then handed her a two-pound coin before he set off back to his office.

'Get yourself a cream cake or something from the shop. See you at teatime Alice!' he called over his shoulder.

Alice stood staring at the box for a moment or two with a puzzled look on her face. In the shop, Mrs Butterfield also stopped unpacking her new stock for a moment and squinted at the black box standing on the beach.

'Whatever is that thing, Alice? Does your Dad know anything about it, love? Never seen anything like that before. Hope it's not some new piece of military equipment; I thought we were supposed to be getting rid of all that.'

'I'm not sure. It looks really weird, doesn't it? I'm going to go and have a closer look.' Alice chose a nice chocolate éclair and Mrs Butterfield put it in a paper bag for her.

'There you go love, keep your money. It's your birthday, isn't it?' Alice smiled and nodded. She put the coin in her pocket and walked back down to the beach, munching the éclair.

It was the kind of black that Alice imagined black holes would be made out of: so dark you get lost in it. She walked round it several times before she noticed the outline of a door on one side, but no handle. Beside the door was another tiny door just at Alice's eye level. She touched it, and it felt like it was covered in velvet. She noticed that her fingers left little blue marks where she'd touched it. She felt all the way round the edges of the little door and suddenly it popped open. Behind was a bright silver panel with lots of numbered buttons, a tiny slot, a screen and a row of round coloured lights, but they were all switched off. It was like one of those machines she'd seen on the mainland where you get money out. When she closed the door again, it clicked shut and sort of breathed out.

Somehow when she stared hard at it, Alice thought that the edges of the box seemed to wobble, like it was about to disappear. She closed her eyes and quickly opened them again, and that time she thought the box was more like a square hole that had been cut out of the picture. Then she noticed that even though the sun was shining, it was as if it shone on everything except the black box, because around its base it had no shadow.

Alice knelt down and touched the sand next to the edge of the box. It was cold and wet. She started to scrape the sand away from the base of the box, like a dog. When she had cleared away a pile about as big as a bucket, she felt the underneath surface of the black box. The dark velvety material continued. Pretending to be a forklift, Alice extended her arms straight out in front of her, placed both hands under the box and pressed upwards. Some sand fell away from the underside, and then the box lifted ever so slightly off the ground. She was amazed: how could this enormous metal box be as light as a feather? Suddenly frightened, she quickly pulled her hands away in case the box squashed them, but it paused for a moment before easing itself back onto the sand, and she even thought she heard it make a little sighing noise.

Alice stood up and patted the black side of the box.

'You're a strange one,' she whispered softly. She watched her bluish hand mark slowly fade through all the colours of the rainbow back to black. She drew a circle on the side of the box, but by the time she drew eyes and a smiley mouth, the circle was already disappearing. She stretched out her arms and measured along one side, like she had seen her Dad measure the rooms when they came to visit their cottage for the first time. The box was three times as long as her arm span on each side. From above it would be a perfect square, Alice thought. She stood back, and judged it was about three arm spans high, too. A perfect cube.

The pile of sand from the hole she had dug seemed to spoil the perfectly formed cube, so she started to push it all back under the box and smooth it over. As she did so, Alice came across something hard and shiny. It was a thin, flat rectangle of metal the size of a credit card covered in wet grains of sand. Something washed up in the last tide perhaps, or maybe one of the ferrymen dropped it, Alice thought. She took it down to the water's edge to wash it off and see whether it had someone's name written on it. The water was icy cold, and she dipped the card in quickly, trying not to get her hands wet. She wiped it on the sleeve of her coat and then held it up to dry.

Written in raised letters it said 'C-Bean Mk.3'. On the front there was a hologram image of a globe that shimmered in the sunlight, and then the back of the card was coated in the same dark black as the box itself. Alice walked back towards the box.

'C-Bean Mark 3,' she said aloud. 'Is that what you're called? The C-Bean. And is this your key, perhaps?' She approached the side where the tiny door was, and gently pushed it to make it pop open. Sure enough the slot inside was about the right width to receive the shiny card. As she was about to post it in, the hologram globe on the card started spinning and then the coloured lights on the panel flicked on, turning first red, then orange and then, one by one, green. Alice held her breath and slid the card into the slot.

'Not everything is what it seems', drawled Dr Adrian Foster, as he cast his eye over the five children seated in front of him. It was Monday morning, his first day as their new teacher. 'And some things can travel a long way from where they come from to tell us something about other times and other places. They are like little clues that pop up now and again when we least expect it. Like a message in a bottle. Like me, for instance.'

He chuckled to himself and nodded like a toy robot, as if to confirm these statements, fixing his gaze of each of the children in turn. He had curly white hair, wore a grey duffle coat with big deep pockets, and trousers that were a bit too short for him. He wore some kind of identity bracelet on his left wrist, and on his feet he wore white sneakers with fluorescent yellow laces the colour of highlighter pens. Attached to a toggle on his coat he'd tied another yellow shoelace that disappeared into one of his pockets.

As Alice absorbed the different aspects of her new teacher's appearance, Dr Foster pulled a long prickly-looking object out of his other coat pocket.

'I forgot to say kids, it's Show and Tell today. So I thought I'd bring in something myself, to show y'all.'

Dr Foster passed the object around. 'Take a look at this, everyone, and tell me what you think it is.'

Dr Foster was obviously used to a bigger class than this in New York, Alice thought, because the word 'everyone' sounded silly talking to five children sitting on a small rug.

Sam F flinched when it was his turn to hold it, and said suspiciously, 'Yuck, I'm not touching that! What is it anyway?'

Sam J sniffed it, then pretended to comb his mop of red curly hair with it. 'Look Sam, it's a brush.'

'No-o-o, it's not a brush,' said Dr Foster, his eyes twinkling at Sam J's rascally nature. Sam passed it back to Edie.

'It's a bit like a hedgehog,' Edie said, holding it in her lap as if it was a small animal, 'Only more lop-sided.'

'Good job, Edith.'

'Don't call me that. I don't like it.' Edie pushed her glasses up her nose and sniffed.

'Sorry – you prefer Edie do you? Anyone else got an idea?' Dr Foster asked, as Edie passed it to Alice. Alice held it gingerly, and ran her finger along the seam that ran down one side. She shook it, and felt something rattle inside.

'Where did you find it?' she asked.

'How d'you know I found it, erm Ali … ?'

'Alice. I dunno. It's just not the sort of thing you would buy in a shop. Not in our shop, anyway.'

'Well, you're right there. I did find it. In a forest.'

Dr Foster was looking really quite merry and excited now.

'Is it a creature?' Alice was beginning to like her new teacher's curious nature.

'Well, that's what people often think. It does look a bit like a creature.'

'So can you eat it?' Sam J asked.

'Not exactly, but you could grow things from it. Shall we open it and see what's inside?'

The children nodded, too intrigued now to speak. Dr Foster pulled on the spare yellow shoelace. He kept pulling at it and at the end of the shoelace was a very special penknife. It was black and silver and very fat, like they had tried to squeeze a lot of different tools into it, but they didn't quite fit and kept poking out.

'I need it back now, Alice.'

She handed him the prickly thing and Dr Foster slid open a little knife and pressed the tip of the blade against one end of it. He ran the knife along it in a straight line where the seam was. Then he folded the penknife back into its handle and slipped it into his pocket. Everyone was watching him with wide eyes. Their teacher's head seemed to twitch with the effort of using the knife. He pressed quite firmly and the thing snapped open, like the stiff catch on an old-fashioned purse.

Alice was concentrating on the case, but the other children were pushing each other out of the way to see what had fallen out. On the floor in front of Dr Foster were six little stones the colour of toast. The children reached out to grab one. Dr Foster picked up the last two and gave one to Alice.

'Well, what d'you know, there are exactly six, one for everyone, including Charlie.'

Alice thought this trick would not have worked so well with Dr Foster's old class, because there would have been too many children for 'everyone' to have got one.

'It's like a wee hamburger,' Sam J said, peering at one.

Dr Foster chuckled. 'And that's just what they're called – hamburger beans. They're a kind of seabean and this is their seedpod, it fell from a tree.'

Alice frowned, remembering the seabean she'd given to her mother, and the C-Bean Mark 3 she'd found on the beach just two days before. There was something strange about this whole Show and Tell thing, but she couldn't work out what it was.

'Where does the seedpod come from?' asked Edie, knowing there weren't any trees on St Kilda for it to grow on.

'Well, it didn't come from this island. Or the next island. Or even the mainland. It came from a cloud forest deep in the Amazonian jungle. Bats drink the nectar of the tree-flower, pollinate the plant and the seeds form. Then when they ripen the seedpod splits open and the seabeans float across the ocean and wash up on a beach somewhere, sometimes even here in the outer Hebrides,' Dr Foster paused to let this image sink in. Alice could see a thick mist forming, and more trees disappearing into the distance than she could ever imagine.

'Dr Foster, how come the seabeans get washed up here?' Alice asked.

'They are carried by a magical sea current.'

'All the way to St Kilda?'

'All the way.'

Dr Foster turned to the wall behind them where a world map was pinned up. He pointed at Scotland with one hand, and at the Amazon basin in South America with the other.

Moving his hand round and round like he was stirring soup, he said 'you see, the current that connects all your lovely remote islands off the coast of Scotland with the coastline of Brazil where the Amazon meets the sea is a nice warm one, called the Gulf Stream. And when things get swept into the sea, the wind blows and the waves roll and they carry things a long long way.'

'Why?' asked Hannah, looking up from a drawing she'd just done of the prickly pod.

'It's just one of the fascinating things about how our planet works, and it's all to do with the tides, the winds, the moon, and the gravitational pull.' Alice thought for some reason that Dr Foster sounded like he was repeating lines that he'd learned.

'I thought the tide just goes in and out, and that when it goes out the sea gets sort of thicker, and then when it comes in, the sea is thinner,' Edie said, staring at the map.

'Well it's always moving about, and bringing treasure when it returns. Beaches are full of hidden treasure. Like this seabean. I bet if we looked carefully, we'd actually find other seabeans on your beach right here.'

As he said it, Dr Foster looked straight at Alice and raised his eyebrows, as if he knew exactly what she was thinking. It made her feel slightly uneasy. She stared back at him but decided not to say anything.

Dr Foster picked up the fragments of the casing and held them gently in the palm of his hand.

'Do you have a nature table, children?'

Edie stood up to show Dr Foster. She was the Nature Table Monitor.

'It's not got much on it at the moment, because it's winter and there aren't any flowers and stuff to collect outside,' she explained to Dr Foster.

'Well, we can start a new collection, then. Edie, can you arrange it while Alice makes up an identification card, please?'

He gave Alice a small white card and a black pen. She pictured the word 'seabean' in her head, and quite liked the way it had two lots of 'ea' in it. When she had finished writing she was disappointed though, and even thought about asking Dr Foster for another piece of card, because the n had ended up too close to the right-hand edge. She propped the card in front of the seedpod on the table and then, after a moment of hesitation, put her hamburger seed next to the pod, because that's where it seemed to belong.

Dr Foster wasted no time on his first day getting to know not just the children but the island as well. Straight after morning break, he said that it was their turn to do a Show and Tell. The children protested and said they had not brought anything to show, so Dr Foster told the children to put on their coats and said they were to take him on a tour of the island.

'But it's too big! It'll take too long,' moaned Sam F.

'Well then, just show me the best bits,' suggested Dr Foster reasonably.

'What about our shop – have you seen that yet?' Edie asked.

'Yes, I went there yesterday to get some shampoo, as it happens.'

Alice was relieved when she heard this, because the one thing she didn't want to have to show Dr Foster was her C-Bean, and he was sure to notice it.

'Do you want to climb our wee mountain – the Conachair?' Sam J wanted to know.

Dr Foster laughed, 'Maybe not today, Sam, but maybe this weekend.'

'How about the First World War gun – have you been to see that?' Sam F asked, getting into the idea.

'Now that sounds like something I gotta see,' agreed Dr Foster. 'Alice, are you coming with us?'

Alice was sitting in the corner of the classroom by the nature table, with a faraway look on her face. Now that the C-Bean had arrived, the island seemed different, like another place. Come to think of it, now that Kit had arrived, home seemed like somewhere else too. And today, school felt strange; Mum wasn't there, and that was both good and bad. There was just a lot of newness to get used to.

As they set off it started raining in a slow steady drizzle. Alice was hoping they would not head for the beach where the C-Bean was. She didn't want Dr Foster to find it. At least, not yet. Thankfully, they headed out of the village away from the beach. Dr Foster had brought a large golf umbrella and the children crowded underneath it as they walked past the first of the cottages and on up the hill to the west. The weather closed in until they could only see about two houses ahead. They showed him the repaired houses with their new turf roofs, and the children pointed out whose was whose. Then they passed the graveyard. Alice hoped no one would want to tell Dr Foster about the babies buried there.

Edie just said as they passed, 'That's where the people who used to live on St Kilda are buried'.

Next they passed the ruined houses and the boys told Dr Foster all about how they had beds that were built into the walls and slept on straw and bits of turf instead of mattresses in the olden days.

Dr Foster listened intently as he trudged on up the hill. 'Heck, you kids know a lot about this island! And what are all these little stone huts?'

'They're called cleitean or cleits. It's where they kept all their food and stuff,' said Sam F.

Alice had fallen behind the others. They were approaching old Jim's underground house. She ran to catch up. As Alice got closer, she could smell Dr Foster's wet duffle coat. It was like an old dog.

'Dr Foster?'

'Yes, Alice?'

'Have you met Old Jim?'

Dr Foster was panting a little as they walked up the hillside. Alice also noticed that his left knee clicked when he walked. He straightened up suddenly, holding the umbrella up high with one hand and putting his other hand against his back to support himself for a moment.

'Erm, no, don't think we've been introduced. Who's Jim?'

'He lives in an underground house just up here. He's my friend,' Alice said.

'Well, maybe I'll meet Jim some other time. I think I've had enough of an introduction to this weather. Shall we head back, kids?'

'Just a moment.'

Alice skipped on ahead and stooped down in front of the entrance to the underground house and called into the darkness, 'Hello? Jim, are you in there?' Alice stood waiting but there was no reply.

The rain had become heavier and more persistent and they began to make their way back down to the village. When they got back to the classroom, Dr Foster went into the back room and came back with a huge roll of paper. He suggested they made a big map of the island for the rest of the day, and that they should all mark onto it the other places they'd not yet managed to show him. Sam F made the first move by drawing on the gun emplacement on the headland, pointing the gun out to sea.

'You know, Dr Foster, the gun has never ever been fired,' Sam said solemnly. He harboured a secret hope that one day, when he was old enough to be one of the army men himself, he might be called upon to fire it.

Edie wrote a list for Dr Foster of all the people on the island, starting with the McLintocks, the Jacksons, the Killigans, the Fitzpatricks, the Butterfields, the Robertson, the Cheungs, and her own family, the Burneys. Next to each person's name she wrote down what they did. It was not a very long list of names, but since everyone had more than one job, it took a long time to write. Then she wrote little numbers next to the names and corresponding numbers on the map showing where they all lived or worked, or both. For Charlie Cheung, she also wrote an email address, because he was still in Hong Kong.

Sam J decided the map should be more three dimensional, and went to get the building blocks out. He put one yellow cube for each cottage, two green ones each for the shop, the church and the school, red ones for the two rows of army huts and, down by the harbour, eight blue blocks to make up the Evaw shed where the wave energy machines were being built. Hannah meanwhile made some very detailed drawings of all the shells you could find along the beach, and all the different kinds of birds that lived on St Kilda. Then she cut them out and put them all around the edges of the giant map.

Alice looked at their efforts. It seemed too bland and ordinary with just the blocks and the list. Even with Hannah's drawings it didn't begin to explain their amazing island. She put some cotton wool on the hillside, to make it seem more like the kind of cloudy wet day Dr Foster had just experienced. Then she made a little enclosure out of salt dough to form the graveyard, and a mound with an entrance to mark on the map where Jim's underground house was.

It was almost finished, and the children were tired. Dr Foster said they could go on their laptops until it was time to go home. Alice checked her email. There was one from Charlie, sent the day before.

Hi Alice. Who's the big sister now then! Let me know what our new teacher is like. Is it snowing or raining? Hong Kong is still full of tourists. Everybody comes here to go shopping, even on Sundays. Got to go. See you in a few weeks! Charlie.

He had attached a picture of himself holding his new mobile phone, standing in a street full of traffic in front of a tall grey building with lots of people walking across a bridge in the background. Alice wondered what the map of Hong Kong Island would look like compared to St Kilda. She tried to imagine the crowds of shoppers, the noise of cars and buses, the feel of the pavements.

As they were all packing up, Alice found a small black cube of Lego on the floor. She picked it up: this was what was missing from the map. In front of the shop, beside the sea wall, she placed the black cube right where the C-Bean had been left.

Alice's Blog

22nd January 2018

So there have been three arrivals actually, not just two. Baby Kit isn't even supposed to be here yet. But he is: by my watch, he's already more than 100 hours old. And, of course, I'm now eleven years and two days old.

The second new arrival is Dr Foster. His knee clicks when he walks and he looks a bit like a sheep. He even sounds a bit like a sheep when he laughs.

But something else has arrived too. There's a very strange cube thing on the beach called a C-Bean. It arrived on my birthday, and so I really thought it was somehow meant to be my birthday present. I mean I kind of decided it was mine: it didn't seem to belong to anyone, and nobody knew what it was.

I bet you're wondering what happened when I went inside it! I wasn't going to write about this, but as it's part of what's happening in my life here, I suppose it should be in my blog.

Imagine stepping inside a whale. Except on the inside there are walls and a floor and a ceiling that keep changing all the time. It was as if it was recording everything about me: how big I was, how I moved, how hot I was, what my voice sounded like and what mood I was in. I bet you're thinking: how did she know it was doing all that? Well, first of all the walls showed my outline, like I was casting a shadow on them, except there was no light shining on me to make the shadow. Then it put the shadow into colours, and I noticed my hands and face were coloured blue (where I was still cold from outside), but my body was red. If I walked around, the shadow images moved around as well on all four walls.

When I said 'hello' the C-Bean echoed like I was in an enormous cave. I said it in all kinds of silly voices and the C-Bean kept repeating whatever I said back to me. Then, when it had got all the information about me it needed, it projected a hologram that was exactly the same size and shape as me into the middle of the room and I could walk all the way round her. I tried to touch the hologram but it wasn't made of anything except coloured light projected in the space. Then I said hello again, and the 3D picture of me said hello back. Then she started copying anything I did, but doing the mirror image, so if I moved to the left, she moved to the right.

I stayed inside the C-Bean for ages, and it felt like I'd made a new friend. I realised I'd got quite thirsty. I didn't say it out loud or anything, but a few seconds after I thought about wanting a drink, this little opening appeared in one wall, like the hatch in one of those vending machines. A fresh glass of water stood there waiting for me. I picked it up and drank it. Then, to test it, I began to picture in my head a chocolate biscuit. The opening disappeared for a moment or two and then reopened, and there on the shelf was just the kind of biscuit I had been thinking about. It was delicious.

After that I imagined all sorts of things, like a pen, a camera, an electric toothbrush, a baby's rattle. Every time, whatever I had imagined would appear, in exactly the same colours and shapes that I'd pictured in my head. Next I tried things that were a bit bigger, like a guitar or an umbrella, to see if they would fit in the hatch. When the opening reappeared, it was just longer or larger. Then I tried to think of something more particular, like our St Kildan postage stamps, or my own teddy, but it managed fine. Teddy looked a bit too clean, though.

Then I thought: if it can do a stuffed toy animal, can it do a real one? That was clever: the real animals appeared, but they were just holograms and images. I had zebras stampeding all around me. I stood in amongst a herd of elephants spraying each other and washing themselves. I watched hundreds of penguins diving off an iceberg right in front of me into the sea. It was so real – you could smell the fish they were eating and hear all the sounds they were making and the room got colder and colder as I watched the sun set over Antarctica. When the room was completely dark, I suddenly wondered if it had gone dark outside the C-Bean too. I picked up the rattle to give to Kit and opened the door to go out.

The sun had set outside too. I could still feel the rattle in my hand when I stepped out onto the sand, but by then it was already invisible, I could only hear the rattling sound until I got as far as Edie's house. By the time I reached our house, it had completely disappeared.

When I woke up the next morning I remembered I'd left the card key in the slot of the C-Bean. After Dad and I had been to church (Mum stayed at home with Kit, but she did at least get dressed), he went off to a meeting in the pub about buying the island, so I said I'd walk back by myself. I waited until he'd gone inside the pub, then I ran down to the beach. I was really scared the C-Bean might have gone, but as soon as I came round the corner past the shop, I could see its straight black edges against the sky.

I walked slowly up to the C-Bean and suddenly felt shy. The big door was shut. I pressed the little door on the panel next to the door and it opened like before and I could see the card was still inside the slot. I pressed some of the buttons but none of them made the card come back out, and anyway the lights had gone out. I walked round the outside to see if there was any other way of getting in, or if it had changed colour or shape at all on the outside, but it was the same smooth matt black on all four sides with no reflections. I went back round to the door and slumped up against it, feeling very disappointed that I couldn't get back in. I felt the door nudge me, and when I turned round, I saw my body had left a blue mark on the surface where I had been leaning. Then I heard my own voice say hello. I said hello back and the door opened. It remembered me! I was about to go back inside, but then I thought how much fun it would be to show Edie, so I closed the door and ran off to fetch her.

It was a real shame, because Edie had a temperature and her Mum said she had to stay indoors. Also, my mum had come round to see where I was. I felt bad that I hadn't gone straight home, and that Mum had to bring little Kit outside because of me. So I went home and helped Mum make Sunday dinner.

23rd January 2018

Just after lunchtime today there was a lot of noise and when we looked out of the window, Mr McLintock was unloading something from the back of his truck into the school yard. Everyone crowded round the window to see what was going on. Dr Foster went outside to find out, and when Mr McLintock had driven off, he came back inside rubbing his hands together, all excited about something.

He said something like, 'Well, kids, that strange-looking thing outside is our new ultra high-tech classroom.' Then, 'We are very lucky indeed. It's a gift from an anonymous donor to help the children of St Kilda. None of the other islands has one.'

I looked through the window and realised with a shock what Mr McLintock had delivered to the yard: my C-Bean! I couldn't quite believe what Dr Foster was saying, and anyway calling it a classroom made it sound very boring. Plus it didn't look nearly as exciting in our schoolyard as it did when it was down on the beach. It also looked a lot smaller.

Dr Foster said the instruction manual was supposed to be arriving by post so until then he had no idea how to use it. I was about to put my hand up and tell him I knew how to open the door, but I stopped myself just in time. I felt a bit confused. Part of me felt it was my C-Bean, my present, my secret. But part of me couldn't wait for the others to see inside and find out about all the amazing things it could do.

24th January 2018

My birthday present from Mum and Dad arrived in the post this morning: it was a big globe that swivels on an axis and has a light inside. It is designed to get brighter and brighter by itself in the morning to wake you up. I've put it beside my bed, so I can look at all the places I want to go one day before I fall asleep. Lori gave me some yummy chocolates and Granny and Gramps gave me a 1000-piece jigsaw with a picture of the other St Kilda in Australia that they'd found on the internet. It has a very nice beach with palm trees, but for a jigsaw it's got a bit too much plain blue sky.

Lori went back with Granny and Gramps on the helicopter on Friday. Part of me wanted to go back with Granny and Gramps and stay with them for a while. They live in Liverpool in a block of flats overlooking the River Mersey. Another part of me wished I was older and that Lori and I were going back to boarding school together in Glasgow, and that I had lots of friends and clothes and make up like Lori. But the biggest part of me wanted to stay here and be with Mum and Dad and Kit. Even though the walls aren't quite thick enough between my bedroom and theirs when Kit cries at night. Also, we are eating a lot of things out of tins, not because Daddy can't cook, but because right now he's either:

a) looking after Mum and the baby or

b) down in the Evaw shed.

He keeps saying 'It's a critical time right now,' but no one is being critical at all. Mum is extra specially kind and lovely at the moment. It's probably because she didn't get out of bed for three whole days.

Anyway, my presents weren't the only things that arrived on the ferry this morning: the C-Bean's instruction manual came in the post too.

On Wednesday morning, Mr Butterfield, who delivered the mail round the island after it arrived off the ferry, brought a package for Dr Foster. It was a bright calm day, and he stood around chatting in the schoolyard for ages. As far as Mr Butterfield was concerned, this was all part of doing a good job as the island postie, and many other messages and pieces of information were entrusted to him on the doorsteps of St Kilda.

Eventually Dr Foster came back into the old classroom with the large brown envelope tucked safely under his arm. Alice's heart skipped a beat when she saw the hologram symbol of the Earth printed on the top left corner of the envelope, the same design as on the key she'd found on the beach. Dr Foster tore open the envelope and pulled out a large black folder full of information about the C-Bean Mark 3.

The children were supposed to be doing some maths exercises, finding number patterns using their hundred squares, which Alice usually loved. But as soon as Dr Foster emptied the envelope they all stopped what they were doing and watched him intently. Alice could feel a noise like waves crashing inside her and she began to feel as if she was breathing underwater. Her secret was about to be revealed.

The night before Alice dreamed about the C-Bean. In the dream, she was back inside it, imagining being in Antarctica again. The C-Bean started to move around like an iceberg in the sea, and she kept slipping from side to side every time it moved. The penguins seemed to be getting further and further away, and then she could see one being tossed high into the air, and suddenly a huge whale came bursting through the wall of the C-Bean, spouting water and lunging towards her. She was gasping for air, and when she reached out to try and save herself, all she kept grasping were babies' rattles, only they weren't like a child's plaything because they were covered in this thick, smelly oil.

When Alice woke, she was breathing heavily as if she had run all the way down the hill to the shop. She opened her eyes and saw the light from her globe and let her eyes adjust while she tried to convince her brain that she was not in the Antarctic, even though her bedroom was so cold she could see her breath. She wondered if she had shouted out loud in the nightmare, because she could hear her parents stirring next door, and Kit starting to whimper. She slid on her slippers and went out into the passageway.

'Mum? Dad? Are you awake?'

'Go back to sleep Alice. It's OK, we're just changing Kit's nappy,' her Dad said in a loud whisper.

'Can I come in your bed? I've had a nightmare.'

'Umm. Well, Mum's a bit tired. Just a minute and I'll come and tuck you in, love.'

Alice stood shivering for a moment, then ran back into her room, jumped into bed and buried her head under her pillow to stifle her tears. In the morning she still had her slippers on.

The C-Bean's instruction manual came in the form of a digital tablet in a smart case, and there was also a small printed booklet containing a 'Quick Start Guide'. Tucked into a pocket inside was another thin metal cardkey identical to the one Alice had used.

Dr Foster laid it all out on his desk and said, 'Well, kids, where shall we start?'

'How do we get inside?' Eager as ever, Sam J blurted out the question uppermost in all their minds.

The C-Bean stood, dark and silent, in the middle of the cracked concrete yard. Alice noticed yesterday that on one side there was a nasty scrape mark where Mr McLintock's truck had winched the C-Bean down with his tow chain and his hook had caught against it. When she touched the scrape mark, the black surface felt spongier around where it had been damaged, and a silvery crust had formed over the surface. After school was over, Alice got a sponge and some warm water from the classroom sink and tried to clean the wound a little. The warm water turned the black surface a vivid electric blue, like the sky on a cloudless day, but it didn't seem to get wet at all. Instead, when she had finished sponging the surface, it just returned to being the densest black imaginable.

'Why don't you all go out in the yard and have a good look for some kind of slot for this cardkey then, while I have a quick read of the instruction guide, and see if we can work it out.'

The children wasted no time. Sam J grabbed the key from Dr Foster's desk and tussled with Sam F to be first out of the door, with Edie close behind holding her new compass and shouting instructions bossily to the two boys. Hannah was busy drawing flowers.

'Hannah, Alice, come!' called Edie, turning back. But both girls stayed put. As far as Hannah was concerned, unless the new classroom was full of paint, paper, pens and pencils, she would not be interested. Alice just wanted to delay the moment when the C-Bean was no longer hers alone. She stared at her hundred square and started counting. She had made a bet with herself that it was bound to take until she got to a hundred before they found the slot for the key. Or at least, that was how long she was prepared to give the others before she went outside and opened the C-Bean for them … ninety-eight, ninety-nine, a hundred. When her finger was on the last space, Alice looked up from her desk. From where she was sitting she couldn't see any of the children out of the window.

She walked outside, calling 'Are you in yet?'

'Nope. Round here.' They were on the far side of the C-Bean, lying face down on the concrete trying to slide the card key underneath the C-Bean.

'Edie thought she could see a little gap just down here.'

'Hmm,' said Alice, 'shall I have a go?'

They handed her the key and she walked up to the door and said in a loud voice, 'HELLO'. She was not sure what she expected to happen. There was a pause, and then the smaller door eased open and the lights flickered on one by one.

'Wow,' said Edie. 'How did you do that?'

'Look, there's a key already in the slot!' Sam J yelled, jumping up and down and clapping his hands together.

Alice paused. The boys were already hammering on the main door, waiting for it to open. She looked down at the other cardkey in her hand, with its globe spinning away. She slipped it into her cardigan pocket. 'Hello,' she breathed so quietly no one but the C-Bean would hear.

Edie was looking down at her compass. 'Look you guys! Look at this!'

Just as the C-Bean's door opened, the north point on the compass started flicking back and forth, and then started spinning furiously.

'Maybe this thing's made out of something magnetic,' suggested Sam F.

'Well?' said Sam J, poking his head inside the door. 'Are we going inside or what?'

'We'd better get Dr Foster first,' said Edie.

Edie was just about to go back inside the school when Dr Foster emerged, followed by Hannah.

'Ah, you've managed to get it to open. Fabulous.'

So, for the second time, Alice stepped inside the C-Bean …

It was as dark and as cold as when she had left it after her Antarctic adventure, but Alice felt hot with anticipation. Dr Foster was trying to find a light switch.

Alice cleared her throat. 'We need some LIGHT,' she said slowly and clearly.

The room started getting lighter so slowly that at first the children all thought their eyes were just getting used to the gloom, like when your parents turn off the lights at bedtime. But after a minute the ceiling, the floor and all four walls started glowing faintly, just bright enough for the children to see the dumbstruck look on each others' faces as they took in their new surroundings.

The inside of the C-Bean was absolutely empty. There was nothing on the floor, or the walls, no shelves, no cupboards, no books, no art trolley, no computers and no furniture. Dr Foster began to look a bit impatient.

'Where's all the stuff?' asked Sam J, reading his teacher's mind.

'Well, on page five of the manual it talks about a Central Resource Table, but I don't see any table!'

'CENTRAL RESOURCE TABLE,' repeated Alice. The two Sams, who were standing in the middle of the C-Bean, began to rise up from the floor on a platform about the size of a double bed.

'Cool!' they chimed. They both laughed and began to tap a slow rhythmic beat on the top of the table between them, and parts of a grid of coloured lights appeared where they'd touched the surface.

'It's a hundred square!' exclaimed Alice. The boys slid off the table and the children found they could fill in the gaps by touching the table here and there, and then watched as different mathematical sequences rippled in rainbows across the square. Once it had completed all the times tables, the table went white.

Under the table was a kind of pit, so the children could sit around it and tuck their legs underneath. Dr Foster sat down too and took off his glasses. Where they rested on the table Alice noticed a tiny coloured outline forming.

'Edie, can you put your compass on the table for a minute?' she asked. Edie took the compass from around her neck and placed it in front of her. The north point was still twitching. A two-dimensional copy of the compass started appearing in the surface of the table. Even Dr Foster was wide-eyed now.

'It's like it can record things,' said Sam F, 'but I bet it doesn't know what they're for.'

'What is a COMPASS for?' Alice asked, and Sam was about to answer the question, thinking it was directed at him, when the table displayed a whole series of moving diagrams of the Earth involving the North and South Poles, with arrows looping from one pole to another. But there were no sounds or words to explain anything.

Dr Foster, his eyes fixed to the table, said 'Ah, it's trying to tell us about magnetic north and how the Earth is like a giant magnet. Your compass is magnetised too, Edie, so that it will always know where north is, and you can use it to work out what direction you are facing.'

Alice thought that Edie's compass was not at all sure where north was at the moment.

Dr Foster continued, a little breathlessly, 'I wonder if there's meant to be sound too? I didn't notice a section about that in the manual. Come to think of it, it did mention a new kind of interactive whiteboard, but I don't know which wall it is – they all look the same.'

'Maybe it doesn't matter which wall you write on,' Alice mused silently to herself, 'but you'd need a PEN.'

A moment after Alice had the thought, a hatch appeared in the wall nearest to Dr Foster to reveal a whiteboard pen. The children watched in disbelief as Dr Foster put his glasses back on and reached out to pick up the whiteboard pen. The hatch then closed up and disappeared.

'Terrific, just what I needed,' Dr Foster laughed, trying to pretend this was nothing out of the ordinary. He stood up in front of the white wall beside him and enquired, 'Does anyone know what latitude and longitude are?'

Edie was first to put her hand up. 'Latitude goes this way,' she said spreading her arms sideways, 'and longitude goes that way,' she moved her arms up and down.

'Good. That's right. Longitude tells you where you are on the earth in terms of east or west, and latitude is a way of saying how far towards the North or South Pole somewhere is. It's a coordinate system. Does anyone want to guess what the coordinates are for St Kilda? What I mean is, how far north, and east or west are we? Anyone?'

No one responded.

'No, I didn't know either, so I looked it up last night at Reverend Sinclair's house. He has some real nice books about St Kilda. I found out that we are 57 degrees 48.5 minutes North, and 8 degrees 34 minutes West. Alice, could you write that up here for me?' Dr Foster tapped the white wall and handed her the pen.

Alice wrote the coordinates slowly and carefully on the smooth white wall. She remembered about the 'seabean' card she was asked to write for the nature table. This time there was plenty of space and the letters could be as big as she wanted. She even put a full stop after the W, but then the pen stopped working properly. Or was it the wall?

Somehow the pen seemed to sink in, as if the whiteboard was soft, like a pillow. Alice touched the surface and it felt damp. She could see her fingers sinking into the space of the wall, and her hand was somehow misting over. She pushed her arm in further until she could no longer see her hand at all.

'Alice, what on earth are you doing?' Dr Foster tried to pull her back, but by then Alice's head had disappeared. Her whole body became enveloped in a kind of thick cloud that was starting to billow into the C-Bean. The other children could hardly see each other through the fogginess, and they reached out to hold each others' hands. But it was too late to hold Alice's hand – she had somehow vanished.

Alice felt a bit dizzy and wondered if this was how it would feel to be caught in a snowstorm, or to jump out of a helicopter in the middle of a thick white cloud. Tiny beads of water clung to her skin, particularly, she noticed, round her ankles. She took a couple of steps, and realised she was wading in icy cold water. Where was she? Not outer space, she decided, as there was very little water there. The air smelled very fresh, like sea air. There was a kind of crying in the distance. She strained her ears to listen, and the crying got louder until she realised it was a seabird calling. She closed her eyes and listened again. Gone. When she opened them, the mist seemed to be clearing, and she could see the rippling surface of the water stretch away in front of her. Behind her the mist was still a thick blanket.

She looked down at her feet submerged in the water, which was extraordinarily clear and was beginning to lap round her knees. Here and there fish darted in silver shoals just above the seabed. She scuffed the white sandy bottom with the edge of her shoe, and caught sight of something black in the water. She reached down to pick it up. A crisp black rectangle with long tendrils trailing from all four corners came up, dripping wet and shiny.

'Alice, where are you?' a voice called. She had almost forgotten about her classmates. Edie's face appeared in the mist, taut with worry.

'Over here,' Alice called, pushing the rectangular thing into her pocket.

Edie waded across, shivering in her waterlogged shoes and tights. Her hair clung in wet straggles round her face and her glasses were all steamed up.

'What are we doing out in Village Bay, Alice?'

'What?' Alice scanned the clearing horizon, and caught sight of the army huts on the foreshore, then the row of little cottages behind, and beyond that the familiar outline of their mountain, Conachair. She felt cheated suddenly. Why here? If the C-Bean could conjure up such vivid images from as far away as Antarctica, why had it deposited them on St Kilda?

'But I thought …'

'We'd better go back to the C-Bean. Dr Foster will be worried.'

Alice followed Edie into the densest part of the mist, and within moments stumbled back into the small square space with its central table. Hannah and the two Sams were huddled on top of the table in their bare feet, while Dr Foster was standing with his trousers rolled up in the flooded C-Bean, squeezing out their soaking wet socks and hanging them over on the edge of the table.

'Oh girls, thank the Lord! Where did you go? There's been a flood. I don't know where all this water came from. Now let's get back to the schoolyard and dry out.'

'But ...' Alice wanted the others to see what she and Edie had seen. She turned back to the misty wall, but it had already hardened over.

'No buts now. You look half frozen, dear. Whatever would your mother say if she knew I let you all get soaked on my first week here?'

Alice sighed, and did as she was told: 'SCHOOLYARD!' Her voice was clear, but had a slightly tearful wobble. It sounded to the others like a protest, but to the C-Bean it was a firm command. There was a sudden jolting movement, and the door flapped open. The children all exited from the C-Bean, tiptoed barefoot across the cracked concrete and back into their warm old classroom.

After lunch, while their socks were steaming on the radiator, Dr Foster had them all outside again in their dry PE trainers, bailing the C-Bean out with the mop bucket and some plastic containers they kept the coloured pencils in. Alice noticed that the C-Bean now had a white salty tidemark running all the way round it about twenty centimetres up from the bottom. She looked down at her legs, then measured them with a ruler: if the water had come up to her knees, that meant it was thirty centimetres deep where she'd been standing. If the tidemark on the C-Bean was less, then it must have been floating.

'My compass!' said Edie suddenly. She ran back inside the C-Bean, and reappeared with it hanging round her neck. 'Thank goodness,' she said, 'the north arrow's pointing north again now. Look.' Alice could tell Edie had been quite unsettled by their little adventure. She put her arm round her.

'Shame we didn't get to take a picture of us two out in the Bay, Edie. You looked so funny standing there in the water. Good job it didn't happen in one of those force nine gales!'

Edie said airily, 'I don't even want to think about it. It was too weird. As far as I am concerned, it didn't really happen.'

'It did happen Edie, I know it did. And it's our secret.' Alice reached into her pocket and pulled out the black object she'd found in the water. 'Here, you can have this as a souvenir.'

Edie took hold of the thing by one of its corners and held it up to inspect it.

Dr Foster looked across the yard, leaning on the mop handle.

'What have you got there, you two? May I have a look?'

Edie showed her teacher. 'What is it? Alice just gave it to me.'

'Ah yes, that's a mermaid's purse. Dogfish lay their eggs in it, and when the time is right, the eggs hatch, and the little fish just swim on out.' Dr Foster paused, but Edie didn't say anything. 'Why don't you put it on the nature table, Edie?'

'Can I write a name card for it, like Alice did for the seabean pod?'

'Sure – there's just time before you all go home. Let's go find the right pen. Not like that pen in the C-Bean. We need one that writes like it's supposed to.'

Alice watched as Edie and Dr Foster went back into the school with Hannah following after them. Sam J and Sam F were bouncing a tennis ball around the schoolyard to each other.

'Watch out,' said Alice, 'we don't want to damage the C-Bean again.'

Something had happened today, something real, something special. The other adventures she had in the C-Bean on the first day, they were imaginary. But today it had somehow transported them from the schoolyard to somewhere out in the bay and back again. It can't have just been an illusion. What about the wet socks, the flooded floor, and the mermaid's purse? So, if it did happen, how did it happen?

Alice went back into the school. The instruction manual lay open on Dr Foster's desk at the page about the Central Resource Table. She touched the menu at the side of the screen and flicked to the index. She noticed there was a listing for 'Using the Interactive Whiteboard' and, lower down, another one titled 'Activating the Transportation Function'. Her heart did a strange sort of flutter as she read it.

'Dr Foster ...' she began.

'Yes, dear?'

'Could I take the manual home this evening and read it?'

'I don't see why not, Alice. Then maybe you could you give us a proper tour of where everything is and how it's actually supposed to work. I guess we must have done something wrong today.'

'OK,' she said, her hands shaking with excitement as she stuffed the digital book into her schoolbag. 'I'll bring it back tomorrow.'

When Alice got home from school, her mum was cooking tea while Kit lay in his basket waving his arms. Alice knelt down to tickle his toes. She watched his little face as he wriggled with pleasure.

'Mum, just think, Kit's a week old today.'

'I was just thinking the same thing, sweetheart. What a week, eh!'

'Yeah.' Alice was looking at Kit's face, but she was somewhere else, her eyes had gone fuzzy, and all she could see was his outline against the red blanket. 'I've had such a strange day at school.'

'What's Dr Foster got you doing, then?'

'You know that cube thing they delivered off the ferry? Well it turns out it's for us. It's a mobile classroom that someone's sent over as an experiment, and Dr Foster let us go inside it for the first time today. Did you know it was coming, Mum? It's called a C-Bean, and it's very strange. It's totally empty so you have to imagine things, and then they sort of happen. I can't explain it really. Anyway, Dr Foster has lent me the instruction manual to read this evening.'

'No, it was never mentioned to me,' her mother replied vaguely.

Alice was thinking about the C-Bean all through her meal, and it wasn't until she'd eaten all her sausages and mash she realised she hadn't put any ketchup on her plate. Kit had fallen asleep in his basket and her parents were busy talking about the Evaw plant, so Alice was able to slip away to her bedroom straight afterwards.

She lay down on her bed. The manual contained a lot of long words, and they were all repeated in Spanish, German and Chinese. In the first section, Alice learned that the C-Bean had been designed in Germany and assembled in Brazil. It was a Mark 3 product, which meant that it was replacing the first and second versions they'd made. Ninety-nine new features had been added. (Why not a hundred, Alice thought, they only needed to think of one more!) She skipped ahead to the section on Activating the Transport Function. First there was a long list of things *not* to do when trying to use this particular function. It said things like, 'DO NOT use a mobile phone or other mobile 5G handheld devices in the C-Bean'; 'DO NOT try to transport the C-Bean to more than one place at a time'; and 'DO NOT use the reset function if the C-Bean is in motion'.

There were too many diagrams of how the electronics worked and page after page of explanation. Alice couldn't understand why anyone would want to make a set of instructions so long and so complicated. Finally she came to a list of standard commands. She was pleased to see she had already mastered some of these – or rather guessed – such as saying 'LIGHT' to make the lights come on. It also said that when the System Administrator says aloud or writes on the wall the name of an item held within the C-Bean's Virtual Storage System, this enables the item to be retrieved through a Temporary Collection Portal. I know all about that, mused Alice, but what about when you just think it? The glass of water had appeared before she said a word about being thirsty. The manual went on: 'After the Access Panel has been activated for the first time using the Cardkey, the C-Bean may be voice activated to allow subsequent access. The C-Bean will remain programmed to respond only to the voice it was exposed to during the Imprinting Stage. This voice is the System Administrator.'

'Cool! So it was my voice the C-Bean was imprinted with that first day on the beach,' Alice murmured. 'But I still don't get how the transport function works …'

She flicked ahead in the manual. Page 99 described the use of the walls as interactive whiteboards (as she had guessed, they all worked as whiteboards). Finally, on page 100, Alice found what she was looking for: it said 'The C-Bean uses geo-stationary satellites to locate a destination on earth to a high degree of accuracy, but to ensure transportation to within a five-metre radius, precise north-south and east-west coordinates must be provided.' It also said, 'The coordinates may be inputted in "voice recognition mode" or in "script recognition mode"'.

Suddenly it all made sense: when she had written up the longitude and latitude coordinates of St Kilda on the wall it had transported the C-Bean to that location. Dr Foster must have remembered them ever so slightly wrong, and that was why they'd arrived out in the bay instead of on dry land.

The following day, Dr Foster promised the children that if they worked hard all morning, they could go in the C-Bean after lunch. Needless to say, they earned their time in the C-Bean. Alice led the way inside. The day before Dr Foster had suggested that, as the C-Bean was so empty inside, the children should bring in some of their own things. He suggested they could make a colour table each week, and put all sorts of things on it that were the same colour. This week's colour was red, so there in the middle of the resource table he'd put a large red apple, only it wasn't a real apple, it was too perfect and shiny. Dr Foster asked the children to gather round. Alice handed the instruction manual back to her teacher.

'Now, before Alice tells us all about what it says in the instruction manual, has anyone else brought something red for our collection?'

Sam J pulled his fire engine out of a plastic bag and put it next to the apple.

'Now that's impressive, son, and d'you know something?'

'What?' Sam asked.

'I happen to have ridden in a real fire truck exactly like this one.'

Sam was all ears.

'You see where it says NYC on the front? That stands for New York City – where I come from. That's why I brought the red apple: the nickname for my city is The Big Apple. And just along the street from where I used to live, there was a Fire Station, with a truck just like this one parked out front. One day we took the children I was teaching to meet the firemen and have a ride in it.' He nodded his head repeatedly after he said this.

Alice tried to imagine Dr Foster in his grey duffle coat walking down the street in a faraway place called The Big Apple, and seeing the red fire engine gleaming in the sunshine. It seemed so far away from St Kilda, just like Charlie's photo of Hong Kong.

Or was it? Alice felt a ripple of excitement in the pit of her stomach as she remembered the bit she'd read about the transport function. What if … ?

'Dr Foster, what longitude and latitude is New York?' she asked.

'Ah, that's a good question, Alice. Well, it's a lot further west than here, and a bit further south too.'

'But where is New York exactly?' Alice persisted.

'Gee, we'd need to look it up …' Dr Foster began, and as he spoke the resource table began to flash with maps, starting with a satellite image of the Earth, and then zooming in and becoming more and more detailed, until the table was covered with a huge map showing a long green rectangle with patches of blue here and there.

'Well, would you believe it?' Dr Foster exclaimed. 'I think this is a map of Central Park, which is smack in the middle of New York.' He started to point out where the zoo and the skating rink were, and every time Dr Foster touched the map, the exact coordinates came up in a box.

'Aha, how interesting!' Dr Foster put his finger on a spot near the bottom of the long green rectangle, just beside one of the ponds. 'Now, here's the answer to your question Alice: 40 degrees, 46 minutes and 55 seconds North and 73 degrees, 57 minutes and 58 seconds West. Fancy that!'

Alice repeated the coordinates slowly under her breath. She couldn't be sure, but it was as if the C-Bean moved slightly. Dr Foster stood up to get a better look at the overall map, and as he stepped backwards, he seemed to fade out a little. His white hair and grey coat became paler and began to merge with the white wall behind him, until all Alice could see were his fluorescent yellow shoelaces. The children fell silent as their teacher drifted out of sight. Gradually they started to hear sounds, including something like the foghorn on the St Kilda ferry, only the booming came in short intermittent stabs. There were some voices in the distance, delicate birdsong, and then a siren, noisy and urgent.

'What shall we do?' asked Edie, searching Alice's face for answers.

'Go after him,' Alice said, peering eagerly into the misty white space. 'I have a feeling we're somewhere else.'

Sam J and Sam F stepped into the fog, their arms extended in front of them as if they were pretending to be zombies. Alice and Edie took hold of Hannah's hands, and followed after them. At first they thought they were surrounded by people, but in the misty gloom they saw that the C-Bean had arrived in the middle of a clump of trees. Dr Foster was sitting on the ground looking completely stunned and rubbing his forehead.

'Dr Foster, are you OK?' Alice enquired.

'Yes, I bumped my head on one of the trees, that's all.'

'Trees?' said Sam F. 'But there aren't any on our island!'

'We're not in St Kilda now, Sam,' said Alice quietly, looking at Dr Foster to see if he had any idea where he was.

'Then where are we?' said Edie irritably. 'I can't bear the way the C-Bean does this!'

Dr Foster got to his feet, and took charge.

'Kids, stay close to me. I'll find out what is going on.'

He moved out of the trees onto a narrow path that ran alongside them. The children followed close behind him. Alice looked back and saw the C-Bean standing blacker than ever as a ray of winter sunshine struggled between the bare branches of the trees. In the distance she could see the tops of buildings many times taller than the tallest tree.

'This is extraordinary!' said Dr Foster as they approached a large pond. 'We seem to be in the middle of Central Park …' He fell silent for a moment or two, taking in his familiar surroundings. A smile crept across his face and he turned to face the children.

'Well, today it seems we're on a very special outing. Now kids, I want you to listen carefully. This might not be a real place at all, it might just be an illusion recreated from the C-Bean's memory bank, but I'm not taking any chances. None of you has been to a big city like this before, and it's very easy to get lost. But there's no point in not doing a couple of things before we go back to the C-Bean. Who wants to go to a real museum?'

The children clamoured 'Yes, me, yes please!'

'And afterwards we'll go to my favourite diner for a milkshake. Welcome to the Big Apple!' Dr Foster cleared his throat and said, 'This way, everyone.'

The park was full of people. They were walking dogs, pushing babies, drinking coffee, jogging, cycling or skating. Here and there snow had been heaped up beside the paths in dirty piles. A little brown dog joined them and started to trot along beside them as they moved around the edge of the frozen lake. They came to one edge of Central Park, and Alice could see a huge building up ahead. It had columns and steps and posters hanging down either side of the entrance. Above was a sign that said 'The American Museum of Natural History'.

Dr Foster stopped in front of it on the opposite side of the road and looked puzzled. 'Well, for some reason it looks closed – let's see, it's Thursday lunchtime, now why would that be I wonder? Kids, wait here while I ask someone. Perhaps it's closed Thursdays.'

He crossed the road and spoke to a girl sitting on the museum steps. Alice could see Dr Foster looking at his watch and asking questions. The boys were marvelling at the constant stream of traffic that passed: cars, buses, yellow taxis and green trams with complicated overhead cables. Edie stood holding Hannah's hand and biting her lip. The little brown dog was sitting at Alice's feet, and she bent down to stroke it.

'Look Edie, Hannah, it's a lost dog.'

Finally their teacher rushed back over the road, smiling as though someone had told him a funny joke.

'Well, it's quite simple,' he said, a little out of breath. 'I don't know why I didn't think of it: in St Kilda it's already lunchtime, but of course here in New York it's five hours behind, so in fact it's only eight o'clock in the morning. I'm afraid it's still breakfast time kids, and the museum doesn't open until nine.'

'Wicked! So can we have breakfast again?' Sam J chirped.

'Good thinking, Samuel! Let's go get ourselves an all-American breakfast, and when we're done, we can come back and look around.'

Dr Foster steered the five children up the next side street until they came to a big wide road called Broadway. Alice looked at all the apartment blocks, with their brown stone steps and metal fire escapes. There were all kinds of cooking and laundry smells coming from the houses. When they turned the corner into Broadway, Alice could see people with briefcases disappearing down steps that went under the pavement, and on every street corner there were flower stalls and newsstands. She tried to keep up with the others, but kept lagging behind, and a little voice trilled in her head again and again, 'You're in New York! You're in America!' It still seemed quite impossible that they really were being marched along a totally foreign street that was somehow quite familiar to their teacher.

Dr Foster stopped outside a small, friendly-looking cafe with seats inside covered in red plastic.

'This is the place, children. I hope you're feeling hungry!' He led them inside, and chose a table in a booth. They slid into their seats and a waitress called Cindy (according to her name badge) came over with six menus and a mug of coffee for Dr Foster.

64

SeaBEAN

The waitress explained all the choices on the menu, which went on for four pages, then left them to decide what they wanted. The pub on St Kilda only served jacket potatoes, with three different kinds of filling to choose from, and they'd never heard of half the things on offer: grits and scrapple didn't sound very nice, but waffles and syrup and Key Lime Pie for breakfast sounded delicious. The children took a long time asking Dr Foster's advice and comparing notes. Finally, the waitress took their order and the menus disappeared.

Alice noticed a machine on the table with words written on little pieces of card inside.

'Dr Foster, what's that?'

'Ah, that's a very old jukebox. If we put in a dime, it plays music. Shall we have a go?' Dr Foster fumbled in his pocket and, among his loose change, found the right coin. They chose a song called 'New York, New York'. Sam F pushed the buttons, and the machine sprang into life. After a minute, they were all singing along, even Edie, who was starting to look as though today's adventure might not be so bad after all.

When they'd eaten all the eggs, bacon, pancakes, muffins and maple syrup they could manage and Dr Foster had paid for it all with his credit card, they walked off down the street in high spirits. Alice checked her watch: it was almost two o'clock in St Kilda time, so take away five, that made it now just coming up to nine o'clock in New York.

Sure enough, the huge entrance doors to the museum were already open when they arrived back, and they clambered up the steps. Dr Foster got a map for each of them, and they stood in a circle to make a plan. Alice saw a poster advertising a new 3D film that was being shown at 11am about making energy from the waves.

'Look, Dr Foster, can we go and watch that?'

'There are hundred of things to see here, kids. How about we split up? I'm going to take Hannah and the boys, but Edie and Alice, you can look round by yourselves if you like.' He looked at his watch, 'So long as you meet me back here at, let's say, three ... Oh ...' Dr Foster stopped mid-sentence, and a look of dismay came across his face.

'I'm sorry to disappoint you kids, but I don't think we're going to have much time to look round the museum after all – your parents will be wondering where on earth we are if we don't get back in time for when school finishes. So in fact we only have about an hour.' He paused, and looked at their downcast faces.

'But we do have time to visit my favourite room. This way!'

Dr Foster led them briskly down the hall, through a hot sticky rainforest exhibit where they could hear the sound of tropical birds and insects, and into a small circular room containing a large display cabinet with a sign that said 'The drifting ocean currents'. Inside it were rows and rows of different shaped seabeans, each one polished by its journey across the ocean. They were round, fat, long, brown, red, grey and yellow. Alice could see hamburger seeds like the ones Dr Foster had given them, and a Mary's Bean like the one she'd given her mother. There were others called 'nicker nuts', 'sea purses', 'the snuff box sea bean' and the 'coco de mer'. Some of them had been made into necklaces and bracelets. There was a map showing where the seabeans had drifted from – Africa, Asia, America and Australia.

'Ours are way better,' Sam J concluded, grinning at his teacher. 'So what's next, Dr Foster?'

They looked round a few more exhibits they didn't quite understand, called things like 'The Polluted Planet', 'Magnetic Reversal' and 'Rising Sea Level'. They even had a quick look at something Alice spotted about nuclear versus wave energy, then the children were ushered back out onto the street again, where the little brown dog appeared to be waiting for them. They all stood waiting for a gap in the traffic to cross over to Central Park, chattering to each other about what they'd seen.

'I don't get it, Dr Foster, why is the sea level rising, and what was all that stuff about how the Earth's magnetism can switch over?' Edie asked.

A loud siren, which seemed to come from nowhere, abruptly drowned out Dr Foster's reply and they all looked round. A fire engine hurtled past them, exactly like Sam J's toy one.

'Wow!' exclaimed both boys, staring after it.

'Well, we've seen all the important things now,' chuckled Dr Foster. 'Let's get back to the C-Bean, quick as we can. It's a quarter after three in St Kilda.'

They crossed the road and the children started to run back to the little clump of trees where they'd left the C-Bean. As they approached, they could see a group of people had gathered around it, and some kind of smoke or mist seemed to be rising from the C-Bean. Alice saw a look of panic came over Dr Foster's face, and it occurred to her in a flash that perhaps the C-Bean was heading back to St Kilda without them.

The children made their way through the crowd of people and found the C-Bean being hosed down by three firemen wearing large yellow hats. The same fire engine that they'd just seen go past had pulled up on the grass behind the trees.

'What are you guys doing?' Dr Foster asked the firemen, his voice sounding peculiarly mechanical all of a sudden.

'Someone reported a kiosk on fire in the Park. Is it yours, sir?'

'Yes. Yes it is.'

Hannah whispered to her sister, 'Someone's been drawing on the side of the C-Bean – look Edie.'

Across the whole of one surface, painted in angry spiky writing, someone had written 'Hadron burn in Hell!', with a background of cartoon-like flames in red and orange.

The firemen turned off the hose. Oddly enough, the C-Bean was not the slightest bit wet after its drenching, but there was no more smoke as far as Alice could tell, just the graffiti. People started to drift away now that the spectacle appeared to be over. Alice walked round to inspect the other sides of the C-Bean. She stood in front of the C-Bean's door, and whispered 'hello', then beckoned to the others as the door swung open, and everyone went inside. Everyone, that is, except Dr Foster. Alice went back out to look for him.

Dr Foster was holding a piece of paper in his hand and was talking to a man in uniform. Alice could only hear snippets of their conversation: 'No, we don't have a permit to locate here … Today… Yes, I realise that … What? A hundred dollar fine!' The little brown dog was circling round Alice's legs. It wagged its tail and barked at her. The man in uniform looked across, frowning.

Alice waved to catch Dr Foster's attention, and Dr Foster said, 'Excuse me for a moment, sir,' and then hurried across to the C-Bean. Alice pulled her teacher inside and clicked the door shut. Then she said loudly and forcefully, 'Where is ST KILDA? Where is a PEN?' Within moments, satellite maps illuminated the central table. Alice touched on the map to enlarge Village Bay, and then touched the spot behind the church where their schoolyard lay. Alice grabbed the pen as soon as it appeared in the collection portal. As Edie called out the exact coordinates, Alice wrote them onto the white wall.

There was a pause. The children were utterly silent, each holding their breath, willing the C-Bean to return home and quickly. In the silence, they could hear a strange snuffling sound. There was a slight jolt and the door opened. Dr Foster's red plastic apple rolled off the table and out through the door, chased by a little brown dog.

The little dog shook itself dry and looked around the schoolyard. The door into the school had been left open, and he trotted inside into the warmth. The children's empty sandwich boxes were on their desks, and the dog sniffed each of them in turn, licking up crumbs. Obviously rather hungry, he went over to Dr Foster's desk where he found an open packet of biscuits. The dog tugged at the wrapping and two digestives fell out, sprinkling a shower of crumbs onto his fur. The dog was just licking his chops contentedly when the first child appeared.

Sam F caught sight of something scuttling away when he entered the classroom. Whatever it was ran and hid under the nature table. He thought perhaps it was one of the St Kilda mice, which sometimes came inside on a cold winter's day and were twice the size of a normal mouse. Having seen so many incredible things that day, he didn't give it another thought.

Dr Foster stood beside the C-Bean and made sure all the children emerged safely, and then followed them back into the schoolroom. He was still holding the hundred dollar fine he'd been issued. Alice saw him stare at it again, raise his eyebrows and shake his head as he walked back to his desk. Then he screwed it up and threw it in the recycling bin.

'Well, kids, it's been quite an unbelievable day. Literally. I bet we'll all wake up tomorrow and think it was some kind of weird dream. I think we've discovered that the C-Bean has immense powers, and if we treat it well, there might be other journeys it will take us on. I'm just glad that the first one happened to be somewhere I know!'

'Can we go on another adventure tomorrow?' Sam J piped up hopefully.

'Not until I've read the instruction manual properly, no. I'm sorry we didn't have time for you to give us the proper tour today, Alice, but

I think in the circumstances I'd better have a good read of it myself this evening. See you tomorrow everyone.'

Alice stayed behind to email Charlie. She needed to share her experience with someone.

> Charlie - Our new classroom called the C-Bean is absolutely amazing. I can't wait for you to come back. Today it took us to New York - really! Alice.

As she shut down the computer, she heard a scuffling noise, and then she felt something warm and wet nudge her hand. When she looked round there was the little dog, sitting quietly on the story rug behind her, his head tilted on one side.

'Oh, it's you. You're definitely lost now! Come here, little one.'

The dog shuffled forwards on his bottom, then stopped and wagged his tail. She could hear a low chuckling bark grow in the back of the dog's throat. When he woofed the sound echoed around the high ceiling of the old school room, and the dog appeared to frighten himself. Alice ruffled his fur.

'Well, I can't leave you here,' she said. 'You'll have to come home with me.'

The two of them sauntered up the grassy street in the twilight, the dog weaving from side to side as it caught new smells, but always returning to Alice's side. The seabirds were calling above the cliffs in the distance. There were no other dogs on the island, apart from the dog that belonged to one of the men who worked on the ferry. This one was quite similar – the same kind of mixed-up mongrel – only he had no collar and apparently no name. A waif and stray that had accidentally found its way from New York to St Kilda. Alice could not imagine what her parents would say.

'Wait here,' she told the dog, and he sat down by the back door.

Alice went in. Her mum was feeding Kit on the sofa. She snuggled up beside them. She was about to tell her mother about the dog, when he appeared in front of them, uttered a soulful little cry, and lay down. Alice's mum jumped, and the baby started to cry.

'Mum, it's OK, don't be scared. This is our new dog, he just got here, and he's called …' – Alice cast her eye around the room looking for inspiration – 'he's called Spex,' she decided, as her eyes landed on her mum's glasses case.

Alice's mum was rocking Kit to stop him crying. She didn't look cross, but she didn't look pleased either.

'Is that so? Is that because he ex-Spex to be looked after?' her mother teased. 'Is he the ferryman's dog?' She paused but Alice didn't answer her. She just tried to look appealing. Taking his cue from Alice, the dog was trying to look appealing too, with his head on one side. Alice's mum laughed.

'Well, it's OK by me for you to have a new friend, but you'll have to ask Dad what he thinks too.'

'Where is Daddy?'

'Down at the shed. He'll be back later. He said he needed to work late this evening.'

Alice took the dog into the kitchen and gave him some leftover porridge in a bowl. Then she scrunched up an old blanket and put it next to the row of wellies.

'C'mon Spex!' she said, trying the new name and patting the bed.

The dog climbed obediently into the bed. Tomorrow she would ask Mrs Butterfield to order in some dog food from the mainland. Over breakfast she would try and convince Dad about keeping Spex.

It rained all night, hard thundering drops plummeting down so fast they sounded like they were making craters in the thick turf roof above Alice's bed. It rained so hard she could not help dreaming of rain. They were sheltering under some trees in Central Park, only the trees were closing in, and she saw they were actually policemen encircling her, and she couldn't get past them to look for the C-Bean.

Everything was a blur of green uniforms and green leaves, all pressing into her face, brushing past her with their wet surfaces … Spex was licking her hand, and Alice woke up.

The dog stared at her sleepy face, barked and ran round in circles, begging her to get up. She looked at her alarm clock: 7.30 am. Alice pulled on her dressing gown and wellies and went down the passage to open up the back door and let the dog out. It was still dark and still raining, but the little dog didn't seem to mind, and ran off sniffing at tussocks of grass and lapping up puddles. Alice laughed and ran after the dog, splashing in the puddles. Spex disappeared into one of the stone storehouses and reappeared dragging a long stick. Alice threw it for him to fetch a few times and then called him back to the house.

'We've got a dog!' she said out loud suddenly. 'Spex, you're coming to school with me. You are officially our school pet. Come on.'

When she got to school the others were already inside the C-Bean, drawing and writing with the digital pens on the table. Dr Foster had asked them to make a record of what they'd seen the day before in New York, and left them to get on while he went to make an urgent phone call. Everything they wrote or drew on the table, the C-Bean seemed to be storing and making into a big display up on the walls around them.

Alice was late because she had been looking for something to use as a dog lead. Spex had obviously never been put on a lead before, and didn't much like the feel of the long scarf she'd tied round his neck, so it had been quite a struggle. The dog walked round the C-Bean trailing his homemade lead and wagging his tail happily as all the children patted him.

Alice said, 'Meet Spex, everyone. He escaped from New York just like Dr Foster!' Then she made him sit beside her at the table. She watched the others working quietly for a while, a whole blank expanse of table in front of her waiting for her to begin too.

All she could think about were the dense green trees in her

dream. Alice stared down at the table and watched as the outlines of branches began to appear, each one growing more and more twigs, overlapping and making complex patterns. It looked like shadows on a forest floor, all moving slightly. Soon the whole table was covered with her interlocking branches and twigs.

'Hey, what's going on?' Sam F rubbed the table with his arm, trying to get rid of the branches that were starting to obscure what he was doing. He picked up his bag from the floor, pulled out his lunch box and his walkie-talkie set and dropped them onto the table, then rooted around inside to find something to try to clean the table with. The noise broke Edie's and Sam J's concentration and they looked up. Hannah was drawing skyscrapers on her side of the table, and had not yet noticed the spreading tree pattern.

Alice stood up. The air in the C-Bean had become warm and steamy as the children's breath mingled with the moisture coming off their damp clothes. The branches were not just on the table, they were appearing above the table too, faint fragments of twisting lengths of bark, then as the holograms grew, vines with huge fleshy flowers and fruits hanging down began to appear. The holograms became stronger and darker, filling up the whole space inside the C-Bean now, so that Alice could hardly see the surrounding walls any more. Spex tugged on his lead and trotted off, his nose close to the ground.

'Spex, wait!' Sam F called, as he tried to grab him, missed, and chased after him. Alice watched as they both disappeared behind a thick clump of trees.

'Edie, Sam, Hannah. Quick – it's happened again! Sam and Spex have gone.'

She stuffed the things back into Sam F's bag, slung it over her shoulder and followed after them.

The children fell into single file behind Spex, moving quickly between the trees in silence. The mist clung to the trees and was even thicker above their heads as they picked their way through the tangled green undergrowth. Alice could hear croaking and squawking from all directions. It was suffocatingly hot and sticky, like when you have been standing in a very hot shower and can hardly breathe because the air is so full of tiny drops of water. Within minutes the children were peeling off their sweaters and tying them round their waists. But they kept on moving.

After a while, the trees starting to thin out, and they found themselves at the edge of a huge empty clearing covered in yellow earth. Sam F stopped abruptly and turned round.

'Where are we? This isn't Central Park is it, like yesterday?' His eyes were wide and sweat was dripping off his chin.

Alice looked around the clearing and realised there were tree stumps dotted everywhere, each one sticking a short way out of the ground. It looked as if they had recently been chopped down. Along one side of the clearing she could see something large and bright green, and behind it a wall of sheer rock. She could hear someone shouting and their echo bouncing off the rock.

'I think we should keep a low profile until we work out where we are,' Alice said quietly. 'Let's watch what's going on from behind those bushes over there.'

Edie looked doubtful. 'I think we should just go back to the C-Bean,' she said.

'No way!' said Sam J. 'This place is like a proper jungle. I bet there are monkeys and everything.'

'And what about those bats that drink nectar, the ones Dr Foster told us about! I saw one of those weird seedpods on a tree back there,' added Sam F.

'Hannah, what do you think?' Alice asked.

Hannah sniffed and looked at Edie, who was standing with her arms folded. She was wearing green flowery leggings that blended into the background and made her look like she belonged in a rainforest.

'I like it here,' she said, 'it smells nice.'

'What will happen if one of us gets lost or hurt or something? What if we get kidnapped, and never get back to St Kilda?' Edie protested, but she knew the others had won. 'OK, but we have to stick together. No one runs off, right?'

The children nodded. Suddenly they heard a sound like a gunshot, and then its echo a moment later. An engine fired up, and the green thing on the far side of the clearing began to move. As it moved out into the sunlight Alice could see it was a tractor with long caterpillar tracks. It was making its way towards them. Without saying a word, the children ran behind the bushes and crouched down.

Spex meanwhile had wandered off and was standing right out in the open when he saw the huge green vehicle approaching. He began to bark. The barks volleyed back to him so loudly off the rock that he must have thought there was another dog, and he stopped, pricked up his ears, and then lay low with his belly pressed to the ground. The children gulped and held their breath, crouching lower.

The vehicle stopped and a man jumped down. He had a dark face and was wearing a yellow baseball cap and dirty overalls the same green as the caterpillar tractor. He pulled off the cap and wiped his forehead, then pulled it back on. He stood still for a moment watching Spex and, as he started to move towards him, his hand reached into his pocket.

Alice saw a flash of metal and was convinced it was a gun, but the man brought it up to his mouth to drink. By the time he put the flask back in his pocket, Spex had slunk away.

The man climbed back behind the wheel again, and turned the vehicle round on the soft yellow earth. The tracks churned up the surface behind it, and blobs of silvery liquid trickled into all the ruts. At first Alice thought it was petrol. It definitely wasn't water. The thought of the water made Alice realise how thirsty she was.

The children waited until the tractor disappeared, and began walking in the opposite direction in search of water. When they reached the rock, Alice remembered Sam's bag and brought out his lunchbox. They shared out the ham sandwiches (Hannah didn't want one) and the carton of apple juice between them, and each had a bite of his apple.

They could hear a constant loud hissing sound in the distance. A bit further on they came across some equipment where the caterpillar tractor had been parked. There was a stack of shallow metal pans, all dented and smeared with the yellow earth, a couple of metal cylinders and several reels of hosepipe.

'Must be water near here somewhere if there's a hosepipe,' remarked Sam F, picking an apple pip out of his teeth.

'Whoa!' shouted Sam J in a choked voice, and Alice could see a look of fear creeping over his face.

They walked to Sam J. He threw his arms out to stop them as they reached him and they saw that one step further on was a sheer drop, taller than any cliff face on St Kilda. Spread out below them was a kind of quarry, with hundreds of workers moving mounds of yellow rock using machinery while others were hosing down piles of rock. The children hadn't heard the sound of the mine because the quarry lay at the edge of a huge cascading waterfall. The hissing sound they'd been hearing had turned into a ferocious roar, louder than the roughest waves that ravaged Village Bay in winter.

Alice's legs were shaking as they all moved back from the cliff edge. When they turned round, they could see the caterpillar tractor returning. There was nowhere to hide this time, so they began to run for cover in the trees on the nearest edge of the clearing. Their feet slid in the yellow mud, and with every step across the clearing more and more lumps of it stuck to the bottoms of their shoes.

'Hey!' a voice shouted. Alice tried to go faster, but the others were much further ahead. She could see Sam F at the back, his bag hanging open, as he tried to keep up with the rest. She saw something fall out of the bag into the mud. She looked back and could see two men coming after them. She stumbled on. The men were shouting again. She saw something black and silver in the mud – it was one half of Sam's walkie-talkie. She picked it up, and spotted a boulder up ahead. Breathing hard, she hid herself behind the boulder and waited. The shouting stopped, and all she could hear was the distant roar of the waterfall.

Alice closed her eyes and counted to a hundred. Then she half-stood and peeped over the top of the boulder. In the mist she could see the caterpillar tractor moving off and a group of men following behind it, carrying their equipment. She could just make out a name written on the side of the truck: *Eldorado Brasil*. She saw one of the men lean over the cliff edge and signal something down to the people in the mine below. He was pointing in her direction. She felt sweat rolling down her back. Another trickle ran into her eye and she could feel its salty sting.

She waited a minute longer, and then called out 'Edie? Sam? Wait for me!'

There was no sign of the others. She scrambled through the undergrowth, and realised she had no idea where she was going, or which direction the C-Bean was. She was still holding the walkie-talkie in her hand and, with fingers crossed, she switched it on.

'Hello. Come in Sam! Are you there Sam? ANSWER ME!'

But there was no reply, just a soft crackle. Now she couldn't tell if it was sweat or tears in her eyes. She stumbled and caught her knee on a thorny vine lying coiled on the ground and disturbed some creatures up above. There was a loud squawking and she saw a flash of vivid blue further ahead. Her knee was bleeding, but she just rubbed it and continued walking.

There was a pile of blue feathers on the path ahead of her. The trees were very close together now and the forest was quite dark, but Alice could make out something moving under the feathers. She put the walkie-talkie down and crept forwards very slowly.

A large bird was clawing the air with its black scaly legs, trying to stand upright. Alice bent down and smoothed its feathers, but she was afraid of lifting the bird because it had a very sharp-looking beak. The bird eyed her with its bright yellow eye, tilted its head, and squawked. She decided it must be some kind of parrot.

'Hello,' Alice said.

'*Olá*,' answered the bird.

The bird managed to stand upright and began a sort of lopsided hopping. Alice laughed. It was showing off she thought, splaying out its tail feathers, organising them with its beak, and chanting '*Olá olá!*'

The walkie-talkie made a tapping sound, then a voice crackled, 'Alice, is that you?'

Alice grabbed the walkie-talkie and fumbled with the button on the side, pressing it and speaking into the mouthpiece.

'Edie, is that you?'

'Negative. It's Sam Fitzpatrick.'

'Thank goodness! That wasn't me, Sam, it was a parrot you heard.'

'Did you say a carrot?'

'Where are you Sam? Have you got back to the C-Bean yet?'

'Negative.'

'Is everyone with you?'

'Affirm … yes.'

'Including Spex?'

'Yup. He's here.'

'Tell him to come and find me Sam.'

'How do I do that? He's a dog.'

'I know, but just try. Say, "go find Alice" or something.'

'OK.'

'Keep this thing on, OK?'

Alice stroked the bird's feathers and waited. Her knee was throbbing now and her throat felt like it was coated with sandpaper. After a moment or two the parrot clambered onto her lap, and then hopped up onto her shoulder. He was using his beak and his claw to open a seed. She watched as he managed to open the seedpod and then remove the seeds. She wasn't sure if she should keep moving or not.

Suddenly the little dog bounded through the undergrowth and ran round Alice, wagging and barking. The parrot flew up into a branch in alarm and squawked loudly.

'Spex!' Alice was so relieved to see him she felt sick and cold all of a sudden. He licked her face and sat at her feet, looking very pleased with himself.

'Where are the others, Spex?' she asked, shivering.

The dog started sniffing the ground and rooting in the undergrowth. He picked up the walkie-talkie in his mouth and brought it to her. As Alice put her cardigan back on she felt the other card key to the C-Bean in her pocket. She studied the silvery image of the earth and ran her fingers over the writing on the front. How were they going to find the C-Bean again? Why had it come to this place when no one had written any coordinates on the wall?

The bird squawked at Spex, and flew into the next tree. Spex jumped up and barked, then ran further along the path the way he'd come. Alice followed, and the parrot flew down, its feathers still dishevelled. She stopped and realised it was slightly injured.

'C'mon, hop on,' she said gently, holding her arm out. The scaly legs gripped onto the sleeve of her cardigan, and she found she could only walk quite slowly with the parrot. The dog ran back from time to time, leading the way. At one point they had to wade across a narrow stream. Spex splashed across. And back again. Alice thought about taking off her shoes and socks, but then thought it was safer to keep them on in case there was anything in the water that could bite or sting her. She moved through the shallowest part as quickly as she could, the parrot still clinging to her left shoulder.

Up ahead, there were more and more trees and the path disappeared from time to time. They had to push their way through the tangle of undergrowth. The bird flew up into the branches, and limped from one tree to another. Just when Alice had no idea which direction she should be heading, the walkie-talkie made a bleeping noise. Alice tried to speak into it, but there was no reply. It wasn't even crackling now. The batteries must have gone dead. She felt as if she might cry at any moment. She swallowed hard. All she had now was the card key. She took it out of her pocket and held it up to the light again. Something had changed. The globe was spinning very slowly. Alice remembered how when she first found it, the globe spun faster when she approached the slot. What if …

Alice moved more quickly now, ignoring Spex and the parrot. After a few metres the globe stopped spinning. She stopped, turned, and set off in the opposite direction. A few moments later the globe started rotating again. She pressed on, and the rotations got a little faster. Alice's heartbeat sounded louder than the roar of the waterfall now. She couldn't hear the dog barking or the parrot squawking, and she could no longer feel the pain in her knee. Just keep going, she told herself, the spinning globe will show me the way.

Alice's Blog

28th January 2018

You know I'm really supposed to be writing about life on this island for my blogs, but it seems that lately we've been spending a lot of time getting stuck in other places, so I don't think this is really going to make much sense to some people reading it. I mean, who's going to believe it when I write about us popping over to New York for the afternoon, or the Amazon rainforest for a couple of hours?

So if you think I'm making it up, whoever you are reading this, it's up to you. By the way, you can post me a message telling me what you think on this website and I can have a look. And if anyone out there knows anything about a C-Bean Mark 3, or has one too, our teacher Dr Foster would really like to talk to you. It had him really worried the last time. He only went back inside the school to make a phone call, and after that the door to the C-Bean wouldn't open. Apparently we were gone for over two hours. To me it seemed like much longer, but then I was totally lost in the middle of a rainforest with a poorly knee, a stray dog and an injured bird, being chased by some men with a caterpillar tractor and not knowing where on earth the others were, let alone the C-Bean.

But when I found the other cardkey in my pocket, I just knew I could find my way back. I beat the others to the C-Bean by five minutes and thirty seconds in the end. I could tell that Edie had been crying because she was frowning and sniffing and wouldn't even look at me when they arrived back, but she didn't say anything because they had too much to tell me.

The boys were so excited they could only explain things with actions and sound effects. They jumped around with their arms near their knees whooping until I got the general idea about the monkeys they'd seen. Then their arms started juddering back and forth and they made a buzzing noise through their teeth as they described how they'd watched some more trees being cut down with chainsaws. But when they got to the last part, both Sams fell silent and let Edie open Sam F's bag and reach inside.

I knew it wasn't an animal because she would be too scared to do that kind of thing. If one of the boys had reached inside the bag, I would have guessed a tree frog or a huge furry spider, or one of the bats they'd been talking about. But it was much more beautiful. Edie stood in a little patch of sunlight, pulled out a large lump of something she'd wrapped up in some tissues, and held out her hands for me to see.

It was knobbly, like a giant piece of popcorn when it's got stuck together with sugar at the bottom of the bowl. Only it was more yellow, and it looked hard like play-dough when it's been left out too long. Except it shone.

Both Sams clamoured, 'Can you guess what it is?'

I was looking at a huge lump of solid gold. Edie said they found it half buried next to a metal pan like the ones we'd seen earlier in the clearing. It was as if someone was trying to hide it and then maybe had run off, and was too scared to come back for it. When Edie gave it to me it was so heavy I had to use both hands to hold it. Sam J said he knew it was real gold because he had bitten it, like pirates do, to test it's not fake, and he showed me the teeth marks.

Then it was my turn. Spex was still snuffling round my feet, so the parrot stayed stubbornly up in the tree until I got Hannah to hold the dog still. I called to the bird, and there was a flash of bright blue and then he landed on my arm. I said, 'Say hello to my friends', and it was like we'd been rehearsing it all the way through the forest, because he said 'Olá' to them, and even did a little bow with his head. Everyone laughed, which made him embarrassed, so he started fiddling with his broken tail feathers.

But that was just the beginning of the Show and Tell session: when we got inside the C-Bean, it had its own story to tell. It started showing us all kinds of data on the walls, including maps and photos of everywhere we'd just been, of the men and the quarry and loads of close ups of all the equipment. I noticed that we were even in some of the pictures. The notes and images were being put into some sort of sequence on the central table, and we could see the yellow earth, and the caterpillar tracks, and Sam's walkie-talkie lying on the ground in one.

Then the C-Bean started to label everything it had photographed: it put words like 'gold panning equipment', 'mercury amalgamation process' and 'cyanidation', whatever that is. I got the feeling they must be all be about something dangerous or polluting because the words flashed red and a yellow triangular warning sign came up beside them. I wanted to read everything to know what it all meant, but Edie was getting really worried about us getting back, so in the end we just wrote up the coordinates of St Kilda (I know them off by heart now) and waited for the little jolt to know we were back in the schoolyard. Just as I walked out of the door I remembered that the manual said the C-Bean was assembled in Brazil. Perhaps it was homesick.

We could see Dr Foster through the window, pacing up and down in the schoolroom. He kept running his hands through his white hair and making funny faces like someone had just stepped on his toe. He didn't even seem to hear us when we opened the door. We walked in quietly and sat down at our desks.

I can't remember what he said to us exactly last Friday. He didn't really even need to say anything. We thought he was going to shout at us for getting locked inside the C-Bean without permission. It seemed like he didn't know whether to be cross or pleased to see us. He kept starting sentences and then sighing and not finishing them. Some of the things he said were more to himself than to us, like 'I should have been there,' and 'It's just not fair'. It took us a long time to realise that he was not talking about our adventure at all, but something much more serious and upsetting.

The phone call that Dr Foster had to go and make earlier that morning was to New York. After he managed to tell us that, there was a long pause, and his eyes went very red. He blew his nose into a large white hanky, and smoothed his hair again. Then he said that there had been a fatal accident in his family. He told us his sister worked in a research laboratory where they did experiments using poisonous chemicals. I might have been imagining it, but I think he even used the word 'cyanide'. He said had to go back to New York. He had to get a plane. The helicopter was coming for him. He had to give her a decent funeral. He was sorry, but school would be closed for a few days.

Dr Foster never even noticed that there was a bright blue parrot in the room who'd been listening very attentively all the way through, not even when our teacher stood up to leave and it did a sympathetic little squawk. I wanted to give Dr Foster a hug, but he just put on his big grey duffle coat, picked up his battered leather briefcase, smiled at us with sad eyes, and left. We all looked at each other, and had nothing to say. All I knew was I couldn't say the word 'dead' out loud.

Edie walked over to the nature table, took the golden nugget out of its tissue wrapper and put it carefully in the middle. Then she dried her eyes on one of the tissues and threw them all in the bin.

We found a jar of sunflower seeds in the classroom and gave them to our parrot. He was hopping from foot to foot with excitement as we fed them to him one by one. When the seeds were all gone, he started squawking 'Peri-gro-so, peri-gro-so'. I could tell the bird was getting upset about something. He flew over to the window and sat on the windowsill sulking. He was still there the next morning.

I asked my parents, do parrots sleep at night? What do they need to keep healthy and happy? These are things we are going to have to find out, because there are only seabirds on St Kilda for company, and he's not the same as them and I don't suppose he even speaks their language. Mum and Dad think I've been given a project to do on parrots while Dr Foster is away.

Dad says I can help him in the wave energy lab if I haven't got anything else to do next week. I said, only if there are no poisonous chemicals like cyanide in his lab. Then he gave me a lecture about how there are way too many poisons in the air we breathe and in the food we eat and the water we drink, and about all the heavy metals that are getting into our eco-systems and ruining our planet.

I said, 'What, like gold?' Dad said, 'Gold's not a heavy metal,' and I said, 'Yes it is, it's very heavy actually,' but he said it was just inert. I asked him what inert meant, and he said, it means that you can eat it and it wouldn't do anything to your insides. But he said they use dangerous chemicals in the gold mines, like cyanide and mercury, to make the tiny bits of gold stick together. Dad said that mercury is a heavy metal and, interestingly, it's also the only metal that's a liquid most of the time.

After he'd told me all that I said, 'Dad, you should be our replacement teacher while Dr Foster is away, you'd be quite good at it!' and he just laughed and said he was too busy.

I kept thinking about the silver liquid in the caterpillar tracks. Was that mercury? Did we find a gold mine?

Later that evening, I asked Mum if she had ever heard of Eldorado. She was singing Kit an old Scottish song she used to sing to me when I was little, so at first she didn't answer. I sat on the bed and waited until Kit was snoring softly in his cot, and then Mum put her arm round me and told me a story about a beautiful city where everything was made of gold. The mayor of the city covered himself with gold too, and they called him El Dorado, the golden man. Mum said she thought it was supposed to be somewhere up the Amazon in Peru or Brazil, but that no one had ever really found it. Then she said sleepily, 'Why do you ask?'

I wanted to blurt out, 'That proves it!' The lump we brought back really IS gold. And wherever we went to wasn't just anywhere, it was Eldorado. It exists. But they've ruined it. All the trees have been cut down. Instead I said, 'I saw the name written down somewhere, that's all.'

29th January 2018

Today was the first day of no school. I stared at the map of St Kilda that's on the wall in our kitchen while I ate my breakfast, wondering what to do. It's a really detailed old map with every little lump and bump marked in wiggly lines called contours. If you go across the lines you're walking uphill or downhill, and if you go along in between the lines, you are walking on a level. Only you can't see the lines in real life. Unless you're a mapmaker. I bet mapmakers walk around and see contours everywhere they go. On the cliffs, the lines are bunched so close together they're almost touching.

I tried to imagine that instead of being one or two miles across our little island was in fact a huge continent, and that the little stream running down towards the sea was actually a massive river like the Amazon. So I bet you can imagine how my heart skipped a beat when I saw a little black symbol marked Amazon's House on the Gleann Mor side of the island! I went up closer to have a better look. It said on the key at the side of the map, 'believed to be the hunting lodge of a fabled female warrior'. We walked all over the island the summer we moved here, but I don't remember seeing this house or hearing that name.

A plan exploded into my head. I ran round to Edie's with Spex and persuaded her and Hannah to come on an expedition to Gleann Mor. Jane, their mum, made us all a packed lunch, and we walked over to Sam J's house. Sam F was there too, and they were playing with the walkie-talkie set, which was working again now they'd put new batteries in it. In the end, we all ate lunch there, and set off with our bellies full of soup and sandwiches. Mrs Jackson gave us some flapjacks wrapped in silver foil and a bottle of water to share between us.

It was spitting as we set off, and Spex darted around in between our legs, shaking himself dry every now and again but making us wetter. He seemed more excited about this adventure than the trek through a real rainforest, probably because he wasn't on the lead.

We followed the stream that runs into the Bay back to where it first appears out of the ground, just past the end of the village. There are stone cleits dotted all over this part of the valley, but they stop when the ground gets steeper. Dad told me once there are over a thousand of them on St Kilda. We could see the radar station spying on us from the summit. We climbed higher up until we were at the bit shaped like a saddle, where you can suddenly see the other side of the island. Well, if I'm honest, we only caught a tiny glimpse of the cove in the distance before the clouds closed in and it became too misty to see anything very much.

Hannah was soaked and shivery. She said she wanted to go back home, but we persuaded her to keep going. Edie and I held her hands and we ran down the other side, so she would warm up. Spex barked all the way down.

I was worried we'd miss the Amazon's House, but we nearly ran into it. It was about the same size and height as the C-Bean, but made out of long thin stones, and instead of a perfect cube, it was circular with a mossy dome on top. We walked around the walls until we found the way in.

'It stinks of dead sheep in here,' remarked Sam J, as he ran his hand along a ledge on the inside wall. The ledge turned into a deep shelf and he climbed up onto it. 'And bird poo.'

'Can we have a flapjack now?' Sam F asked. Edie opened the

silver foil and we all helped ourselves, including Spex who ate the remaining crumbs as well. As our eyes adjusted to the gloom, we could see other shelves and cubbyholes built into the walls. Here and there stones were missing, and you could feel gusts of wind and rain coming through the cracks. I could see something that looked metallic in one of the cracks, and when I reached out to pick it up, there was a sound like a sword being pulled out of its scabbard. I asked the others if they could hear something like scraping metal, but they said they couldn't.

After the others had gone back outside, I examined the metallic thing. It was smaller than the C-Bean's cardkey, attached to a chain, and had rounded corners. It was dull and dirty, but when I rubbed off some of the dirt, I could see it said RAF and had a long number and some initials punched onto it: D.C.F.

In the stillness I could hear another noise, like a woman clearing her throat. Without saying a word, I put the metal thing on a chain back into the recess, zipped up my coat, and stood very still. It felt like someone was breathing just in front of me, and for some reason I imagined I was standing face to face with the female warrior who once lived here. I stared hard at the space in front of me. She didn't move or make a sound, but I could feel her warm hands touch my hair. I couldn't be sure but I think she also whispered Kit, Kit, Kit. It might have been a bird or the wind, of course. But whatever it was, it really made me shiver.

I ran outside. The others were down by the water where Spex was sniffing trails of scent. The sea in the cove looked strange – like it was burnt – and it moved in a sort of syrupy way.

When I got closer I could see that Spex was not sniffing but picking things up and carrying them and then putting them down again higher up the slope, away from the water. His tail was wagging with delight because he had found something that needed to be done, but when I saw what it was, I yelled at him to stop.

I counted a hundred birds. They were all different species – skuas, fulmars, petrels, guillemots, gannets, kittiwakes – all lying on top of each other, all dead. They'd been washed up by the last tide and stank of rotting fish. Their feathers were sticky with this thick black film. The boggy grass was covered in the same stuff, all the way up to the last high tide mark, where a long line of rubbish and seaweed had collected, all stuck together like treacle toffee.

The skies had cleared a bit. I looked out to the horizon. I'd heard about tankers that crashed into rocks and split open, spilling their cargoes of oil everywhere. I knew it had happened in other parts of Scotland before. But there were no ships in sight. We decided we needed to tell someone what we'd found, and we knew there would be someone up at the radar station we could tell. They could get a message to the mainland, and send someone over to investigate.

Halfway up the hill, the rain started again in earnest, and we were walking straight into it. I could feel it lashing my face, even with my hood pulled close against my cheeks. We lost sight of the radar station, and although we had Edie's compass we still couldn't work out which way we were walking. A soggy Spex followed me, his tail between his legs, waiting for me to show that I had forgiven him for moving the birds.

We never did find the radar station that day, but we did

manage to make it back to Village Bay before it got dark.

In the local online newspaper it said that Mr McLintock called a meeting in the pub and five men hiked over to Gleann Mor the next morning. They could see for themselves that something had to be done about the damage the oil had caused. Everyone was angry, and a reporter arrived by helicopter from Glasgow with three environmental experts to work out what had happened. Dad says he's even more determined now we're not going to let the island be sold to those Russian oil people. But we haven't got much time. There was another piece on the website which said that the school was closed on St Kilda for the time being, because of a death in the teacher's family, and that he had returned to New York to attend his sister's funeral, who had died 'under suspicious circumstances'.

There seems to be altogether too much sadness here at the moment. Even our parrot is down in the dumps. I don't think he likes the cold, and he is definitely not a fan of peanuts. I got him some from the shop yesterday, but he seems to prefer pork scratchings.

2nd February 2018

It's been raining non-stop for three whole days. I've emailed Charlie in Hong Kong six times, but he hasn't replied. So I've decided to add some more to my blog.

The reporter told Dad last night that one of the environmentalists thinks the birds did not all die because of the oil slick. Instead they might have been poisoned by the fish they ate. So they've sent samples of the contents of their stomachs in test tubes on the ferry today, to be tested in a lab in Glasgow. We rang Lori there yesterday to wish her happy birthday, but she said she hadn't heard anything about all these catastrophes.

Today we did every jigsaw we have, including the one of the Australian St Kilda I got for my birthday. We played every game we could think of and Edie won every time. Out of pure frustration, Sam J and Sam F had a big fight. The only thing I could think of to make them stop fighting was probably not such a great idea. I suggested, as Charlie was not replying to any of my emails, that we could, if we wanted to, pay him a visit.

Everyone went quiet and looked at each other. We knew school was meant to be off limits, but no one had said anything about the C-Bean. Just a short trip, I suggested, and we'd come straight back.

They didn't need much convincing. We've decided to do it tomorrow, while there's a special emergency meeting about the oil slick going on.

A strong smell of garlic drifted into the C-Bean, but even then the children had no way of knowing if it had worked or not. Once again, the walls had become cloudy and porous and all they needed to do was to walk through it to find out if they had arrived, and if so, where exactly.

'Well, are we going out or not?' For once, it was Edie who seemed impatient to find out. The others nodded. This time, they'd come prepared: Alice had left Spex at home that morning, she'd brought the C-Bean's instruction manual with her, and they'd all brought lunchboxes.

Even when they were out of the C-Bean, they still seemed to be in the middle of a cloud. In the far distance they could hear the hum of traffic and strange incantations that sounded like someone singing very out of tune through a loudspeaker. The sounds seemed to be coming from below. Alice thought they must have got Charlie's coordinates wrong, and that somehow they'd ended up in the sky. But then she realised she was walking on a kind of hard grey surface. She bumped into another wall that felt at first like the C-Bean, and heard someone else do the same.

'Hey, what's this? Did the C-Bean move?' Sam F demanded.

Alice knocked on the side of the other smooth flat-sided thing, and a deep metallic boom resonated and seemed to echo away down a long tunnel. Feeling her way around the side of the metallic object, it started to curve away and then she found a large rectangular opening. The cloud was thicker still around the opening.

'Hello!' Alice said very quietly, just to test it.

'*Olá!*' came the echo.

Then there was the unmistakeable sound of squawking and feathers flapping.

'Who brought the stupid parrot? I thought we agreed to leave him behind.' Edie's sense of adventure was vanishing already. But so too was the cloud, and the bird's blue shape slowly emerged from the billowing whiteness, silhouetted against a large silver air-conditioning duct.

'Hey, we're on top of a roof!' Sam F said suddenly, peering over the edge of the nearest ledge at the streets far below.

'Guys, this is not just any roof – we're on top of a skyscraper!' Sam J announced, his arms outstretched, like a mountaineer who'd just climbed Mount Everest.

All around them the city was densely packed with tall buildings standing upright like the bristles on a hairbrush, and where they stopped the sun was setting behind a huge expanse of silvery water dotted with all kinds of boats.

'I'm scared,' said Hannah, and sat down quickly, wrapping her arms tightly round her knees.

'Question is,' said Alice, thinking out loud, 'are we on top of the right skyscraper? Are we even in the right city? This looks like New York did. Say we are in Hong Kong, how do we know for sure this is Harbourside Tower 6?'

The two Sams were moving around the roof among a maze of pipes and boxed-in machinery. One of them found a hatch with a stiff metal fastening. Between them, they levered it off, lifted the hatch door and flopped it back onto the roof. The parrot flew over and perched on the edge of the opening. They spied a ladder inside, and called out.

'Over here!'

Alice and Edie looked at each other, and then in a single movement they both scooped Hannah up and carried her over to the hatch. She buried her head in her lap and did not even peep until she found herself inside the opening on the top step of the ladder going down. Hannah wasn't the only one with wobbly legs: they all felt a tiny bit nervous. The open hatch let a pool of light into the hallway below. Alice followed Hannah down.

As they started walking along the first corridor, blue lights set into the floor like an airport runway came on automatically. The walls were covered in silver and black stripes, and each apartment had a pair of doors that looked like a big fridge-freezer, with a wide one and a narrow one, and two long metal handles side by side in the middle. On a plaque next to each door was a number.

The boys were jumping from one blue light to the next, with the bird waddling along the carpet behind them.

'What did Charlie say the number of his Grandpa's apartment was?' Edie asked, studying each one in turn. 'We're up to 3106 here.'

'Number 3003,' Alice said.

'Well, everything here starts with 31, so maybe he's on the floor below.'

They found another set of silver doors, three in a row, with a button beside each one instead of a number.

'These must be the lifts,' said Edie. 'How do we call one?'

Sam J pressed all three buttons and they stood waiting. No one was prepared to admit it, but none of them, including the parrot, had ever been in a lift before, they'd only ever seen them on TV. Above the lift doors were arrows pointing up or down. Suddenly there was a loud ping and one set of doors opened. The parrot squawked loudly and started flapping when he saw another blue parrot reflected in the mirror at the back of the lift. Alice had to pick him up and carry him inside. Sam F pressed the button that said 30, and a second later the doors opened again and they stepped out into an identical corridor. Except, as Hannah pointed out, the runway lights were pink, not blue.

The children walked past more silver and black stripes. They passed a cleaning lady in white overalls pushing a trolley along. She smiled and said something they didn't understand. And then, there they were, facing the door with 3003 written beside it.

'Aren't you going to knock, Alice?' Sam J asked in a singsong voice.

'What if he's not there?' Edie said, biting her lip. 'What if it's just his grandpa at home – we can't speak any Chinese.'

They all stood rooted to the spot. The smell of garlic was stronger than ever.

'OK, here goes.'

A maid in a white apron answered the door, and looked quite surprised to see a group of five children and a blue parrot standing there. Alice asked in a clear voice, 'Is Charlie at home? We've come to see him.'

The maid smiled and welcomed them in with a sweep of her arm. She didn't say anything but she seemed to understand what Alice had said. They stepped onto thick grey carpet, and she gestured to the collection of shoes in the lobby.

'I think we're supposed to take our shoes off,' hissed Edie.

They lined up their shoes, which still had traces of St Kildan soil mixed with a yellow Amazonian variety stuck to the soles. Then they tiptoed in their socks behind the maid into the living room.

Charlie was sitting cross-legged on the floor opposite an elderly man at a glass table, and they were both eating with chopsticks out of little bowls. Charlie had his back to them and turned when he heard the maid enter the room. He nearly choked on his food when he saw his school friends standing there. He put the chopsticks down and stood up.

'Hi!' Alice said. She felt shy all of a sudden, and looked down at her socks. The Sams were giggling. Edie shot them a look of contempt and then said, 'We came to see you, Charlie.'

'I can see that, but how on earth …? Ah well, it doesn't matter, come and meet Grandpa; we were just eating our supper. Dad's not back yet. Is that … a parrot?'

'Yup,' said Edie. 'Alice found him when we went to the Amazon in the C-Bean. He wasn't supposed to come with us here. But we did leave Spex at home.'

'Spex? Who's that – a new kid in our class?'

'No. He's a dog. He came back with us accidentally from New

York.' Edie said, pushing her glasses up her nose and rolling her eyes to show she knew it all sounded a bit ridiculous. The children looked embarrassed. There was a long pause.

'Cool,' said Charlie, 'now let's eat.'

Alice felt a surge of relief, and let the parrot hop off her arm and onto the sofa. Charlie moved across to the kitchen area to fetch five more bowls of garlic chicken and rice and then arranged more cushions around the table. The children sank gratefully onto their knees and picked ineptly at the rice with their chopsticks. Hannah opened up her lunchbox instead because she didn't eat chicken. Then Charlie said something in Chinese to his grandpa and the old man nodded. He wore a grey tunic and looked very wise and wrinkly.

'Lak dis,' Charlie's grandpa said, showing them how to hold the chopsticks. He chuckled with amusement as they all tried to coordinate their fingers and thumbs around the two sticks. Charlie poured out some pale looking tea that smelled of flowers from a china teapot into seven tiny cups and handed them round. Alice noticed none of the cups had handles.

'So …' he began, casually running his hand through his mop of black hair, 'Have you got something to tell me?' Charlie looked expectantly at Alice. She raised her eyebrows and pointed up at the ceiling.

'We arrived on the roof just before. You know, in the C-Bean. It was quite easy really.'

'Can I go up and see it?' he said eagerly, wiping his fingers on his checked shirt and looking much younger than almost twelve at that moment.

'Yeah. But we kind of hoped you'd show us a bit of Hong Kong while we're here.'

Charlie turned to ask his grandpa something.

'Grandpa says we can go and take a look around the harbour before it gets dark. C'mon.' Charlie picked up his mobile phone from the kitchen counter and they said goodbye to his grandpa, who bowed his head very solemnly. The maid was in the hallway arranging their shoes in a line facing the door, ready for the children to put back on.

In the lift, Charlie thumbed a text to his Dad while the Sams counted out loud from thirty down to zero, but they weren't counting quickly enough: the lift glided like silk down to the ground floor in less than ten seconds.

Alice was looking at her watch and frowning. 'Charlie, what's the time?'

'Six-fifteen.'

'Oh,' said Alice, and worked out St Kilda was eight hours behind Hong Kong. Their footsteps echoed across the marble floor of the entrance lobby as they walked towards a revolving door. Just as the children were about to go through it, the parrot got in a panic and starting flying in circles around the lobby.

The security guard was dozing at his desk, and woke up with a start when the bird squawked loudly in his ear as he flew past. The guard jumped to his feet and pressed a buzzer, but Charlie quickly ran and opened up the emergency exit at the far end of the lobby. The alarm went off but by then Alice had managed to coax the bird down. She carried him on her shoulder out of the emergency exit, leaving the alarm ringing incessantly, and several bright blue feathers whirling above the fan on the security guard's desk.

The street was teeming with people pouring in all directions from office buildings. Alice could hardly see the pavement. She looked up instead and saw wires and signs hung across the street like knitting that had come undone. Charlie was beckoning her to follow, and she could see the others were right behind him. There was a large shopping centre ahead with huge screens all over the façade showing advertisements for things in giant complicated symbols, but she couldn't understand any of them. Charlie dived down a side street that was lined on both sides with market stalls, each with its own plastic canopy and bare dangling light bulb. Alice wanted to look at all the things they were selling, but she didn't want to lose the others like she had the last time. A little way ahead, Charlie stopped.

When she caught up they were standing in front of a stall that seemed to be selling all kinds of shrivelled up dead animals, some in jars, others in transparent plastic boxes. Dead snakes, rhinoceros horns, beetles, spiders, birds, and many other creatures and parts of creatures Alice couldn't identify.

'What do people buy this stuff for? Souvenirs?'

'They make medicines out of it. Chinese people believe it will make them live longer. Some things they eat as a delicacy – like those bird's nests.' Charlie was pointing at some yellowy-brown saucer-shaped things wrapped in cellophane.

'Bird's nests?' Sam J wanted to check he had heard right.

'Yeah, these ones cost five thousand Hong Kong dollars a box.'

'No way!'

Alice stood fingering one of the smaller boxes containing an almost transparent seahorse. She noticed that Edie was standing well back, holding tight onto Hannah's hand. The air was close, and people were pushing past with bags of groceries. They walked to the end of the night market and turned into a quieter, darker road. The Sams were whispering about something. There was a very strange smell. On the corner there was a fruit seller sitting on an upturned crate. She had arranged all kinds of fruit on a sheet of grubby cardboard in front of her. One of the fruits was as big as a football and covered in brown spikes.

'Charlie, what's that?' Alice asked.

'Ah, they're durians. It's called the King of Fruits here. That's what the smell is; Dad says it's like sick mixed with dead rats and smelly socks!'

'Do people really eat it?'

'Yeah. I've tried it. It's a bit like onion-flavoured custard. But it smells so bad on the outside, you're not allowed to take it in the subway trains or in any of the shopping centres.'

Alice reached down and touched the fruit. It was like an enormous seabean. The fruitseller picked it up and handed it to her. She cradled it in her arms, thinking how it weighed about the same as her baby brother. But it felt rough and cool like a rock.

'Charlie, have you got any money? I really want to buy this thing.'

'What for?'

'To put on the nature table at school.'

'You're mad, Alice.' Charlie laughed and fished in his pocket for some money to haggle with the fruit seller. A minute later Alice was walking happily along, swinging the heavy fruit in a plastic bag.

'C'mon, this way,' Charlie shepherded them all across the road. The parrot squawked as if to reinforce his instruction and transferred himself to Charlie's shoulder, sensing he was now the leader. Through a brightly lit doorway they saw a group of men in green overalls crowded round a television cheering loudly at a horse race on the screen. When it was over, they handed each other money. The six children crossed the road in the darkness and realised there were no more buildings here, just a wide pavement. Alice could hear the sloshing of water against a wall. The sound was suddenly so familiar, she closed her eyes and was right back in Village Bay down by the seawall, listening to the waves lapping against the pier. She breathed in, hoping to smell the strong clean St Kilda air, but this air was full of diesel, rotting fruit and fish.

All along the harbour, fishing boats had drawn up, and fishermen were busy hauling their catch in crates onto the dockside. The two Sams ran on ahead to look in the boxes. There were men hosing down the decks as the boats bobbed and knocked against the harbour wall.

'Look at the size of these fish!' Sam J was riveted. 'That one's got like a sword coming off the end of its nose.'

'And some are still alive!' shrieked Sam F.

'We've got enough pets now,' said Edie firmly, but they all stood and looked at the writhing mass of silvery fish in the nearest crate. All except Charlie, who was sending another text.

There was one boat that did not look the same as the others, or at least it was not unloading fish. There was a crate on the dockside with some tall metal cylinders in it that looked like silver fire extinguishers. The boat was bright green, and on the side Alice could see a logo with a name. There was something familiar about it. She went a little closer and saw the name was written in a logo she recognised: Eldorado Brasil.

Alice stopped swinging the shopping bag, and her stomach lurched as she remembered the caterpillar truck. She could see someone inside the boat's cabin looking at some maps. On the deck were eight or nine other crates containing rows of the same dull metal cylinders. The man in the cabin came out, and when he looked up she felt sure she recognised the same dark face and yellow baseball cap she'd seen before in the rainforest. He glared at her, or rather at the parrot, who flinched on her shoulder, his claws gripping her collarbone tightly. Alice could sense that the man and the bird knew each other.

Just as Charlie said, 'It's dark, we need to get back to the apartment,' a surly-looking gang appeared, and Alice saw they were the same men they'd just seen gambling on the horse race. A short fat man lunged for the parrot, but Charlie caught his arm as Alice ducked and ran towards the fishermen. She called to the boys 'Sam! Sam! Run!'

The boys obeyed instantly, but she couldn't see any sign of Edie or Hannah.

The parrot flew from Alice's shoulder onto the deck of one of the fishing boats, and squawked excitedly. He kept saying 'vamos, vamos' to the men. The fishermen, thinking he was after their catch, began shouting at the him, and slid their boxes across the wet dockside out of reach. The man in the yellow cap jumped ashore and was now coming towards them. Alice waited behind some crates until he got close and then swung for him with the durian. She caught him by surprise. The man slipped, and unable to regain his balance, fell backwards into the water. The other men didn't stop to rescue him, but came after Alice and Charlie, who were by now heading back towards the night market, calling for the parrot to follow.

Charlie had taken one of the metal cylinders from the crate and, holding it like a baseball bat, swung it at two of the men. He missed and held the cylinder out in front of him to keep the others at bay, all the while running backwards along the dockside. Finally he turned and ran, the cylinder tucked under his arm.

Alice stumbled after him, past the fruit seller and up the busy street that was now crowded with tourists. She pushed past them, craning her neck upwards looking for the parrot, willing him to follow her. She could hear police sirens, and emerged at the crossing opposite Charlie's apartment building. She could see the security guard standing by the plate glass window, watching as the commotion built up in the street outside. She turned back and saw Charlie, Hannah and Edie a few metres away. But there was no sign of either Sam.

'Alice! This way!' She looked back across the street. The boys had opened the emergency exit and beckoned to her. When the lights changed, she slipped through the crowd, crossed the road and stood on the pavement, calling for the startled bird. At last she caught sight of some blue feathers, and he swooped in through the door just ahead of her. The security guard was at the other end of the lobby facing away from them, and there might be just enough time to run across to the lifts before he had time to react.

She pummelled the buttons outside the lifts, summoning them under her breath. Alice and the two Sams got in the one that arrived first, the parrot shrieking *perigroso, perigroso* like a demented old lady. There wasn't time to wait for the others, because the security guard was already heading their way. The doors slid shut and they began their ascent to the thirtieth floor.

Alice banged on the door to Charlie's grandpa's apartment but there was no reply. An alarm started ringing again in the corridor, and when Charlie, Edie and Hannah stepped out of the next lift, Alice said hurriedly 'Let's go up to the C-Bean and wait there until it's all quietened down.'

Charlie nodded, and led the way up the final flight of stairs and onto the roof, still carrying the metal cylinder. The C-Bean loomed mysteriously in the moonlight, surrounded by the billowing clouds of steam from the air conditioning units. Alice said 'hello' as she approached the door, and stepped back to let Charlie go in first. She stood and waited for all the children to come out of the hatch. But there was no sign of the parrot.

She looked up into the night sky, willing him to return, and suddenly he exploded out of the hatch and started to wheel around above the building. He flew higher and higher, his squawks getting fainter as he got further away, until Alice thought she would never see him again. She was about to close the door of the C-Bean, when a vision of blue flashed through the cloud of steam. The bird landed rather ungracefully and then waddled across to the door, muttering to himself and shaking his head from side to side. Alice ushered him into the C-Bean and closed the door gently behind him.

Charlie was talking to someone on his mobile phone. The other kids looked exhausted and sat on the floor. Alice's mind was still racing through the streets down below. She put down the durian finally.

'That thing really does smell, Alice, why'd you have to get it?' asked Edie.

'She did knock the man that was after us into the water with it,' pointed out Sam J.

'Yeah, that was way cool, Alice,' murmured Sam F.

'Did any of you recognise him? The parrot did – in fact I think he was after the parrot, not me,' said Alice.

Charlie finished his call. 'Sorry, that was my Dad. He says I'm grounded. I can't believe it, you guys show up, I ask if I can show you round, and it's only just gone dark, but Dad gets crazy with me, says there's all kinds of bad people who hang out down by the harbour.'

'Well, we did run in to a few,' Alice observed.

'I suppose so – who were those guys, do you think?'

'Pirates!' said Sam J.

'Yeah, right,' said Edie dismissively.

'What's in the cylinder, Charlie? Maybe that will give us a clue,' Alice suggested.

Charlie looked at his impromptu weapon for the first time. The label was in Chinese but written in characters he couldn't read. There was, however, a warning symbol they could all recognise: a skull and crossbones.

'See, told you it was pirates!' Sam looked triumphant.

'Der! That just means that whatever is inside it is dangerous,' said Edie sarcastically.

'*Perigroso, perigroso,*' chirped the parrot nervously.

'Is that what it means when he says that – danger?' Alice wondered.

The C-Bean, which had been completely unresponsive until then, flickered into life, and across the four walls started to display hundreds of words written in black in all different languages and writing systems. The words pulsed round the walls for a few seconds, and then stopped, and certain words turned red. The children stood up to inspect the red words. Both 'danger' and 'perigroso' appeared. When they touched the words, the C-Bean said them out loud.

'Wow,' said Charlie, 'this thing is amazing! How does it do all this stuff?' Among all the other words, he recognised the Chinese character for danger: wei. It looked like a person curled up in a ball hiding under a roof.

Alice had an idea.

'Charlie, put the cylinder on the table, so the label is facing down.'
Charlie held the cylinder on its side so it wouldn't roll off, and the
table, which had been blank until now, began to process information.
A strange diagram like a hundred square began to appear, only
each coloured square had letters written in it as well as numbers.
The diagram was not a complete shape, but was jagged along the
top. It looked a bit like a city skyline. One of the squares down
near the bottom right began to flash. It had the letters 'Hg' written
inside it. Alice touched the square and beside the diagram a single
word appeared: mercury. Then a map appeared next to it, showing
where mercury came from. There were places marked in grey where
mercury ore was no longer mined, and only one place was coloured
red, to indicate mercury was still being mined: China.

'That's it. It's mercury. Dad told me about it. It's a poisonous metal
they use to extract gold. Someone must be smuggling it from Hong
Kong to the gold miners in Brazil, Charlie!' Alice's eyes shone with
fear and excitement.

'What on earth are you talking about, Alice?'

'The boat in the harbour had the same logo on it as the one I saw
on a truck in the rainforest: Eldorado Brasil. They must be connected.'

'Shhhh,' said Edie, 'Can you hear something outside?'

They all listened. They could hear footsteps and then there was a
loud knock on the side of the C-Bean.

'We better get going,' said Edie.

'What about Charlie? He can't come back to St Kilda with us.'

'I'll text my Dad and say I'm staying over at a friend's.'

'But you're grounded.'

'Well, I'm not going outside now, am I? We don't know who's out
there. C'mon, how do you work this thing?'

While Charlie texted his father, Alice took a deep breath and said
'TO ST KILDA'. The children waited in silence. They could hear

footsteps walking round the perimeter of the C-Bean, and people using walkie-talkies. In another moment they were gone.

Alice knew something had gone wrong because they couldn't seem to open the door to get out of the C-Bean. Nor had the walls become porous for them to step through like before. But they had arrived somewhere. Outside they could hear music and a crowd of voices, and a series of loud bangs that sounded like gunshots. Except every time the bangs stopped, they could hear voices cheering.

Suddenly there was a knock on the door, and someone shouted, 'Hurry up in there, I need to pee!' They had a strong accent, but it was not Scottish, Chinese or American.

Charlie said, 'Now what do we do?'

Alice was rummaging around in her schoolbag for the instruction manual. She opened the digital book and thumbed anxiously through the index. There were entries for problem diagnosis, system malfunction and manual or remote override. The problem section listed all kinds of issues, including 'C-Bean non-responsive' and 'involuntary system shut-down'. Both entries suggested that the C-Bean could be malfunctioning due to electrical storms, magnetic interference, or excess heat or cold. Its operating range was given as being between 50 degrees centigrade and minus 50 degrees centigrade. It had been hot in Hong Kong, but Alice felt sure it was nowhere near the maximum.

'Charlie, was there any telecommunications equipment on the roof of your apartment building?' she asked.

'Could be. The whole building has wireless 5G super-broadband access.'

Then Alice remembered Charlie had been using his phone as they departed.

'Something has messed up the transport function. We're going to have to reset the C-Bean.'

'How do you do that?'

'I don't know – we'll just have to follow the instructions in here.'

Sam J was munching a sandwich from his lunchbox, and Hannah was drawing pictures of the strange fruit and shrivelled up animals she'd seen in her sketchbook.

'How long will that take? Cos I need a pee too,' Sam J announced.

Alice scanned through the section titled 'How to reset your C-Bean Mark 3'. First, it said, evacuate the cabin.

Fine, we can't do that, thought Alice. Then, using the external keypad, re-key the serial number which is embossed on the card key, followed by three Xs. Then hold down the green button for ten seconds.

'How on earth do we do that when we can't even get out?' wondered Alice aloud.

'Do what?' Charlie asked impatiently. 'Let me see!'

'The reset routine only works if you are outside the C-Bean. We're stuck inside.'

'Isn't there some kind of code word we can use, or something?' Edie suggested.

'Genius, Edie!' said Alice.

Alice tried to think. When she said Hello, the C-Bean opened the door to let her in. So what if she simply said Goodbye?

They heard a mechanism unlatch, and the person outside flung open the door and burst in with a bemused look on his face.

'Who are you?' Sam F was staring at the boy and blocking the doorway like a proficient nightclub bouncer. 'This is private property, OK?'

'I thought this was the loo block, mate,' the boy said, rolling his eyes. 'That's the trouble with festivals – never enough places to pee.'

'Festival? What festival?' Sam continued his interrogation with a rising note of panic in his voice.

'St Kilda Festival, you dimwit. What's this, some kind of meeting of the Melbourne Secret Society?'

Sam F pushed past the boy, and stepped out onto a sandy patch of dried up grass in front of an esplanade of palm trees. It was pitch black and very hot, and coming up the middle of the esplanade was a loud marching band. The man at the front was wearing a leopard skin tunic and beating a drum. High above his head, and merging with the night sky, waved a large dark blue flag covered in stars with a tiny Union Jack in the corner.

Charlie stood beside Alice, blinking in disbelief. The others came out of the C-Bean like frightened rabbits and stood with their hands over their ears as the procession filed past.

'Welcome to Australia, aliens!' the boy said, and walked off.

Suddenly the night sky exploded into colour. Fireworks lit up crowds of faces picnicking under the palm trees, and illuminated the suburban houses that ran along the edge of the esplanade. In the other direction, the children could see in the brief intense flashes of light a pier stretching out into the sea, and a long sandy beach.

Alice recognised the scene from her jigsaw puzzle and grinned.

'Awesome! This is the other St Kilda. Remember – the one Reverend Sinclair told us about once? Where the people from our St Kilda arrived by boat over a hundred and fifty years ago.'

'But why have we arrived here?' Charlie looked perplexed.

'I dunno. The C-Bean must have been thrown off course – it understood the instruction for St Kilda, but because of the interference from your mobile, it came here instead of Scotland.'

'Cool,' said Charlie, watching a huge white firework die away to blues and reds.

They could smell some delicious food cooking, and realised that the C-Bean had landed next to a cluster of brick-built barbecues, where people were grilling fresh fish.

'I'm hungry,' Sam J said, salivating in front of the nearest barbecue.

'We haven't got any money,' pointed out Edie.

'I have,' said Hannah, and fished some coins out of her jeans pocket.

'It's Scottish money. You need Australian money here.'

'We can try. I've got some Hong Kong dollars too, remember – c'mon,' said Charlie.

The men running the barbecue were starting to pack up, and said the children would get something to eat for free if they mucked in. Sam F and Sam J looked ecstatic: they were both given striped aprons to wear, and a knife each to slit open pitta bread to make grilled fish sandwiches.

'Where are you kids from exactly? Sydney?'

'No, we're from the real St Kilda,' said Edie solemnly.

'Whad'ya mean the real one – this is the real McCoy here!'

'We're from an island called St Kilda off the west coast of Scotland.'

'I thought no one lived there any more,' said one of the chefs.

'They didn't until five years ago. We went out to live there because our parents are setting up a wave energy plant,' explained Alice.

'Oh, now I get why you guys are here. This is now the main environmental festival of the year, ain't that right, Geoff? All kinds of alternative energy people are here as well as all the music and stuff. Including the wave guys – there are a several wave energy companies operating in Australia too. Beats using charcoal. That's best left for barbies, eh Geoff! You like tomato salsa on your fish, kids?'

They handed the children a portion of food each, a couple of bottles of homemade lemonade, and a leaflet about the festival.

'Tonight's the last night – crikey it's already ten-thirty – only another few hours to go 'til next year,' Geoff remarked.

The six children thanked the two men, and wandered over to the seaside promenade to sit on a bench and eat their food. Alice recalled it was only seven-thirty when they left Hong Kong, so they were a few hours ahead again. Another place, another time zone. It was all a bit dizzying. She stared out to sea, and instead of trying to place herself somewhere in time, she tried to picture where she was on her illuminated globe.

'That's Antarctica out there,' she said after a minute or two.

'How do you know?' Sam J said with his mouth full.

'Well, Melbourne is at the bottom of Australia, and there's nothing below it except miles of sea, and then tons of icebergs, and then the South Pole.'

'Hey, there's penguins!' said Sam J.

'Don't be stupid, there aren't any penguins in Australia,' Edie protested.

'Look, here!' Sam pointed at an advert in the leaflet, showing a picture of some little penguins waddling along the beach near St Kilda, looking like a family going home after a day at the seaside.

The children all laughed and both Sams started doing imitations of penguins waddling.

'Where's our parrot?' said Alice suddenly. 'I don't remember him getting out of the C-Bean.'

They finished their food and threw the napkins into a bin on the seafront, then walked back to the C-Bean. There inside was the bird, cowering under his wing and refusing to move.

'I think he's a bit traumatised,' said Alice, concerned.

'What should we do?' Edie asked. 'I vote we go back now. We've got to work out how to get the C-Bean to work again properly, right?'

Alice picked him up and gently wrapped him in her cardigan. She emptied her bag and put the parrot inside with just his head poking out, saying 'There, there,' like she'd heard her mum say to Kit when he was crying.

'Nah,' said Charlie, still poring over the leaflet. 'I vote we take a look round the festival just until it's over. There's all sorts happening.'

As Charlie was the oldest, the decision went his way. Edie was already fretting and saying they had to all stick together.

As they moved towards the main street, they could hear someone making a speech through a loudhailer. A crowd had gathered round a small platform, waving banners and placards saying 'Stop Poisoning our Rivers!' and 'Whales and Dolphins Deserve Better!' Alice persuaded the others to stand and listen.

A man in a flowery shirt took the loudhailer from the person standing next to him. He had rolled his sleeves up and Alice could see sweat pouring down his neck. He loosened his tie and cleared his throat.

'You want to know something?' he began. 'In the past year two whales and three dolphins had been found beached on the Melbourne coastline. The Yarra River is still as polluted as ever, with heavy metals present in the water long after the gold mines had closed upstream. In my opinion, and it's one supported by a number of leading experts I can tell you, mercury and other substances are getting into the food chain and severely affecting the wellbeing of our marine mammals, making them confused and disorientated.'

Alice was trying hard to follow, but the man's voice was becoming quite emotional: 'That's why,' he went on, 'they are getting beached. It is wrong, and something needs to be done!' He lowered the loudhailer from his mouth and stepped down from the platform. The crowd applauded and cheered. Alice thought he sounded just like her dad when you got him started on something he cared about.

Charlie was moving off. The bird was fidgeting inside her bag, so Alice lifted him out and onto her shoulder. They walked on up the street, where there were stalls giving away free T-shirts and mugs as well as leaflets about a whole variety of environmental causes. Sam J spotted a stall about the Phillip Island penguin colony.

'Hey look Alice, they're called Fairy Penguins. It says there are hundreds of them near here!'

Alice was thinking about the hundred dead seabirds she'd counted at Gleann Mor. She wanted to ask someone about it. Just then someone tapped her on the shoulder. She turned round and a very tall woman with piercing blue eyes was looking not at her, but at the parrot.

'What are you doing with a rare endangered species?' she demanded suspiciously.

Alice shrugged. 'We found him. He was injured.'

'Found him? Where?'

Alice didn't know what to say. Who was this woman, and why did she want to know? Charlie stepped in, 'It's none of your business, my Dad got him from an animal rescue place in Hong Kong.'

'Let me take a look at him. I'm a vet. I have a stall over this way. I work for an Animal Protection Agency. Come with me,' she commanded. The children looked at each other. They were tired of running away, so they followed meekly after her.

The woman took the bird and placed him on the table behind her stall. 'If I'm not mistaken, this is a Spix's Macaw – it's native to Brazil and as far as I know is now virtually extinct in the wild, did you know that?' she said accusingly, as she spread out his wing and tail feathers.

'No, we didn't know,' Alice said, wondering if the vet was going to confiscate their parrot.

'Hey, cool, Alice,' said Sam J. 'We can call him Spix!'

'Yeah, then we've got a Spix and a Spex,' added Sam F.

Spix clucked approvingly at his new name. Although he appeared a bit affronted at the vet's examination, he sensed he was in expert hands.

'He says things,' said Sam J.

'Ah yes, they're very good mimics,' the woman said, sounding a little more relaxed.

'He says stuff like "perigroso",' Sam went on amiably.

'Hmm, Hong Kong you said. Why does he say things in Portuguese, I wonder?' said the vet.

'Is he going to be OK? His tail, I mean?' Alice asked, changing the subject.

'Yes, there are no broken bones. But he should be living in a rainforest, not being kept as a child's pet.' She gave Spix a seed from her pocket and watched him shell and eat it. 'No problems with his eating and drinking?'

'No, I don't think so.'

'They eat the fruit of the swamp almond tree where they come from, but a lot of the forests where the tree grows are being devastated. So the bird's natural habitat is slowly being destroyed. Here – read this.'

The vet handed them another leaflet with a picture of a parrot very like Spix on the front cover. Spix hopped back onto Alice's shoulder, and bobbing his head, said over and over, '*Muito mau. Vamos, vamos.*'

'What's he saying?' asked Sam F.

'If I'm not mistaken, he's saying something like "Very bad, let's go",' laughed the vet.

The children wandered back towards the seafront. They had been swept down a different street by the crowds leaving the festival, who were now congregating at the tram stops and bus stops, waiting to go home. They could see a huge sign marked 'Luna Park' up ahead, and could hear screams and fairground music spilling out. The children stared longingly through the ticket barriers at the whirling and cavorting rides inside. Then they walked around the perimeter of the amusement park, where some little striped tents had been erected. There were signs propped up outside each one, offering fortune-telling, crystal ball gazing and palmistry.

An old lady with curly white hair stepped out of one of the tents, and smiled at the children. Alice looked at her apprehensively, and the woman beckoned to her. There was something familiar about her.

'Come child, I can tell you are troubled. Let me show you something.'

Charlie said to Alice, 'Have you ever had your palm read or been told what will happen to you in the future?'

'Can they really do that?'

'They say they can. Lots of people say it's all guesswork.'

'Shall I go, Charlie?'

'Yeah, why not? We'll wait for you right outside. I'll make sure nothing happens.'

Alice followed the woman into her tent, and sat down on the little stool. The old lady sat opposite, behind a table covered in a cloth marked with what looked like a noughts and crosses grid.

'I practise Kumalak, my dear Alice. It's a system of fortune-telling from Kazakhstan that's been used for more than a thousand years.'

'How do you know my name?'

'What is your question?'

'I don't know what you mean?'

'The one thing you want to know, tell me, what is it?'

Alice thought hard while the woman chanted mechanically under her breath. She felt she wanted to ask a lot of questions. But what did she want to know exactly? She felt as if the sea was surging through her, oily black waves crashing through her chest. She felt dangerous chemicals tingling in her fingertips and on the tip of her tongue, and the sharp dryness in her throat she had felt in the rainforest. There were monkeys, parrots, chainsaws and her baby brother creating a cacophony in her tired brain.

She took a deep breath, and felt the old woman in front of her disappear and instead the female warrior was there again, confronting her from long ago, her warm hands touching her hair.

'I want to know why.'

The old woman nodded and pulled out a little bag. She emptied out a pile of beans from the bag and divided them into three piles. Alice counted forty-one beans in total. The old lady began by touching each one to her forehead, dividing them up among the nine squares in front of her, according to some ancient formula. She looked up at Alice from time to time, as if she was trying to work out what she was thinking. At last the beans were all distributed to her satisfaction, and the woman spread her hands out on the table.

'There. Now let's see,' she began. 'The number three is about the three realms of nature: animal, vegetable and mineral. For you, these have become powerfully interconnected. Your question of why?" seeks to learn the links between them and how these become broken, in nature as well as in your own life.'

Alice tried to concentrate on what the old lady was saying. She felt so tired, and the sound of seagulls outside was making her homesick. The woman continued.

'Three beans in this square tells me you are caught up in a vivid journey, full of strange encounters, and that from this you are gathering new strength. You are far from home, and even there you have encountered changes, dangers and unsettling news. You must return, and apply what you have learned.'

Alice felt a little overwhelmed. It was as if the woman had looked at her under a microscope and seen all the fuzzy teeming particles as an overall pattern. But it still didn't make sense. She just knew that she was on the other side of the world and she needed to get back home. The woman smiled knowingly to herself, and scooped the beans back into the bag.

Alice looked in her pockets for something to give her by way of payment. At first all she could find were a few seeds the vet had given her. Then she found the two-pound coin Dad gave her on her birthday for the cream cake. She laid the coin on the table, thanked her and left.

'So are you going to marry me and live happily ever after, then?' Charlie teased when she came out. He grinned but Alice looked stern and serious.

'Nothing like that, no. C'mon, we need to get back to the C-Bean,' she said, and strode at great speed down the street towards the esplanade.

Alice took great care inputting the correct St Kilda coordinates this time, and made Charlie switch off his mobile phone. The jolt came sooner and more fiercely than usual. Even after the C-Bean had apparently arrived at its destination, it seemed to rock unsteadily on its base. Alice could hear wind gusting and waves pounding right outside. There was a sudden crack of thunder and the C-Bean shuddered.

'Great. I've arrived back home in the middle of the worst thunderstorm ever,' said Charlie, rolling his eyes.

'At least we made it,' remarked Alice.

'I sincerely hope so,' said Edie.

Silence.

Another thunderclap tore open the door suddenly. To begin with all they could see was a mass of angry clouds and rain sheeting down onto a choppy grey sea. It was impossible to tell if it was night or day. In the midst of a flash of lightning Alice could see it was their St Kilda, sure enough: across the bay she could see the familiar misty outline of the smaller island of Dun. In the same moment she realised, however, they had not arrived in the schoolyard, but were instead perched precariously on the jagged landing rocks along the coast, just above the gun emplacement.

As they all moved towards the door to peer out, the C-Bean tipped abruptly towards the sea, and the children clung onto each other in terror. Over the roar of the waves, Alice barked at the others to go back to the far side of the cabin and stay there. As a result, the C-Bean shifted in the opposite direction and seemed to wedge itself into the rocks. Charlie crawled on his hands and knees back to where Alice stood gripping the edge of the door, and they both looked out and assessed the situation. Edie let go of Spix, who was struggling to get free and join Charlie, but he was blown out of the door before he could manage to land on Charlie's shoulder.

Chapter 9: On the Rocks

Alice leaned out, calling 'Spix! Come back!' An enormous wave crashed on the rocks below and threw up a huge spume of spray. The last thing she remembered was that she couldn't see the parrot. Then a sudden gust of wind must have slammed the door shut and caught Alice sharply on the head and knocked her out cold.

The old lady was throwing hundreds of seabeans up into the air, crying 'Kumalak, kumalak'. Alice was running around trying to pick them all up again and put them back in the little bag. Every time she picked one up, it turned into a dead fish, or a dead bird, and the seabean was its beady silver eye staring up at her. The silver eyes became blobs of silver liquid that trickled out, and Alice tried to pick it up, but it was impossible. It spilled through her fingers in tiny silver balls and ran in all directions…

When she came to, Alice's head was throbbing violently. Edie and Charlie had done their best to clean the wound on her scalp with salt water and had wound a sweater around it.

'Are you feeling OK, Alice?' Edie asked. Alice was lying in her lap and it was pitch black inside the C-Bean.

'A bit sick,' she admitted. 'How long have I been unconscious?'

'About half an hour,' said Charlie from a dark corner. Alice could hear the other children breathing.

'I think the C-Bean is pretty badly damaged, Alice,' said Edie, breaking the news to her friend as gently as she could.

But Alice was only dimly aware of where she was. 'It smells in here, have I been sick?' she asked.

'No, it's that spiky fruit you got, remember!' said Sam J, and he rummaged around in the dark to find the malodorous durian and pulled it out of its plastic bag.

Alice was feeling distinctly nauseous now, and retched loudly. Charlie crawled across the floor to open the door. The wind had dropped, but the sudden movement caused the C-Bean to lurch again and shift position. The durian rolled rapidly across the floor, making a strange ticking sound as its spikes grazed the floor, and fell into the sea below. Charlie watched as it resurfaced, and laughed.

'Well, that's two passengers down. Only six more to go. Who's next?'

'I don't know what you think is so funny – your Dad'll be worried sick about where you are,' said Edie reproachfully.

'Let's not talk about being sick, shall we. The smell is bad enough in here as it is,' retorted Charlie. 'Alice, are you up to a bit of rock-climbing?'

Alice groaned softly, and said, 'No way'.

Charlie had an idea. 'Edie, what's your Mum's phone number?'

He switched his phone back on, thumbed the number, including the Scottish dialling code, and waited for someone in the Burney house to answer. There was no reply.

'Any other numbers I should try?'

Alice said weakly, 'Call my Mum, Charlie, she'll be at home with Kit.'

Charlie tried again. 'Mrs Robertson? Is that you? It's Charlie.' The line was very crackly and he could hardly hear what Alice's mum was saying, and then the line cut out.

'How long have we been away roughly?' Edie asked.

Alice managed to lift her arm and look at the glowing hands on her watch. 'Five hours or so.'

'Perhaps we should try and call the air rescue people,' said Edie. 'They'd be able to get us off the rock safely.'

'Air rescue,' repeated Alice drowsily, and passed out.

She could hear helicopter blades scuttering round above their heads. Next she was dangling from a long rope with someone's arms wrapped round her. Seawater in her eyes and nose. Then there was a blanket that smelled of something strange. Dad's face with anxious eyes. Someone stroking her hair.

Alice missed the worst of the trouble their trip to Hong Kong had caused. It was two days after they'd arrived back on the island before she regained consciousness properly. The worst was definitely when the grown-ups realised Charlie Cheung was among the children that had been rescued, but there was no sign of his Dad. Charlie was more concerned there was no sign of a parrot, and that's when Edie's mum, who was treating all the children for shock and hypothermia, decided that Charlie must have hit his head too.

A few days later Charlie brought round the newspapers for Alice to read. Several newspapers had sent reporters over from the mainland to cover the story of the island children who had been blown onto the cliffs in their mobile classroom/stranded on the mountain in a storm/abducted by aliens, depending on which paper you read. They mostly reported that by the time the Scottish authorities had contacted Charlie's Dad in Hong Kong, he'd already filed Charlie as a missing person when he didn't return home that evening.

One of the reports also noted, but made clear the events were not necessarily linked, that bizarrely the police had also carried out a raid in the vicinity of the Cheung's apartment building. There had been reports, it said, about a cache of illegal mercury found at the harbour as well as sightings of a UFO on the roof of Harbourside Tower 6. Neither the alleged mercury nor the UFO had been found.

'So how long have you been grounded for this time, Charlie?' Alice asked as she handed back the newspapers.

'Forever, I should imagine. Dad thinks I took my air ticket from the apartment and flew back to Scotland by myself, and was brought over from the mainland in the air rescue helicopter. As far as he's concerned it's the only logical explanation, so that's what I've let him believe. But the good thing is, I've been grounded here. Dad flew back yesterday, and we're staying put now.'

'That's great.'

They fell silent. Alice sat up in bed and felt the bandage covering her left eye and most of her head. She could hear Spex barking outside.

'What do you think of Spex?'

'That's another story. When you lot disappeared, apparently he did too, so they all thought that wherever you were, Spex was with you. Then it turned out he'd been staying with Old Jim in his hovel up the hill. The next morning, Mr McLintock saw Spex pestering some grey seals down on the beach.'

'I like that he found Jim. One lonely waif and stray meets another.'

Alice's Dad came in carrying a tray of scrambled eggs and toast.

'Hi Charlie, feeling better? Here's your lunch, Alice. Eat up. Then, if you're feeling up to it, we can have a gentle stroll down to the Evaw shed this afternoon, because today is Launch Day!'

'You're launching the wave energy machines already?' Charlie was incredulous.

'Yes, your Dad said the last tests he ran in Hong Kong on the control system worked a treat, so we're going for it – two months ahead of schedule!' Alice's Dad rubbed his hands together with excitement. Then suddenly he looked all gloomy and forlorn.

'It's just a shame about the hundred thousand pounds we still need to buy the island – that's going to be an impossibly difficult task to achieve, I'd say, considering we've only got about ten weeks to go before the deadline. Shame. Those wretched Russians and their oil rigs. Everyone was looking forward to having a massive party to celebrate stopping all that!'

Alice's Dad got up and left the room.

'We've got to do something, Charlie, it's not right.'

'Yeah, but time's not exactly on our side, is it?'

'Anyway, what about the C-Bean's control system?' Alice asked, changing the subject.

'Ah. Sorry, more bad news. There was no sign of the instruction manual when they searched inside. Or the mercury cylinder. And there are no plans to get the C-Bean off the rocks for now. They are saying it's too difficult and they're going to leave it there 'til the weather is better, and then try to winch it off the rocks. But it'll be expensive. I suppose there's a chance we could get it working again.'

Alice looked bitterly disappointed and pulled the covers over her head. Charlie waited a few minutes for the sobbing to stop, and then slipped out of her room. In the end, both Alice and Kit slept through the Evaw launch, but their mother watched from the kitchen window as the last of the huge pieces of machinery and long orange floats were manoeuvred out into the sombre grey sea.

Alice's next visitor was waiting patiently by her bedside when she woke the next morning. The first thing she saw when she opened her eyes were fluorescent yellow shoelaces.

'Dr Foster!'

'Alice, it's so good to see you again. Gee, what a lot of things have happened while I've been gone!' Alice thought he reminded her of someone else, but she couldn't think who it was.

'I'm so sorry about the C-Bean. We shouldn't have gone in it without you there. I'm sorry we've got it stuck on the rocks.'

'Now don't fret about all that, Alice. Normal school is starting again on Monday, so I thought I would bring you over some books to read, if you are feeling up to it.' Dr Foster sounded more business-like now.

Alice nodded. She was staring at her illuminated globe and wondering if they'd ever go on any more adventures in the C-Bean. She closed her eyes and drifted off to sleep.

She dreamed she was in the C-Bean, but inside it was as if she was floating in a warm pool with her baby brother in her arms. She was kissing him and feeding him sunflower seeds and he was making appreciative little gurgling noises. When she looked down he seemed to have a little fishy tail like a mermaid. The tail was swishing backwards and forwards in the water, so Alice let go to see if he could swim. He paddled towards the table in the centre, which was like a little island in the middle of the pool of water, and grabbed onto the edge.

'Good boy,' she cooed, 'good boy!'

Spex licked her face, and Alice was awake again. Judging by how fast his tail wagged, he obviously thought she was talking to him in her sleep.

The first day Alice felt well enough to go back to school, the sun was shining. She saw primroses flowering in the grass and puffins returning to nest in their burrows on the cliffs. When she arrived at school, the classroom smelled a bit strange, like someone had left some very sweaty socks on the radiator overnight. Dr Foster had placed a large bag on his desk.

'Now come over here, kids, I've got something exciting to show you.'

The six children came forward to stand in front of Dr Foster's desk, feeling a little uneasy.

'Remember on my very first day I showed you a seabean, and I told you that sometimes you can find things washed up on the beach from far far away? This morning I went for my morning stroll along the bay, and caught sight of a large round object on the beach. At first I thought it was a coco de mer, which is a kind of seabean that can float many hundreds of miles, but now I think it's something quite different. See what you think. It's got a very strange smell.'

He unzipped the bag and pulled out Alice's durian. On one side the spiky brown skin was broken and they could see the inside of the fruit. Some of the spikes had been snapped off by the storm waves, and it no longer looked as fresh as when they'd bought it. Alice and Charlie exchanged glances, and then Charlie put up his hand.

'Yes, Charlie?'

'You can get those in Hong Kong. It's called a …'

'… King of Fruits,' the children all chimed together, and laughed.

Dr Foster looked very surprised and pleased at the evident enthusiasm of his students.

'Very good! Now, Charlie, can you make up a card for it, and as it's King of the Fruits, you can put it over there in pride of place on the nature table.'

Dr Foster pointed to the nature table, and noticed that something else was already occupying pride of place. He walked across to the table, and the children started fidgeting nervously. Sam J pulled his face and pretended to bite his finger.

'Now, what's this? I see something's been added to our little collection while I've been away.' In between the mermaid's purse and the hamburger seedpod sat the gold nugget. The teacher picked it up and turned it slowly in his hands.

'Now that's heavy. Where did you find it?'

Silence.

'Come on; let me in on the secret. Whatever is it?'

More silence.

'Well, I have an idea of what it is, but it seems quite improbable …'

Sam J could hardly contain himself.

'It's a lump of gold and we found it when …'

Edie butted in, 'Well, it looks like gold, but actually it's a rock that we found near Gleann Mor and we painted to make it look like a lump of real gold.'

'Is that so? Well, it's very realistic – and very heavy. If it was real, it would be worth a lot of money.'

Sam F raised his eyebrows. 'How much would it be worth, Dr Foster?'

'Let's weigh it, shall we, and work it out.'

The lump turned out to weigh 2.5 kilogrammes. Dr Foster said he thought that gold was worth about sixty thousand dollars a kilo.

Edie was the quickest. 'Dr Foster, that's a hundred-and-fifty thousand dollars' worth of gold. I mean if it was real, that is.'

'Very good, pity it isn't, that's what I say.'

Alice felt faint and went into the toilets to fetch herself a glass of water. She stared out of the window at the green slopes of Conachair stretching into the distance. How much did Dad say they still needed to buy their island? A hundred thousand …

Her train of thought was broken by a noise outside the window.

'*Perigroso, muito mau, muito mau.*'

'Spix!'

Alice was overjoyed to see the missing parrot hopping along the stone wall outside. He looked up at her and ruffled his feathers against the wind.

Alice opened the window and held out her arm. The bird squawked and flew across and landed first on the windowsill and then hopped onto her arm.

'*Olá!*' crooned the bird.

'So you're back!' laughed Alice, thrilled to see him again.

Alice's Blog

Monday 19th February 2018

At last someone has responded to my blog. Well, it's more than just someone, it's the actual designer of the C-Bean, a lady called Karla Ingermann from Germany! You can read what she wrote in the column next to this one, but the most important thing she told me was that we can't leave the C-Bean out of action for more than a hundred days, or its operating system will lock up and stop working altogether. Anyway, Karla says she is prepared to come over and help us get it going again. As it's already been a week since the C-Bean got stuck, that leaves us ninety-three days to fix it. At least that's two more weeks than we've got to come up with the money for the island.

So Charlie and I are trying to think of how to persuade Mr McLintock to pay for it to be rescued off the rocks where we got stranded, and get it brought back to our schoolyard. Even then it might not work any more, but I think it's worth a try. I know Dr Foster wants us to get the C-Bean back, but he says it will cost a lot, and right now the islanders are only concerned about buying the island, so there isn't going to be any spare money for the C-Bean.

My head is finally feeling better – they say I bruised my skull really quite badly, and that I've got to go for a special test in Glasgow, to make sure everything is all right. They are going to put me in a scanner thing and take pictures of my brain in slices. But it's only to make sure – Mum says she thinks I'm perfectly fine.

Dad says the launch phase of the wave energy plant is going

well – the machines are now properly anchored out in the sea to the west of St Kilda, where the biggest, strongest waves are, and it's already generating power. But it's not yet hooked up to the part that actually collects the power and feeds it into the National Grid – that's the part Dad is working on now. We hardly see him at the moment because he's always working down in the shed.

There is one worrying thing that's happened: the cylinder containing the mercury, which we brought back with us from Hong Kong, has been washed up on the beach. Charlie found it, but unfortunately the lid had come off and the thing was completely empty. So somehow all the mercury got into the sea during the storm. This is not good news, especially after finding the dead birds on the other side of the island. It might take years, they say, for the grass and the sea to recover, and for the fish and birds to re-establish themselves.

Also, about the gold nugget: we couldn't tell Dr Foster, but it is real. If we could just think up a way to sell it, the money we'd get for it would pay for everything: the rest of the money needed to buy the island, and depending what we get, maybe enough to pay to rescue the C-Bean and get it fixed.

I've had one idea, but it might not work. I am thinking about telling my sister Lori, because she is going to meet us in Glasgow when I go for my scan, and while Mum and I are at the hospital, perhaps she could go and sell it to a gold dealer or something.

Tuesday 20th February 2018

There was a huge commotion in Village Bay today: Spex came running up to the houses barking his head off before it was even light, and nobody knew what was the matter with him. He kept running down towards the water and then running back again. Mr McLintock went down to the beach in the dark with his torch to take a look. He came running back and woke up the whole village. Spex was right: there was an emergency. A female minke whale was beached on the shore. Dad and I got down to the beach a few minutes after Charlie and his dad. The whale seemed very confused and didn't have the strength to push herself back into the water.

'It must have happened at about 2 am when it was high tide,' Charlie's dad said. 'I think it's important to keep the whale's skin wet until the next high tide this afternoon, then there's a chance she could get back into the water and swim away.'

Mr McLintock went to get his truck and his fire hose. The men connected the hose to a pump from the Evaw sheds. It just about stretched as far as the little inlet of seawater at the side of the bay, but only if they sprayed the water high into the air, and then it more or less landed on the whale.

Edie's mum's managed to take samples of blood from the whale to send to the environmentalists at the lab on the mainland. While she pushed a hypodermic needle into its thick browny-grey skin, I stroked the side of the whale. It mostly felt soft and rubbery but there were rough patches where barnacles had attached themselves to her skin.

The minke whale was at least ten metres long and lying on her side, so every time she blew air out of her blow-hole, the people standing on that side of her got a blast of warm fishy air. But the smell wasn't nearly as disgusting as being shut in the C-Bean with a durian.

All morning the men kept on spraying her with water. I asked Charlie's dad why he thought the whale had got stranded, and he said sometimes it's just that they're ill, sometimes they get confused by deep-sea signals from submarines, but nowadays they think it's more likely to be because of poisonous chemicals in the sea water. That was what I was afraid he would say. I remembered the man in Melbourne giving the speech saying whales can get disorientated due to mercury poisoning. I felt terrible: what if the mercury from our cylinder had got into this whale's body or brain while it was feeding in the bays around St Kilda?

By about one o'clock in the afternoon the tide was coming in fast, and the whale started to try and move herself with her fins. We were all soaking wet and frozen, but no one was prepared to leave the beach until we had done everything we could to get her back in the water. Then, by my watch, at 1.28pm she was finally afloat again, and swam off into the deeper water of the bay, blowing out through her hole very happily.

Dad said, 'Right, I don't know about you lot, but I'm off to have a nice hot bath!' Everyone laughed, and we all went back up to the village.

So we have successfully performed one rescue operation, but rescuing the C-Bean is now really urgent. We only have a couple of months to think of something.

Today I had a meeting with Charlie, Edie, and the others during school lunch break and we decided that we should definitely try to sell the gold nugget. Sam F took lots of pictures of it this afternoon with his camera so he would remember it, and then I brought it home in my schoolbag. Tomorrow Mum and I are being taken by helicopter for my head scan in Glasgow. So tonight I am going to phone Lori while Mum and Dad are out at an islanders' meeting in the pub.

Tonight is also the first time I am babysitting for Kit – Mum says he'll be an angel, that it's only for a couple of hours and he's usually asleep by seven, so I should manage OK.

Wednesday 21st February

Kit was not much of an angel. He cried pretty much the whole time his mum and dad were gone, and I still had to phone Lori. I had Kit on my lap feeding him with a bottle in one hand, and the phone in the other. Lori didn't answer the first time, so I left a message, and then she rang me back. She said she was in the tuck shop getting some sweets when I rang.

'Lucky you,' I said, 'I've got stuck with your baby brother and he won't stop crying.' Just to prove it, Kit let out a particularly loud yell at that point, and then Lori went quiet.

I don't usually ask my sister for help, it's only something I'd do when I'm desperate. For one thing, she'd want to know all about the C-Bean, and how on earth we got this gold nugget, and I didn't want to have to tell her everything. But I knew I needed her help.

I took a deep breath. 'Lori, you know how the islanders need another hundred thousand pounds to buy the island?'

'Yes.'

'And it would be cool, wouldn't it, if we could help make it happen?'

'Yes. Where is this leading, Alice?'

'Well, I've got a sort of winning lottery ticket, and I need you to help me cash it in while we are in Glasgow tomorrow.'

In the end it was that simple – she just said yes! What I didn't tell her, though, was the lottery ticket weighs 2.5 kilogrammes and is made of solid gold. I'll have to find a way to tell Lori that tomorrow.

Thursday 22nd February 2018

Mum kept the helicopter waiting twenty minutes while she explained everything to Edie's mum about Kit's routine and made sure she'd left enough milk for him. I could tell she was cross with Dad because at first he said he would take me to Glasgow, but when he lost all of Tuesday because of the minke whale, he said he had slipped behind on his schedule and needed to make up the time if they were going to start the wave energy plant by the end of April.

The pilot was not very pleased about being kept waiting either, but he still said I could sit in the front next to him, which was really exciting. Dr Foster brought my classmates out to watch us go. I made a thumbs-up sign to them and pointed to my bag so they knew I'd got the gold nugget with me. The island slipped away from under us as the helicopter swooped into the sky, tail first. I could see the whole village spread out below across the mountainside, just like the map, with scatterings of sheep and stone cleitean. After a while you couldn't tell which was which. Then I could see over the ridge and down into Gleann Mor, where the sea didn't look too oily in the early morning sunshine. The last thing I saw was the smooth black sides of the C-Bean wedged between the white and grey rocks. As we flew higher, I could see that it was already covered in bird poo.

Lori was looking pretty anxious in her pink jacket with the collar turned up and her hair blowing in the wind when we landed on the huge 'H' on the roof of Glasgow General Hospital. I managed to get her on her own when we went to the toilets, while Mum talked to one of the nurses about the tests I was having.

Straight away, while we were still walking along the corridor, Lori was asking, 'Where's the lottery ticket then? What kind is it? How do you know how much you've won? The newsagents don't have much cash in their tills, you know. You don't really know how it works, Alice.'

I took a deep breath and said, 'This is not a normal lottery ticket.'

'What is it then?' Lori was getting impatient.

I pulled her inside the first toilet cubicle, opened my bag so she could see the gold nugget. At first she just stared at it, and then she laughed.

'What the hell is that, Alice?'

'It's 2.5 kilogrammes of pure solid gold that we found in one of the stone cleitean on the island and it's worth about sixty thousand dollars a kilo so Edie calculated that it should sell for over a hundred thousand pounds,' I lied without even pausing for breath.

'Whoah there! Don't be an idiot, Alice. Let me get this right: you want me to just walk into somewhere, hand over this lump of metal, and say, here, weigh this, and convert it into cash please?'

'More or less, yes. But a cheque would be safer, made out to The New St Kilda Trust Fund.'

Lori was silent, then finally she said, 'OK, I'll give it a go.'

Five hours later I was in the helicopter flying back to St Kilda with a huge cheque in my purse and an even bigger smile on my face. Mum thought it was because I'd been told my brain was fine. She said I'd been very brave. Little did she know that my brain was actually on fire after what had happened.

Lori is so cool I still can't believe it! She found out there was some antique metal dealer in a little back street in Glasgow and took it there. She told them she had been left the nugget by her great-great-uncle, who used to be a gold prospector in Australia. Once they had checked it was real gold, they wrote her the cheque there and then.

When she handed it to me, she said, 'Alice, you're starting to seem really grown up all of a sudden. You're not so much of a kid sister any more.' I beamed, and told her I was really proud of her too, and we hugged each other.

Charlie, Dad and Edie were waiting to meet us off the helicopter. It was dark when we landed, and Hannah and both Sams were already in bed. I wanted them to all be there when I told them, but for now I couldn't even tell Edie and Charlie with both my parents there. I just kept the huge smile on my face, and tapped the side of my nose knowingly. I made a money sign by rubbing my fingers together. Charlie raised his eyebrows: how much? I signed two ones and four zeros at him.

He shook his wrist in approval, like he'd touched something very hot, and Edie clapped her hands. I've never seen them both so excited.

It was only later, as I stared at the long number - £110,000 – on the cheque under my duvet, that it occurred to me that it must have been Old Jim who secretly donated the £500,000. That's what he had been trying to tell me on my birthday when he wrote in his notebook. But where he got the money from, I have no idea.

Friday 23rd February 2018

This morning, before Dr Foster arrived at school I showed the others the cheque for the New St Kilda Trust Fund. We were all so excited none of us could concentrate properly all day. We've decided to put it in an envelope addressed to Mr McLintock, but we're going to give it to Mrs Butterfield in the shop to give to Mr Butterfield, who will deliver it tomorrow morning. We'll tell Mrs Butterfield it came on the ferry and got mixed up with Dad's Evaw post.

As far as the minke whale was concerned, however, today was no laughing matter – the whale's blood showed up not just mercury, but lots of other toxic chemicals from the sea too. She could easily get beached again on another island, where there might be nobody to help her that time.

Saturday 24th February 2018

Our plan worked, and by lunchtime everyone in the pub was apparently talking about the second cheque that had arrived from an anonymous donor. Mr McLintock was so happy, he proposed a toast 'To All the New St Kilda Islanders!'

Then Dad proposed another toast 'To the Future of St Kilda', and beer slopped everywhere as they all clunked glasses. No one could really believe that the island was now ours.

When Dr Foster saw our faces looking through the window, he called us all inside and proposed a third toast, 'To the Children of St Kilda'. The pub erupted with a loud 'Hear, hear!' Everyone on the island has been really nice to us since we were rescued from the rocks. They all said the storm must have been much worse than they thought to have blown our wee classroom onto the rocks like that.

Then Dr Foster stood up and made a speech. He said that he wanted to thank the people of St Kilda for making him feel so welcome here. There were more shouts of 'Hear hear!' again as well as 'Get on with it, Adrian!' Dr Foster took another sip of his beer, and then said, 'So, in the interests of all our kids, I think the extra ten thousand quid we've been sent should be spent getting their classroom winched off the cliff, fixed up and returned to the school yard.'

Mr McLintock slapped him on the back, and said loudly, 'A grand idea. So be it!'

By the end of the afternoon, the celebrations in the pub had turned into a full-on party. The grown-ups drank even more than they did at Hogmanay, and when it got dark someone let off a few fireworks. Even Spex and Old Jim came out to watch them. Spex barked at every single one.

I was sitting on the seawall down by the harbour rocking my baby brother in his buggy, and eating fresh chocolate éclairs from the shop with Charlie, Edie, Hannah and the two Sams, while Spix flew around making Kit laugh by squawking 'olá

olá'. It was our own little celebration: soon we would have our C-Bean back again and have other adventures. For now, we were happy to watch the last of the fireworks in the night sky.

We all agreed they weren't nearly as good as the fireworks we'd seen in the other St Kilda, but right now there was nowhere we'd rather be in the whole world than right here on our own little island.

Map of St Kilda

SeaWAR

Book II

Contents

On a remote Hebridean airbase near Benbecula, a missile is launched. There have been many missiles tested from this location, but this is something new: it carries a nuclear bomb. Its target is a unique stack of rock called Levenish forty miles west, home to thousands of gannets and other seabirds, one of Scotland's sanctuaries. The missile hits the target and the stack is blasted to pieces on impact, shards of rock and bird raining down into the sea below.

A few hours afterwards, a military plane flies over the ocean to check on the damage the test nuclear warhead has caused. The RAF pilot steers a course through the billowing plume, catching occasional glimpses of the shattered rock below, not hearing the anguished cries of the remaining birds over the noise of his engine. He makes a few mental notes for his report, then smiles and tips the plane to turn back to base: the mission would appear to have been a success.

A few kilometres away, another man watches through binoculars from his post in a remote radar tracking station on the island of St Kilda. He makes a note of the time of the explosion and a small drawing of the sinister mushroom cloud in his brown leather notebook. Underneath the drawing in an urgent, rapid scrawl he writes:

THIS MOMENT IS A TURNING POINT THAT
CAN ONLY LEAD TO RUIN...

Alice's Blog

1st May 2018, 8am

Today is the day! The same helicopter that brought Granny and Gramps and my sister Lori over from the mainland when my baby brother Kit was born in January is coming to get the C-Bean off the rocks.

I should explain that our poor C-Bean Mark 3 is nearly dead. It's now just this pathetic abandoned cube wedged on the rocks at the end of our village on St Kilda, washed up there by the last storm. Or at least that's what all the grown-ups think. Looking at it now in that sorry state, no one would ever believe it's actually a mobile classroom, let alone a high-tech teleporting device with untold powers! Over the last few weeks we've watched it turn from a mysterious alien object like the blackest piece of outer space to a disgusting lump of junk covered in bird poo, barnacles and fish guts. Who would ever know it was once capable of transporting us kids from this remote Scottish island to anywhere in the world with just a single command?

It's probably a good job no one really knows - otherwise we would never have got away with such wild and dangerous adventures. It's only because they think it's teaching us things in a safe but exciting way that the adults ever agreed to get it airlifted off the rocks, because this whole rescue mission is awesomely expensive. Everyone around here thinks it got blown there during a very rough storm, but in actual fact it was due to a slight error in our navigation when we were coming back from the other St Kilda in Australia. That was weeks ago.

8pm

What can I say? It was like a scene from an old James Bond film – the helicopter just plucked the C-Bean from the rocks and held onto it like a giant seabird clinging to its prey. All six of St Kilda's schoolchildren, that's me, Charlie, Edie, Hannah and the two Sams, were watching anxiously from the beach. I don't include my sister Lori, because she's sixteen and still at school on the mainland until July. We wanted everyone to come and watch, but the adults said they were all too busy getting things ready for our annual May Day party. All, that is, except my friend Old Jim, who's ancient and a bit eccentric – the one who lives in an underground house made of earth at the end of the village. For some reason he took a keen interest in the rescue mission, and managed to hobble all the way down to the gun emplacement just near the village shop to watch things earnestly, while our little brown dog Spex, who's adopted Jim as his owner, ran around barking.

There was one other special person who came to watch – the C-Bean's designer, Karla Ingermann. She's flown over from Germany to help us get it going again. She seems a bit shy around the adults but adores my baby brother. Today she pushed him in his buggy all the way up the concrete road to video the C-Bean being rescued from the radar station up at the top.

The worst bit was when there was a loud ripping sound and the C-Bean lunged downwards. It skimmed the surface of the waves and swung out of control from side to side for a few seconds. Then the pilot managed to tilt the helicopter upwards and lurch away at a steep angle. He was aiming for the cluster of buildings just past the jetty. The best bit was how he managed to just clear the old stone storehouse by a hundred millimetres, before he lowered the C-Bean into the schoolyard right next to the chapel.

So it's been the best May Day ever. There was no school, and everyone was on holiday. We had this massive outdoor party – we set out chairs and tables and ate a feast with two lambs from the next-door island of Soay that we roasted on a spit. Then we lit a celebration bonfire. We do that every year to celebrate May Day as a tradition, but really, for us kids, this year's party was all about getting our C-Bean back. For the adults, I suppose it was more about the fact that out in the bay, for the first time ever, my dad and Charlie's dad have managed to get the new wave energy machines working to generate enough power to keep the whole of St Kilda and the rest of the Western Isles going all day, every day. I'm pleased for our dads because they've worked really hard, and it's making them both ill. They've got itchy skin and their hair is starting to fall out!

Oh and there's one other important thing I should mention – this year, May Day marks the day that St Kilda finally belongs to us! They've paid for it with the anonymous cheque we gave them from selling the gold nugget we found, and the money that I think Old Jim must have secretly given them, and now we've signed all the documents, and so that's it – it's ours!

To make it more special, the village committee decided to plant a tree. This is really something because there are no trees whatsoever on our island, so it will be St Kilda's first and only tree. But not for long – the plan is to plant one tree every year on May Day from now on, so when us kids are grown up there'll be like a whole forest! Edie and Hannah's dad went over to the mainland last week and chose a stubby little Scots pine, which they brought back on the ferry, and left it standing outside Mrs Butterfield's shop until this afternoon. Now it's been planted right in front of the vicar's house. Mr Butterfield made a special plaque for it. It says:

ST.KILDA'S FIRST TREE

PLANTED ON THE FIRST DAY OF OUR INDEPENDENCE

MAY 1ST 2018

After we'd planted it, we all sang a hymn, and then our parrot Spix appeared out of nowhere, flew around in a circle over our heads and then landed in the tree squawking, 'Olá, olá!'. Everyone clapped and then Spix took a little bow.

Monday 14th May 2018

Karla's been running loads of tests on the C-Bean for almost two weeks now, but there's not been a flicker of life. She says all its systems were down. All the wonder seems to have gone out of it. And its door is still hanging half off its hinges. I can hardly believe now that we were transported all the way to New York, Brazil, Hong Kong and Australia in that sorry looking thing. It smells of seaweed and is going kind of rusty. You can see gaps now where the black coating has been joined together because there are crusts of this yellowy-brown stuff forming. I'm sure there's more of it appearing every day.

Now that my brother Kit is four months old, our lovely temporary teacher from America, Dr Foster, has gone back home, which is a bit of a shame because we all really liked him. My mum is back as our schoolteacher, which is OK except that now I've got to call her Mrs Robertson again and it feels weird. She let us look inside the C-Bean the day after it was rescued. Hannah was the most upset. She keeps doing all these mad drawings of forests and fairgrounds and foreign cities and loads of other beautiful other places she says are inside the C-Bean, but my mum has no idea what she's on about. As far as Mum knows, the walls have always been that dark and slimy and there never was a table that appeared in the middle of the C-Bean with amazing illuminated maps and images. The two Sams begged Mum to let them clean inside it, but Karla said not to do anything for the time being. She has at least ordered a new hinge mechanism for the broken door, which is on its way from Germany, and she's said that while she's waiting for it to arrive, she's got to wade through millions of lines of computer code, trying to figure out what's wrong with it.

I suppose I should say what she looks like. Karla is twenty-eight with short spiky red hair. She's a quiet, skinny sort of person with a freckly face and glasses with thick lenses that make her eyes look smaller than they really are. She never smiles, only ever wears black, and doesn't seem to want to talk to any of the other adults. And she sniffs a lot. On the first day she got here, Edie whispered to me at break-time, 'I don't trust her, she's fake'. But then Edie is always looking for the bad side to things. Sometimes I wonder if she really wants them to turn out wrong.

Karla asked Mum for permission to turn the little broom cupboard next to the schoolroom into her office, and now she works in there night and day, peering at the smallest, fastest, coolest, thinnest laptop Charlie says he has ever seen. He says it's made in Finland and doesn't need a power cable because the battery works on thermopower waves. I guess that's just another kind of wave energy. Charlie's just twelve, but he's a complete computer nerd so I'm sure he knows what he's talking about. All I know is, that thin black thing of Karla's makes our school iPads look really old-fashioned.

Mrs Butterfield says Karla only goes back to sleep in the guest room over the pub in the wee small hours when it's already getting light and Mrs Butterfield is sorting out the shop before opening time. She thinks that Karla must be allergic to something on St Kilda because she is always sniffing and sneezing and has bought nearly all the packets of tissues Mrs Butterfield had in stock.

It was 8 am on 15th May, half an hour before school was due to start, and Alice wandered down the village street with Spix, her bright blue parrot, stalking her all the way. A fine Scottish rain had been falling since first light. Alice was daydreaming about the C-Bean's door opening mysteriously that first day it arrived on the beach, and how it recorded everything about her, and even projected a holographic image of her that talked back in her voice, and how she only had to imagine something and it would magically appear a few seconds later in a small recess in the wall.

Alice found herself alone in the schoolyard. She walked round and round the C-Bean's ruined exterior, singing an old Gaelic sea shanty they'd just learned and trailing her hand over its bumpy surface. Still humming the tune, she stopped in front of the tiny door concealing the access panel. She pressed the door very gently, and after a moment or two she could see it was trying to force itself open. She ran her fingernail around the perimeter of the door to dislodge the rusty, salty substance and ease it open. The cardkey she'd found in the sand on the beach on the first day was still in the slot. Alice closed her eyes and ran her fingers gently over the keypad inside, humming softly to herself. The buttons felt cold. She breathed warm air on them, talking under her breath, 'Come on C-Bean, you can do it. Remember me, Alice. Your friend?'

She opened her eyes a crack and thought she was imagining it at first. Was one of the lights on the panel glowing faintly? She breathed onto the keys again. They were warm to her touch now, and seemed softer somehow, like skin. She hummed a line from the song again, like a lullaby, and very slowly the row of lights starting pulsing red and green in sequence. Alice smiled a secret smile, and kept singing to the C-Bean, coaxing it back to life. After a few minutes it was humming the same pattern of notes back to her, very softly, but definitely making its own sounds. She wanted to run into the office and tell Karla, but she didn't dare leave the C-Bean at this critical moment of its recovery. She didn't want to call for her to come, either, in case the sound of shouting upset the C-Bean, so she stayed by its side until she could see Charlie in the distance leaping across the dykes, taking a shortcut to school. She beckoned wildly to him.

'Charlie, go and get Karla, tell her something's happening,' Alice said breathlessly when he was close enough to hear.

Karla immediately made a conference call to Germany from her tiny office. As the rest of the children arrived for school, they caught snippets of the conversation but none of them could understand any of it. All they knew was that Karla seemed very excited and kept sneezing and repeating the words '*biomimetische Funktion*'. After she ended the mobile phone call, Karla came into the classroom and told Mrs Robertson that some rather experimental things got added to the design of the C-Bean during its production process.

'I see. Why was that?' asked Alice's mother, putting six ticks in her register.

'It was in order to get around a few … malfunctions it had defeloped,' Karla admitted, and sneezed loudly.

The Sams started giggling because of her accent. Hannah, meanwhile, was drawing a picture of Karla on her iPad, and Edie was sitting with her arms folded, looking suspicious as usual.

'What kind of experimental things, Karla?' asked Charlie.

'Exactly as Alice found out just now – it responds to human warmth and touch and soothing sounds. Who thought it vood be possible?' Karla seemed completely amazed, and it made her accent stronger and more difficult to understand, perhaps because she was thinking too much in German.

'I knew about that the first time I found the C-Bean,' murmured Alice, almost to herself.

Alice was sent to get more tissues for Karla from the shop. When she came back, she couldn't resist loitering for a while by the C-Bean in the schoolyard.

'You can do it,' she breathed, her face very close to one of its walls. She touched one of the ridges of rust. To her amazement, it started to shrink very gradually under her fingertips. She worked her way slowly round all four sides until the rust had all but vanished. Then she eased the broken door open until there was a wide enough gap to slip through, took a deep breath and stepped inside.

There was a strong slimy fishy smell, like a pair of wellington boots that have been left with seawater inside. Every surface inside was still grimy and mouldy. Alice stood in the middle of the C-Bean with her eyes closed and focused her thoughts on the cleanest white bed sheets she'd ever seen, until she could picture them blowing and billowing in the wild St Kilda wind and could smell the sharp fresh air. After a while she didn't need to imagine the clean smell – she just knew the C-Bean was producing it itself, completely blotting out the fishy smell, and it had added in the sounds of the waves and seabirds to complete the atmosphere. When Alice opened her eyes again, the walls were clean, bright and alive. She was surrounded by a kaleidoscope of images from all over the island. It was as if the C-Bean was happy to be home and was busily sorting through its memory bank. Alice clapped her hands with joy, and ran out to get Karla.

By the time everyone trooped inside the C-Bean, including Spix, it was replaying moving images of the rescue mission, a silent witness to its own sea adventure. The children could see Old Jim in his ragged black clothes watching, as well as a colourful bunch of children shouting and waving down on the beach, right up until the cable started to break and it almost dropped into the sea. Curiously, as the C-Bean got to the part when it landed in the schoolyard, Alice realised that the movie had been filmed from where Karla had been standing, up by the radar station.

'Look, it's us!' chorused the Sams in unison.

Then the walls went blank again. Spix squawked loudly, as if in protest.

'Hmm, not quite fixed, then,' Edie couldn't resist saying.

'Oh come on, Edie. It was quite traumatic for the C-Bean, nearly getting dropped like that,' ventured Alice. Disappointed, the other children drifted back to class, but Alice stayed, her curiosity working overtime.

Karla went back to the office and brought out her shoulder bag containing her laptop. She sat down cross-legged on the floor of the C-Bean, scrolling through dense lines of computer code, looking for something in particular. Spix was fidgeting around on the floor, taking sunflower seeds from Alice's hand. Charlie was sent back to fetch Alice.

'Hey, your mum says you can't spend all day in here.'

Just then, the C-Bean started making a low crackling sound and the same complicated code – masses and masses of black symbols and numbers containing secret instructions – began moving up the walls around them. Suddenly one line appeared near the floor, highlighted in bright yellow. The C-Bean locked onto that one piece of information and then began duplicating the single line of code so it appeared on every surface, getting larger and larger. They all stared in amazement.

'Look!' said Charlie, 'it's worked it out for you, Karla. That's where the problem is.'

Karla looked up and smiled for the first time ever. When she glanced back at her laptop, the same line of code on her screen had been highlighted, and it appeared the C-Bean was busy making alterations by itself. The code was changing before her very eyes, without her needing even to touch the keyboard.

'Charlie, can you be a kind one and go back to my office and get my mobile phone? I again must call the guys in Germany, right this moment!'

Charlie went off to get it, and Alice started singing her song again, happy in the knowledge that the C-Bean might actually work. She could feel the wind picking up outside, coming down off the highest mountain, Conachair, into Village Bay to meet the incoming waves. It whistled round the schoolyard, as if it too was as impatient and excited as Alice felt. A sudden gust whipped up against the broken door and banged it shut. Spix let out a loud squawk. A shudder ran through the C-Bean's structure, and the walls went dark.

Karla sniffed loudly then cleared her throat in the dimness. Alice could still see her face because of the glow from the laptop screen.

'Alice, can you please to check the door for me?' There was a tiny note of panic in her voice. She started rummaging in her bag for a tissue.

There was a thin line of daylight visible along one side where the door didn't fit properly anymore. Alice started to crawl towards it on her hands and knees. She experienced her own moment of panic then, when she realised the last time she'd crawled across the C-Bean like this was when it got stuck on the rocks coming back from Australia and she'd banged her head badly. She was just about to reach out for the door when the C-Bean started shivering. Soon the whole thing was vibrating and quivering. Karla's laptop slid off her lap and across the floor, then crashed into the wall opposite and stopped working. Alice stood up carefully in the dark and tried to push the door open, but it was stuck fast. They were trapped inside, unless Charlie could get it open again from the outside.

It was not easy trying to think with the C-Bean shaking so much. Alice sat on the floor and tried to calm it down, making 'shhh, shhh' sounds like she used to soothe her baby brother Kit. The movement of the C-Bean was making her feel quite nauseous. She could hear Karla muttering as she tried to get her laptop to reboot. Alice closed her eyes. There was another high-pitched scratchy noise building up from somewhere, like an old radio or TV that wasn't tuned in properly, something Alice's dad called white noise. It crackled and buzzed louder and louder. Karla started pummelling the walls with her fists and calling out.

'Charlie, Charlie, we're stuck! Help!' She paused, then blurted out, 'Alice, we are going to need to do a factory reset, now, quickly!'

'OK. But how do we do that?' asked Alice, trying to remain calm.

'We reset the date und time. Sorry, but I get fery – how do you say it – *claustrophobic*. I don't like being in small confined spaces. It makes me panic.'

Alice imagined the word 'reset' in her mind. She concentrated on each letter individually, as if she was making a handwritten display card. As she visualised the 't' at the end, a glowing white rectangle appeared out of the gloom on one wall of the C-Bean. At the left end of the white rectangle was a single vertical line, a cursor that blinked on and off. Karla stared in amazement.

'It wants us to input something,' she said impatiently. 'But what?'

Alice thought for a moment and then looked at her watch. She uttered a string of numbers, barely audible over the white noise.

'15-05-18, 08.45.'

The numbers appeared dutifully one by one behind the blinking cursor, and then paused. The C-Bean had steadied itself, and was now just rocking slightly to and fro. They both stared at the digits and waited. Nothing happened.

'It isn't vorking!' wailed Karla.

'Oh,' said Alice, realising her mistake. 'Reset.'

There was a sharp jolt and the C-Bean's door flew open. The pod's interior was suddenly flooded with sunlight, and they both squinted. Karla stood up and exhaled slowly, like she'd been holding her breath the whole time it had been wedged shut, and then ran out of the door, clutching her laptop and her bag. Spix rearranged his tail feathers and followed her. Alice stood in the doorway, her eyes still adjusting to the brightness.

What with the wind and all the shuddering and quivering, the C-Bean had moved quite a long way from the schoolyard and was now down by the shoreline facing the water, in almost the same place where it had been nearly dropped in the sea by the helicopter. The waves were breaking a few metres from the base of the pod. Alice groaned as she realised another winching was going to be necessary. However, miraculously, the problem with the door seemed to have been rectified – she found she could now click it shut behind her with no problem. She was just wondering how they would afford to move it all over again, when Karla came running back.

'Where are we?' she cried, looking confused and somewhat stricken. Alice thought the claustrophobia must have still been affecting her.

'On St Kilda,' Alice said gently as she looked around her.

There was something odd, for sure. She counted the houses in the village and found that there were six missing. The Scots pine wasn't there. Above the village, there was no concrete road winding up to the radar station on the ridge, just a dirt track. Nor was there a gun emplacement on the headland. And when she turned and looked out to sea, she couldn't see the wave energy station, either. Some things were where they should be, though – the school, the chapel, the little walled graveyard and, further up the slope, she could still make out the entrance to Old Jim's underground house.

'Erm. Let's go up to the schoolhouse and find the others,' Alice suggested.

They started to trudge up the beach towards the school and the chapel. As they got nearer, a bell started ringing. A handful of children ran out of the classroom into the yard. Alice waved. But her classmates looked very unfamiliar somehow. They had all dressed up in olden-days clothes – the girls were wearing white smocks over brown dresses, and the boys wore britches and caps and hand-knitted woollen sweaters. Then it occurred to Alice that it wasn't their clothing that made them seem unfamiliar – these were not the St Kildan children she knew. She studied their faces. No Edie, Hannah, Charlie or a Sam among them. She stopped walking and stood still.

'Vat is wrong?' Karla asked.

'I'm not sure,' said Alice. 'But I think resetting the C-Bean has altered the clock a bit too much.'

One of the boys caught sight of Alice and Karla and called to the other kids. They stood in a line by the schoolyard wall and watched, pointing and whispering to each other as Alice approached, feeling somewhat shy. She was suddenly very conscious of her own clothes – jeans, a stripy rainbow-coloured fleece, and wellington boots with a yellow daisy pattern. And then there was her bright blue parrot, which hopped and fluttered along beside her.

'Hi. I'm Alice, I … live here,' she said brightly when she got close enough to talk without shouting over the sound of the wind.

Their spokesperson said, 'Good morning, miss. I'm Donald Ferguson. I've always lived here. You don't look as if you come from these parts.'

'Hello, Donald. This is my friend Karla, and this is my parrot, Spix,' continued Alice, trying to ignore the last remark. 'Can we speak to your teacher?'

'Aye, she's inside. It's ma mother. You can call her Dora.'

Alice smiled. At least one thing was familiar – having a mother for a teacher was definitely something she knew all about.

'Can I just check something out with you before we speak to … Dora?'

'Aye, mebbe,' Donald cocked his head on one side, curious.

'What's today's date?'

'I know, I know!!' All seven children put their hands up eagerly, wanting to answer Alice's question.

'Well?'

'Fifteenth of May, nineteen eighteen!' they chorused triumphantly.

'A hundred years into the future, yes.' Alice said it for what felt like the hundredth time. It seemed very strange to be standing here in her own classroom, surrounded by the same cream walls and high ceiling, saying those words. She looked around her. Instead of an interactive whiteboard there were maps printed on curling, yellowing paper hanging on the walls. The children sat in two rows in stunned silence, staring first at Alice, then at Spix, then at Karla. In front of each of them were a slate and a piece of chalk instead of an iPad. Mrs Dora Ferguson, their teacher, was obviously in a state of shock, because she kept rubbing her hands together in an endless washing motion and pushing imaginary strands of hair back into the neat little bun on the back of her head. Finally, she turned to the blackboard behind her, picked up a piece of chalk, and slowly wrote the number 2018 on the board in large curling numerals. She gazed at it longingly for a while and then turned back to face Alice with a look of awe on her face.

'But how can that be?' she asked. 'How did you get here?'

'In something called a C-Bean. It was given to us earlier this year as an extra classroom, but it turned out to have special powers. I didn't know about this one until just now. It's never travelled back in time before,' Alice said matter-of-factly.

'A seabean, you say? Like the ones that get washed up on the beaches here sometimes.'

Alice smiled, remembering her own mysterious little seedpods – a Mary's bean and a hamburger bean.

'Well, it's a lot bigger than any of those, and it's shaped like a cube. You can come and see if you like – it's down on the beach right now.'

'I see. And your friend … who is she?' Dora asked tentatively.

Karla had not said a word since they'd arrived at the school, and was standing rigidly by the door, clutching her shoulder bag in front of her as if for protection.

'Oh, this is Karla – she's the C-Bean's designer. She's from Germany,' Alice said cheerfully by way of introduction.

There was a gasp from several of the children, and Alice could hear them whispering 'She's a German!' to each other. Dora looked at Karla with a very grave expression.

'Oh, that is not good. Whatever are we going to do now?' She sat down heavily in the chair behind the teacher's desk and rested her head in her hands.

Alice turned to Karla. Claustrophobia suddenly seemed to be the least of her worries. The children were fiddling with their inkwells, fidgeting and squirming in their seats.

Dora looked up suddenly and asked them to file outside. They obeyed her at once, trooping out in a line, heads down.

With her pupils gone, the teacher tried to compose herself. She leaned forward and ran her hands over the old-fashioned wooden desk in front of her, as if she was feeling for some tiny lost item. She smiled politely, stood up and cleared her throat.

'You must realise, surely, that we are in the middle of a war. It might not seem like it on this remote island, but we have been at war for the past four years. Do they not teach you about this war in the future? So many people have been killed. We don't know when it's ever going to end. The Germans just won't give up.'

Dora looked accusingly at Karla as she started pacing up and down the aisle between the two rows of desks, darting anxious glances out of the window at the C-Bean. From here it looked like an ominous black tombstone standing on the foreshore.

Alice suddenly remembered the commemorative plaques inside the chapel, listing all the men who'd died in the First and Second World Wars. She murmured an inscription to herself: 'First World War, 1914–1918'.

'What did you say?' asked Dora, wheeling round and fixing Alice with a stare.

Alice was about to repeat what she'd said, but there were two things that occurred to her in that moment. One good – she could tell Dora this war was going to end soon – this year even; and one bad, that it was going to be followed by an even more horrible war against the German Nazis – the Second World War.

Instead she said quietly, 'I know a bit about the war, yes'.

'And your friend?'

'Karla knows too. It was a long time ago, and Germany and Britain are friends now.'

'Is that so?' Dora said slowly, mulling over this new information. 'But we are going to have to keep this very hush-hush for now. I mean, the people on this island are very nervous and suspicious because of the war effort, and they will naturally think that Karla is some kind of spy.'

Alice found the notion quite exciting, but decided not to say anything. Karla just looked tired and embarrassed. She had slumped into a chair by the door. She didn't look anything like a spy, Alice thought, feeling quite sorry for her.

'Alice, I think that in the circumstances it would be best if you and Karla and your parrot were to go home right now in your time-travel machine, and never come back.'

Something in the way Dora said this made Alice realise it was actually the last thing the teacher wanted to happen. Although she was afraid, she was also curious and wanted to learn more, as any good teacher would.

Alice looked at Karla, who shrugged. Then Dora had another idea.

'Your seabean – can you make it invisible?'

'I don't think so, although ...' Alice said slowly, remembering that it could produce objects that would then disappear once you took them outside the C-Bean.

'I read about this magician in London who can make things invisible by throwing a cloak over them, so there must be a way,' Dora insisted.

'Why don't you come and see it for yourself?' Alice suggested. The children were jostling each other impatiently outside the door now, waiting to be called back inside.

Dora hesitated, and then without a word she removed the apron she was wearing, hung it tidily over the back of her chair and reached her overcoat down from the peg beside the blackboard.

She opened the door and made an announcement.

'Children, we are going for a walk to see something of great interest, and nobody is to misbehave. Do you understand?'

As they walked past the chapel, Alice looked in through the open door. The wall where the plaques should be was empty. Donald came up beside her. They were the same height. He had an earnest look in his brown eyes that reminded her of someone, but she couldn't think who it was.

'You're aliens.'

'I suppose we must seem like that. But I can assure you we're not from another planet.'

'Have you read *The Time Machine* by H.G. Wells?'

'No, but I've heard of it,' Alice answered.

Donald was a bit out of breath as he jogged along beside Alice, who was, out of habit, counting her footsteps and only half listening.

'It's about a man – the Time Traveller,' Donald continued, 'and he builds a machine that lets him go to the future. Is that what you are – a time traveller?'

He stumbled on by Alice's side waiting for an answer. They were almost back at the C-Bean.

'*Olá!*' Spix got there first and triumphantly announced his arrival, which made all the children laugh.

'A hundred and sixty-seven,' Alice said out loud when she took the final step and stood in front of the C-Bean.

'I thought so,' said Donald, as if her bizarre answer proved it.

The children fell silent as they stepped inside the C-Bean. Even Donald, who'd been talking non-stop all the way down the hill, was now dumbstruck by the tiny, empty interior. After a while, he couldn't contain himself any longer and a torrent of questions poured out.

'Where are all the buttons and dials? Where's the clock to tell it what year to visit next? How do you control it? Where do you sit? Why is it all dark and empty? Is it powered by steam or coal?'

Alice was unsure of some of the answers. She wanted to show them what it could do, but she also felt shy and protective of the C-Bean's incredible powers. So it was Karla who spoke for the first time.

'The C-Bean is an adfanced piece of Western technology, that uses biomimetic micro-electronic self-organising systems to orientate itself and learn about the enfironments it finds itself in. These unique attributes make it an ideal learning enfironment, and so we – *wie sagt man auf Englisch* – adapted its original use for the education market early in 2116. I mean in 2016 …'

Karla's voice droned on like a voice-over from a science documentary. The children were all open-mouthed now. Even to Alice she sounded like a strange alien intelligence from a distant future.

'I don't know what all that means, either,' said Alice, as if reading their minds, 'but I want to show you something. Watch this.'

Alice began, softly at first, to sing the words of the old Gaelic sea shanty that had made the C-Bean come back to life, and soon it was displaying all over its four walls moving images of old wooden fishing boats being tossed at sea, huge nets being hauled in, piles of silvery fish heaped up on jetties, and women in headscarves gutting them and throwing them into buckets. The children, their eyes wide as they watched the scenes playing out all around them, also knew the song and started to join in, shyly at first; then Dora began to sing too in a high, strained voice and their voices grew louder, until they were all singing heartily.

The C-Bean, bolstered by their lively sing-song, embarked on an ambitious imaginary sea voyage, the wind blowing freely, sails flapping, and up in the clear blue sky overhead seabirds were wheeling and diving. Alice smiled as she noticed Spix trying to copy them by flying around in the confined space. She was remembering the time she and Edie found themselves out in Village Bay because Dr Foster had got the coordinates for St Kilda ever so slightly wrong. Just like that time, there was a slight lurching movement beginning, and a certain mistiness gathering in the waves around them, as if the walls were becoming a little bit porous …

Alice noticed that Karla was the only one not singing. Instead she had pulled a tiny camera out of her shoulder bag and was photographing everything that was happening in the C-Bean with a serious look on her face. Alice thought Karla was probably feeling claustrophobic again – even though the C-Bean was producing lots of outdoor images, they were still in a confined space. So Alice stopped singing, and the sea voyage subsided, along with the lurching motion. The mist cleared and the walls hardened over.

The children uttered a disappointed 'ohhh!' in unison and Dora, shaking her head in disbelief, laughed and said, 'Yes, I think that's enough now'. But Donald was persistent.

Chapter 3: Invisible

'What else can it do? Let's go somewhere real and get out and look around, like you did, Alice!' The other children looked terrified and excited in equal measure at their classmate's suggestion. Donald tried again.

'Mrs Ferguson, what about going to see that Crystal Palace down in London you were telling us about yesterday? You know, in Hyde Park where they had the Great Exhibition in 1851? We could go there! I mean *then*!'

'Well, Donald, I don't think that's such a good idea. We might get stuck there and be unable to get back. Alice – is that a possibility?'

'We've always got home before,' Alice said truthfully.

'Let's at least try. Please!' Donald urged.

There was an eager, fidgety silence among the children. Dora smoothed her hair and chewed her lip, and made more washing motions with her hands. Then she buttoned up her coat and said, 'All right, Alice, can you take us there? It would be extremely interesting, I have to admit. I've never even been to London before.'

Alice smiled and said, 'Neither have I'.

Alice requested a pen, and the children gasped when one just appeared as if by magic in a recess in the wall of the C-Bean. Then she called up the geographical coordinates for Hyde Park, London, and using the pen wrote the date and time very precisely, this time including the century – 15/05/1851, 09.30 – and their destination on the white wall behind her. The children were sitting on the floor watching her every move. Karla was filming the whole thing.

'Don't forget about making it invisible,' Dora reminded Alice; and so to please her, Alice added the word 'invisible' after the date, and underlined it twice, even though she had no idea if it would work.

As she did so, it suddenly occurred to Alice that here she was, just a few months after she'd found herself accidentally in New York's Central Park with her 2018 classmates and their teacher Dr Foster, trying – this time on purpose – to transport the C-Bean from St

Kilda to London's Hyde Park with a group of schoolchildren from 1918, to a time even longer ago – one hundred and sixty-seven years, to be precise.

There was the slightest of jolts, and then the door clicked open. The C-Bean had landed on a long red carpet, and Alice thought for a moment that somehow the Victorians knew they were due to arrive from the future, and had rolled out the carpet specially. But as it turned out, the C-Bean had simply landed awkwardly on the spot where two main routes crossed.

There was a steady hum of excited voices. It felt stiflingly hot. Spix, who had been perched on Alice's shoulder, suddenly let go and whirled up into the space above their heads. Alice looked up and gasped. They were inside an enormous greenhouse with a very high glass roof. All around her were gleaming Victorian inventions, some with steam pouring out of them. Hundreds of people were milling about between them, the women all wearing bonnets and long dresses, the men in long-tailed coats with top hats. Huge colourful flags and drapes were hanging down from an upper level. Alice could vaguely remember a biscuit tin at her Granny's house with a picture on it that looked very similar. She turned round to look at the C-Bean, to try to imagine what people in 1851 would make of this dark and mysterious invention from the future. But the C-Bean wasn't there!

Alice had a momentary panic until she realised that the 'invisible' command must have worked. She stretched out her hands. The ends of her fingers made contact with its velvety outer surface, even though she couldn't see it. She realised they were going to have to remember this exact spot if they went off exploring and wanted to find it again. Alice surveyed her surroundings more carefully. There was a vast green combustion engine to their left and some sort of golden oriental pagoda to their right.

Dora had the children grouped around her skirts and was

pointing things out and explaining what they were. Alice thought the teacher had a sparkle in her eye that hadn't been there before. One of the children, a little girl of about seven or eight with rosy cheeks, came up to her and held her hand. Alice could see that Donald was itching to explore, whereas Karla seemed reluctant to leave the C-Bean. She stood in her black jeans and black leather jacket, clutching her shoulder bag with one hand and blowing her nose nervously with the other. Alice thought she looked as if she wished she, too, were invisible like the C-Bean.

Donald grabbed Alice's arm and asked, 'Have you ever seen a real tree before? Apparently there are three elm trees growing in here. I just overheard a man tell some people it's down that way,' he said, pointing. They set off down the red carpet, Spix swooping and squawking above their heads, the little girl still holding Alice's hand, with Dora and the others struggling to catch up. Donald was in the lead, ploughing a furrow through the crowds.

The elm trees were huge and very still. It seemed that the glasshouse must have been put up around them, because they were definitely growing in the ground. Alice and Donald walked round and round the biggest one in the middle. Spix settled happily on one of the branches. He kept crying 'Olá, olá!' which appeared to amuse the Victorian visitors, who were trying to catch a glimpse of Alice's exotic bird, assuming it was one of the exhibits. But Alice and Donald, coming as they did from an island with no trees to speak of, were more interested in the elms. A seedpod had fallen off one and landed on the red carpet. Alice picked it up and studied the hard nut in the centre surrounded by a delicate papery fringe, like the beige wings of a moth. She put it in her jeans pocket.

They wandered part way down another aisle, somewhat unsure of what to do next.

'I think it might be time to go back now,' said Dora, sensing that all the children, Alice included, were a little overwhelmed by the crowds and the heat. No one disagreed, and they all trooped back in the direction of the C-Bean. They could see Karla still standing awkwardly on the red carpet.

'It is a relief you are coming back,' she breathed when they got nearer. 'The infisibility function is starting to wear off – look!'

It was true – people were becoming aware of the C-Bean's presence, which was slowly turning into a golden mirrored surface. There were several ladies standing around it, adjusting their bonnets and expressing fascination at being able to see their own reflections in what seemed to be a huge mirror made of gold. Just then, a child accidentally ran into it. Where his forehead bumped the C-Bean, a patch of blackness started to appear.

Donald suddenly blurted out, 'Alice, they've called the police, look!'

Alice turned and saw two uniformed policemen in domed helmets marching towards them along the red carpet, waving truncheons. She remembered how they got into trouble with the police in New York for parking the C-Bean in Central Park without a permit. A look of terror flickered across Dora's face at the prospect of being arrested and detained by a Victorian police officer and, in an effort to prevent this from happening, Alice hurried everyone back inside the C-Bean, clicked the door shut and quickly barked out St Kilda's coordinates from memory.

A fter the usual jolt there was an expectant pause.

'How do we know if we're back?' Donald asked.

'We don't – we just open the door and find out,' said Alice matter-of-factly.

'Can we get outside quickly, because I feel … how you say … a bit sick,' Karla announced.

Alice opened the door. For some reason they had arrived up near Old Jim's underground house. Karla dropped her bag on the floor and ran out onto the hillside to be sick in the grass. Dora and the children hung back in the C-Bean, also a little stunned at what had just happened. Alice looked outside to see if the C-Bean had recovered its visibility. She was surprised to see that in one way it had and in another it hadn't. Its outer surface was now camouflaged to look like a very large stone enclosure or *cleit*, the kind that are dotted all over the island and in which the old St Kildans used to keep food and fuel dry over winter.

Alice chuckled to herself, 'That's very clever.'

'What's clever about that?' remarked Donald, scanning the scene in front of him. 'I don't think your time machine quite worked that time!'

Alice turned towards the village. She could hear the chapel bell ringing in the distance. She could make out a group of islanders entering the front door of the chapel. It looked smaller than before, until she realised there was no schoolroom built on the side. Along the main street half the houses were missing – all the ones with the tar-black roofs. Nor, she discovered to her dismay, was there a storehouse, a pier or a landing jetty. Things were getting into the habit of disappearing!

Dora stood on the threshold peering out, the other children pushing to try and get a look for themselves.

'It's not 1918, is it, Alice?' she said quietly.

Donald cleared his throat and announced firmly, 'Alice and I will go and investigate'.

'Please be careful, both of you, and come back as quickly as you can,' Dora sighed. She gazed up at the sky with a faraway look in her eyes. Seabirds were calling – it sounded like home, but it wasn't. The sound made Alice stop dead in her tracks. She suddenly realised Spix had not come back with them.

'Spix! We left Spix!'

Donald could see she was upset. He stood biting his lip with his arms hanging limply, anxious to explore but aware Alice needed some words of comfort.

'I'm so sorry, Alice. But you know, we left him in the best birdcage ever built – he'll love flying around there and entertaining everyone all day!'

'I suppose so,' Alice said, brightening a little at the thought. 'Poor Spix!'

She looked at her watch. It was gone 10 am. It occurred to her that Spix wasn't the only thing she was feeling anxious about. She had been missing from her own time well over an hour now – what must her mother be thinking? What must Charlie have told her mother when he realised that Alice and Karla had somehow got stuck in the C-Bean just as it was beginning to work again?

'Let's go this way to the chapel, Donald.'

Alice took a deep breath and started to follow the dyke that ran along above and behind the old turf-roof houses, so they wouldn't be noticed. There were sheets and clothes hanging out to dry in the backyards. A few chickens were pecking in the grass. As they got near, the last of the islanders were just entering the chapel – an old man with his arm around his wife, who was weeping into a handkerchief. The door closed softly behind them and the bell stopped ringing. Alice held her finger across her lips to tell Donald to stay silent, and they crept over the wall and went to stand under the window.

A service was just starting. It was all in Gaelic, but Donald could understand and was listening carefully. To Alice, it all sounded very sombre. There was a lot of intense talking in low voices, and when the congregation finally sang a hymn, it sounded more like wailing than singing. After a while, the bell started ringing again, a single plaintive note carried away on the sea breeze. The door of the chapel creaked open, and Donald and Alice moved swiftly round to the end of the building so that no one would see them. Donald seemed desperate to tell her something. He pointed for them to move further away, down to the shore.

'What is it?' Alice whispered as they hid behind some rocks.

'Not good,' announced Donald. 'It was a funeral. For a week-old baby.'

'Oh,' said Alice. 'How sad.'

They both fell silent for a moment and watched as a forlorn huddle of women formed outside the chapel and began talking amongst themselves. One of them cuddled another baby wrapped in several shawls. The men were still inside.

'They said it was the fifth newborn baby to die this year, and another is already sick. They were saying lots of prayers for them. Then there was a big discussion about whether they should all emigrate to Australia. Apparently there's going to be a chance to leave in the next few months on a ship. Some people want to, and others don't want to give up on their life here. They've got hardly any food. I know what that's like ...' Donald bit his lip and looked unsure of himself for a moment.

'Go on,' said Alice softly.

'We had the same problem when I was little – we'd all been starving hungry for weeks, and we waited ages for them to send us emergency supplies from the mainland, but for our family it came too late. My Dad had already died.'

'Oh, you poor people!' Alice let out a heartfelt sigh. She

remembered the vicar telling them just a few months ago at school about the babies in St Kilda who kept dying only days after they were born. They got ill because of some oil that was put on them that was meant to keep them healthy, but she couldn't remember the whole story. And the other thing – about Australia – she knew a bit about that too, how most of the people who left on the ship became ill and died on the way, only a few actually making it all the way to the other side of the world. But she didn't know about the islanders starving. Her stomach starting churning in sympathy, and she felt sorry for these hungry, helpless people. She forced back the tears by thinking hard.

'So,' she said at last, 'it must still be 1851, because I remember now that's the year before people left for Australia.'

'We should get back to your Seabean,' Donald nudged her elbow. 'I don't want to be sent to Australia!' He was trying to make a joke, and Alice smiled.

'You're right, Donald – that would be too weird. Let's go back.'

They ran back along behind the wall, stooping low and picking their way between the tussocks of rough grass still laden with dew. Alice glanced down into the graveyard and saw a freshly-dug oblong hole, the earth mounded up alongside. It was obviously for the baby. There were other new-looking graves, too, with little wooden crosses, where a child no bigger than a doll was buried.

Back in the C-Bean, Dora and the children were busy playing games it had generated to keep them amused – dominoes, chess and backgammon. The children were chattering away, engrossed in the novelty of moving the digital pieces around the C-Bean's white walls with their fingers and waiting for it to respond. Dora looked up.

'Well?'

'It's still 1851. We weren't clear enough about the time when we set off back – I'm not used to this function yet,' Alice said apologetically. 'Where's Karla?'

'She disappeared over the hill. I didn't dare call for her,' Dora said.

'Donald, can you go and find her?' Alice asked.

Alice noticed that the little girl who'd held her hand was playing outside the C-Bean with the pen it had produced to write the coordinates earlier. For some reason, it had not disappeared when it was taken out of the C-Bean this time. Alice wondered whether by resetting the C-Bean, it had changed the way the objects it produced behaved – instead of evaporating when they were taken outside, it seemed now that the things it made were permanent.

An idea formed in Alice's head.

'What's your name?' she asked the child.

'Elsa.'

'Elsa, may I have the pen, please?'

She took the pen back inside the C-Bean and began to write a list of items on one wall in large capital letters – oats, milk, eggs, sugar, butter, flour, carrots, cheese, apples, bananas, oranges, honey, bacon, potatoes, sausages. Then she smiled to herself, and as an afterthought added her favourite item of food – *ketchup*.

An opening appeared in the wall next to where she was standing, and there in the recess was a large wicker hamper piled high with all the things on the list, including a large bottle of tomato ketchup sticking out of the top. Alice lifted the hamper from the recess and started to drag it across the floor towards the door.

'Is that a picnic for our lunch?' Elsa asked, watching her closely.

'No, this isn't for you, sorry,' Alice said, as she manoeuvred the hamper out through the door.

Donald had found Karla and was walking back towards the C-Bean with her.

'What's all that for?' Donald asked.

'It's for the starving villagers. I want to leave them something before we go.'

'Good idea,' Donald remarked approvingly.

They each took a handle and carried the hamper across the grass and into the graveyard enclosure, where they put it down beside the open grave.

'Look! They're coming,' Karla called.

Alice and Donald both looked up, startled. They could see the villagers were moving in a slow procession up the main street towards the graveyard, four men at the front carrying a tiny coffin on their shoulders.

'Wait, there's one more thing I need to leave for them!'

Alice ran back to the C-Bean and scribbled something else on the wall – *medical kit*. She added out loud, 'For the babies! Please, quickly!'

A second later, the C-Bean produced a neat-looking green box with a white cross on top. Alice grabbed it and ran outside.

'It's too late, they've seen us!' Donald muttered.

Ignoring him, Alice darted into the graveyard and tucked the kit inside the basket with the food. She could hear the rustling of skirts and shuffling footsteps not far behind her, and a stern voice said something in Gaelic, which she imagined meant 'Who are you?' But Alice didn't turn to look this time. She just fled back to the C-Bean, her heart pounding in her mouth. She didn't want to have to explain she was from the future for a second time that day.

Alice was very clear with her instructions to the C-Bean this time, and spoke the date out loud as well as writing it on the wall. There was a brief but unnerving jolt that possibly signalled they had switched centuries – or so they hoped. Alice checked her watch – it was now almost 11 am, but was it 1918? And why hadn't the door opened?

They all stood, stiff and tense, waiting. Alice could just make out a man's voice speaking very slowly into a loudhailer, in an accent similar to Karla's. His words were muffled through the walls of the C-Bean, but it sounded like: 'You must take cover immediately. We intend to begin bombardment in five minutes.'

'What's going on out there?' Donald asked impatiently. 'Come on, I want to get out and see.'

They could hear people running and a panicked voice shouting, 'Where are the children? They're not in here!' Someone passed even closer and replied, 'They must have been captured. Come on, you heard what they said. We've got to get to safety.' Alice tried the door again, but it would not budge. She thought for a second, then commanded, 'Manual override!' – but still the C-Bean did not respond.

A few moments later there was a series of loud bangs. They were so ferocious it sounded like a building exploding. Alice could hear what sounded like rocks and stones coming crashing down, and then something large hit the top of the C-Bean, making the door fly open. A shard of timber blocked their exit, and the air outside was filled with dust. It was impossible to tell where they had arrived, but it was a place none of them wanted to be – there was more rapid firing, and each time something hit its target the noise was deafening. Dora shouted above the din that she didn't think anyone should venture forth – they were safer inside the C-Bean for the time being. The children had clustered around her, coughing and choking as the dust drifted into the C-Bean. All except Donald, who was standing alert and ready for action. There were brief pauses between the rounds of gunfire, and in one of these, he scurried out of the C-Bean, climbed through the rubble and disappeared into the dust cloud outside.

Alice was unsure what to do, but she felt responsible for landing them in this mess. Dora was trying her best to calm the bewildered children. She gave Alice and Karla a look that said, 'Do something!' There was another volley of shots, and their deadly echoes, followed by the sound of something else being destroyed further off. Then silence. Alice beckoned to Karla and turned towards the door to pick her way out of the C-Bean. She felt sure they must be in a large city where war was being waged, but which city and which war? Perhaps they were still in Hyde Park, but in 1918. The air was full of the smell of burning and gunpowder. But mixed in there was something familiar – a fresher, cleaner smell.

Alice groped her way forward and the dust cleared enough for her to see that she was standing in front of the shattered remains of a stone building. As she walked a bit further, she noticed there was grass underfoot, and the sound of waves breaking. When the dust cleared some more, Alice could see a familiar shoreline stretching out in front of her that confirmed they had arrived back home in St Kilda. But there was no sign of Donald, and the whole place looked battered and deserted. All around buildings spewed forth flames and black smoke. One house was almost completely destroyed. The clean fresh smell was the sea. Alice stared out into the bay. There was a dark shape moving slowly underwater, a whale of some kind perhaps. It was slowly submerging and retreating.

She heard a noise behind her and turned abruptly. A boy in school uniform was running towards her, covered in dust with blood running down his forehead. As he came closer, she realised it was Donald.

'Did you see, did you see? It's a German U-boat – I mean submarine – look, Alice! I reckon it's run out of ammunition now!' He sounded strangely excited – as if he had waited a long time for something this real to happen that would make him believe once and for all that his country was truly at war.

'How did you get hurt?' Alice asked, and asked Karla for a tissue to wipe away the blood.

'I'm fine, leave it,' Donald mumbled, pushing Karla away, his eyes trained on the horizon. Karla put the tissues back in her bag and took out her camera. She started taking photographs of the German submarine. They watched it turn and leave the bay to go round the headland.

'You can see its periscope!' Donald spluttered as it withdrew beneath the waves. Karla turned the camera inland, and began photographing all the damage.

Alice and Donald surveyed the wreckage too.

'They've decimated the storehouse, look! And the wireless station!'

It appeared the commander of the German submarine must have also been suspicious of the stone cleitean dotted around the bay, because a lot of them had been blown to smithereens.

Karla suddenly blurted out in a panic, 'The C-Bean, where is it gone?'

All three of them ran back to the schoolyard and, seeing Dora and the children emerging seemingly out of thin air, realised that it must still be there. Karla moved towards them.

'It's just being infisible again. I can feel it.'

But Alice realised there was no way of knowing if their invisible time machine was damaged or not. She could only hope it had been in some way protected by the surrounding buildings.

There was an eerie silence on the island, partly because there was no wind. Alice turned to speak to Donald. He was shaking violently. She remembered seeing a film about the Gulf War once, and her mum had explained to her that soldiers often behave strangely when they are in a state of shock.

'Where do you think they all went to take cover, Donald?' she asked gently.

'Over there somewhere, maybe in one of the ditches,' he said, jerking his thumb backwards over his shoulder but unable to turn and look in that direction. Alice scanned the area beyond the village. There was no one in sight.

'I'm sure they're all safe, wherever they are,' she said.

Donald suddenly turned and ran in that direction.

Alice watched Donald stumbling along the village street and then diving into what must have been his own house about halfway up.

'Alice! Karla! What's happening? Is Donald hurt?' Dora called out anxiously from the C-Bean.

'As far as we can tell, the island has been attacked by a German submarine,' Alice reported. 'But it's gone now, and I think it's safe to come out. Donald's hurt his head and he's a bit shaken up. I think he's gone home.'

Dora picked her way carefully over the rubble, and turned to help her pupils clamber out. She looked around at the scene of devastation and her hands started making washing motions again without her realising. They all stood in a quiet huddle.

'We were so undefended. I suppose this was always going to happen, but why now?' she asked of no one in particular. 'Look at the mess! How are we ever going to get straight again?'

A tear rolled down one cheek and she brushed it away. 'Just so long as no one was ...'

But she couldn't bring herself to finish the sentence.

'Donald thinks they are all hiding in a ditch.'

'I sincerely hope so. I must return the children to their parents.' Dora put her hand over her mouth, unsure whether to say sorry, thank you or both to Alice, who had a very forlorn look on her face. Karla surveyed the scene blankly through her thick glasses and started shivering.

'Come with us, Alice – you too, Karla. We all need to get over the shock.'

'Are you sure? Maybe it would be better if we didn't – there are some things we can't possibly explain.'

Before they could make a decision, Alice spotted two men in uniform walking briskly towards them, one of them armed.

'Take the children to safety, Mrs Ferguson,' said one of the men. 'You're safe now – we'll take care of things from here.'

The man gestured with his gun for them to go. Dora nodded, shepherding her charges in front of her and beckoning to Alice. Alice grabbed Karla's hand and started to go with them.

'Not you,' the man said gruffly, lifting his arm and barring her way with the gun. Alice stood rooted to the spot, feeling the weapon against her throat.

'The two foreigners come with us,' the other man said, pointing at Karla and Alice.

Alice's Blog

16th May 1918

I've persuaded them to let me have some paper and a pencil. Maybe there's a chance that someone will find what I've written, but the main thing is I have to record everything that happens to me here, otherwise I'm worried I'll lose track of time. We've been gone over 24 hours now. What must Mum and Dad be thinking?

Karla is in the same situation as me, only it's more serious for her, because she really is an enemy: not only has she admitted she's a German, but she also had some very strange futuristic items in her shoulder bag such as her laptop and her camera, which have of course been confiscated. That made her really grumpy, and now she frowns all the time and mumbles a lot in German.

With me, they're just not sure. No matter how much Dora has reassured them I'm just an ordinary eleven-year-old Scottish schoolgirl, they won't believe it because they think I must have brainwashed her into saying that. As far as they're concerned I also represent some kind of unknown threat, because I don't speak Gaelic, I am wearing strange clothes, I don't have any identity papers and I seem to have mysteriously arrived from nowhere. All of which is, of course, true.

I've heard about prisoners of war, or PoWs, but I've never really thought about what it meant before. I am sure there aren't many prisoners who are kept locked up all day in a damp stone cleit like this one and have to sleep on straw mattresses at night, which are very itchy. Donald and Dora are allowed to visit us, and brought us oatcakes Dora made for us.

Karla is really struggling in here because of her claustrophobia. She says she doesn't mind the dark, it's the fact that it's a confined space and she feels trapped. She says she wants to escape, but there's someone outside the entrance to the cleit guarding us at all times.

He tried to scare us last night by telling us that this particular cleit is haunted by someone from centuries ago called Lady Grange. I thought he was just winding us up, but when I asked Donald about it, he said it's true, there was a woman called Lady Grange who was once imprisoned in this very hovel. Someone quite posh, but a bit feisty, from Edinburgh. Her mean old husband wanted to get rid of her apparently, and smuggled her here against her will. It's all a bit spooky. This morning Donald brought me a book about her that he found in the schoolroom. It said that in all the thirty years she was a prisoner here she was only allowed to write three letters, and that only one of those ever made it to the mainland. Just before she was about to be rescued by the person who got that letter, her guards took her to the Isle of Skye, where she died. The story keeps going round and round in my head. I must be going a bit crazy because I thought I could hear Lady Grange crying - until I realised it was Karla.

She won't admit it, but I've heard her. Her eyes were all puffy this morning behind her glasses. It made me feel really homesick because all I could think about was my brother Kit crying for a feed in the night, and then I got really upset. Last night Karla was talking in her sleep. I thought I was dreaming, because she kept saying 'Kit, I'm sorry, but the mission is a failure. We have to go to Plan B.' Except that she pronounced B as 'bay'. I know she's fond of my baby brother, but it was still weird that she should be talking in English to him like that in her sleep.

When we were eating breakfast this morning I said to her, 'Karla, what's Plan Bay?' She looked kind of embarrassed, as if I had found something out I shouldn't have. She told me her company had made her sign something called a 'confidentiality agreement' when she started working for them, so she was 'not at liberty to say'. Donald tells me he'd heard that she said the exact same thing to the army officers when they took her off for questioning yesterday. So I told her she needed to be a bit less secretive, or she will never be allowed out of this place. It was meant as a piece of helpful advice, but she took it the wrong way. Now she won't talk to me at all. I can still hear her sniffing in the darkness, though.

17th May 1918

Karla has vanished! Whoever was guarding us during the night must have fallen asleep, because when I woke up this morning, she had gone. Donald came to see me before school, and told me they've mounted a search party to look all over the island for her. But I'm more worried that she will go back to the C-Bean and somehow make it take her back to 2018 without me. So I have been trying to send the C-Bean urgent messages in my head not to let her control it. Donald says that the C-Bean is still there, but people have started noticing something strange, because although it's managing to remain invisible most of the time, occasionally there is a flicker when it's suddenly visible for a moment or two and you can see this weird black shape appearing.

He managed to hand me a note without the guard noticing. I waited until after they took my breakfast tray away before I opened it. Donald's obviously also been worrying about Karla taking the C-Bean and leaving without me, so he's come up with his own Plan B, and is going to come and get me later to help me get home. They're holding a big meeting this morning in the chapel to decide what to do about me, and about recapturing Karla. Donald says he's stolen some sleeping potion from his mum's medicine cabinet and slipped it into the guard's tea flask, so later this morning, when it's taken effect, Donald's going to rescue me.

Donald was hiding behind the wall in the graveyard. He had been watching the guard taking slurps from his flask since about 8 am, and when he saw him slump sideways in the doorway just before 10 am, he ran across to the cleit and whispered into the dark interior.

'Alice, it's time.'

They half walked, half ran down the village street towards the chapel. They both knew they would have to remain absolutely silent, since the C-Bean was standing right beside the building where the whole village was assembled to determine Alice's fate. They crept round the back of the chapel and into the yard. It looked empty. Alice's heart was thumping. What if the C-Bean had already gone? She groped around until she ran into one smooth wall, and heaved a sigh of relief. She worked her way round the sides until she had located the access panel and popped it open. Her stomach lurched when she could feel that the cardkey was missing from its slot. She knew instinctively that Karla must have taken it, and had no idea if the C-Bean would work without it. Donald watched as she ran her hand over the keypad to warm the keys, but the tiny lights did not come on. Alice didn't dare sing the sea shanty out loud, but instead started coaxing the C-Bean under her breath, until eventually the door clicked open. Donald and Alice stepped into the pod and quietly closed the door behind them. It was pitch black inside.

'LIGHTS!' Alice commanded, and the C-Bean was instantly flooded bright white. She was not used to such brightness after being imprisoned in the gloomy cleit, and she was slowly adjusting to it when she heard a quiet but firm voice say, a little sarcastically, 'So you made it. Well done, both of you! Stand with your hands on your heads!'

Alice turned and was shocked to see Karla scowling at her and brandishing a silver penknife. She was even more disturbed when she realised it must be Dr Foster's penknife because it had that yellow shoelace tied to it.

'Right, Donald, you get out now,' Karla's determined voice instructed.

Donald didn't move a muscle, he just kept his eye on the blade glinting in the bright light. All three of them stood absolutely still for what seemed like ages, and then suddenly Karla lunged towards Donald.

'Karla, no!' Alice shrieked as Donald stumbled backwards and fell against the door.

'I'fe been waiting for you, Alice,' she said between gritted teeth. 'This wretched thing will not go anywhere without you. I'fe tried everything.' Karla waved the knife around the interior and stared accusingly at Alice.

Donald saw his chance and moved quickly, grabbing Karla's wrist from behind and twisting her arm, and managed to bring the knife sharply downwards. As he did so, the knife grazed his arm and it started bleeding profusely. Karla's face was now wild with anger and she started wriggling like an animal to free herself from Donald's grip. Donald pulled Karla's arm behind and up her back, but he was shaking again and looked quite frightened.

Alice felt confused and upset to see Karla behaving so strangely, but she knew she needed to do something. She blurted out 'Handcuffs!' and the C-Bean produced a pair. She grabbed them from the recess and Donald managed to wrestle them onto Karla's wrists and remove the knife and the shoulder bag she'd been holding. Karla then seemed to go limp. Donald let go of her. At first she looked as if she was about to drop to the floor with exhaustion, but then suddenly and without warning she crashed out of the door and ran up the hillside. They could hear the familiar sound of her being sick in the grass again. Donald shut the door and leaned against it, panting and still holding her bag.

'That was scary! Are you sure she is who she says she is?'

'You're telling me it was scary. She's been acting so weird the last couple of days. Is your arm all right?' Alice asked in a breathless voice. She pulled a tissue out of her pocket and dabbed the wound.

'Never mind that. Time to go! I'll deal with her. She won't get far now she's got handcuffs on.'

'Neither will I, Donald, unless we get the cardkey back from her and put it in the slot!'

'Maybe it's in her bag,' Donald said, fumbling through its contents. 'Is this it?'

'Yes! It goes in the slot inside the access panel, OK?'

Donald nodded.

Alice tried to calm herself. Her stomach was still tied in knots even though their ordeal appeared to be over, until she realised there was something else nagging at her deep inside. All the time they'd been imprisoned in Lady Grange's cleit, Alice had wanted to escape back to her own time, but right now she found that she was sad to be going. She wanted to give Donald something, some sort of memento. There was nothing in the C-Bean except the knife, which carried all the wrong kind of significance. She felt inside her jeans pockets. Yes, it was still there.

'Close your eyes and hold out your hand.' She gave him the elm tree seedpod.

Donald looked at his palm and smiled.

'I have something to give you, too.'

He took Karla's camera out of his pocket and gave it to her.

'I stole it from the cupboard at the wireless station. I wanted to give you her other machine too, but it wasn't there. You may as well keep this too,' he said, handing her Karla's bag.

They stood silently. Then Donald whispered, 'Can I come with you?'

Alice shook her head and looked down at her wellington boots.

'It's not a good idea, Donald – it could mess everything up. It might have worked in The Time Machine, but we don't know what would happen if someone really did go forwards in time …'

Silence. She took hold of his hand.

'But I will come back, I promise.'

Donald cleared his throat. 'When?'

Alice thought for a moment. Then she had an idea.

'I'll come back on 29th August 1930.'

'Why then?'

'You'll find out, but I can't say.'

'But that's ages, Alice!' Donald rolled his eyes. 'I'll be a grown-up!'

'Let's just hope I recognise you, then, and that you remember who I am!' she joked.

Alice watched as Donald stepped out of the C-Bean, clutching the elm seed and smiling at her.

'I'll put the cardkey in now, all right?' Alice nodded and he closed the door.

'Right, I hope this works – St Kilda, Scotland, 17/05/2018,' she whispered.

Instead of the usual routine, the C-Bean did something Alice hadn't seen before. Its walls shimmered through a whole sequence of invalid commands and numbers, like someone was interfering with its memory banks. Next there was a series of images of a place she didn't recognise – the interior of a laboratory building with long grey curving corridors. One image showed the C-Bean itself under construction, standing in a brightly-lit factory space, surrounded by people in green gowns and masks who looked like they were performing a surgical operation.

Then the walls went white and the C-Bean played various audio snippets it must have recorded of Karla's voice getting more and more desperate as she uselessly barked out orders to try and make it depart for 2018. At one point Karla sounded confused, because she said something like 'OK, Plan B then: 16/05/2118.' Another voice replied sharply to Karla's request:

'Negative. Unauthorised command.'

There was a long pause, during which Alice could hear someone moving around, the door of the C-Bean opening and shutting again, and then she heard Karla's voice say, 'Removing cardkey. Activating remote override.'

The walls went black at that point, and a single line of code came up on one wall at eye level. The only actual words Alice could recognise among the string of numbers and letters were 'Operation SeaWAR'.

Alice had no idea what was going on. She stood tense and still in the middle of the space with her arms folded, and waited. More strange images started appearing on the C-Bean's walls, of a missile being fired from a base somewhere and then arcing over a huge expanse of ocean dotted with small rocky islands. She saw images of a rock that looked like one of the stacks near St Kilda exploding, shown as a set of time-lapse photographs of a huge cloud forming in the sky above, billowing upwards and outwards in the shape of a mushroom. On another wall, the C-Bean was running through a huge quantity of other data – graphs, maps and mathematical formulae, like a scientific report – but Alice had no idea what any of it meant.

'I don't understand,' she said aloud, shaking her head.

With that, the C-Bean promptly stopped its technical show-and-tell, and produced a recess containing a large sheaf of paperwork in a brown folder tied up with string. Alice lifted it out of the recess. On the front cover was a red stamp stating 'Top Secret' printed over black type that said 'On Her Majesty's Service' and 'Nuclear Weapons Research Programme – Annual Report 1960'. At that moment, the door opened. She stuffed the folder along with the camera into

Karla's shoulder bag and stepped warily out of the C-Bean, already sure she was not in 2018.

The C-Bean had arrived way off track this time, and was standing next to the radar station on the top of Mullach Mor, the second-highest point on the island. There was a strong wind blowing. The pod had taken its disguise capabilities to a new level too, appearing this time like a small electrical substation or generator unit, painted on the outside in a dull military grey, with a large yellow and black label on the door that said 'DANGER: HIGH VOLTAGE'. Alice patted it approvingly, and looked around her.

Through the patchy mist, she could see the road going back down the mountain and could make out the village as a crescent of tiny roofs some way below her. On closer inspection, a few of the roofs had fallen in and there were thirty or so khaki green tents erected on the grass between Main Street and the beach. Alice also noticed that the concrete road leading up to the radar station actually stopped halfway up the hill, and the rest was just a dirt track as before, with tools lying around and sacks of cement piled up indicating that the road was currently under construction. What puzzled her even more than anything was the fact that out to sea there appeared to have been a fire on board a ship, because the bay was filled with a massive cloud of smoke. It had a very distinctive shape, like a tree or a mushroom, exactly like the images she'd just been seeing inside the C-Bean.

Alice was about to head off down the track to investigate further when she caught sight of somebody speaking into a handset inside the radar station. He had a beard and rather untidy hair and was wearing a rough woollen sweater. Alice thought he looked about Karla's age, late twenties maybe, with earnest brown eyes and a deeply furrowed brow. Alice ducked down below the window ledge and crept closer to listen.

'Come in, Benbecula. Yes, sir, picking up some unusual activity in the last hour. Blast zone larger than usual. Seems to have hit Stac Levenish, from what I can make out, plume considerably larger than anything I've seen, now dispersing. Have to say, sir, it looks not unlike what the Yanks dropped on Hiroshima in 1945. I'll put it all in my log, and I've taken photos for the record, but I just thought you should know. Right. No problem. Over and out.' There was a click as the man replaced the handset, a scrape of boots across the wooden floor, and suddenly the door was flung open.

He surveyed her quickly, then a rapid grin flashed across his face.

'I've been expecting you!' he said. 'Robertson, right?'

Alice stood up from her crouched position.

'Alice Robertson, yes. Who are you?'

'James Ferguson. Dad told me about you.'

'Your dad?'

'Yes, my dad, Donald Ferguson.'

They both stared intently at each other and for a fleeting moment Alice thought she could see some similarity between this James and her friend Donald, just as James's gaze shifted from her face to the grey cube behind her. He raised his eyebrows and made a clicking sound with his teeth, then strode over to the C-Bean and knocked against its walls with his knuckles.

'This it, then? Pretty good camouflage.'

'I suppose ...' Alice began.

'Well, we have some catching up to do. Have you brought the papers?' he was looking at the bulging shoulder bag.

'I have been given some papers, yes, as it happens,' said Alice slowly, wondering how he could possibly know she would be bringing them, or that she would be arriving at all. It certainly had not been part of her plan.

'It's not safe to talk up here, let's go back to my place, get some lunch. Lie low for a bit.'

And with that, James collected his things, locked up the radar station, slipped the keys into his pocket, and strode off down the steepest part of the mountainside. Alice trotted behind him, trying to keep up as they moved through the long wet grass. The smoke cloud in the bay filled the eastern sky and was drifting towards St Kilda.

James lit a small stove, and put the kettle on to boil. He unwrapped some bread and cheese from a tea towel in his little kitchen, and put a jar of pickled beetroot on the table beside it.

'Help yourself,' he said, while he washed two mugs and swilled out a yellow teapot.

'Is this the same house as your dad lived in?' asked Alice, looking around the simply furnished room with its bed, armchair, table and stove, and remembering her friend darting into a house the day of the submarine attack.

'Certainly is. When I was first stationed here earlier this year, they wanted to put me in the old wireless station, which was done up as proper living accommodation, but once I'd worked out which house had belonged to my family, I repaired the roof and moved in here. It was the first one to get done up.'

'Do you work here all year round?'

'Yes. The War Office has been granted the right to have a missile tracking station here, but the National Trust for Scotland are in charge of the island. I'm the operator in charge of monitoring things up at the new radar station.'

Alice had so many questions bubbling up inside her, but something in James's manner assured her they would have time to work it all out. For now, she just needed to check one thing.

'James. What year is it?'

'1957.'

'OK. And was the island evacuated in 1930?'

'Yes, all thirty-six of us that were left, when I was a baby. I was the last one to be born on St Kilda. That's my claim to fame!' He laughed and clapped his palms against his thighs, making the table wobble. Hot tea slopped onto the breadboard.

'And your dad?'

James looked down at his feet and paused for a moment before he answered her.

'He's dead, sorry to tell you. Got himself involved in active service in the Second World War as a pilot, survived pretty much the whole war and was then brought down during some mission in July 1944. The whole crew perished and they never found the bodies. He was a pretty brave guy, though, got awarded the Victoria Cross – funnily enough for taking out a German submarine when he was stationed in Italy. I have it here.'

James pulled open a drawer in a carved wooden chest beside his bed, and took out a navy blue box. Inside on a bed of dark red velvet lay Donald's medal. Alice lifted it out, remembering his boyish blood-stained face in the midst of his first experience of war – just an hour before in terms of her time.

'He talked about you a lot, Alice. Told us all kinds of fantastical bedtime stories when we were growing up, about this girl who could travel through time, and what she got up to in her time-travel machine.'

Alice smiled. 'I'm sure most of it was made up.'

'Well, I know one part was true. Did you not notice something in the backyard?'

James took her outside and round to the rear of the tiny dwelling. There, growing among the tussocks of grass, was a small but determined-looking elm tree, its slender branches twisting and swaying in the fierce St Kildan breeze. Alice chuckled and did a quick calculation in her head. There was no doubt in her mind it was the elm seed that Donald must have planted back in 1918 after she left, which meant it was now thirty-nine years old.

'So after you left Dad in 1918, after that German sub attacked, what happened next?' James asked conspiratorially once they were back inside his cottage.

'I don't know, because it hasn't happened yet.'

'What do you mean?'

'Well, I was trying to get back to 2018 just now, and I ended up here. From what I can make out, the C-Bean will only travel back in time to the same date and time but in a different year.'

Alice looked at her watch, 'Let me check to make sure: I make it 12 noon on 17th May, right?'

James consulted his watch. 'Correct.'

'Something weird happened in the C-Bean when I was trying to issue the command, and I've ended up here.'

'To be honest, I wasn't surprised you showed up today – first there was a weird explosion out in the bay, then just as you arrived I was picking up something else odd too, a radio signal up at the station. On a frequency no one's ever used before.'

Alice remembered the folder and pulled it out of Karla's bag.

'You asked to see this,' she reminded James, and pushed the bread and cheese aside to make room for it on the table.

James's eyes grew wide as they fell on the stamp on the front cover. Without a word, he tugged at the string holding it all together, and took a deep breath before opening it.

'1960 … crikey, that's three years into the future. Where did you get this?' he breathed.

'The C-Bean … obtained it,' Alice said in a hushed voice.

James was rifling through the pages, as if he was looking for something he knew would be in there. There were detailed maps of Scotland in one section – Alice recognised the familiar outlines – with red dots marked all around the coast. There were other maps of clusters of islands elsewhere, on pages entitled 'Nuclear Test Sites'.

'I knew it,' James suddenly declared triumphantly, stabbing his forefinger at a map Alice could see was of St Kilda. 'The idiots!'

'What is it? What have you found?'

'That wasn't just a routine missile they launched from Benbecula earlier. It was a nuclear warhead!'

Alice glanced at the page he was studying and her stomach turned when saw printed in block capitals the words 'Operation SeaWAR'. As if reading her thoughts, James continued, 'Bet that's why you've been thrown off course – I knew about them detonating bombs in the Australian outback and off Christmas Island in the South Pacific, but I had no idea about plans to test them here in Britain! Didn't we learn anything from Hiroshima back in 1945?' He growled under his breath and shook his head.

'They said the death of more than a hundred thousand people was the price we had to pay to end the war and that it would never happen again, but look, this is the report of us Brits carrying out a test explosion of a nuclear bomb right here off St Kilda!'

Alice looked at the photographs dated 17th May 1957 and realised they were the same time-lapse images that the C-Bean had been displaying just before she arrived. It must have been happening in real time.

'And what's more, I was right – they are storing weapons-grade nuclear material somewhere on St Kilda, as well as planning to dump spent nuclear fuel rods and warheads here. It says this is the first British site to be selected,' James said angrily.

He was running his finger impatiently down page after page.

'Doesn't say exactly where they are dumping stuff, but I'm sure I'll find it. I've been picking up unidentified ships from the radar station arriving from the north side of the island and delivering something I thought was suspicious, so I've been logging their movements – but so far no one has acknowledged what's actually going on.'

James sat back and tugged his beard, his face going through a sequence of pained expressions, finally settling on that deeply furrowed brow Alice had seen earlier.

'OK, we've got our work cut out. We'll take a boat trip round the perimeter of the island and check it out thoroughly. I don't know why I haven't done it already.'

'But I need to get home,' Alice said, 'I'm not sure I should stay that long.'

James looked at her and scratched his head.

'I promise we'll be back by teatime and you'll be on your way, but there's no point you going back unless we know for sure.'

'Know what? And who are 'they' exactly? You keep saying 'they'.' Alice was feeling a bit cross – what James was saying just didn't make sense to her.

'You've arrived in the middle of what everyone's calling the Cold War, Alice. It's not a war that's being fought in the open, like a real battle as such. Countries like America and Russia are spying on each other. They're accusing one another of lying about how many and what kind of weapons they each have, and all the while they're both busy secretly designing and building a deadly nuclear arsenal! Now, as if it couldn't get any worse, it seems Britain is building up a deadly stockpile of its own. They've been calling me a conspiracy theorist for years Alice, but now I almost have proof. However, your Top Secret file isn't going to be enough – we need to get some actual hard evidence. I'm absolutely positive we are either making, storing or testing nuclear weapons right here on St Kilda, Alice. Probably all three. And it's got to be stopped!'

James made various growling noises again and started making preparations for their expedition, his movements quick and deft. He filled a metal canister with water and proceeded to pack a small rucksack with binoculars, a compass, two gas masks and a boxy-looking camera in a brown leather case. He looked in the chest by his bed, took out three rolls of photographic film and stuffed them in a side pocket. In the other side pocket he put a box of matches.

'Got what you need?' he asked, already a little absent-minded at the prospect of this expedition.

Alice looked in Karla's shoulder bag. There was a packet of tissues, a granola bar and her camera.

'This could be useful,' she said, switching on the camera. 'In fact …' she scrolled through the last few photographs, and it felt strange seeing images of St Kilda that had in reality taken place thirty-nine years ago, even though from Alice's point of view they'd only just been taken in the past hour.

'James, look – I have some pictures of your dad here.'

'Really?'

James put the rucksack down and took the camera gingerly in his hands, as if it were an injured bird.

'What do I press?'

'Here, like this.'

Alice watched as he scanned her scenes of war-torn St Kilda, with his own father, a twelve-year-old boy, caught in the thick of it. James sniffed and a tear rolled down one cheek. Alice offered him one of Karla's tissues from the bag. The last picture was of Dora's face appearing in the doorway of the C-Bean, her features wracked with worry. James blew his nose loudly and suddenly grinned.

'That's Granny Dora, if I'm not mistaken! She looks so young – incredible.'

He was distracted for a moment by the force of his own memories. Then he shook his head, stroking his beard.

'Right, this is no time for nostalgia. Let's go.'

Outside, the wind had dropped. James took a direct route once again, striking a line towards the jetty, with Alice struggling to keep up. She still had no clear idea of what they were going to look for, or what James was so keen to find out.

James stopped to load film into his camera, and then started taking photographs of the plume, which Alice could see was drifting slowly towards the neighbouring island of Boreray.

'Who's on St Kilda at the moment, James? What are all those tents doing in the Village?'

'That's RAF and army people who are here to construct the

facilities. Luckily for you, they're not around today, thank goodness – went off on some recce.'

'Recce?'

'You know – a reconnaissance mission – to Boreray. Oh and a couple of high-up War Office guys are supposed to be arriving later today to check on progress if the weather holds; and in a month or so some nature conservation guys will descend on the island for the summer. They're planning to come every year from now on, to mend walls and log bird colonies and such. Mind you, by the time they get here I wouldn't be surprised if the whole place is radioactive.'

'What does "radioactive" mean, exactly?'

'Well, for starters, it means you should be wearing one of these.' James pulled the two gas masks out of his rucksack and slid one down over his face. He pulled it away from his mouth to add, 'It's dangerous stuff. Makes people really ill in all sorts of ways. Some scientists even think it even causes cancer. That device they detonated today is only a fraction of the size the Americans dropped on Hiroshima and Nagasaki in Japan, but it looks like it's wiped out a massive bird population in the first few seconds. Officially, I'm keeping an eye on things, but unofficially, I'm keeping notes on all this top secret activity, in order to get the evidence to support my theories.'

'Theories?' Alice asked, struggling with her mask.

'Britain is getting involved in the nuclear arms race, and it's only a matter of time before it all goes horribly wrong. The Americans and Russians are way ahead of us in terms of developing technologies of mass destruction. If we are all at it, there'll soon be enough nuclear weapons to destroy the entire planet, and even if only a couple of them went off it could kill half the world's population straight off, pollute our seas and farmland with radiation for the next hundred years and leave the survivors suffering the consequences of radiation sickness for the rest of their lives. I want to do something to stop it right now, before it's too late. That test explosion you saw today is just the start – there'll be much worse to come.'

'And you think there's a secret stash of radioactive nuclear stuff right here on the island?'

'That's one of my theories, yep. And if the past few weeks are anything to go by, a new shipment is due today. If we hurry we might just catch them red-handed delivering it. Now, keep your mask on, Alice.'

They were jogging past all the military tents down to the shore where there was a small wooden dinghy with an outboard motor moored against the jetty. James slung his rucksack into the bottom of the boat and started untying the rope. Alice noticed the name SEABEAN was painted in green capitals on the back of the boat.

'I like what you called it,' she said through the mask, but James didn't hear her. He just pointed for her to step aboard and put on a lifejacket.

Alice zipped up her fleece and then pulled the lifejacket on and settled herself on the wooden seat in the middle of the boat. There were oars in the bottom, but James started up the engine and they pulled away.

'We'll take some more photos of the explosion on Levenish and then go round to the north side and take a look from there – that's where this new radio signal seemed to be coming from!' James shouted through his mask over the roar of the engine and the slop of the waves. Alice just nodded and pressed her knees together to try to avoid shivering. They skirted alongside the neighbouring island of Dùn, moving towards its southernmost tip. The grey sea was choppy and waves were coming over the bows of the boat. Alice realised she had never been round St Kilda in a boat before and it was much bigger than she'd previously thought. The cliffs soared above them, a seething mass of wildlife. She felt a little nauseous with the lurching motion of the boat and the smell of petrol, and was worried she might be sick in the mask.

James then took them several hundred metres out into the middle of Village Bay and stood in the middle of the boat to take more photographs of the devastated sea stack with his camera. The boat was moving around a lot in the waves and Alice gripped onto the rail, hoping James would not take too long. Gannets and fulmars were diving and squealing all around them, still in a state of alarm. Floating all around the boat were the remains of hundreds of dead birds, their feathers burned and charred. James shook his head with disapproval at the devastation, and then they moved east towards the cliffs opposite, below the mountain of Oiseval – the same route the German submarine had taken in 1918.

As James took the tiller again and steered the dinghy round the headland, Alice thought she could hear another boat's engine in the distance, but couldn't be sure – the wind and the birds were making so much noise. Ahead of them Alice could see two large brown birds attacking a group of fulmars by diving towards them at speed and tipping their wings so they lost balance and dropped into the sea. The fulmars in a panic dropped their gulletfuls of fish and the brown birds seized the fish for themselves, amid much squawking and commotion.

Alice pointed to the scavengers and shouted, 'Look out James! Bonxies!'

'What are they?' James shouted, watching the birds in astonishment.

'Haven't you seen them before? Their proper name is Arctic skua – our teacher Dr Foster told us they are the real villains of the seas. They don't bother catching their own fish, just steal everyone else's.'

'No, never seen anything like that before,' James called, watching their antics intently.

From behind them, there was a sudden roar, and when Alice turned towards the sound, a much larger boat painted a dark military grey had emerged from behind a stack of rock and was coming straight at them.

'James, look out!' Alice shouted as the boat sped past, sending up spray and making their dinghy rock violently from side to side. Alice read the name on the stern – *Dark Hunter*. At that moment James turned, lost his footing and fell overboard, his camera still around his neck. Someone on the other boat was shouting something through a loudhailer, but Alice couldn't hear properly. Meanwhile James had disappeared under the water. Alice checked on all sides of the boat but there was no sign of him. *Seabean's* engine was still idling. Her heart thumping in her chest, Alice moved to the back of the boat and sat down next to the tiller, trying to remember which way to push it to steer a boat left or right. The other boat was turning up ahead, about to come back in their direction. Alice managed to turn *Seabean* to face the cliffs, and then spotted James waving about ten metres away. She edged nearer and he clambered aboard, shivering and dripping wet.

'Go, Alice, just go! That's one of the Navy's new fast patrol boats. Head for those rocks, I know a cave under there where we can hide.'

Alice opened the engine's throttle and the boat surged forward, the bows rising high out of the water. She could hear the other boat behind them, but didn't dare look round.

'Are they following us?' she called to James, who lay in the bottom of the boat in front of her. He didn't answer. Alice pressed on towards the rugged coastline of St Kilda. She could see a darker archway in the lower part of the cliffs, and aimed for that, hoping it was the cave James meant.

'James, are you OK?' she yelled again. Still no response. Something whistled past her head and cracked off the rocks ahead of her. And again. She realised the other boat was firing at theirs. More bullets whined past. Alice ducked down as low as she could. One bullet glanced off the edge of the boat, leaving a deep scorch mark in the varnish. They were nearing the cave entrance, so she had to slow down. Alice risked a quick look over her shoulder. She could see the dark silhouette of a man standing on the deck of the boat behind, operating a gun. She shuddered and turned to face forward – the *Seabean* was entering the mouth of the cave. A seal barked at them from the rocks, then wriggled into the deep water, its echo bouncing off the cave walls. Alice realised they would be safe here, since the entrance to the cave was much too small for the larger boat to pass through. She decided to try and moor *Seabean* alongside the rocks where the seal had been basking and see if James was all right. But there was no mooring, so she just made the engine cut out.

James was still lying face down in the boat. Alice moved forwards, calling his name. He felt cold and didn't seem to be breathing. Alice tried not to panic, and remembered how Edie's mum felt your pulse. With some difficulty she managed to free James's left arm from under him and squeezed the inside of his wrist. She realised to her relief he was alive but unconscious. There was no sign of the camera.

'OK, now what?' Alice muttered to herself. She looked at her watch. It was coming up to three o'clock. She could hear the *Dark Hunter's* engine humming just outside the cave. She could feel her own pulse racing. James groaned suddenly and tried to roll over. The bottom of the boat was full of water. Alice helped him to sit up, opened his rucksack and made him sip some water from the metal canister he'd brought.

'Have they gone?' James asked after he'd taken a few mouthfuls.

'Not yet, no,' Alice whispered, taking a slurp herself and wiping her chin.

Her eyes had got used to the dimness of the cave now, and she stared around her. Higher up on the rocks beside them she could see that some equipment had been stacked. It looked like drums of explosives and coils of rope, and ten or twelve spherical devices painted black.

'Look up there, James – what are they?' Alice asked, dreading his reply.

James rubbed his eyes and stared in the direction Alice was pointing.

'Good God! Naval mines, if I'm not mistaken.'

'What are they for?'

'They are basically bombs that are planted underwater to blow up submarines. We used them in the war to create safe zones for own ships and also to attack enemy U-boats. There are ships called minesweepers that go around making sure the sea is safe from mines for other naval vessels. I've picked up reports that the American navy is planning to use dolphins to detect and lay mines in future.'

'Really? That's not good,' Alice said, frowning. 'Have these ones exploded yet or not?'

'They look intact to me. Goodness knows what they're using them for in the Cold War. Have you got that other camera, Alice? We should take some shots of them.'

Alice took Karla's camera out of her bag and offered it to James.

'You do it – I have no idea how that thing of yours works!'

Alice took a panoramic shot inside the cave, moving the camera in video mode steadily from left to right until she was facing the mouth of the cave.

'I think they've gone,' James remarked. 'We should get going.'

He tried to ease himself up, and winced with pain.

'What's the matter, James? Where is it hurting?'

'My ankle – I must have twisted it as I fell into the water. Can you be captain?'

Alice nodded, and was about to pull the starter rope when James waved his arms for her to stop.

'Use the oars, Alice, until we get outside. I want to be sure they've gone.'

Alice used one oar to push them away from the rocks, then struggled to manoeuvre both oars into position. Facing the back of the boat, she began to pull them through the water in small circles, gaining momentum, while James steered with the tiller.

'More to the left, Alice,' he muttered. 'That's it. Not much further.'

Alice's hands were cold and wet, and the oars kept slipping.

'OK, pull them in now. We'll just drift out.'

As they re-emerged into the daylight, the sound of James's voice changed, no longer echoing off the cave walls. He was peering through his binoculars, scanning the cliffs in both directions.

'We can't go back to Village Bay, Alice. That's where they will have headed. We'll have to go round to the Gleann Mor side and walk back.'

'How are you going to do that with a twisted ankle?' Alice asked.

'We'll just have to.'

They landed later that afternoon in Gleann Mor, cold, hungry and exhausted. There was no beach as such, so having wedged the *Seabean's* mooring rope with a knot between two rocks, they gathered their belongings and made a start inland. What with their wet clothes, James's swollen ankle and the fierce southwesterly wind, they made very slow progress up the valley. Alice was instinctively heading for the pass at the top, just below the radar station. But James was in a lot of pain, and she could not imagine how they were going to make it back to his house. Then she had another idea.

'We'll rest in the Amazon's house, James – do you know it?'

'Aye, it's that haunted stone dwelling near here. I've not been inside it. People have said there's something odd about it.'

Alice felt drawn to the place ever since she'd had a strange experience there a few months before, when she thought she had felt the presence of the ancient female warrior. It made her shiver even now, and it wasn't just the cold this time.

She could see the outline of the stone dwelling in the distance. James's limping was getting slower and slower, but eventually they made it. Alice had nothing with which to strap up his ankle, and no blankets to keep him warm. She spread the contents of James's rucksack out to dry on the stone ledges built into the walls. Alice remembered finding an engraved metal tag on a chain on one of the ledges last time. There were a few other ragged bits of metal debris strewn around, but she couldn't see the chain anywhere. James slumped down, unable to walk any further.

The only things that had survived their sea voyage were the canister of water, Karla's camera and a soggy granola bar. Alice split the granola bar in half, and ate her portion as she pondered her next move. As a bare minimum they needed food, dry clothes and something to support James's ankle. She might not manage to get James safely back to his house, but she could leave him here so long as he was comfortable, and if she was lucky she might even make it back home to 2018 before nightfall.

Alice left James sleeping and zig-zagged up the last section of the valley. It was steep and she was tiring quickly after the exertions of the day. As she rested by a pile of rocks halfway up, she thought she could just make out the outline of the C-Bean flickering faintly against the sky. But she must have been so tired she was imagining it, because when she finally reached the ridge, all she found there was the radar station. Telling herself that the C-Bean must have made itself invisible again, she ran around desperately hoping she would somehow bump into it. But however much she searched the area beside the radar station where she'd left it, she could not find the C-Bean's smooth walls anywhere.

Alice pressed on. As she reached the village, she could hear voices and a boat chugging in the bay. It was difficult to say for sure in the gathering twilight, but she thought she could just see the outline of the *Dark Hunter* that had pursued them earlier. She realised they must have been the War Office men James had mentioned would be arriving. Alice wasted no time, and quietly let herself in to James's house. There was a torch on the shelf by the front door, and she used it to look around for the items they needed. She found crackers, a jar of salmon paste, a bottle of lemonade, dry clothes and a blanket, matches, a couple of candles and some aspirin, but no bandages, so she took a long knitted scarf instead. She stuffed everything into Karla's shoulder bag and then, as an afterthought, went back for James's pillow. There was a brown notebook under the pillow, which she decided to take as well. She thought about making up a flask of hot tea for James, but she didn't know how to operate the stove and anyway it was a lot to carry back up the mountain and over into the valley on the other side.

All set for the return journey to Gleann Mor, Alice crouched outside James's front door and listened intently, scanning the village and the tents for any sign of human activity. One or two tents were lit from inside and there was a light on in what Alice knew as Reverend Sinclair's house. No doubt that was where the War Office men were staying.

She groped her way between the rocks and cleitean that were dotted everywhere in the grass, heading towards the wall that ran along behind the village. She paused for a moment to catch her breath, then climbed over it, and began the climb back up to the ridge. It was almost dark when she reached it and her legs had turned to jelly, so she half ran, half fell down into Gleann Mor, and managed to find the stone house where she'd left James. It was silent inside, and smelled strongly of bird droppings.

'James, are you there?' Alice called, softly in case he was still asleep.

But James wasn't there. She put all the things down, turned on the torch and looked round, inside and out, calling his name into the darkness. Nothing. In the end she was so exhausted, she made a small bed for herself with the pillow and blanket and curled up to sleep.

As the sun was breaking over the ridge to the north-east, she could feel its rays boring into her face, and when she opened her eyes she thought she could see the outline of a man in a flying jacket standing in front of her. Alice called out 'Who are you?' but the person drifted away. The light was too strong and made her head throb with pain, so she closed her eyes again. Her throat was dry and she felt sore where her wet clothes had chafed her skin the day before. In a panic, she awoke fully. It was 7 am.

There was still no sign of James, no footprints, nothing. A stream trickled past the stone dwelling. She lay on her stomach beside it and drank some of the cool fresh spring water. She ate some of the crackers, then repacked Karla's shoulder bag including the torch and James's notebook, leaving the rest of his things there. Then she set off to look for him. She headed for the radar station once more, harbouring a small hope that as she rounded the summit she would see that her beloved C-Bean had returned.

No such luck. And worse still, the War Office men were inside the radar station with the door open. She crept up to the back of the building and held her breath.

'Where the dickens do you think Ferguson's gone?' said one in a gruff, angry tone.

'No idea. His last report was filed yesterday morning. He knows things he shouldn't have got wind of, that's for sure. Lord knows what he was up to yesterday, and who that girl was he had with him. They must have gone into hiding somewhere.'

'Well, she is obviously working for him. Hope he doesn't try and pull a stunt like that again. He'll get court-martialled for it.'

'Yes sir, he's finished.'

'He obviously knows about the cave.'

'Knows too much, that's for sure. Probably working for the other side, I shouldn't wonder.'

'Commies! No matter, we'll search his place later, see if there's anything there. Bound to have got some dodgy evidence together by now.'

Alice let out a little involuntary gasp as she remembered she'd left the top secret file in the house. She didn't want James to get into any more trouble, so she realised to her dismay she needed to go back and fetch it. Alice darted round to the front of the radar station and surveyed the hillside in front of her. There was no cover, and the only thing she could do was run as fast as she could down the hillside, hoping they would not see her. But they were on their guard and within seconds she heard one of them shout, 'You, girl, wait!'

But Alice didn't look back, she just kept running. The footsteps behind were gaining on her rapidly. Out of breath, she turned and saw both men had guns and were moving expertly through the grass. Ahead of her were some stone cleitean. Alice ducked inside the biggest one, hoping they would not see where she had disappeared. Fighting back angry tears, she crawled to the darkest corner and waited.

Alice's heart was still racing, but she was fairly sure the men couldn't have seen her duck inside the cleit or they would have found her by now. She held her breath and listened hard for several more minutes with her eyes shut. When she finally opened them, all she could make out were a few chinks of daylight coming through gaps in the stone walls, along with the wind. Her eyes slowly adjusted to the gloom inside the cleit. There was something quite familiar about its size and height. She vaguely thought she could hear Karla sniffing in the darkness, but decided her mind must be playing tricks on her – it just felt like the cleit where they'd been imprisoned in 1918. The sniffing got louder, and someone cleared their throat.

'I don't suppose you've brought me paper and a pen as I requested.' It was not Karla's German accent, but a crisp, faintly Scottish female voice.

There was a rustle of fabric and a tall, gaunt woman appeared a few feet from where Alice was crouching. The woman wore a long dress with a very full dark blue skirt and a cream lace neckline. She had pale, papery skin, green eyes and red curly hair piled up on top of her head with hairpins, and wore a choker of pearls around her throat. On closer inspection, Alice noticed the woman's boots were dirty and worn, and the hem of the dress was caked in mud. She seemed confused when she saw Alice.

'Oh! Who, pray, are you child? Why are you here? – my breakfast tray has already been returned.'

'My name is Alice. I am trying to escape from those men.'

'As am I,' the woman said wearily, and smoothed a hand over her skirt. 'I have been detained here against my will for years and years. No one has come for me. It's a national disgrace.' Her voice grew quickly shrill and angry, and her eyes took on a fiery look.

Alice bit her lip, and then in a very quiet voice asked, 'You wouldn't by any chance be Lady Grange, would you?'

'I am she, yes, it is true,' the woman said airily, with what was left of her noble manner, and then added with a tut, 'Never was there ever such an unladylike place as this!'

'So it's true…' Alice murmured to herself. She couldn't remember how long ago this lady had been imprisoned on St Kilda, but it was several centuries for sure. How had she slipped so far back in time? Alice was deeply puzzled, but also aware that this new turn of events had in any case saved her from being captured by the War Office men in 1957. Had she somehow accidentally stepped inside the C-Bean without realising or remembering? After she bumped her head badly back in April, they said at Glasgow General Hospital she might suffer occasional lapses of short-term memory. Had something just happened up on the mountainside that she was unable to recall?

Lady Grange was pacing up and down, muttering to herself as if she too was searching for some lost memory. Alice stood up and looked around the cleit. In one corner there was a straw mattress, similar to the one she had slept on when she was imprisoned, and a foul-smelling bucket. Right beside it was an elegant little chair and an antique writing desk, on which stood a small vase containing a tall, straggly wild flower.

Lady Grange watched as Alice approached the table. It seemed so out of place in this rough interior.

'What is the use of a writing table if they never let me write?' Lady Grange scoffed, and flung herself down on the mattress. After a while she asked in a softer, more curious tone, 'Pray tell me, how is it you speak English? Why have they dressed you in such strange attire? And what is in your bag, child?'

In all the palaver, Alice had forgotten she still had Karla's shoulder bag with her.

'Actually, I have some food. Are you hungry, Lady Grange?' Alice asked politely, as she pulled out the bottle of lemonade, the rest of the crackers and the jar of salmon paste.

'No, I have no need of sustenance now. My stomach it too disturbed today.' There was a long pause, and then she said, 'You can call me Rachel if you like, since you're a fellow prisoner. I am guessing it is the first time you have been held against your will.'

'The second time, actually,' Alice admitted, opening the bottle of lemonade slowly and listening to the long hiss as the bubbles escaped.

'I also have paper and a pencil, if you're interested.'

Lady Grange sat up instantly, her eyes alert and blinking. It was too dark to see properly inside the cleit, but sensing the woman's urgent need to write, Alice laid James's brown notebook on the writing desk and opened it at an empty page. Lady Grange fairly snatched the pencil from her hand, and then seated herself very carefully at the desk.

'Oh for a candle!' she wailed despairingly.

Alice searched the cleit and found an ornate brass candlestick on the ground, but no candle. Then she remembered James's torch.

'Just a moment, I have something better.'

Lady Grange was startled by the sudden brilliance of the torch's beam. She looked at Alice with fresh eyes, and her tone became more humble.

'Who *are* you, my dear? Do you come from foreign shores?'

'No, I live here, like you. Just in another time.'

Lady Grange frowned. 'What time are you speaking of?'

Alice looked at her watch and her stomach turned a somersault as she remembered how long she had now been missing.

'Friday 18th May 2018, 8.30 am, to be exact. I should be arriving in the schoolyard on St Kilda right now.'

When she heard this, Lady Grange stood up abruptly from the desk and backed away from Alice, and James's torch and notebook fell to the ground. Alice stepped forward to pick them up, as the room seemed to spin slightly, and she felt strangely dizzy all of a sudden. The last thing she heard was Lady Grange's shrill voice saying, 'What is happening? This must stop at once!'

Alice's Blog

Saturday 19th May 2018

It's such a relief to be home! Either the C-Bean came back to fetch me or it had been standing there on the hillside all along — disguising itself so well as a stone cleit that it even had me fooled. When I crawled inside it to get away from those men in 1957 I had no idea! Charlie found me all disorientated, lying on the floor of the C-Bean clutching James's torch and notebook. He said he thought he saw Karla dressed in a funny costume run out of the C-Bean the moment it appeared back in the schoolyard, but it was actually Lady Grange. Nobody knew anything about her existence until late yesterday afternoon when Mrs Butterfield found her sleeping in the store behind the shop. She'd stolen a whole pad of paper and a set of gel pens and had been feverishly drawing and writing, apparently.

She's been given Karla's old room above the pub now, and Karla's wardrobe of black clothes. She thought they were boys' clothes at first, but in the end she seemed glad to change out of her tatty old dress. She keeps talking about needing to get back to Edinburgh, only she hasn't got any money to pay for the ferry crossing. So Mrs Butterfield says she can stay and work in the shop until she's got enough together to cover the journey. But she keeps wandering off, and people say they saw her wandering all over the island yesterday. It's like she was imprisoned in that cleit for so long that she just needs to roam freely now. Edie's mum rang the doctor on the mainland and he's sending over some special medicine to help calm her down. No one has any idea how she got here, or why she arrived dressed in a sort of theatrical costume.

All in all I'd been gone for three whole days. As far as my parents were concerned, Karla and I were stuck inside the C-Bean without food and water and they couldn't get it to open. Charlie assured them that the C-Bean could provide us with things to eat and drink via its vending function, and that it probably had its own oxygen supply too, but they were still freaking out – mainly because of my recent head injury. Anyway, they were more bothered about me than about Karla. They think Karla has gone AWOL – that's 'absent without leave' - and they've put out a Missing Person announcement on Scottish radio and on the Internet. I couldn't understand at first why everyone seemed so suspicious about Karla, until Charlie told me that while I was gone, he found her passport with a completely different name on it in her office. It turns out she doesn't work for a company making high-tech learning pods for the education market like she said, and when Charlie's dad made some enquiries, the police on the mainland looked into it and said she had a criminal record as a computer hacker. So she is a spy after all! Charlie thinks it's really hilarious that Karla's now a prisoner of war in the twentieth century and instead I've come back with another prisoner that I've accidentally freed from the eighteenth century.

I suppose it's pretty cool that I've rescued Lady Grange, because it was really unfair what her husband did to her, but I still feel bad about what happened to Karla. Then yesterday Charlie and I managed to get the files off her camera onto our computer and we now reckon she's been spying on us the whole time - by the looks of things she's not really the C-Bean's designer at all, and came here under a false name to nick the idea and email loads of information about it back to Germany so they could try and make one of their own.

When we showed my parents Karla's photos, Dad gave us a passionate lecture about 'industrial espionage' and 'reverse engineering' – he's always been worried about that kind of thing – like whether someone would steal his ideas for the wave energy machines before they were built. Poor Dad - the whole thing with me disappearing has made him more stressed and sick than ever – he gets headaches all the time now, and his skin is even more red and itchy. I feel really bad about it, and what's more Charlie said his dad is feeling worse too.

On the plus side, Charlie and I have checked up on a few things that went right about my time travel adventure. For instance, I was so happy when we looked up the births and deaths in the chapel's ledgers and saw that the newborn babies stopped dying after 1851, and there is even a note dated 16th May 1851 saying they prayed and gave thanks for the mysterious hamper of food and medicines!

Sunday 20th May 2018

I've been worrying a lot about what happened to James after I left him in the Amazon's house, and whether he is OK. What if the War Office men found the file I gave him? So we've been trying to find out what happened to James and to Donald. This morning Charlie and I looked up on the Internet what 'court-martialled' means, and apparently it's some kind of law court for when soldiers have done something wrong. Charlie thinks that when they said he must be 'working for the other side' they meant the Russians, and that James was therefore some kind of spy too, but I don't think he was. He just didn't want Britain to carry on making all those nasty bombs and ruining St Kilda in the process.

When we went to church this morning, it was really weird seeing Donald Ferguson's name listed on the Second World War plaque in the chapel as one of the St Kildan men to have perished in 1944, just like James told me. What's more, we also found Donald's dad's grave in the graveyard. James, however, is a bit more of a mystery. Apart from what we already know, that is: he really was the last baby to be born on St Kilda, on 3rd August 1930, and his mother was called Elsa Gillies. The rest is a bit hazy. His name appears on a list of all the people working on the island in 1957, but it doesn't say what happened to him after that. So I don't know if he was caught and punished, or escaped, or what! There were a few other things on the Internet but we have no idea if any of it relates to James. For example, there was a James Ferguson nominated for a Nobel Peace Prize in 1977, but it doesn't seem likely it was the same person, and another James Ferguson who filed a patent for a synthetic black material called Obsidon in the UK in 2002. We also found a news report from the same year which said the production plant in China that won the contract to manufacture Obsidon had burned down.

The only other clues about James are in his notebook, which Charlie and I have gone through really thoroughly, but there is not much we could understand. He was obviously keeping a kind of diary about the government's plans to make and store nuclear weapons in Scotland, like he told me. There is even a drawing of the same mushroom cloud after the explosion on 17th May, and underneath he's written something about it all leading to ruin. Weirdly, there are some entries dated 1960, where he's written down a load of ideas and maths calculations about time travel, including a diagram of the C-Bean, no doubt based on what Donald told him. He was obviously getting muddled up about dates, what with all his fantasising about travelling to the future, because he's even written underneath one diagram 'Activation date: November 2017'. He got one thing wrong from Donald, though: it's titled 'C-Bean Mark 2'.

Tuesday 29th May 2018

The C-Bean Mark 3 has disappeared! It was there in the schoolyard when we came home from school yesterday afternoon. Mum had been doing a history lesson about the Second World War in the C-Bean with us, and it showed us black and white films with Japanese survivors telling their stories about the awful things that happened to their families and their cities after they dropped the atom bombs. Charlie and I were asking her why people still wanted to make nuclear weapons when they knew how horrible the effects could be, and then the C-Bean did this strange thing it had never done before — an alert message flashed up on all the walls saying, 'File missing. Could not retrieve data.' Afterwards I wondered if it was because I'd given that particular file to James.

The thing I'm most upset about now the C-Bean has disappeared is that Charlie and I were planning to go back to 1957 and check to see if James is OK. I'm still hoping that the C-Bean has just gone invisible for some reason and we will run into it soon. But I've got a nasty feeling this might all be Karla's doing.

The C-Bean had been missing for several weeks. Alice and Charlie had almost got out of their daily habit of arriving early for school so that they could search the schoolyard, looking for any kind of clue as to its whereabouts. One weekend, Alice had traced over a map of the whole village and they'd divided it into a hundred squares to search the bay more systematically. All six children had checked their bit of the map thoroughly. The only things they'd found were a toggle that must have fallen off Dr Foster's duffle coat, a few old coins, a shell from a bullet, which they decided must have been one the German submarine fired, and, in the back of Sam F's garden, the stump of a tree, which Alice realised was where Donald had planted the elm tree in the Fergusons' back garden.

Old Jim came out to see what they were doing on the first day. He stood in front of his underground house for ages, nodding his approval, and coughing violently from time to time. Spex ran backwards and forwards between them, barking excitedly. The second day, Jim only came out for a little while, and stood there shivering even though it was quite a warm day. In the end, Alice and Edie were worried about him, and helped him back inside to bed.

Alice began using James's notebook to write down her own theories and observations. On one page she drew a picture of the half-grown elm tree as she remembered it. Opposite she drew their new tree, the Scots pine, and wrote underneath it, 'Actually the SECOND tree to have been planted on the island'. On another page she made a detailed drawing of the C-Bean Mark 3, with all its special features and capabilities labelled and listed so she wouldn't forget them. She also printed out some of the pictures from 1918 that she'd managed to get off Karla's camera and stuck those in, but she didn't date them. The notebook became a source of comfort, she took to sleeping with it under her pillow like James had done, and after a while she started carrying it everywhere she went, so that she had images of the C-Bean with her even if she didn't have the real thing anymore.

On the last day of the summer term, their teacher Mrs Robertson asked the children to write and draw pictures of the best memories from their past school year. For Alice, this was finally too much, and she fled out of the classroom in tears, unable to even begin to put down on paper what had started to seem a crazy dream that never really happened. She ran as far from the school as she could get, and ended up near Old Jim's underground house. She plunged her hands into her pockets and stood with the fresh summer wind whipping her face and hair, staring out to sea. Her fingers curled around the edges of the notebook in her left pocket. In between the gusts of wind she caught the sound of Jim's coughing. Alice turned and called out his name. Spex crept out of the house and greeted her, quietly wagging his tail.

'Hey Spex, is Jim still poorly?'

Alice ruffled the fur round his neck and bent down to crawl through the low doorway. She groped her way in the darkness to where the coughing was coming from. Jim lay on his bed amid a pile of rugs, pillows and blankets with a dirty sheepskin flung over him. The dog sat down dutifully by his side. Jim's skin was sallow and flaky, and his hair and beard were longer than ever. Alice fetched him a mug of water from a pitcher he kept by his little camping stove. He sat up and drank a little. Alice touched his forehead. It was burning.

'You need to see a doctor, Jim,' she said.

He looked at her blankly, watching her lips move. She realised he hadn't heard what she said, so she pulled out her notebook and pencil to write down the word 'doctor'. Jim fixed his gaze on the book, and a flicker of recognition came over his face. He reached across and grabbed the book from Alice's hand. She offered him the pencil, thinking that he wanted to write something down for her, but he waved the pencil away and began to flick through the pages, more feverish than ever. When he reached the page where there was a drawing of the C-Bean Mark 2, he pointed at the page repeatedly and then at his chest. Alice peered at him with wide eyes as she came to a slow realisation … What? Could it be?

Alice did a quick mental calculation – if this *was* him, he must now be eighty-eight years old. She could hardly believe he had been living here right under her nose all this time – no wonder Alice had always felt like they'd always known each other! Old Jim was James Ferguson!

Alice looked harder at Jim's wrinkled face and a huge grin spread across her face. He started chuckling and was struggling to sit upright in bed. His laughter became louder and more raucous, which made him cough and cough until his face went blue. Then he seemed to forget how to take another breath, and his body went limp as he slumped back down onto the rugs.

'Jim, Jim, wake up!'

Spex joined in, barking and licking his owner's face. But Alice knew it was too late.

The vicar held a funeral for old James Ferguson in the chapel a few days later. The summer term had just ended, and Alice asked if they could wait a day longer until her older sister Lori came back from boarding school on the mainland, so she could be there to give him a send-off too. It was a shame Dr Foster wasn't there, Alice thought, but just about everyone else turned out for it. Everyone was wearing black – including Lori, who usually made a point of only wearing fluorescent colours, although she still insisted on wearing her high-heeled shoes. Everyone except Lady Grange, that is. She decided Karla's black jeans and T-shirts were not suitable for a funeral so she washed her dark blue dress and put that on instead. Alice thought she looked very regal.

It was a sad affair and many of the villagers shed a tear or two, Alice included. But no one cried louder than baby Kit, who for some reason was very restless that day. Alice carried Kit in her arms all the way up to the graveyard in the procession to see the coffin being buried, and it occurred to her at that moment that it felt right for the last person to be born on St Kilda before its evacuation in 1930 to be the first to be buried there after the island's reinhabitation. It seemed nicely symmetrical. Even so, Alice was still having difficulty connecting the old man she had known all this time with the much younger friend she'd made called James in 1957. She still had so many unanswered questions, and now she felt she would never know the answers.

After everyone had trooped out of the little oval graveyard, Lori walked over to her sister.

'C'mon, Alice, don't make such a big deal of it. He was just some old man.'

Alice stared at her sister in disgust.

'OK, be like that, Ali. I'm going to the wake in the pub with Mum and Dad and the others. You'll have to give Kit his tea.'

Lori stomped off in her high-heeled shoes and left Kit and Alice in the graveyard. Alice realised she was just as upset about the loss of the C-Bean as she was for the loss of old Jim. Kit started crying again.

'Shhh, shhh, Kit, my little kittiwake, don't cry. He's up in heaven now,' Alice sobbed in her baby brother's ear, but she had no idea what heaven really was, and no way of knowing if it even existed. She just knew Jim's body was buried under that mound of fresh brown earth, alongside the babies from long ago. Maybe Jim himself was still in the past, maybe he was in the future, or perhaps he was right there with them – except that he was now invisible, just like the C-Bean. At least with Jim they'd put a marker where he could be found in the graveyard, unlike the C-Bean. With this thought Alice began to wander home.

After she'd finally settled Kit down for a nap, she lay on her bed and flicked through Jim's brown notebook once more, wondering if she'd made a mistake in not asking for it to be buried with him. She kept going back to the drawing he'd made of the C-Bean Mark 2, and was trying to make out what he'd written beside it, but it was a lot of strange maths. She began doodling a crude map of the island, adding the route they'd taken around the island by boat, the site of the nuclear weapons store, and the Amazon's house. She put down the pencil. She was beginning to doze off when there was a knock on her door.

'Come in,' Alice said sleepily.

'Hi Alice, are you OK? I just thought I'd pop round.' It was Charlie.

'Yeah, just feeling a bit sad, that's all.'

'I know something that will cheer you up.' Charlie seemed quite fired up for some reason, and was wandering around the bedroom beating his right fist into his other hand like it was a baseball glove.

'What's that?' Alice asked, yawning.

'Just a minute.' Charlie knocked on the window to attract someone's attention, then beckoned them to come inside.

Within seconds, Sam J and Sam F burst into Alice's bedroom and shouted in unison: 'We've found something. A secret cave. Under the gun.'

'Really?'

'Yes, and that's not all. We think the C-Bean's down there.'

The C-Bean's disappearance had been the source of much speculation on the island among the grown-ups, who had never known an item so large go missing, even in the wildest St Kildan storm. A week after it disappeared, they registered it with the Hebridean police as 'stolen', but the police made no progress investigating either that or the other disappearance on the island, namely Karla Ingermann. The detective on the case suggested the two disappearances might be linked, which made Alice think her hunch about Karla interfering with the C-Bean was right. But knowing the C-Bean's new-found ability to make itself invisible, she clung on to the hope that it was just a matter of time before they found it again.

But it was not quite how Alice imagined. After Jim's funeral, the two Sams had gone down to the jetty to mess about by the old gun emplacement. The gun was permanently pointed out to sea, trained on the horizon. It had been waiting to be fired ever since it was put there at the end of the First World War, unused for a century, waiting for an enemy attack. In the absence of a playground, to the island children it was a robust piece of play equipment that had led to endless imaginary games.

Once Alice had got the two seven-year-old boys to calm down and tell their story properly, she found out that during the course of their game that day, Sam F and Sam J had discovered they had somehow worked the gun's rusted bearings loose and they began to rotate it. When they had managed to turn the gun halfway round, so that it was pointing inland towards the chapel, they discovered that the turning motion was actually a mechanism that opened up a secret chamber beneath the gun mounting itself. When they climbed down into the chamber, they were convinced the C-Bean was down there, but they couldn't make it open.

'Alice, you have to come NOW and see,' they implored – as if she needed convincing. Alice was already bundling the sleeping Kit into his buggy. She put Jim's notebook in her pocket, and let the Sams lead the way, running and skipping with excitement, down to the headland, with Alice and Charlie taking turns to drag Kit's buggy down the rough grassy street behind them.

'Do Edie and Hannah know?' Alice asked as they went past their house.

'No – shall we get them to come down too, do you think?'

'Well, it's only fair,' Alice pointed out, and knocked on the door of her other two classmates.

Edie opened the door. She looked a bit glum.

'Hi Alice.'

'Get your boots and coats on and come with us, the boys have got something to show us apparently.'

James Ferguson's wake was still going strong when they passed the pub, and no one noticed when all the island children went past, heading for the gun emplacement late that afternoon.

Sam J ran on ahead and stopped at his house to get a torch, while Sam F fetched his walkie-talkie set from next door. The two of them sprinted the final hundred metres, and even from this distance Alice could see that a large dark hole had opened up in the ground beside the gun.

The children all stood round, peering down into the chasm below. Alice made sure she'd secured the brake on Kit's buggy. There was a rusty iron ladder hooked over the metal rim of the chamber.

'You first, Alice,' the Sams said in a hushed tone.

'Why me?' she enquired, biting her lip.

'Because you're the one who'll know how to make it work. Here, take this, and this.'

They handed her the torch and one half of the walkie-talkie set. Alice remembered using it when they were trying to escape from the Amazonian rainforest. Despite being right here on St Kilda, this moment seemed much more thrilling and dangerous.

Alice worked her way carefully down the ladder, the torch and the walkie-talkie tucked under one arm and her heart beating fast. The handrails were damp and there was a metallic smell. When she stepped off at the bottom, she could see a dark cubic object looming, but it seemed to be wrapped in polythene. Was this really their C-Bean? She looked up and could see the silhouettes of several heads leaning over the hole above. The floor of the cave was puddled with seawater. Alice flicked on the torch and waded across to the C-Bean. She started to pull at the polythene sheeting. Beneath the layers of plastic, the surface of the C-Bean was mottled and grey, perhaps because it was going mouldy in this damp, airless environment.

'Charlie, come down, but be careful, it's a bit slippery.'

While Charlie descended into the chamber, Alice ran her hands over the C-Bean's walls until she could feel the access panel, then pressed to make it open. It was a bit stiff and in the end she had to use the pencil from her pocket to loosen it. When she shone the torch into the recess, a puzzled look came over her face – instead of the digital LED buttons and the slot for a cardkey there was just a large manual switch, like a power overrider. Below the recess with the switch was an empty shallow metal drawer. Alice slid the drawer in and out, but it didn't do anything.

'Come over here, Charlie – this is really odd.'

Charlie examined the drawer and then looked at the handle.

'Looks just like the master switch at the Evaw plant they used to get the whole thing fired up and working.'

'That's just what I was thinking, Charlie! But why's it different? Who's changed it?'

'Dunno. But look at this, Alice!'

Charlie had pushed aside more of the polythene to reveal a somewhat faded notice taped over the door itself. They both read the words out loud in unison: 'War Office Property. Unauthorised Entry Forbidden.' There was a date scrawled along a dotted line underneath and someone's signature, but it had got wet at some point and they couldn't read what it said.

'What do you think happened, Charlie? Shall we try and get inside?'

'No idea. Looks like it's been here a while.'

Alice gingerly lifted the switch. It made a loud grinding noise, and it took both of them to force it all the way up, but finally there was a small whirr and a click, as if some gears had slotted into place. Charlie peeled the sign off the door, and they waited, but the door remained resolutely shut.

'Talk to it, Alice – you know, like you did before.'

Alice stroked the side of the C-Bean and cooed softly, 'Come on baby, open the door for me, it's Alice'.

There was a low buzzing sound and then a crackle. A child's voice said, 'What's happening? Can we come down? We're getting bored up here!' Alice realised it was just Sam F on the walkie-talkie.

Charlie flicked on the other walkie-talkie and reported 'We can't get it working. You might as well stay up there for now. Sorry, guys. Over.'

Hannah's voice called down, 'Sing the sea shanty, Alice'.

Alice started humming the tune, but she didn't hold out much hope. She ran her hands over the C-Bean's surface, but it didn't change colour at all. And it had a rougher texture than she remembered. There was something not right about it, like it had been interfered with in some way, and she felt sure it could no longer respond to her.

Charlie, meanwhile, took the torch and started exploring the rest of the cave.

'Hey, Alice – look over here!'

The torch beam lit up one corner of the cave to reveal a tunnel.

They had to walk one behind the other because it was quite narrow. It appeared to have been blasted out of the rock and a rope handrail was fixed at intervals to the wall at waist height. Alice walked along the tunnel in silence. She couldn't seem to get out of her mind the image of James's wrinkled old face lying in his underground house. They emerged after a few minutes in a vast concrete-lined room with a metal walkway around the edge and in the centre a large tank full of water. After a few seconds, a set of overhead lights flickered on, perhaps triggered by their movement. Charlie and Alice both froze.

The water in the tank glowed green, as if lit from below. At first Alice thought it was empty, but then she noticed standing upright in the water were hundreds of thin metal rods that had been slotted into the compartments of a submerged steel basket, like cutlery in a dishwasher. At the far end of the pool there were several larger cylindrical items, also submerged. Alice could hear an alarm going off faintly, and noticed three red warning lights flashing on the wall opposite.

Charlie looked incredulous. 'What is this? Do you think our dads know about it?'

On the wall just behind them Alice noticed the same ominous yellow-and-black danger symbol that James had shown her in the top secret file, and her heart started pounding.

'I don't know, but look, I think this stuff is radioactive, Charlie. If the alarm's gone off, it must be leaking or something. We should get out of here, just in case. I've got a horrible feeling we've stumbled across the nuclear waste dump that James suspected was on St Kilda all along.'

'Yep, bet you're right – come on, then,' Charlie replied with a grim look on his face.

They walked quickly back to the first chamber where the C-Bean was standing. They paused in front of it for a moment before climbing the ladder.

'You know why we can't get inside it, don't you Charlie?' Alice asked in a quiet voice.

'Why?'

'Because this is not our C-Bean.'

All the next day Alice couldn't stop thinking about the luminous underground tank with the strange cylinders in it. She had to let James know what they'd found under the gun emplacement. It was so frustrating to see the other C-Bean standing there when they were unable to get inside. She either needed to get their own C-Bean back, or get the other one working. If only Jim was still alive, she could maybe ask for his help. She felt like she could hear the alarm ringing constantly in her head as if it was saying, 'Do something!' Charlie thought they should tell the adults what they'd found. But Alice stubbornly clung to the hope that she could think of another way to deal with it.

After tea that evening she walked up to Jim's underground house to try and coax Spex out to eat something, and maybe even come back to her house. Ever since Jim had died, the dog just wouldn't come out and sat by the bed whimpering. She took a plate of warm chicken to entice him, a bowl of fresh water and a cardboard box.

'Spex, where are you?' Alice called as she stepped inside the dwelling.

She found him curled up asleep on the dirty sheepskin rug. He roused himself and half wagged his tail when he saw Alice. While he ate the food, Alice started putting Jim's things in the cardboard box, as her mum had suggested. There was only one item of furniture other than the bed, a large oak sea chest against one wall. It was black with age and had carved panels on all four sides. Alice opened the lid and looked inside. There was a musty smell coming from the blankets laid on top. She lifted them out. Underneath, to her surprise she found the ornate candlestick she recognised as Lady Grange's. Beside it lay a bible, and beneath that, wrapped in brown paper, was the top secret government file that she'd given him in 1957, now somewhat tattered.

She closed the lid of the chest and was about to leave with the box and the dog. She looked around the dwelling one last time, and felt she should make Jim's bed. She smoothed the rugs and quilts, then picked up the pillow to plump it and noticed a leather-bound notebook lying under it on the mattress. It looked exactly the same as the one she had, but this one had a red cover instead of a brown one. She opened it to look at the first page. It was a diary of sorts, and the first entry was 1st June 1957. James must have started another one when he realised the brown one had gone missing. Alice laid the notebook in the cardboard box with the other things and took it all home.

Her house had developed a strange unsettled atmosphere over the last few days. Her dad was ill in bed. Alice couldn't remember that ever happening before, and it was making her mum really stressed. When Alice walked into the kitchen, her mum was on the phone to Evaw's head office in Edinburgh.

'Yes, I know, Les, but the odd thing is Dr Cheung and my husband both have the same symptoms. I know they have been under a lot of stress lately, but the sickness is getting worse, not better. I really think someone needs to fly over and do a health and safety check on the plant. Perhaps there's something wrong. Mmm. OK. I'll call you again tomorrow, Les. Is nine am OK?' Mrs Robertson put down the phone and sighed.

'Mum, is Dad going to be OK? I'm really worried!' Alice whispered.

'I sincerely hope so, sweetheart. I see you persuaded Spex to come back. Maybe that will cheer your dad up. Did you get Jim's things? Was there much in that hovel of his?'

'Just his mother's bible and a candlestick, but I think I know who it belongs to. And this old red notebook. Is it OK if I go round to Charlie's for a bit? I want to tell him something.' Alice asked, stuffing the notebook into Karla's bag.

'Yes, so long as you're back by nine.'

Alice loved the long summer evenings on St Kilda, when the sky just faded to a dull glow but never went completely dark, and it was warm enough not to need a coat when you went outside. But tonight, the greenish glow on the horizon only reminded her of the weird tank in the cave. She looked across at the gun silhouetted on the headland and the roof of the Evaw office nearby. Something suddenly occurred to her and a feeling of dread shuddered through her. What if their fathers had been exposed to a radioactive leak coming from the cave? What if that was what was making them sick?

She ran the rest of the way, burst into Charlie's house without knocking, and darted through the living room where his mum was reading a book and into Charlie's room, panting for breath.

Charlie looked up from his computer. 'Alice, whatever's the matter?'

'Radiation sickness! That's what they've got Charlie! That chamber's leaking right next to Evaw's shed, that's why they're ill. Look it up on the Internet – I bet you I'm right!'

Charlie peered at his laptop screen and they scrolled through a list of symptoms. Vomiting, fatigue, headaches, dry cough, burning, rapid heartbeat, hair loss …

'Wow, Dad's got all of these. Mum's going crazy. He's so ill he's in bed.'

'So's mine. What are we going to do? Maybe Jim was affected too. He had the same cough and high temperature, you know. I think that tank we found in the cave may only be the tip of the iceberg – what if they've stored loads more in other caves or under the sea out there in the bay, just like James predicted?' Alice blurted out, her eyes wide and her breath uneven. She paused and pulled something out of her pocket.

'And look, I found this, Charlie.'

Alice handed Charlie the red notebook and he starting flicking through the pages.

'Whose is this?'

'I found it under Jim's pillow. For all I know he's probably written stuff down about the radioactive waste in here. It's some sort of record of his theories and inventions - look at all the diagrams and calculations, Charlie.'

The two children pored over the pages. The dates of the entries were entirely random – one page was from the 1950s, the next 1971, then 2000, then back to the mid-1960s. Suddenly Alice caught sight of a detailed drawing of the power lever they'd seen on the other C-Bean.

'Hey, Charlie, look at that!'

The next page was a sketch of the metal drawer, which James had labelled 'Instant mailboat'. Charlie scratched his head.

'Maybe the C-Bean in the cave is a prototype that James built after he'd seen our one. That would explain why it's different. The War Office must have found out he was building it and confiscated it from him – which is why it's down there covered in notices and polythene!' Alice was lost in thought for a moment, staring at the sketch. Then she gasped and clapped her hand over her mouth.

'Charlie, I think I know what the drawer is for! We can use it to communicate with him.'

'How come?' Charlie asked, popping a piece of chewing gum into his mouth and offering Alice some.

'No thanks. Don't you remember, in the olden days people on St Kilda used to send messages to the mainland in miniature waterproof containers called *mailboats* when they needed help. It's James' idea of a joke, calling it an "instant mailboat"! I reckon he was trying to invent a device that would let you send a message instantly from one time to another in an emergency.'

Alice looked at her watch. It was almost 9 pm, but she felt there was no time to lose.

'Charlie, we need to try it right now. This *is* an emergency. Maybe James can help us find a way to make our dads better.'

Alice tore a page from the red book and wrote a note on it addressed to James, telling him that their fathers were sick, and that they thought they'd found the nuclear waste dump that he'd been looking for in a hollowed-out chamber beneath the gun. She signed and dated it, Friday 27th July 2018.

They slipped out of the back door without Charlie's mother noticing, and headed down to the gun emplacement. The mechanism was very stiff, but between them they managed to rotate the gun towards the chapel and open the hatch just enough to be able to squeeze through and climb down. They had forgotten to take a torch, so they had to grope their way towards the C-Bean in the dark. Alice reached it first and felt her way to the access panel and opened the little door.

'Right – let's give it a go, Charlie.'

Charlie pulled the lever back down to its starting position and Alice slid open the metal drawer, placed the folded note inside and closed it again.

He lifted the handle, and they could both hear the gears whirring and clicking into place like the previous time. Then they stood in the dark and waited. Water was dripping from the roof of the cave onto their heads. Alice shivered. Silence.

'OK, let's come back early in the morning and check it,' said Charlie.

They were halfway up the ladder when there was a muffled scraping sound, followed by the faintest of clicks.

'Did you hear that?' Alice squeaked. She jumped back down off the ladder and stumbled across to the C-Bean. She felt inside the access panel and her heart skipped a beat.

'The lever – it's moved, Charlie – I was right!'

'Well, open the drawer then and see.'

Alice pulled the drawer and felt inside. The letter was still there. Disappointed, Alice picked it up and then suddenly realised it was not her note. This one was in an envelope, and it was sealed up.

It was almost too dark to read the letter when they got above ground. Charlie closed up the cave entrance, trying to make as little noise and possible, but even so Mr Butterfield heard them as he was heading for the pub.

'What are you two kids doing out this late? You shouldn't be playing with that gun,' he shouted.

'I left my sweater here earlier,' lied Charlie.

They waited until he was out of sight and then Alice tore open the envelope. It was unmistakably James's handwriting.

My dear Alice

So pleased you worked out how to operate the mailboat feature! The rest of my C-Bean experiment has been a bit of a disaster so far, but I'm still working on it. Thanks for the tip-off about the nuclear waste dump. I've got a contact now who's quite high up in government. They told me St Kilda is still on the list as a preferred waste site but so far no decision has been made as to whether they will actually use it. Rest assured, Alice, I will do my best to make sure they go with one of the other options that would be much less damaging.

Yours, James

PS I wonder if you could send me a few materials I need to get my C-Bean prototype up and running. I need ...

'Hey, Alice, what the hell do you think you're doing out here?' It was Lori, who had obviously been sent out to look for her. Alice could see her sister's fluorescent pink jeans approach them in the deepening twilight. She hid the letter behind her back and glanced at her watch. It was nearly ten o'clock.

'Mum's been getting worried. What have you got there? Let me see. Are you two writing love letters to each other, or what?' Alice could tell by Lori's tone of voice that she was being ridiculed. She passed Lori the letter, and was grateful James had omitted to date it.

'Where did you get this?'

'We found it …' Alice faltered.

' … in Karla's office, among her papers,' Charlie butted in, covering for her.

'Why's it addressed to you then, Alice?' Lori was nothing if not persistent.

'And who's this James? Is he your "boyfriend"?'

'Shut up, Lori – it's a letter from a … scientist. I asked him to look into whether there's a possibility that it's a nuclear accident or some kind of radioactive leak that's making our dad and Charlie's dad ill, if you really want to know.'

Lori fell silent and read the note again.

'I see. Does Mum know about this scientist friend of yours?'

Alice shook her head. Lori stuffed James's letter into her back pocket.

'Well, we'd better go back and tell her you've been snooping around the German spy's office. You can't keep disappearing like this – it's freaking her out.'

'Lori, don't be mean. Think about it. Dad's sick. I just want to help, that's all.'

With that, Lori walked off. Alice rolled her eyes at Charlie, and they both followed Lori up through the village. Charlie peeled off at his house with a silent wave and a shrug, as if to say don't worry, it'll be OK. But Alice was fighting back tears of anger. She could feel them pricking in her eyes, and she swallowed hard before running to catch her sister up.

'Wait up, Lori – I've got something else to tell you.'

Lori wheeled round to face her, but instead her gaze fell on something unexpected behind Alice.

'What the ...'

Alice turned and saw Lady Grange running half-naked towards them, locks of curly red hair flapping around her face. She tripped on a tuft of grass and fell over.

'Lady Grange, what on earth's the matter?'

The woman lay writhing on the ground, delirious and distraught, tugging at her clothes and hair. Alice ran back to help her to her feet.

'I had to get out of that box, Alice! It was too bright, and there were too many pictures. Get me the nurse! I need some more of her magic medicine. Where is Karla hiding? I need to hide too, or they'll find me. I know they will!'

'Lori, can you go and get Edie's mum? Tell her Lady Grange is ill again. She knows what medicine to give her. And bring a blanket.'

Lori scurried off in the dark, while Alice knelt down and stroked Lady Grange's hair to calm her down. She was puzzled – why did she mention Karla, and what did she mean by a 'box' – could she possibly have found the C-Bean?

'Do you know Karla? They've made me wear her clothes and live her life and I don't want to any more. I am not her!' Lady Grange implored.

'No, of course you're not Karla. Nobody said you were. It's OK, I understand.'

Alice left a pause, then asked gently, 'Lady Grange, what box are you talking about?'

Lady Grange pointed vaguely above the village. 'Up there! I couldn't get out. I was stuck inside it for hours, but no one came.'

Alice stared into the gloom at the silent mountain ridge. Could the C-Bean have returned to where it had been left in 1957, and Lady Grange had somehow found it when she was roaming around? Alice's heart was pounding, but she knew there was no way she could go and look until tomorrow. She could just make out two figures hurrying towards her.

'Come on now, dear, let's get you to bed. My, she's got a shocking temperature,' Edie's mum Jane said in her 'I'm-a-nurse' voice, wrapping a blanket around Lady Grange's shoulders and easing her up.

Lori stood a few feet away, biting her bright orange fingernails.

'Will she be all right?' Alice asked. 'She seems very confused.'

'Let's hope so. There are too many ill people on this island – it's enough to make us evacuate it all over again!' Edie's mum said emphatically. With that, she led Lady Grange away.

The two sisters walked back home in silence. Alice wanted to ask Lori to give the letter back, but she decided not to. Now there was a chance their C-Bean had reappeared, maybe there was no need.

Alice was woken in the morning by her dad. When she opened her eyes she was convinced she must still have been dreaming, because he was fully dressed and looked completely well again. No redness on his face. Even his hair had grown back.

'Come on, sleepyhead. It's your favourite day of the week – Saturday! I've been up hours, already taken Spex for a walk, and your mum's come up with a plan for us to make up a picnic and all go for a family walk up Conachair in the sunshine.'

Alice hugged him and remembered the letter.

'Is Lori awake?'

'No. Why don't you go and wake her, and we'll all have breakfast?'

Alice crept into her sister's bedroom and nudged the sleeping hump of bedclothes.

'Hey Lori, guess what? Dad's well again!'

The hump spoke: 'Why'd you have to wake me to tell me that, you idiot? Since when was he ill?'

Alice frowned and went back to her room to get dressed. She

needed to check for sure, so she ran down to Charlie's house and let herself in. They were all sitting round the table having breakfast – there was Dr Cheung, tucking into bacon and eggs and looking bright and breezy with a full head of hair, just like her own father.

'What can we do for you, Alice?' Mrs Cheung enquired. Charlie just winked at Alice.

'Nothing … see you later!' Next she ran to Edie's house. Edie opened the door.

'Did Lady Grange sleep here last night? Is she OK?'

'Lady Grange? No, why? She'll be in her room above the pub, as far as I know.'

'Of course. Silly me. See you later.'

'Wait, Alice. What's going on?'

But Alice skipped off back home for breakfast happy in the knowledge that, despite the risks, they'd successfully managed to reverse the damage that had been done to their island and their health.

The two girls took it in turns to carry the picnic basket up to the ridge. It was a beautiful mild day, and Alice watched as her parents walked hand in hand up ahead, Kit bouncing on her father's back in a baby carrier, and Spex bounding backwards and forwards between them all, happy to be part of the family again. They picked a spot with the best view of the bay. Lori spread out the picnic blanket while Alice stared out to sea, completely distracted for a moment. She could see the Evaw machines anchored just below the surface, collecting wave energy, but in her mind's eye she could also still picture the mushroom cloud looming above the bay.

'What are you looking at? Aren't you going to help me, Alice?'

'Thank goodness.'

'What?'

'Nothing.'

'You're a weirdo, Alice.'

Later, while they were eating, Alice noticed something out of the corner of her eye. She felt sure she could see a brief flickering shape appear from time to time further down the mountainside, just on the flat piece of ground near the radar station. She kept her eye trained on the spot, and sure enough it happened again. This time the square shape was unmistakable – it was the C-Bean, no doubt about it. She hoped that no one else noticed the strange sight of it momentarily materialising and then disappearing again, like a mirage. She could hardly contain the surge of excitement welling up within her.

'Come on, Spex – chase me!'

She practically ran the last few hundred metres to the summit of Conachair, her arms outstretched like a little kid pretending to fly. Because in truth, that was how she felt.

On the way back down, Alice's mum made a suggestion.

'Why don't you two girls camp out tonight? The weather's fine – it'd be fun.'

Lori looked only vaguely interested, but Alice jumped at the idea, a secret ulterior plan already forming in her mind.

'Can we ask Charlie and Edie to come too?'

'Does Charlie have a tent?'

'Yes, he has a four-man one, actually.'

'I'm not sleeping in a tent with Charlie,' announced Lori.

'Well, why not let Charlie sleep in our two-man and you three girls can use his then,' said their mother, always ready with a solution. 'You could even take Hannah too, if Jane says she can, since there'd be room.'

'Can we camp over in Gleann Mor?' Alice asked nonchalantly, wrapping her arms around her father's waist. She wanted to gain them a bit more time away on this trip.

'Yes, you're both old enough now, I suppose – but take Spex with you, for protection,' advised Alice's dad, stopping to admire the view one more time. 'Just look at the wave machines from up here – don't they look fantastic! What an amazing achievement, Alice, don't you think?'

'Yes. We've changed history, Dad,' Alice said proudly, even though they were talking about two different things.

Alice managed to grab two minutes alone with Charlie to tell him her plan. They were rolling up sleeping bags and stuffing them into drawstring sacks in his room. The others were down at the shop buying provisions.

'So, once the girls are asleep, we can creep back up to the place on the ridge where I saw the C-Bean, and I reckon we'd be back in the tent before they wake up.'

'It sounds a bit risky, but we can give it a go.'

'Please let's do it. I really need to find out if James is OK.'

'Well, we know he was OK, because he survived well into his eighties!' teased Charlie.

'You know what I mean,' Alice giggled, thumping him in the stomach.

The expedition over to Gleann Mor went without a hitch, except that Edie was a bit grumpy about the whole thing. They were rewarded with a spectacular sunset. The whole valley was bathed in a peachy pink light, making their faces glow orange. In actual fact it was a bit chilly, so Charlie lit a campfire using barbecue coals in a tin tray, because there was no wood around to light a real one. Alice realised they'd pitched the tents near the stream she had drunk from the morning she woke there, cold and alone, in 1957. With their colourful tents, and having Spex with them this time for company, the place felt much less desolate. Lori started telling them made-up ghost stories while they warmed up the baked beans they'd brought and buttered some bread for tea. Alice looked like she was listening, but really she was remembering her own strange encounters in this valley, and about losing James there. When it was her turn to tell a story, she didn't need to make it up. But she realised it didn't have a proper ending.

'You can't end a ghost story like that,' objected Edie when Alice's voice trailed off with the words 'That's all'. 'The man can't just vanish and leave the girl wandering around all over looking for him. And anyway, how did he go off when his ankle was hurt?'

'Well, that's my story – it's someone else's turn now.'

After that they ate in silence. Charlie rinsed off the plastic plates in the stream and then went inside his tent. Spex followed him.

Alice lay very still in her sleeping bag, listening to the other two girls dropping off to sleep. She didn't move a muscle until she was sure she could hear them making the kind of steady breathing patterns that meant they were sound asleep. She wriggled out of her sleeping bag without unzipping it and lifted the flap of the tent door she'd deliberately left open (so she could 'breathe', Alice had told them). Charlie had done the same, and she found him sitting on his sleeping bag, fully dressed and ready to go, his hand over Spex's muzzle so he wouldn't try to greet Alice. They moved away from the campsite and up the slope, without speaking a word until the dying embers from the campfire were just a pale orange dot.

'Did you bring your torch?' Alice whispered finally.

'Yep. Are we near the spot?'

'Not much further.' It was still not quite dark on the horizon to the west, and the remaining light made everything look as if it was different shades of blue. Just then, up ahead, Alice saw a much darker flicker, a straight edge, and then the vertical line was gone. Now she knew what she was aiming for.

'This way, Charlie.' They moved off the path and made their way diagonally across a large patch of thicker grass, Spex sniffing his way through the undergrowth. As they got closer, the glimpse of an edge turned into a steadier slab of black. The closer Alice got to it, the more substantial the C-Bean became, as if she was calling it into being with her very presence.

Suddenly, they were standing in front of it.

'It seems bigger, doesn't it?' Charlie whispered.

'Much,' Alice agreed, and touched it for the first time. She could swear it trembled, but it was probably her hand, not the C-Bean. The door opened and they both stepped inside.

Alice sat on the floor, stroking Spex and basking in the soft white light that emanated from every surface around her. For some reason she felt she was finally home. It was strange, when most of the time the C-Bean seemed to make her go anywhere *but* home. It was like something in her blood, her pulse even, was connected to this pod.

'Right, we haven't got all night. What's the deal?' Charlie paced impatiently in circles around her. His footsteps made something on the floor shift around. Alice noticed there were sheets of paper scattered on the floor, and started to gather them up. Someone had written pages and pages with a pale lilac felt-tip pen. The writing began small and neat, and became larger and more angry-looking and then it looked like the pen must have run out.

'Lady Grange. It must have been what she wrote when she was stuck inside here. Look at this, Charlie.'

'Can't we look at that later, Alice? There isn't time now.'

'OK, you're right. Let's go and find James – we still don't know why he wasn't in Gleann Mor when I went back for him.'

'So, chalk it up!'

Alice asked for a pen, and wrote very specifically on the wall in huge swirling writing: *28th July 1957, Gleann Mor, St Kilda, Scotland,* so that the C-Bean could be in no doubt about the place and time.

For no apparent reason, just before the command was acted upon, the C-Bean asked Alice for permission to perform a software update.

'What shall I say, Charlie?'

'It might add some useful new features – go for it!'

Alice gave her consent, and it announced in a dull monotone that it was adding two new patches, effectively upgrading it to a C-Bean Mark 4. There was a wavering sensation, when not only the C-Bean but even Alice's body and Charlie's too seemed to flicker and fragment slightly. She had never consciously experienced the dematerialisation process before, but this time it was a truly physical, and not entirely pleasant, sensation. It occurred to her that perhaps they shouldn't time travel too often, in case it did something bad to your insides.

It was most peculiar to step back out of the C-Bean in the very place where they'd pitched their camp earlier and find there was no longer anything there. No tents. No children. No campfire. And then the C-Bean itself did the oddest thing – in a matter of seconds, it vanished, leaving nothing on the ground except the cardkey. Spex sniffed it inquisitively. Even that looked slightly different, too. There was still a logo of a spinning globe on it, but it was black and rubbery.

'That's the updated C-Bean Mark 4 for you,' joked Charlie, and he picked it up out of the grass and tossed it to Alice. She examined the black card and then slipped it into her jeans pocket.

'What now?'

'We walk over to James's house.'

They decided not to use Charlie's torch until they were inside the house, and what it revealed when they flicked it on was quite a shock – not only was James nowhere to be found, but his place had been ransacked. Everything had been turned upside down, and Alice knew immediately what the War Office men had been looking for. She imagined that James must have gone into hiding somewhere, and taken the file with him, since she knew he still had it in his possession the day he died. But it upset her when she caught sight of a navy blue box trampled on the floor, and found that Donald's medal had been taken. All that remained was the imprint of the cross in the red velvet.

Charlie was eating a biscuit he'd found in the kitchen cupboard.

'I think it's safe to say James has done a runner,' he said with his mouth full. Spex was sniffing around his ankles for crumbs. Then the dog seemed to latch onto another, stronger scent, and barked. He trotted out of the house and down the street.

'Let's follow him – seems like he's onto something,' Alice said, reluctant to return to the present just yet.

'In the pitch dark? What if we get caught by the army people you said were here?'

'It's midnight, Charlie, they'll all be fast asleep, and we won't make a sound.'

'OK. No barking, Spex,' Charlie hissed, his jaw tense.

Spex, silent and obedient, moved off at quite a pace, and Charlie was right – it was finally dark. The dog looked like he was heading towards the jetty at the bottom of the village. They both jogged to catch up with him. None of the houses had any lights on, but there was some washing hanging in a couple of the backyards. Alice realised that the nature conservationist team must have arrived. Spex carried on past the jetty and up the headland on the other side, stopping at the gun emplacement, wagging his tail and circling round it.

'You don't think …' Alice ventured.

'Could be.'

They shoved the barrel of the gun round towards the chapel. It moved with considerably more ease than in 2018, and the hatch opened without a sound. Spex was so excited that he almost fell into the hole. Charlie flicked on his torch and shone it on the ladder so Alice could climb down. He then handed her the torch and lifted the dog down to her, not wanting to risk leaving him above ground in case he started barking.

'James, are you down here?' Alice called out.

She surveyed the chamber while she waited for Charlie. Scattered all over the floor were half-eaten cans of food and a variety of tools. Spex picked through them, eating any morsels that he found. Propped against one wall were a number of sheets of metal next to something that looked like a half-built raft or base. It was obvious this had been James's laboratory where he was attempting to assemble his prototype C-Bean. There was a drawing with measurements written on it lying beside a box containing some kind of mechanical item, which Alice then recognised was the power switch. James had obviously ordered it from somewhere but had yet to incorporate it into his design. His undated note to her must have been sent from a time much later, when his homemade C-Bean was almost complete.

'Alice, it's not here,' Charlie said quietly.

'Huh?'

'The other chamber. I mean there's no way through. Look – the rock hasn't been touched.'

Alice flashed the torch beam across to where Charlie stood.

'They must have blasted out that chamber some time after 1957, then,' Alice mused.

'Well, anyway, he's not here, so let's go.'

They climbed back up the ladder, and then Alice remembered Spex. She went back down and found him curled up on a rough woollen sweater that had been dropped on the floor next to the tools.

'C'mon, Spex,' Alice coaxed, and tugged at James's sweater. The dog stood up and stretched. Alice saw something shiny on top of a piece of paper in the dent where the dog had been lying. She picked up the shiny object, which was warm from the dog's body. She turned it over in her hand. It looked just like the metal tag on a chain she'd once found in the Amazon's house, and was engraved with some information including those same initials Alice had noticed before – D.C.F. The piece of paper was a note from James.

'Charlie, give me the torch a minute.'

My dear Alice
Glad you found your way down here. Sorry to disappoint you by not being here to meet you. As you can see, they have searched high and low for any incriminating evidence in my possession, but I've

hidden it well, and so far they have not discovered this lab of mine, where as you can see I am now more or less living. Dad told me about it. He said they discovered the cave when they installed the gun up here towards the end of the First World War but it was a well-kept secret among the islanders. The only other person who knew about its existence was that Karla woman, but she's long since gone.

There's something I want you to do for me now, if you don't mind. It's about Dad. Remember how I told you that he was brought down in a seaplane in World War II? Well, some other information has come to light since I last saw you and, amazingly, it seems he must have crashed on St Kilda. Dad was trying to land in the bay at Gleann Mor but must have misjudged the landing and the wind direction somehow. The conservation people told me in the pub yesterday that they'd found human bones and wreckage in the valley there, so I'm convinced he didn't die instantly. They also found this dog tag there, in the Amazon's house, with his number, blood group and initials on it: DCF. So I know it was really him. Dad must have died there. I want you to take the C-Bean and go to the crash site in Gleann Mor and see if you can find him. I was trying to finish my C-Bean in time to go myself and rescue him, but it was more tricky than I thought, that's why I need you to go.

The crash took place just after midnight on 29th July 1944. Good luck, Alice – I know this will mean as much to you as it does to me. Just make sure he lives, that's all I ask.

JF

Alice gulped when she got to the last line. Charlie was reading it over her shoulder.

'That's tonight Charlie!'

'Looks like we've got our work cut out,' he said grimly.

'We better get out of sight of the village before we use the C-Bean,' Alice said thoughtfully, putting the dog-tag in her pocket and feeling it make contact with the new black cardkey.

Charlie picked up James's sweater and they left the chamber in silence, leaning against the gun to close up the hatch and leave it just as they found it. Spex sensed a change in their mood and walked sombrely beside them. They avoided the army camp, climbing diagonally behind the village up to the ridge.

The radar station was locked up and in darkness, and Alice thought it was safe to summon the C-Bean on the adjacent spot where it had arrived once before. She looked at her watch. It was exactly midnight. She pulled the dog-tag and cardkey from her pocket. Putting the dog-tag around her neck, Alice took a deep breath, held out the new cardkey and stood still.

She could hear Charlie sniggering to himself.

'What's so funny, Charlie?'

'What are you going to do next – say "Abracadabra"?'

'Erm … I don't actually know,' Alice answered, aware she was failing to see the funny side of things.

She closed her eyes and thought for a moment.

'Whoah – well, whatever you did, it's working!' Charlie spluttered.

Alice opened her eyes and the C-Bean stood before her. She flipped open the access door and slotted in the cardkey. The door opened and Alice stepped inside. Charlie threw James's sweater on the floor and Spex immediately lay down on it again.

'Right, we're going to need to take some things with us.'

Alice picked up the pen and began making a list on the wall, like she had done once before. It was strange to think that it was Donald who'd helped her carry the hamper of food and medicine out of the C-Bean to leave for the starving villagers back in 1851, and now here she was, making up an inventory of food and medicine to help Donald himself survive his own catastrophe.

'We might need crutches, Alice. James didn't say what his injuries were,' Charlie suggested.

Once they had assembled all the equipment they could think of in the middle of the C-Bean's floor, Alice announced their destination as before – *29/07/1944, 00.15, Gleann Mor.* The same destabilising feeling of being simultaneously fragmented and then rapidly put back together came over her, as the C-Bean recalibrated its time frame yet again to perform this mercy mission. Judging by the look on Charlie's face, he was feeling distinctly odd too.

Worse than this feeling of being physically rearranged was Alice's sense of dread at the prospect of what they might find when they stepped out of the C-Bean to confront the wartime carnage of Donald's crashed plane.

Alice's Blog

Sunday 29th July 2018

What an intense few hours! I never want to go through something like that again as long as I live. I didn't know what to expect when we left the C-Bean, but I think I was at least counting on a calm summer's night. Instead we found ourselves in the middle of the most horrendous storm. Stupid really, I should have thought of that — I mean, why else would Donald have crashed?

Anyway, Charlie and I struggled headlong into the wind and the rain with all the stuff, but it was pretty dark and we could hardly see anything. We were about to go back and ask the C-Bean for tarpaulins or some polythene sheets to keep everything dry when we heard a man's voice calling out in the darkness, obviously in a lot of pain.

I called out, 'Donald, is that you?' and tried to walk towards where the sound was coming from. I kept tripping over bits of the wreckage that were strewn everywhere on the hillside. Eventually we found him sheltering in a section of the fuselage that had landed in a gully. He was lying awkwardly, still wearing his leather flying jacket, with one leg propped up. I was no expert about what kind of condition he was in, but it didn't look great. There seemed to be blood everywhere, and his face was barely recognisable.

'What do we do?' I asked Charlie helplessly, but he just stared in shock. I gave Donald some water and some painkillers and he seemed to come to his senses a little. He wanted to know if we'd been in the plane too, and asked where the others were. I sent Charlie off to look around, but he came back looking worse than ever. He still hasn't told me half of what he saw last night. But as dawn came, I could see that it can't have been pleasant. In fact, I don't think I can write any more now. It's too upsetting.

One thing, though – Spex was instantly drawn to Donald. It was like he sensed the connection between Donald and James, or maybe he simply felt he should stay by a wounded man. Mum once told us at school about these dogs in Belgium during the war who were trained to stay with injured soldiers until help came. Spex did exactly the same. So when he wouldn't come, I put Donald's dog-tag around Spex's neck and left the two of them there.

Monday 30th July 2018

Charlie is traumatised and I don't know what to do. He won't get out of bed, and refuses to eat. He told his parents he had a vivid nightmare, but I know the awful truth. I stayed with him for ages this evening, just holding his hand. He says he wants to cry but he can't.

Lori's not much help. Of course she doesn't know what we went through – as far as she's concerned, Charlie was spooked by the ghost stories she told us, and she said in front of his parents that she thought he was being utterly pathetic. She's also on my case about the fact that when she and Edie woke up, Charlie and I were both in the same tent together. I couldn't leave him, though – he was shaking too much. So now Lori keeps taunting me about Charlie and me being in love, and how she's going to tell Mum and Dad. It's her that's being pathetic.

Tuesday 31st July 2018

I woke up in a panic this morning, really needing to know if Donald survived or not. What if he didn't? What if nobody saw the flare we let off in the hope that some plane would fly over looking for him? What if Spex left his side and wandered off? What if his leg went bad and he got that thing called gangrene where your leg has to be amputated? Should I have moved him or just left him where he was? It was a terrible thing to inflict more pain on a person even when you were trying to help them, but even getting him into the C-Bean was a huge feat. After that I let the C-Bean take over. I had barely enough energy to issue the command 'Diagnose please, treat injuries'. The C-Bean set to work, producing a hospital bed for him to lie on and showed me various little movies to explain to me how I needed to cut off the jacket and trousers and apply dressings to the wounds. Thankfully he hadn't lost so much blood that he needed to be given any extra. I don't think I could have done that. Poor Charlie couldn't cope at all and sat outside while all this was going on. I asked the C-Bean to put out a Mayday alert so that Donald would be picked up. He was even able to drink some hot chicken soup before I wrapped him all up in a load of blankets and then Charlie managed to put up a little army tent beside the C-Bean and helped me get Donald comfortable inside it.

I wanted to help Charlie feel better and stop worrying about Donald myself, so today I went down to the cave and sent James another note via the mailboat drawer. At first I thought that someone else had been down there, because the polythene that had been draped over the other C-Bean had gone, as had the sign that Charlie tore off the door. But then when I saw James had fixed a label to the switch mechanism, I realised that he'd somehow managed to keep his lab and his C-Bean project hidden from the War Office. The other chamber where the tank had been was also gone, and the rock wall was now untouched and looked just like it had in 1957. In my note I asked James if Donald was rescued OK, and how everything turned out. I couldn't believe it when he simply sent back a black and white photograph of his dad, in full military uniform, proudly wearing his Victoria Cross and also a second medal for his services. At his side was a small brown dog. James had scrawled on the back of the photo 'Dad and Spex, on the occasion of his medal ceremony, 30 November 1945, with love and thanks'. Charlie smiled when he saw it. He even got out of bed this evening and ate dinner at the table with his mum and dad. Progress!

Wednesday 1st August 2018

In all the events of the past few days, I forgot to say what happened with the C-Bean Mark 4. It turned itself invisible again when we arrived back in front of Charlie's tent, and I just put the new cardkey in my pocket. But then disaster struck because the next day Mum washed all our clothes from camp, and the cardkey accidentally went in the washing machine. I have no idea if it is waterproof or not, but ever since then it's been pulsing alternately hot and cold – one minute it feels like a lump of burning coal, and the next it's like holding a lump of freezing liquid nitrogen. Well that's probably exaggerating a bit, but either way, you can't bear to touch it. Charlie thinks we should wait a few days to see if it recovers, and then try and use it again. For now I have hidden it in the drawer by my bed along with James's brown notebook and Lady Grange's sheaf of notes.

I still have no idea what happened to Lady Grange while she was inside the C-Bean. I've asked her but she doesn't seem to remember. All I have are the sheets of paper she wrote in lilac ink, but I can't read most of it, and the bits I can seem to be mostly her recreating the letters she wrote when she was imprisoned on St Kilda in the past.

There are a lot of things I can't read in James' notebooks either, because James's handwriting is so bad or it's just too difficult to understand, but some strange things have come to light about the time before he came back to live on St Kilda. Charlie's got the red notebook at the moment — he says he wants to read it properly and check some facts. So far he says he's sure that it was James who was nominated for a Nobel Peace Prize in 1977, for his anti-nuclear warfare work — he wrote about how excited he felt the day he received the letter telling him he'd been selected! As far as we can tell he was working for some sort of government computer project after that, about time-coding. Judging by the entries written during the 1990s, he was living somewhere in Germany and employed by a company there to solve potential Millennium Bug glitches in their computer systems.

It seems he was also the guy who invented a material called Obsidon — he wrote pages of formulae about it. There is something that struck me as weird, though — he stuck in an article from the Scottish Herald dated January 2003. It was a photo of James with a caption underneath asking people to come forward if they could identify this man. Apparently there was a warrant out for his arrest, and he was accused of causing the fire at that factory in China where they were manufacturing Obsidon. So did James go AWOL like Karla? Is that where all the money that old Jim donated came from? Is that why he came back to St Kilda to hide in the underground house?

Alice was dreaming that she was choking. Something bitter and hot was burning the back of her throat. When she forced open her eyes, the room was filled with smoke and intense heat. Then she noticed flames coming from the drawer by her bedside where the C-Bean key was kept. She scrambled out of bed and raised the alarm.

'Mum, Dad, Lori – the house is on fire, quick, wake up!'

She ran to Kit's cot and lifted him out, still asleep. The smoke was making her eyes stream. Her parents were groping their way across the room towards her, half awake and coughing. Lori stood in the bedroom doorway like a statue, unable to take in what was happening. Alice grabbed her by the sleeve and pushed her into the kitchen. Alice's dad opened the back door and they all tumbled out into the cold night air, panting and gasping for breath.

Smoke was pouring out of the house now. Through Alice's bedroom window they could see the first flames take hold. Alice's mum took Kit and shouted, 'Mike, get the hosepipe from round the back! Alice, go and get help!'

'What about all our stuff?' wailed Lori, sobbing.

Alice ran blindly down the village street, knocking on every door she passed, not even stopping to explain why she was waking them all in the dead of night. They would find out quickly enough – the flames were now visible from a hundred paces. Their whole house was on fire!

When she reached the pub at the other end of the village, she turned and saw a surging mass of people half walking, half running up the main street in their night clothes, all carrying buckets and blankets into the cloud of smoke, to try and extinguish the blaze. Alice could hear Mr McLintock revving up his truck to bring the water hose. She pushed open the door of the pub, ran up the stairs to Lady Grange's room and flung herself on her bed in floods of tears.

Lady Grange rolled over and squinted at her.

'Whatever is the matter, child?'

'The key to the box you found on the mountain, it's made my house catch fire, Lady Grange. What shall I do? It's all my fault!'

Once the blaze had been brought under control, some of the men ventured inside the house to try and retrieve any items that weren't already burned or damaged. The fire hadn't reached as far as the living room or her parents' bedroom, but it did appear that it must have started in Alice's room, just as she feared. The family decamped to Edie's house, but Alice was inconsolable. However much anyone said it wasn't her fault, she stubbornly maintained that it was. Never had she needed the C-Bean so much as now – to be able to correct the effects of time. It felt so unfair that she had been able to deal with Donald's injuries, the nuclear dumping, their dads' radiation sickness and even stop the babies from dying, but she didn't know how to change things in her own life. All she wanted to do was return things to a time before the fire happened, but since the C-Bean's cardkey appeared to have been not only the cause of the disaster but also consumed in it, she now had no means of getting the C-Bean back.

'You can't change the way things are, Alice – it's just something that's happened, and everyone's safe, no one was hurt. Think of it like that.' Edie was taking a more philosophical approach to consoling Alice, who was lying on Edie's bedroom floor watching Kit playing with some building blocks.

'I suppose you're right.' Alice made a tower out of the blocks and the baby knocked it down and laughed. She stroked his fine red hair and he looked at her with his big blue eyes as if he could read her mind.

'I just feel so guilty, Edie. I should have realised there was something wrong with that Mark 4 cardkey when it started getting all hot. I should have thought that it could catch fire. Why did I put it next to my bed? And now James's notebook has been destroyed too.'

'It's not important, Alice. Anyway, the red one is safe at Charlie's house. Don't blame yourself.'

'Lori still blames me.'

'Just ignore her – she'll get over it. She seems pretty happy about the idea of you all going to stay at your grandparents' flat in Liverpool, since it means she can go on a massive shopping spree there and buy loads of new clothes.'

'That's another thing, Edie. I really don't want to go on this trip to Liverpool. I mean I want to see Granny and Gramps, but I'd rather they came here.'

'Well, there's no more room in our house.'

Alice's parents had decided they would take a holiday for the rest of August with her grandparents in Liverpool, while the work was done to rebuild their own house. The plan was to 'get everything back to normal', as Mrs Robertson put it, by the start of September, before the school term was due to start. Charlie's parents needed to go back to Hong Kong to visit his grandfather who was not well, so it had been decided that Charlie would also go with the Robertsons to Liverpool. The following morning, Alice's dad would be down at the jetty, overseeing the delivery of a whole load of building materials and replacements for their lost possessions that were due to arrive on the ferry.

Alice sighed. She suddenly felt utterly exhausted and realised that Edie was right – no one was hurt, and that was what really mattered. Plus, she still had the red notebook.

She crawled into her sleeping bag and was lulled to sleep by Kit's wordless baby talk. A little later, her dad stuck his head round the door to check on them.

'Everything OK, Edie?'

'Sort of.'

'She'll feel better in the morning when we get on that ferry. Thanks for being such a good friend to Alice. I'll be back to put Kit to bed in a sec.'

Alice woke early and slipped out of bed. She grabbed a piece of paper and a pencil and walked down to the gun emplacement wearing her wellies and Edie's old dressing gown. Alice leaned on the barrel of the gun to write, then when she was done she moved the gun through ninety degrees and disappeared underground, reappearing a few moments later holding a small package.

It was starting to rain. Alice walked briskly back up the street to Charlie's and knocked on his bedroom window. All she knew was that the package was addressed to her in James's handwriting and contained more than just a single sheet by way of a reply. Charlie pulled back his curtain and smiled. He was still in his pyjamas. She waved the package at him and let herself in by the back door. They sat on Charlie's bed and tore open the package.

The first part was a short note written in pencil on a scrap of paper.

Dear Alice

I am so sorry to hear about your fire. It must have been awful for you.

I think in the circumstances there are some things you ought to know, things that I have only just found out myself as a result of asking you to save my father's life.

During his recuperation in military hospital, they encouraged him to write down his life story as part of his rehabilitation. As soon as I learned that your rescue mission to 1944 had been a success, I went to visit him in Glasgow, and he entrusted his memoir to me, saying he didn't want anyone to read it, since he had written things down that he had told no one else. I enclose Dad's memoir for you to read – it's incomplete but it will help explain a few things to you, as it did for me too. It has certainly helped me progress my own work, and to this end I am sure you will be delighted with the item contained in the box I have also enclosed here. Be sure to read it all the way through before you open the box, Alice!

Yours truly,
James

The memoir was written in small, neat old-fashioned handwriting on seven or eight sheets of blue airmail paper, by someone with a lot of time on his hands. As soon as Alice spotted the words 'Karla' and 'traitor' on the first page, her heart jumped. She scanned the pages rapidly, and as she finished each one, she handed it to Charlie to read. After half an hour she came to the end, her mind spinning as she waited for Charlie to get through the last page.

'So that's why it disappeared! Can you believe it – Karla took our C-Bean remotely using her laptop, once she'd mended it!' Alice exclaimed.

'Yeah, what a crafty operator, nicking the spare parts she needed from the stores at the Wireless Station while the army thought she was a Prisoner of War employed to decode any German messages they picked up. How sneaky is that?'

'I know. Donald must have been so angry when he found out and then they didn't believe him. I did wonder if it was Karla interfering, actually, but I didn't know why,' Alice admitted. 'She must have been more desperate than we realised to get back to her own time. No wonder she tried to attack Donald and me with a knife! But I don't understand why she sent the C-Bean back to us like that. Maybe she *is* on the island somewhere.'

'Nah. He says she vanished on 21st July, which is a few days before Lady Grange found it again here, so I reckon she returned it the same way she stole it – remotely – but she must have had to make some dodgy adaptations to it. I'm sure that's why the Mark 4 cardkey caught fire.'

'I think you're right, Charlie. Remember when I left 1918 in the C-Bean and there was a recording of Karla trying to control it, and the C-Bean said something then like 'Activating Remote Override'. Do you think she summoned it back once she'd mended the laptop and then engineered the whole Mark 4 upgrade thing then?'

'Dunno. But it's all toast now.'

Alice looked downcast.

'There's one thing, Charlie – I feel really bad about not going back to see Donald like I promised before they evacuated the island in 1930. He sounds so disappointed in the memoir.'

'Yeah, but Alice, think about it – that part hasn't happened yet. It's still in your future. You can still go.'

'How, exactly? Even if we could get the C-Bean back, which we can't, we're leaving for Liverpool later today on the ferry and we won't be back till the start of September. They leave St Kilda for good at the end of August, remember?'

Neither of them spoke for a few minutes. Charlie started packing his things to take to Liverpool. Alice stared out of the window at the rain beating down. She pictured Donald all those years ago in 1930, waiting for her down by the jetty, trying to delay the moment when he boarded the ferry in case she turned up.

'Hey, you can open the gift James sent now!' Charlie reminded her. Alice sniffed and unwrapped the package. It was the dark blue medal box. Inside, rolled in a soft white cloth, was a flat object. She felt it through the cloth. It wasn't cross-shaped, and it was too big to be Donald's dog tag. Alice unrolled the cloth, and what fell out stunned them both – it was a cardkey to the C-Bean Mark 3.

'Wow. How on earth … Karla?'

'Who knows where that came from?'

'Anyhow, it's not much good to us now,' Alice said forlornly, fingering the hologram logo of the globe on the cardkey.

'Unless ... Look, Alice, look what's happening!' Charlie began.

She looked down and noticed that as she ran her fingers over the globe, it started spinning, and when she put the card down the spinning stopped a few seconds later. She traced the outline of the globe again, and this time a faint outline of the C-Bean began to appear in the room beside them.

'Do you think it will still work now it's a C-Bean Mark 4, Charlie?'

'Dunno. We could try.'

'Come on, let's go now,' Alice blurted. 'We haven't got much time!'

Alice ran to the schoolyard clutching the cardkey, with Charlie trailing after her with his mobile phone in his hand. There was a low mist hanging over the bay and it was raining hard. They were both still in their pyjamas, but it didn't seem to matter. She took shelter in the chapel porch, and started running her fingers over the hologram and singing the sea shanty softly under her breath. The outline of the C-Bean flickered into being, like a darker, thicker patch of mist in front of her, and then faded.

'I can't make it stay, Charlie!'

'Let me try.' He took the card from her, and she stepped out into the yard, moving nearer to the outline as it emerged. She touched the smooth sides, and the dark surface seemed to get firmer and steadier. She stretched her arms out wide, touching its suede-like surface, and pressed her cheek against the wall, as if she was holding it. Her warm breath was mingling with the mist, which was starting to envelop her, becoming a dense fog. It was so thick that Alice could hardly breathe. She had her eyes open but all she could see was whiteness. She could no longer feel the wall of the C-Bean and dropped to the ground with disappointment. It wasn't until that moment that she realised she was inside.

The walls gradually hardened over, and the mist cleared to reveal a recess in the wall that contained a pile of clothes. Alice picked them up and examined each item. They looked like something her grandmother might have worn as a child – a rough cotton blouse, a hand-knitted cardigan, thick socks, brown leather shoes and a pinafore dress made out of a beige tweedy fabric. Without thinking, she changed out of her pyjamas into the outfit, just as Charlie opened the door and stepped inside. The C-Bean seemed to register his presence too, because another set of clothes appeared in his size, also a little old-fashioned.

'You'll be pleased to know the cardkey's gone in OK,' he reported to her as Alice handed him the clothes.

'Erm … what are these?' he asked.

'Looks like the C-Bean has plans for us.'

There was a loud rap on the door. Alice looked at Charlie with a start. Charlie was pulling the shirt over his pyjama top when the door opened.

Lori stepped inside and stood with hands on hips, staring at their odd attire.

'What's going on with you two? Is this some kind of secret fancy dress club? Whatever you're up to, it's not what this classroom's supposed to be used for! Does Mum know you're in here?'

Alice and Charlie looked at each other.

'She'd better come with us,' Charlie mumbled.

Alice nodded and another set of clothes appeared in Lori's size. Charlie handed them to her. The door closed behind her.

'I'm not wearing these – you've got to be kidding. Look, this is ridiculous, what's going on?'

But Alice wasn't listening to her protests. Instead she just whispered a date and time that neither Charlie nor Lori could quite hear.

The C-Bean shuddered, rocked and then seemed to melt away. They found themselves standing on the foredeck of a ferry steaming into Village Bay. The ferry sounded its horn and within minutes the passengers around them were disembarking onto St Kilda's jetty. Alice followed along after them, and noticed a newspaper that had been left on one of the wooden benches. She picked it up and handed it to Lori, pointing to the date at the top of the page – 4th August 1930. Lori's eyes flashed with confusion and humiliation, but Alice could also sense her sister's excitement. She studied Lori for a moment. Maybe because her pinafore dress was a bit too short and showed her knobbly knees, she seemed much younger than sixteen,

Alice thought, more like a kid.

'Come on, you'll get used to it, Lori,' she laughed. 'Think of it as an unusual school trip. We're going to pay Old Jim's dad a visit. It'll be fun.'

Alice and Charlie strode off the boat onto the jetty with Lori lagging behind in a wake of questions.

'Do Mum and Dad know about this, Alice? I mean about going back in time? How many times have you done this? How did you even know about it?'

'Oh, we've only done it a few times,' Alice answered casually. 'I don't know why, but right from the start I seemed to be the one that just knew how the C-Bean worked, perhaps because I found it first.'

They headed up the village towards James's house. Alice knew which one it was straightaway because she could see the branches of the little elm tree swaying in the wind in the backyard. Lori was open-mouthed, taking everything in. The islanders were obviously preparing for their imminent evacuation – bundles of their belongings were being packed into trunks and wooden crates all the way up the village street. A couple of men were pushing handcarts down to the jetty to load some of them onto the day's ferry – in fact more things seemed to be leaving the island than arriving.

As the three children approached the Fergusons' house, they could see a man moving boxes through the doorway of the Post Office next door.

He turned to face them, and then straightened up, with a puzzled look on his face that said, 'Do I know you?' He was wearing a postman's hat and a badge that said 'D Ferguson, Postmaster, St Kilda'.

'Hello, Donald,' Alice spoke. 'It's me, Alice – remember?'

A smile spread across his face as he looked down at the clothes she was wearing.

'Dressed for the occasion, then? I can hardly recognise you without your flowery wellington boots, Alice!'

She laughed and they hugged each other. Donald was much taller than Alice, and he planted a kiss on the top of her head.

'Donald, this is my friend Charlie, and this is my sister Lori.'

Charlie shook hands shyly, and Lori sort of dipped in a silly little curtsy. Then Donald turned and grinned at Alice.

'By my recollection, Alice, you're a couple of weeks early. But as far as I'm concerned you arrived on the right day – just in time to meet our new addition, born yesterday! Come on inside.'

Elsa Gillies was clearing away dishes from the table when they stepped into the Fergusons' house. His wife looked quizzically at Donald when she saw the visitors, and dried her hands hastily on her apron. She was a small, neat person with rosy cheeks and dark brown hair. A child tugged at her skirt, and in the corner of the room Alice could see a newborn baby lying fast asleep in a basket. Standing beside the baby was the ornate candlestick that had belonged to Lady Grange, the candle's flame burning bright and steady. Alice stared at it for a moment. She was picturing it back in Lady Grange's cave.

'Congratulations, Elsa. I'm Alice. I knew your husband when he was a boy.' She then realised that must sound strange coming from an eleven-year-old child, so she changed the subject.

'What have you called the baby?'

'He hasn't got a name yet.'

Alice peeped into the basket and stroked the baby's cheek.

'Hello, James,' she said.

'Hmm, I like that, Alice,' murmured Donald. 'James … what do you think, Elsa?'

All at once Alice was aware that whatever she knew about Donald's future – the war, the plane crash, his rescue, James's life – could not be revealed to Donald. She felt certain it was one of the golden rules of being a time-traveller. Instead she should concentrate on what had already happened or was about to happen.

'So you're leaving at the end of this month, is that right?' she enquired. Elsa was making tea in the yellow teapot Alice recognised from James's house.

'Yes, we have arranged to go to Glasgow,' Donald explained. 'The Post Office have offered to relocate me. I'm to be postmaster of a branch on the outskirts of the city.'

'That'll be a massive change for you all, won't it? I've been to Glasgow once – it's a big place,' Alice ventured.

Charlie was playing with Donald's older son and Lori was helping Elsa make up a tray of teacups and a plate of oatcakes.

'You should take it easy,' Lori said to her. 'I can't believe you're up and about if the baby was only born yesterday.'

'I'm OK,' Elsa said, smiling and pouring the tea, but she looked tired.

They all fell silent, and there was just the sound of James's brother pushing a wooden truck along the floor.

'Well, drink up, Alice. There are a couple of things I want to show you while you're here. How long are you staying?'

Alice checked her watch. 'Only an hour or so, I'm afraid. We are leaving St Kilda this afternoon ...'

She didn't know how much Donald had told Elsa about where she came from, but what with the new baby, his wife seemed to have many more important things on her mind to care. So she added, 'Part of our house burned down in a fire and we have to go and stay with my father's parents in Liverpool while it all gets fixed.'

'I'm sorry to hear that. Did you lose many things?'

Alice shook her head, not wanting to reveal that this tiny baby's precious notebook was amongst the items that had been lost.

'So, what did you want to show us, Donald?' she asked.

'Our elm tree! It's quite big now – come and see,' he urged, leading them round to the back of the cottage. Alice ran her hands over its leaves, nodding her approval.

'I'm glad you like it, Alice. Let's call in next door now and say hello to Dora. She won't be the only one to be amazed to see you again. There's someone else you know living at her house these days,' Donald said with a mischievous chuckle.

'I can't imagine what you're talking about,' Alice said, already intrigued.

'Don't be long, Alice!' Lori called from the doorway. 'I'm staying here to help Elsa so she can have a rest.' Lori couldn't resist doing the big sister routine.

Dora looked a lot older and thinner but she still wore her hair in a bun. She stared in wonder at Alice and Charlie, rubbing her hands together and peering at the clothes they were wearing.

'I am sure I knitted that cardigan, Alice – where did you get it? Come over here, Charlie. I think I may have also knitted that wee jumper you're wearing.'

She touched the wool and laughed. Another cackle of laughter seemed to be coming from a cloth that was draped over a box in the corner of the room near where Donald was standing. He grinned and with a sudden flick of his wrist he pulled the cloth off the box like a magician.

'Ta-da!' he crooned.

'*Olá!*' croaked another little voice.

Alice stared in amazement at the bright blue parrot as he moved from side to side along the bar in his cage, looking embarrassed.

'Spix!' She was speechless for a moment.

'Parrots live a very long time. He must be getting on for 90, we think.'

'But how on earth …' Alice's question trailed off as she walked over to the cage to look more closely at the bird.

'I had to go to London on business once in the late 1920s, and while I was there I ran into a funny little man with white curly hair who told me he had a business importing exotic birds and animals. When I told him about a parrot I once knew that spoke in Portuguese, he demanded that I went with him to his shop and there was Spix. I used all the money I had just earned to buy him.'

Alice opened the cage and Spix flew out and perched on her shoulder, croaking '*Muito mau, perigroso!*' and bobbing his head with excitement.

'He's been a good friend to me, but he's yours, Alice,' Dora said firmly, smiling. 'I never thought I'd see you again! You don't look any older, mind.'

Alice stroked the bird's blue feathers. 'Well I'm only a couple of months older than when we first met, that's why.'

'I see. Well in that case I'm not sure whether I should give you the other thing back or not.' Dora opened the lid of a very familiar black sea chest behind her and started sifting through its contents, just as Alice had rummaged in it when she went to clear Jim's house out a week or so before.

'Ah. Here it is. I've forgotten what she called it. Odd-looking thing, like one of those typewriters people have nowadays.'

Dora handed Alice Karla's laptop. Its black casing was slightly warm to the touch.

'I'd forgotten you still had it, Mother,' remarked Donald. 'Karla was obsessed with getting that machine working again. No one believed me when I told them she was stealing things from the Wireless Station – she was after tiny bits of wire and metal – and she fiddled away at it for days. She told me she was making a "solar battery" for it, and then one day she just vanished. They all thought she must have been smuggled off the island one night by the German secret service when she was supposed to be decoding their messages for us.'

Charlie took the laptop from Alice, flipped it open and pressed the power button.

'It's dead, right?' asked Alice.

'Yep. We'd need to figure out how the thermopower battery

works if we want to get it going again.'

'It says something on the bottom, a date – look,' Dora said, showing them a small label stuck on the base of the machine.

Alice and Donald were both peering over Charlie's shoulder and said out loud in unison, 'Checked 1 April 2118'. Charlie chuckled.

'Well, someone got that wrong by a century!'

'Unless …' Alice was frowning – something didn't add up here.

'Unless what?' Donald asked her.

'What if Karla didn't arrive on the island from Germany in 2018? We already know she didn't actually work for the firm she said she did, and that Karla Ingermann isn't the name on her passport. What if she's from the future? I mean, from *our* future. Charlie, you said yourself you'd never seen a laptop as advanced as this before. What if she *is* a spy, working for a rival company to whoever made our C-Bean, and they sent her back from the future because they wanted her to work out how to make one just like it? What if that was why she took all those pictures? And what if that C-Bean Mark 4 upgrade we allowed it to perform happened because Karla was making changes to it from the future – I mean trying to sabotage it? Maybe she made its operating system go corrupt, and that's what made the cardkey catch fire!'

Alice's brain was on overload, wheeling through all the possibilities. Spix kept squawking *'Muito mau, muito mau!'*, as if he could read her mind.

'Slow down, Alice. So what you're saying is that Karla could have summoned the C-Bean back to 1918 remotely using this laptop, in order to get back to her own time?'

'Yes, that's exactly what I'm saying.'

'Well, it would explain the time she went missing in 1918 and also when the C-Bean went missing in 2018. But I still don't get why she would have returned it to us.'

'I've no idea either. But I bet when we get this thing going again there'll be stuff on it that might tell us why.'

They said goodbye and left Dora's house. Donald wanted to take Alice and Charlie on a tour to see the gun emplacement. They both pretended to be surprised when he whispered to them that there was a secret cave underneath.

'It made all the islanders feel a lot safer when that got installed in October 1918, I can tell you, after what happened in May. You never know, the cave might come in useful at some point in your future,' remarked Donald, giving Charlie a wink.

The three of them were sitting on a bench in the sunshine in front of the chapel while Spix flew around in front of them. Although the islanders were familiar with the exotic blue bird, Alice felt a little conspicuous sitting there with Karla's laptop, even though their clothes made them blend in, but people seemed too caught up with their preparations for departure to notice Donald's two companions.

'What will you do when you leave, Donald? I mean with the house.'

'Elsa and the women have talked about it. They plan to lay the table in each house with a freshly-laundered cloth, and leave a candle burning and a bible open at the book of Exodus. It'll be a sad day. People have survived on St Kilda for centuries. It doesn't seem right that we're the generation that's giving up, when our lives are probably much easier compared to those of any of our predecessors. But it's good to know that people come back and live here again eventually, Alice. Knowing that makes all the difference, even if I can't share it with anyone here.'

'What does Elsa know?'

'You don't remember her, do you?'

'No, should I?'

'Elsa was one of my classmates. She was eight when you came in 1918. So she knows where you're from. She was there – she came with us to see the Great Exhibition. Don't you remember that little girl who held your hand?'

'Yes, of course. Elsa.' Alice wasn't thinking about the little girl – instead she was wondering where Elsa had been in 1944, and why James hadn't mentioned her.

'Look, here comes your sister.'

Lori was half walking, half running down the street towards them.

'I really think we should go back now, Alice,' she puffed, a little out of breath.

'OK,' Alice said slowly, feeling in her pocket for the cardkey.

'Where did you leave your Time Machine this time, Alice?' Donald asked.

'It has developed a habit of becoming invisible, remember!' Alice stood up and smoothed her pinafore. 'But you get it back with this,' she said, showing him the cardkey.

They walked down to the schoolyard and Donald and Lori watched in amazement as the C-Bean just materialised in front of them. Donald ran his hands over its smooth walls. The door opened and Spix flew straight in, followed by the three children. Alice lingered in the doorway, not sure what to say.

'Well, goodbye, Donald. I'm glad our elm seed grew, and I can't tell you how happy I am to see Spix again! I haven't got anything to give you this time, sorry. But do me a favour – before you leave St Kilda on the 29th, will you leave me a letter in the secret cave for us?'

'Yes, I'll do that. Will we meet again, Alice?'

'I ... have a feeling we might. Look after James for me.'

Alice managed to suppress all the many things she had bottled up inside that could not be said.

It took a while before Alice noticed that the laptop she was clutching was getting hotter. It was only when Lori asked why it was so warm inside the C-Bean that Alice realised Karla's laptop was the cause. She put it down on the floor suddenly and examined her fingers – they were burning from holding it.

'Ice, I need ice,' she stammered and a bucket of cubes appeared in a recess.

'Lori, don't just stand there – can you pass it to me!'

In a state of shock at the C-Bean's powers, Lori finally responded and Alice plunged both hands into the ice.

'We need to get back quickly. This thing's overheating for some reason.'

They were all sweating. Lori took a cube of ice and rolled it over her forehead. Spix had spread out his wings and was lying awkwardly on the floor. Charlie took off his sweater, knelt down and gingerly opened the laptop using the sweater like an oven mitt.

'Look! It's started working again. Maybe it's overheating because it's trying to charge itself using C-Bean's thermopower!'

He nudged the laptop round with his elbow to face the two girls. The screen displayed a red dialogue box that blinked the question 'Allow remote override function?'

'No way! That proves we were right about one thing,' Alice said grimly.

'You really think Karla is trying to control it again now?' Charlie asked incredulously.

'Impossible to say for sure. We just have to try and beat her to it. St Kilda schoolyard, 4th August 2018, NOW!' barked Alice, her face sweaty and her eyes shining.

The C-Bean did not respond. The heat was getting unbearable. Then the same red dialogue box appeared on the wall beside them, and below it was another box into which someone with the username KROB2090 was typing. They watched as a sentence formed itself, the words blinding white against black:

> **'Product Recall by order of Hadron Services Ltd.**
> **C-Bean Mark 4 total system shutdown scheduled**
> **12.00 hours, 04/08/2018.'**

Alice looked at her watch. It was 11.45. She felt her stomach clench up.

'Charlie – the shutdown's happening in fifteen minutes!'

'What's going on, Alice? What are you talking about?' Lori wailed.

'*Perigroso!*' squawked Spix in a high-pitched voice.

'*Hadron.* I know that name from somewhere,' Alice wondered out loud, ignoring her sister. She screwed up her eyes. She pictured the name written in a crazy scrawl of fiery reds and yellows. Then she remembered it was in New York when they came back to Central Park and found the C-Bean with graffiti all over it. 'Hadron burn in hell!', someone had written.

'Alice, you need to do something to stop the shutdown from happening! Whoever KROB2090 is, they're trying to ground us for some reason,' Charlie urged in a panicky voice.

'Yes, but why?'

'I don't know. But I don't want to be stuck in here for the rest of my life! Think!'

'Alice, this is all your fault,' Lori blurted tearfully. 'I can't believe this is happening!'

'Get a grip, Lori! I'll figure it out if you can both just be quiet.'

They all fell silent. Alice sat down cross-legged on the floor, and Spix settled next to her. She stroked his feathers and closed her eyes. Flowing through her mind were images of the time she was diverted away from the War Office men in 1957, when the C-Bean took her back to Lady Grange's time. But they were somehow mixed up with James's prototype C-Bean, which they'd found in the secret chamber. It was as if she had no control over her own memories, as if the C-Bean was sifting through its own database using her brain. She forced her mind back to the first time she was stuck inside it with Karla when they ended up in 1918 by accident.

'I've got it!'

She opened her eyes. Playing over all the walls like a silent movie were all the events she'd just been recalling, like a visual log of her activities over the last few months, including the day Alice and Karla were arrested in 1918, and the terrible night she rescued Donald in 1944. Lori was watching with a look of awe and horror on her face.

'Alice, what have you been through?'

'Charlie, remember how we did a factory reset back in May?'

'Yeah, but you ended up a hundred years ago, remember. I want to land in the present, thank you.'

'What if this time we reset it to a date that's ever so slightly into the future?'

'Can you even do that?'

'We've got to be back in time to catch the ferry, remember! To our *real life*,' Lori pointed out impatiently.

'OK – I don't know if it will work, but here's the plan. We reset the C-Bean to 11.50 tomorrow, which is about the time we were due to get there anyway if we'd gone by ferry and train. We'll text Mum and

Dad to say we'll meet them there.'

'They'll never believe that story,' Lori argued.

'But will it actually stop the shutdown?'

'I don't know, Charlie, but it will buy us a bit more time while KROB2090 figures out some other way of recalling the C-Bean.'

'You can't do this, Alice!' Lori was dripping with sweat.

'Lori, we've got no choice. It's our only option. Unless you want to be stranded in 1930 for ever! I promise when we get to Liverpool we'll tell Mum and Dad everything. Deal?'

Lori sighed and nodded meekly.

'Ready, Charlie? Let's give it a try. Charlie – before we do this, can you use your mobile and send a quick text to my parents, and one to yours too. Then switch it off.'

'Right, I'm on it.'

Alice cleared her throat.

'Pen!' she commanded, wanting to issue the command accurately.

Consulting her watch, she picked up the pen and wrote slowly and deliberately on the wall, 'Liverpool, England, 05/08/2018, 11.55.'

'Wait up! I'm not arriving in Liverpool wearing this ridiculous outfit. You've got to tell this thing to get me something different to wear.'

Alice rolled her eyes and stopped writing.

'We haven't exactly got much time left Lori, but OK, new clothes all round!'

A recess opened up in the wall behind Charlie like a mini wardrobe containing three new outfits on hangers. Alice smirked.

'I think the fluorescent one's yours, Lori,' she said as she checked her watch again and updated the time code to 11.58 and added the final full stop to her command line.

Lori was just about to change when the C-Bean seemed to jerk violently, there were some weird flashes, and the interior was then plunged into darkness. There was a strange booming sound coming from outside the C-Bean.

Charlie cleared his throat.

'Do you think it worked?'

'I sincerely hope so. Did the texts send?' Alice asked anxiously. Charlie turned his phone back on to check.

'Apparently, yes.'

'Well, let's get changed and try to get out of here.'

They all fumbled around in the dark trying to work out which outfit was which, discarding their 1930s clothes on the floor.

'Hey Alice, look!' Charlie whispered, doing his belt up.

'What is it?' Lori asked.

To Alice's utter amazement and relief, a new dialogue box had appeared on the wall, and across it flowed the words:

> '... Reset complete. Remote override function cancelled. Timeline temporarily revised by system administrator. Timeline reverting in 3 minutes ...'

'I don't know exactly what that means, but I think we should get out of here before it reverts back to being yesterday,' Alice said, opening the door to a blast of summer heat coming off the concrete in front of her. Spix burst out, his blue feathers merging with the clear blue sky overhead.

For some reason, the C-Bean had decided to arrive with its cargo of children at the new Liverpool Passenger Terminal, just as a vast white cruise ship moved out into the Mersey. The booming sound was the cruise ship's foghorn announcing its departure for the Caribbean. Hundreds of passengers stood on deck waving goodbye to their families and friends who lined the dockside. No one seemed to pay any attention to the C-Bean – perhaps they thought this black cube was nothing more than a buoy that had come loose from its moorings, floated across the sea and been randomly washed up here, like an enormous seabean.

No one, that is, except a man with curly white hair who stood out from the crowd because he reminded Alice of her old teacher Dr Foster. As Alice stepped out of the C-Bean and removed the cardkey from its slot, she noticed the man turn to look at her and begin to edge away from the crowd of people. He was carrying a battered leather suitcase and walking purposefully towards them.

'Come on Alice, we've got to go,' Lori said, pulling her sister in the opposite direction. 'Mum and Dad and Kit will be arriving at the train station in about twenty minutes. Let's be there to meet them.'

But Alice hung back as the man approached. She noticed he was waving to get their attention.

'Charlie, look – isn't that Dr Foster?'

The man had broken into a trot in an effort to catch up with them. Alice could hear his knee clicking as he got closer.

'Alice, wait, I need to talk to you!' he panted. 'There's something wrong with the C-Bean! Come, let me tell you about Plan B before it's too late.'

Alice stiffened. It really was their teacher, Dr Foster, but there was something odd about the way he spoke – for some reason his voice sounded as if it was computer-generated. Wondering how to respond, she glanced at her watch and stuffed the cardkey nervously in her pocket, when Spix suddenly let out a loud cry and started to chase Dr Foster, who was now running along the dockside towards the C-Bean. Alice noticed that the black cube was starting to wobble and flicker. She watched in astonishment as it slowly changed into a shimmering golden object in the heat. Since everything seemed to be happening in slow motion, it occurred to her that perhaps the dazzling gold C-Bean was only a mirage created by the heat. But before Alice even had a chance to say anything to the others, Dr Foster, the parrot and the C-Bean merged into one luminous thing and then slowly vanished.

Alice shook her head and blinked, her eyes fixed on the spot they had just vacated, as if willing them back into existence, but it was now nothing more than a bright afterimage that remained even when she closed her eyes. She was aware that Charlie and Lori were both calling her to come, but she was somehow unable to move. She could feel the warm sun on her eyelids and a strange dizziness came over her. Surging out of the centre of the glowing afterimage in quick succession was a steady flow of familiar faces from her immediate past: Karla Ingermann, Donald, James and Dora Ferguson, Lady Grange in her long blue dress, and lastly, rushing towards her and barking like mad, Spex. The barking didn't stop until Alice opened her eyes and saw the little brown dog was running in circles around her feet, his tail wagging, and a brand new collar and lead around his neck. Alice felt the dizziness pass and crouched down to stroke him. She noticed that his fur was going grey around his muzzle and he was limping slightly.

'Spex, where on earth did you come from? Is it really you? Come here little fellow,' Alice ruffled the wiry fur on his back.

'You poor thing. You look so old!'

There was some kind of tag attached to Spex's collar. Alice held it up in the sunlight, expecting it to be Donald's Second World War dog-tag. But it wasn't. It was a heavy gold disc the size of a two pound coin, which was coated black on one side. Engraved on the black side it said *Øbsidon 0902*, and on the reverse was the word 'Børk'.

'Bork... Hmmm, did they give you a new name eh?' Alice asked, taking hold of the lead. 'Never mind, you're still our old Spex, come on, let's go and meet Granny and Gramps and the rest of the Robertsons.'

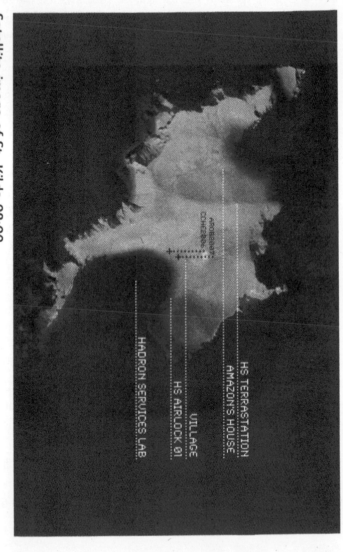

Satellite image of St. Kilda 08:00
10.09.2118

HS TERRASTATION
AMAZON'S HOUSE

VILLAGE
HS AIRLOCK 01

HADRON SERVICES LAB.

AROBERDA
COHEERDA

SeaRISE

Book III

Contents

A solar storm has been raging for months. There is hardly any difference between night and day – the sky is constantly alive with a shimmering brightness, cycling rapidly through a vivid array of colours in the Earth's outer atmosphere. No one calls it the Northern Lights any longer, since the phenomenon can be seen just as clearly at the Equator.

All that can be seen of the small forest in Village Bay on the island of St Kilda, planted by the inhabitants of the 21st century over an 80-year period, are a few scorched and torn upper branches reaching upwards out of the sea like pitiful drowning limbs. The vertical tide marker the islanders installed alongside the jetty 50 years ago when the sea level started to rise rapidly is now completely underwater. At high tide, waves lap the front doorsteps of the arc of cottages long since abandoned, and at low tide their broken windows look out over a salty bog – ideal for wading seabirds, if only they were still around. But their colonies are greatly reduced in size, the birds either dead or departed owing to the ravages of this infernal weather.

There is apparently just one human inhabitant left on this lonely island – a solitary figure with rusty hair wearing breathing apparatus and a long silver coat to protect him from the solar radiation. He emerges like an amphibian from under the sea each day via a hatch beneath the old gun emplacement. Maybe he comes up for air or because, despite the risks, he needs to take readings: air quality, temperature, radiation levels, sea level.

Today, he struggles for longer than usual with the hatch, which is slowly rusting over. He hesitates, perhaps concerned that he might not be able to access his subterranean chamber this time if he closes it behind him. Leaving the hatch open, he adjusts his oxygen supply and then begins his slow trudge up to the terra-station on the mountain ridge where his monitoring equipment is stored. Battling against the fierce, hot wind, he puts up the hood of his silver coat and proceeds uphill.

Alice's Blog

Monday 27 August 2018, Liverpool

It's so frustrating! If only we could crack the password on Karla Ingermann's laptop and get into its hard drive, then maybe we'd be able to figure out why the C-Bean disappeared like it did three weeks ago when Charlie, Lori and I arrived in Liverpool. We've been trying ever since we got here. Maybe we can't get it to work because it overheated when we were in the C-Bean.

Since we reset the C-Bean one day into the future to avoid being stuck in 1930 forever, Charlie's been convinced Karla was trying to summon the C-Bean remotely. He thinks she's the reason it disappeared right after we arrived, taking Dr Foster and Spix with it. He could be right because I'm sure that's how she escaped from 1918 back to her own time - I mean, by controlling the C-Bean remotely - no one else knows as much as she does about its computer code!

I still have absolutely no idea why Karla would want to capture our old teacher - or our parrot - but it's made me wonder if there is some kind of connection between Karla and Dr Foster that we don't know about. It was when he said 'I want to tell you about Plan B' on the dockside in Liverpool that I got suspicious, because Karla also talked about Plan B in her sleep when we were imprisoned in Lady Grange's cleit in 1918, and next morning when I asked her what Plan B meant, she got really nasty. So I have a funny feeling there could be something on her hard drive that will explain the link between the two of them, and maybe even tell us what Dr Foster tried to warn me about Plan B and why he thought there was something wrong with the C-Bean.

Anyway, the laptop's our only hope now. Mum took the Mark 3 cardkey away from us the minute she found out that we'd used the C-Bean to get to Liverpool. So now we can't even try to summon it back and see if it's still working.

Wednesday 29th August 2018, Liverpool

Today it's 88 years exactly since my island St Kilda was evacuated in 1930. I'm trying to imagine what it must have felt like to have to leave your home and go and live somewhere on the mainland forever. It's a bit like what's going to happen to me next year when I leave St Kilda to go to my sister Lori's boarding school in Glasgow. Only I'll get to come back home in the holidays. There are only a few days of the summer holidays left and, to be honest, I'd quite like to be back on St Kilda right now – Granny and Gramps' flat is a bit crowded, what with seven Robertsons and Charlie all staying here.

It felt strange getting a postcard from St Kilda this morning. Edie sent it. She wrote on it that she's really looking forward to visiting our new school in Glasgow in October. Mum calls it our 'Induction Programme'. We will be staying in Glasgow in a dormitory for three nights and in the daytime we'll be doing things like experiments in a chemistry lab and acting out a play and stuff. I can't wait to go because they have loads of really cool things we don't have, like a theatre, a library, a swimming pool and a tuck shop.

Friday 31st August 2018, Oban

Last night I had this weird dream that Village Bay was flooded and my baby brother was floating away in his Moses basket and I had to swim and rescue him. Maybe it's because we're getting the ferry back to St Kilda today, or it could be because

Charlie and I watched a film called *Noah* yesterday. Except there weren't animals being rescued in my dream. In fact there weren't any animals at all. Or any birds. Just too much water. All I can remember is that I was worrying about rescuing the C-Bean but I knew I had to save Kit first. Because weirdly, even though I know for a fact it floats, the C-Bean was sinking.

I don't know why I told you that. I might not even upload this. I think the dream was just a sign that things feel a bit 'out of sorts', as my Mum puts it. Like when I tried to log back into my blog about St Kilda on Gramp's computer yesterday, the settings had been changed and I couldn't get into it. I've emailed the website administrator but they hadn't replied by the time we left Liverpool. So for now I'm writing my blog in a notebook and I'll type it and try again to upload it when I get back.

We're catching the new super-stormproof ferry from Oban to St Kilda today - it's going to be running every three days from now on all through winter, even when the waves are atrocious. Dad says he's started noticing funny things with the waves out beyond Village Bay where the Evaw wave energy machines are. He says some days there are strange whirlpools in the water instead of long rolling waves and they're getting these weird readings from the monitoring equipment. Plus he's noticed loads of dead sea creatures floating on the surface. Some marine biology experts are coming over from Portugal in a couple of weeks to look into it.

And lastly, I have one other thing to report - Lady Grange is completely well now and she's decided to stay on St Kilda. Mum told me yesterday Lady Grange is going to be her new teaching assistant at school. Apparently, she's going to be teaching us history and handwriting, which makes sense for someone who's from the 18th century and likes writing long letters.

The light inside Alice's globe beside her bed grew brighter and brighter until she half opened her eyes. It was much better than an alarm clock as a way of waking up and, besides, it was her secret reminder of all the places she'd been around the world. Alice scrunched up her pillow and half sat up in bed. She could hear her parents moving around in the kitchen, the clatter of things being put out for Saturday morning breakfast, the odd gurgle from her baby brother Kit, Spex pushing his dog bowl around the flagged floor as he licked it clean.

Alice wriggled in the warmth under her duvet and stared up at the glow-in-the-dark stars on her ceiling. It felt good to have her old bedroom back exactly how it used to be before the fire. And it was good to be back on St Kilda, even if it was the end of the summer holidays. School was starting again on Monday – her last year at their tiny island primary school of six children before she could join her sister Lori at high school on the mainland. Alice was even glad to have her mother back as their teacher again. 2018 had felt very disjointed so far, what with the arrival of baby Kit, and the arrival and departure of Dr Foster, their replacement teacher, followed by the appearance and suspicious disappearance of the C-Bean's designer, Karla Ingermann, quite apart from all the crazy comings and goings they'd had in the C-Bean itself. And now, with Spix gone – apart from their dog Spex – the only character still left on St Kilda from all their time travel adventures was Lady Grange.

It made Alice feel dizzy just thinking about everything that had happened in the last eight months, and she had already decided that, this school year, the past would remain in the past, while Alice herself would remain in the present and wait impatiently for her future to begin, just like any normal 11-year-old kid. Anyway, now that the adults knew about the C-Bean's time-travel function, it was useless thinking they would have any further adventures in their 'rather too mobile classroom', as her dad put it. Her mum – that is to say Mrs Robertson – had been required to write a full report for the Hebridean School Board about what had taken place when Alice, Charlie and Lori vanished the morning they were supposed to leave by ferry for Oban, and then just turned up in Liverpool the next day, apparently in the C-Bean. Alice could scarcely imagine how her mother had managed to explain this particular event, and was grateful for her mum's sake that not everything had come to light – as Alice saw it, apart from James and Donald Ferguson, it was beyond any adult's imagination to grasp the full extent of their time travels.

'Alice, are you getting up now? Breakfast is ready,' her mother called.

'In a minute!' Alice slid sideways out of bed, feeling the strands of her orange shaggy rug tickle between her toes. She stood up, pulled on her dressing gown and shuddered just like Spex when he was shaking off water. Then she took a deep breath, opened the drawer of her bedside cabinet and took out the Mark 3 cardkey that her mum had given back to her, James Ferguson's red notebook and the photo of his christening, together with his letters and Donald's sheaf of wartime memoirs. Alice knew these things all meant a lot to her, but she also realised they were a strange burden she'd been carrying. Even the things that no longer existed still weighed heavily – the other, older, brown notebook that had belonged to James and the Mark 4 cardkey, both destroyed when their house caught fire. This was all that was left.

'Time to move on,' she murmured to herself, pulling an old shoebox from under her bed. She emptied out the random assortment of toys, birthday cards and dead batteries, and placed her historical items inside in a neat pile. She put the lid back on and then, using a black felt-tip pen, wrote in capitals on the lid of the box:

1ST SEPTEMBER 2018
TIME CAPSULE OF ALICE ROBERTSON

It would need a better box, she decided, slipping the pen into her dressing-gown pocket. But she already knew where it should be left – in the secret chamber under the gun emplacement. She slid the box back under the bed, and decided she would perform the ceremony with her schoolmates Edie and Charlie after their first day back at school on Monday.

Early on Monday morning, Alice pushed Kit's buggy slowly along the main street of the Village down to the Burneys' house with Spex running on ahead, thinking he was being taken for a walk. Edie Burney's mother was going to take care of him and Kit during the day from now on, so that Alice's mother could teach the children again.

Alice had an odd feeling, as if she was in several places at once. Except, she realised as they reached the Burneys' front door, they were all the same place – her own village street – but since she'd now walked down it in no fewer than five other periods in time as well as her own – 1851, 1918, 1930, 1944 and 1957 – it had a very peculiar effect on her.

'Spex, sit. Good boy.' She patted his head, but he looked bitterly disappointed that his walk had already come to an abrupt end. Alice knocked on the door, just like she had in the 20th century when it had been Dora's house. Her dad once told her this feeling when you think you've done something or been somewhere before was called 'déjà vu' – he reckoned that although it feels as if something's already happened, it's just your brain playing tricks on you. Except that, for Alice, this was real déjà vu – she had walked through this very same door in 1930, the day they got Spix back. As the door opened, Alice had her eyes half closed and was picturing her bright blue parrot in its cage in Dora's living room. Spex slunk inside the house, tail between his legs. Edie's mum smiled and lifted Kit out of the buggy.

'Come here, my little lamb! Alice, run along now, you'll be late. You look like you're not quite awake yet, sweetheart: did you eat enough breakfast?' Mrs Burney asked.

'I'm fine, thanks. I was just remembering something,' Alice said, turning to leave, one half of her still in 1930.

The class was sitting in silence when she arrived and there was a tense mood hanging over everyone. Alice slid into her seat and darted a quick look at Charlie. He raised his eyebrows in a mock question and nodded towards their teacher, who was engrossed in reading a letter. It had evidently just arrived, since Mr Butterfield was hovering at her elbow as if expecting Mrs Robertson to write an instant reply for him to deliver by return. Alice peered at the papers on her mother's desk, and spied an envelope with the logo of a spinning globe on it. It was from the C-Bean manufacturer and Alice knew immediately it could mean only one thing – Karla.

Mrs Robertson cleared her throat and looked up to address the class. Six pairs of eyes were trained on her face.

'OK, kids, this is how it is. Sorry to be the bearer of bad news, especially on our first day back. Our C-Bean has, as you know, caused some concern among the authorities, and it seems that this has escalated to a very high level now, with the Ministry of Defence getting involved for some reason. The German company that manufactures these education pods have written to say they need to recall the C-Bean for a complete refit, but I've also received another, more serious, letter from the Ministry of Defence, who are sending a Scottish officer over to the island next week, apparently in order to impound the C-Bean and carry out a full enquiry. They say 'suspicious circumstances' have been brought to their attention, and they want 'our complete cooperation'.

Her mother looked up at the row of disappointed faces. The two Sams were simmering with fury and confusion. They kept looking out of the window at their beloved black cube standing innocently in the schoolyard, and then back at each other. In the end, they could not contain themselves.

'But they can't take it away – it's ours!' Sam F blurted out.

'Yes, that's not fair, Mrs Robertson. It was a present!' chimed Sam J.

'I know, I know, but I don't think they will let us keep it, boys, I'm sorry. Not now. Not after what's happened.'

Alice felt sure that the suspicious circumstances they'd mentioned had nothing to do with the excursion to Liverpool and probably had more to do with Karla disappearing and not being who she said she was, and who knows what else. It seemed to Alice that it would be better if the Scottish officer took the C-Bean away than if it was returned to Karla's company. That is, if it even belonged to them.

Edie put up her hand.

'Can we still have lessons in the C-Bean until it's taken away, Mrs Robertson?'

'I'm not sure. It doesn't say anywhere in the letter that we shouldn't use it in the meantime ...' Mrs Robertson's voice trailed off with uncertainty. Charlie had the look of someone with a light bulb switching on above his head.

'Well, if it's going to be taken away from us, we should at least have a final goodbye celebration – how about we have a sleepover in it, like they do at the Science Museum in London sometimes, you know, with our sleeping bags?' he suggested casually, except that Alice could hear the sense of urgency in his voice – she'd heard it before.

Mrs Robertson glanced up at Mr Butterfield, then at Lady Grange who was sharpening pencils beside her, and shrugged her shoulders.

'Great idea – why not, Charlie? You can all do that on Friday evening, if you like. Now let's get on with some work, shall we?'

Mr Butterfield tugged one end of his moustache for a moment, and then said 'Right, that's sorted then. I'll be off, Jen – got to do my "mailboat" duties.'

'Mailboat,' Alice murmured, picturing all those messages people used to send in the olden days from St Kilda in strange little home-made packages, all sealed up to float across the sea like messages in a bottle, hoping for food, medicine or salvation. She thought about how she'd sent her own messages back and forth in time to James using the 'instant mailboat' drawer on his prototype C-Bean. If only she could send some kind of mailboat now, to appeal for the C-Bean's salvation or, at the very least, to stop it from being taken away.

Alice's Blog

Monday 3rd September 2018

I can't believe they're taking away our C-Bean. It's the worst news ever.

After school today we all went back to Charlie's house to talk about it and try to think of a way to stop them, but no one came up with anything. We ended up just arguing about my Time Capsule idea. Charlie and Sam F both wanted to put a load of other stuff in it, so people in the future would know something about our life in 2018, like that we eat etc. Edie thought it was stupid and said the food would go off, but Charlie insisted it was worth it. So we raided his mum's kitchen cupboards and decided to put a jar of Scottish honey, a packet of rice, some teabags and a tin of baked beans in the capsule. Hannah wants to put in some drawings she's done of all the lovely nature on St Kilda, you know, birds and flowers and mountains and stuff. I can't decide what I want to put inside. Sam F and Sam J want people in the future to know what technology looked like in 2018 so Sam F put in his walkie-talkie set and Sam J added his wind-up torch. Edie said she wasn't going to put anything in because it was a silly idea, so to annoy her Charlie added a pair of pink plastic chopsticks he'd been given and said 'If you think that's silly Edie, it's so they can eat the rice'.

Edie started to sulk then so Charlie went to ask his dad for a better time capsule box. He came back with this sturdy metal container with a complicated catch that the army left behind in one of the old huts they've just demolished. It has a label on one side that says 'War Office Property'. When I saw that,

I realised James used a box just like it to make the instant mailboat drawer on his prototype C-Bean.

Charlie's dad came to see what we wanted the box for. We asked him how long a time capsule should be left until it gets opened, and he reckoned a hundred years is about the right amount of time. He told us that when he was a little boy growing up in Hong Kong they'd found a box like ours in his neighbourhood when they were digging the foundations for a new skyscraper. The box had been buried in 1880 and had some very interesting Victorian items in it that are now in the Hong Kong Museum.

Just before we closed up our time capsule for the last time, I told the others to wait. I suddenly knew what I wanted to put inside it: my hamburger seabean from the nature table at school. That'll be something very interesting for someone to find a hundred years from now and put in a museum, especially if as Dad says the ocean currents have all changed by then and seabeans aren't getting washed up here any more. Maybe there won't even be seabeans in a hundred years' time if we carry on cutting down the rainforest – the trees they grow on won't even exist, so people in the future won't have ever seen one.

Both the Sams said it would be epic if we threw our time capsule off the top of the cliffs, but nobody else agreed. We had another long argument and in the end Edie and Hannah agreed with Charlie and me that we should leave it in the underground chamber under the gun emplacement. So we hid it under a pile of stones in one corner of the chamber. Charlie thinks that one day in the future an archaeologist will find it.

After tea on Friday evening the children returned to the schoolyard in their dressing gowns and pyjamas. Lady Grange was on hand to supervise laying out their beds for the night inside the C-Bean.

'This is too much! Why did you bring so many of your belongings, children?' she fretted, as they piled into the C-Bean with their pillows, sleeping bags, snacks, books, pens, teddies and electronic gadgets (including Karla's laptop, because Charlie thought that bringing it inside the C-Bean might allow them to get around the password issue somehow). The last to enter the pod was their class pet, Spex, who already had his beady eye on the bag of food.

'Looks like you've brought enough midnight snacks to sink a battleship,' Mrs Robertson remarked when she arrived, having put Alice's brother Kit to bed.

'But not enough to sink a C-Bean,' Charlie joked back.

'So listen up, kids. Seriously, there's to be no funny business tonight, do you understand? No getting the C-Bean to take you to any foreign places and especially no getting it to move you forwards – or backwards, for that matter – in time. We don't want a repeat of The Liverpool Incident, do we, Alice?' Mrs Robertson looked pointedly at her daughter.

'Mum, it's just a sleepover, OK? We won't do anything. Promise!' Alice protested.

'Right, I'll leave you to it, then. Don't eat too many sweets or you'll never get to sleep. I'm putting Charlie in charge of lights out, as he's the oldest,' Jen Robertson said.

'Well, technically that's Alice's job, Mrs Robertson. The C-Bean doesn't usually obey my commands.'

'OK, Alice. No later than ten o'clock, then.'

Alice looked at her watch and nodded. It was almost nine o'clock.

'But we've got to have our midnight feast at midnight, Mrs R!'

'That's why it's called a midnight feast!' the two Sams implored.

Their teacher raised her eyebrows for a moment, then laughed and shook her head.

'OK, I'm off. Lady Grange will tuck you in.'

Lady Grange bid them all goodnight by muttering a little blessing, starting with the eldest.

'Hannah, are you feeling unwell? You are very quiet,' she observed when she came to the youngest.

'She's fine, aren't you Hannah?' Edie nudged her sister, who was drawing something on her iPad.

Finally Hannah spoke: 'Lady Grange, what do we do if we need to go to the toilet in the night?'

'The school is not locked, my dear, and I will leave a candle burning, so you can go inside to visit the – what is it you call it – the "loo"? Goodnight, dear children.' Lady Grange smiled and blew them all kisses, then stepped out of the C-Bean and gently closed the door behind her.

There was a bit of an argument about who was going to sleep next to whom, but when the C-Bean started to make the floor go all springy and fluffy no one seemed to mind anymore where they slept. They bounced around for a bit, with Spex barking in excitement, until Sam J spilled his drink and Sam F complained he'd got crumbs in his sleeping bag, and then things settled down.

'Erm … so, guys, what now?' Charlie asked in an exploratory tone.

'What do you mean, "what now", Charlie? We're just going to sleep, right? No funny business, remember?' Edie said testily.

'OK, whatever,' Charlie said, rolling his eyes.

'What about some stories?' Sam J asked.

'Good idea,' replied Alice, and thought for a second.

'Well, since we can't go on any actual adventures this evening, how about we listen to *The Time Machine* by H. G. Wells?' she suggested, remembering that Donald Ferguson had told her it was his favourite book.

'OK, that sounds cool,' replied Sam J, zipping up his sleeping bag and settling back into his pillow. The C-Bean's walls dimmed to a cosy glow and a voice began:

> The Time Traveller (for so it will be convenient to speak of him) was expounding a recondite matter to us. His grey eyes shone and twinkled, and his usually pale face was flushed and animated. The fire burned brightly, and the soft radiance of the incandescent lights in the lilies of silver caught the bubbles that flashed and passed in our glasses…

The C-Bean's walls were flickering to suggest the flames from the fire, and images of what Alice supposed were the 'lilies of silver' waved in the firelight. The storyteller's voice sounded exactly like Donald's and Alice found herself counting how many children there were in the C-Bean just to check if he was among them. But there were still just six of them. She pictured the Time Traveller in ragged black clothes, like Old Jim. The voice continued, but after a short while Alice realised she was struggling to give it her full attention, because half of her was drowning in a flood of vivid memories brought on by being back inside the C-Bean.

> You must follow me carefully. I shall have to controvert one or two ideas that are almost universally accepted. The geometry, for instance, they taught you at school is founded on a misconception.'
>
> 'Isn't that rather a large thing to expect us to begin upon?' said Filby, an argumentative person with red hair.

Sam F butted in, and the C-Bean immediately paused its narrative. 'This sounds really boring, Alice. Do we have to listen? Can't we play a game instead?'

Given his red hair, Alice was vaguely imagining a grown-up version of Kit playing the part of Filby and questioning how time travel worked. She began asking herself whether some of the things she'd been taught were also untrue.

'You don't have to listen if you don't want to, Sam,' she said dreamily, stroking Spex's head. 'Go on ...' she urged the C-Bean.

'... Nor, having only length, breadth, and thickness, can a cube have a real existence.'

'There I object,' said Filby. 'Of course a solid body may exist. All real things –'

'So most people think. But wait a moment. Can an instantaneous cube exist?'

'Don't follow you,' said Filby.

'Can a cube that does not last for any time at all, have a real existence?'

'Is this a story about our C-Bean, Alice?' Hannah asked.

'Sort of ...' Alice was already half asleep, and couldn't tell or care anymore if she was hearing the story or making it up. Did their cube really exist? When she made it vanish, did the C-Bean no longer exist in space and time? And, if that was so, would there be anything 'left' for the Ministry of Defence to take away?

The Time Traveller continued.

Time is only a kind of Space. Here is a popular scientific diagram, a weather record. This line I trace with my finger shows the movement of the barometer. Yesterday it was so high, yesterday night it fell, then this morning it rose again, and so gently upward to here. Surely the mercury did not trace this line...

In her mind's eye, Alice was picturing an old man poring over weather records, his wrinkled fingers following a line of liquid mercury that trickled across diagrams and rows of figures. It reminded her of the rivulets of mercury they'd seen in the muddy tyre tracks at the gold mine in Brazil and the contents of the mercury cylinder they'd brought back from Hong Kong. The last thing Alice heard before sleep took over was:

The Time Traveller smiled round at us. Then, still smiling faintly, and with his hands deep in his trousers pockets, he walked slowly out of the room, and we heard his slippers shuffling down the long passage to his laboratory...

Alice was woken by Hannah shaking her shoulder.

'Alice, I need to go to the toilet, but I can't get out – the C-Bean's door won't open. Can you make it open for me?'

The interior of the C-Bean was in darkness, full of the sounds of sleeping children and the occasional whimper from the dog. Alice focused her eyes on the luminous hands on her watch – 00.03. So much for their midnight feast!

'OK, just a minute,' Alice whispered, easing herself out of her sleeping bag, trying not to disturb Edie lying next to her. She crept around the edge of the C-Bean to the side where the door was, and breathed the command 'Open'.

Nothing happened. She tried using the 'goodbye' command instead, issuing it a little louder. They both waited, listening. There were clanking sounds outside. It sounded like Mr McLintock was in the schoolyard for some reason, reeling in the thick tow chain on the back of his pick-up truck.

Something clanged against the roof of the C-Bean, and there it was again, the tow chain noise. This time it was unmistakably the sound of winching, a chain being pulled up one link at a time, clink-

clink-clink. The C-Bean shifted and swayed slightly, and there was a sudden airborne sensation, like it was being lifted up. It occurred to Alice with a sudden kick of horror in the pit of her stomach that the Ministry of Defence people had already come to take the C-Bean away without realising there were children inside. The others were all waking now, brought round by the lurching motion.

'Is there an earthquake?' Sam F asked drowsily.

'Charlie, Edie, wake up,' Alice hissed, 'something weird is happening.' She felt Hannah's hand creep into hers and grip tight.

The C-Bean, like the children, seemed to rouse itself and slowly come to its senses – the floor hardened over, and the walls grew brighter. And brighter, and brighter.

'That's actually hurting my eyes now,' said Charlie, shielding his face with his hands.

'It's not my eyes – it's my ears that are hurting!' Alice replied, grimacing with pain.

'Me too,' said Edie, her face wracked with worry.

The others just stared blearily, only half awake.

'What's that whooshing noise?' Sam J asked. 'It sounds like a fireman's hose.'

'Sounds like our camping kettle when it's just about to boil,' mumbled Sam F.

Right on cue, the kettle sound became an excruciating whistle that made all the children clap their hands instantly to their ears. Spex started to howl in pain. The whistle turned into a long penetrating wail that gradually petered out into a pathetic whine.

'Who's outside making that noise?' Sam F moaned.

'It's not outside, Sam. The C-Bean's making that noise,' Alice murmured.

'Like it's crying,' whispered Hannah.

They all fell silent, squinting at each other, blank and motionless.

Through the glare, Alice noticed out of the corner of her eye a dark line appearing low down around the perimeter of the C-Bean's walls. She watched as the line rose slowly up the walls, like a blackout blind being pulled upwards, changing the blinding white walls into a deep murky grey. After a few seconds they were enveloped in the dark grey, instinctively turning their faces to the ceiling as it closed over their heads. They were all holding their breath. It suddenly felt suffocating inside the C-Bean. Hannah burst into tears.

Alice remembered how claustrophobic Karla got inside the C-Bean and for the first time understood what it felt like. It was a sort of crushing, hemmed in sensation that made it hard to breathe. Was the C-Bean malfunctioning for some reason? Had they done something to affect its settings? Alice recalled once again what Dr Foster had said just before he disappeared: 'There's something wrong with the C-Bean ...'

'We've all got to get out. Now! Something's not right!' Alice cried.

She felt as if she was tumbling head over heels in the air, but her body was standing still. The tumbling feeling seemed to conjure up images that started to whirl out of the grey walls on all four sides, like dark matter hurtling towards them. Alice noticed they were actually images of countless catastrophes – tsunamis, earthquakes, hurricanes, solar storms and raging bush fires, leaving scenes of human and natural devastation in their wake as they washed past. The children, still holding their breath, stared at scenes of people anxiously fleeing with tiny bundles of belongings, or sitting in bedraggled huddles on boats amongst floating detritus as their flooded cities were washed away around them, people fighting over an air-dropped delivery of food, and running in vain from some huge, cresting wave that was about to overwhelm them.

Just as it was all getting too much, the C-Bean switched to a different sequence of images, this time showing cities by night where all the streetlights and the lights inside buildings were gradually being extinguished. By the end, the whole planet was shrouded in a bleak and mysterious darkness. It looked so final that it seemed as though the Earth was about to stop rotating on its axis.

'Look!' Charlie said in a choked voice, pointing at one wall. A clock was ticking away, bright green numbers racing through the decades. Alice watched as it passed from 2050 to 2110 in less than half a minute, the numbers finally slowing – 2111, 2112, 2113, 2114…

'It's predicting the future, right?' she murmured breathlessly.

At 2118 the clock froze and the walls went blank again. An eerie silence hung in the air, although Alice could still feel a ringing in her ears. There was a slight motion to the C-Bean, as if it was shaking after all its exertions.

Then a female voice intoned a routine message that seemed at first quite familiar to the St Kildan children, because it sounded like a shipping forecast. But as they listened, Alice realised it was actually a series of dire environmental warnings.

OXYGENATION 19%, FALLING. AIR QUALITY: POOR, FALLING. MEAN SEA LEVEL: +5M, RISING. MEAN SURFACE TEMPERATURE: 30 DEGREES CENTIGRADE, RISING. RISK OF SOLAR RADIATION: CRITICAL.

There was a pause, and then a male voice added:

REMOTE OVERRIDE COMMENCING.
LEVEL OF ALERT: CODE 9.

The report ended and clicked off. Charlie smirked grimly at Alice. 'Do you still want to get out? Doesn't sound too nice out there in 2118.'

'I feel dizzy,' said Hannah.

'Me too, Hannah, me too,' Alice whispered.

The awful whooshing, whistling noise had started up again. Their centre of gravity shifted and it felt as if the C-Bean was being plunged down into deep water. Alice could feel the pressure building in her ears and the sound of a clanking chain outside, like before. Suddenly it seemed to stop and the C-Bean was yanked violently back up again. The children all toppled over and landed in a sprawling heap on the floor in amongst their belongings. The winching sound continued for another few minutes. Then the C-Bean blacked out.

The children stood up in the darkness and felt for each other's hands and waited, too afraid to speak. Alice started to hum the Scottish sea shanty that had brought the C-Bean back to its senses once before, this time more in an effort to calm its occupants than to restore the machine itself. The C-Bean did something in response that seemed to Alice as if it was taking a register – it started to scan each child in turn, producing a 3D hologram replica of them, appearing one by one like ghosts out of the darkness, their names hovering in luminous green capitals above each holographic head: EDITH BURNEY, HANNAH BURNEY, CHARLIE CHEUNG, SAMUEL FITZPATRICK, SAMUEL JACKSON, ALICE ROBERTSON. It then added, in smaller letters below the names, their dates of birth and other information about each of them: height, weight, eye colour, hair colour and blood type. It then scanned Spex too, and above his hologram it said 'CANINE OF UNKNOWN ORIGIN'. Alice remembered how, the first time she went inside, the C-Bean had scanned her as part of getting to know her, but this time the process felt altogether more hostile and officious, as if they were being treated as criminals and it was collecting evidence about them. For the first time, Alice had a nasty feeling the C-Bean was betraying her for some reason. Was it because it was being controlled remotely again?

When the data collection process was complete, one wall of the C-Bean flickered on to show a framed image that looked like a television screen, and a man with scruffy reddish hair wearing slippers and a white lab coat appeared. Alice guessed he was about 50 years old. There was something a tiny bit familiar about him, but she couldn't work out why. He frowned into the camera as he tried to adjust something on a hand-held device.

'Are you sure it's in remote override mode now? How do I know? Oh, I see. Right.'

The man looked up and cleared his throat to speak.

'ATTENTION PLEASE. THIS C-BEAN MARK 4 HAS BEEN RECALLED ON THE GROUNDS OF SERIOUS MISCONDUCT. THE SIX OF YOU ARE BEING HELD ON SUSPICION OF MALICIOUS DAMAGE TO THE NATURAL COURSE OF EVENTS AND WILFUL MANIPULATION OF STATUTORY TIME. UNDER PRESENT LAW, THIS CARRIES THE HARSHEST PENALTY: TS100. FOR NOW, YOU ARE TO BE DETAINED INDEFINITELY WITHIN THE DEVICE ITSELF, PENDING OUR INVESTIGATIONS. YOU WILL BE INTERROGATED IN TURN. FOOD, WATER AND MINIMAL OXYGEN LEVELS WILL BE MAINTAINED, BUT YOU ARE FORBIDDEN TO SPEAK TO ONE ANOTHER OR TO COMMUNICATE IN ANY WAY. THE PUNISHMENT FOR ATTEMPTING TO COMMUNICATE IS SOLITARY DE-CONFINEMENT IN SK ZONE 1, WHERE YOU FACE THE RISK OF SOLAR RADIATION, MALNUTRITION, DEHYDRATION AND CERTAIN DEATH. YOU HAVE BEEN WARNED …'

The screen image flicked off, and a stack of six cardboard trays appeared in a portal in the wall, each with a water bottle, a small paper cup containing three or four coloured tablets and, in an open disposable carton, a portion of brownish food that smelled disgusting and looked like the sort of puréed mush baby Kit would eat.

'Yuck! Spex can have mine – I'm not eating that!' Sam K said, horrified.

'I think the catering options are the least of our worries, mate,' Charlie muttered, scooping out a mouthful with his finger to taste. 'Mmm, worse than eating durian.'

'Shh, we're not supposed to talk, remember,' Edie said, her finger across her lips.

Charlie pulled his mobile phone out of his dressing-gown pocket to check for a signal. He showed Alice, wordlessly pointing at the screen – there was no 5G, but it had detected something called 'Hadronet' and the pointer on the map app indicated they were still on St Kilda. Alice looked at him and shrugged. It certainly felt like they had been transported somewhere else, but maybe they'd just imagined it. She was feeling very sleepy and could hardly even remember what had just happened, perhaps because there was already not quite enough oxygen for all of them.

Fearing the consequences of not eating what they'd been given, the children each took a tray and sat cross-legged on the floor, grimacing as they ate the revolting rations. Sam K managed one mouthful before shoving his tray towards Spex, who gratefully ate the rest. Charlie pointed at the tablets and looked at the others as if to ask what are these for?

'THAT IS YOUR DAILY MANDATORY DOSE OF VITAMIN PILLS, POLLUTION INHIBITORS AND HEADACHE TABLETS, CHARLIE. YOU MUST SWALLOW THEM WITH EVERY MEAL.'

The voice sounded as if the person was in the C-Bean with them, which made all the children jump and turn round. But there was no one there. It was not the man speaking this time, but a quiet female voice with a German accent. Alice knew that voice. She shot Charlie a look and mouthed the word 'Karla' at him.

Edie was collecting their trays and tidying up the C-Bean. She picked up Karla's laptop, nearly dropped it and started blowing the palms of her hands. Alice realised the machine must have started to overheat again. Edie pushed the laptop towards the wall with her toe. The heat from the laptop seemed to activate the C-Bean's scanning function again, because it created a hologram the same size as the laptop, then put up a short description in green capitals floating in space above the 3D image that confirmed Alice's suspicions:

ITEM NUMBER EW9UW9-TOFQFF. PROPERTY OF HADRON
SERVICES LIMITED. ASSIGNED TO AGENT KARLA ROBERTSON,
BORN LOS ANGELES 2090; USERNAME KROB2090; CHECKED
AND ISSUED 1 APRIL 2118, NEXT SERVICE DUE 1 APRIL 2119.

At first Alice thought the information must have been logged incorrectly and that the system had muddled up her name with that of the C-Bean's designer, Karla Ingermann, until she remembered that KROB2090 had been the username of whoever had previously tried to recall the C-Bean when they were stuck inside it, trying to get from 1930 back to the present. So it was Karla, just as they suspected – but why had she chosen to use Alice's surname? Was the spy trying to assume her identity? Alice could not work it out, nor could she understand Karla's connection to Hadron Services. The names Hadron and Hadronet rolled repeatedly round in her head as Alice tried to piece the bits of information together despite her thumping headache. She swallowed her headache tablet and looked across at Charlie, who was leaning against one wall, also lost in thought, his fingers pressed against his temples. He looked up and mouthed the word 'hadron' to Alice, and then started making the shape of a circle with his hand, looping round and round, speeding up the motion as he did so while mouthing what Alice thought were the words 'particle accelerator'.

The woman's voice that sounded like Karla started again.

'COMMANDER HADRON HAS ADVISED ME THAT NOT ONLY
WILL EACH OF YOU BE SUBJECTED TO AN INDIVIDUAL
INTERROGATION BUT YOU WILL ALSO BE REQUIRED TO
PERFORM CERTAIN DUTIES. YOUR FULL COOPERATION IS
REQUIRED. WE WILL START WITH THE ELDEST. WHEN YOUR
INTERROGATION COMMENCES, THEN AND ONLY THEN, WILL
YOU BE ALLOWED TO SPEAK. THIS WAY, CHARLIE.

None of the children had noticed but, while the woman was
speaking, the C-Bean's walls had become cloudy and porous, and
when Alice peered into the mist she could just make out a long curving
grey corridor. Spex was sniffing the ground cautiously. He looked like
he was about to run off into the mist when a bright red canine-looking
droid with flashing eyes appeared and issued a crisp and authoritative
bark. Spex slunk back and cowered behind Alice's legs. The droid's
head rotated through 360 degrees as it assessed the new arrivals and
then it suddenly did something that shocked them all – it selected
Charlie by firing a tiny dart into his arm. Alice could see a small bead of
blood forming on his skin. A fine nylon thread now joined the robot
to Charlie, like a fishing line. He grimaced and clutched his arm in
alarm as the droid started to move along the corridor, forcing the poor
boy to follow. The children watched as Charlie, slightly unsteady on
his feet due to whatever the dart had injected into him, disappeared
out of sight – or rather until they realised the walls of the C-Bean had
misted up and hardened over again.

After he'd gone, despite there being one person fewer in the pod,
it suddenly felt more confined and airless than ever. There was also
a sort of smell that reminded Alice of the anaesthetic gas they had
given her when she went to have her head injury checked at Glasgow
hospital.

'One, two, three, four…' she murmured, looking round and watching as, one by one, Edie, Hannah, Sam J and Sam F all passed out. She was trying to count to ten, but she could feel herself collapsing under her own weight, and realised they had all been drugged.

Alice's Blog

Sunday 9th September 2018 (or should that say 2118?)

We've been trapped inside the C-Bean now for more than 48 hours. Yesterday we were all drugged and Charlie was taken for questioning and has not come back. We're all really worried about him. I can only hope he did what Commander Hadron said, and it's just a matter of time before he comes back. If it wasn't for my watch it would be impossible to keep track of time because there are no windows and no connection to the outside world in the C-Bean, and even though our meals seem to arrive at regular intervals, they all look and taste the same so you have no idea whether it's breakfast, lunch or dinner.

It helps me to keep track of time if I write things down as they happen in my notebook. And anyway, there's not much else to do inside the C-Bean anymore except read or play on our digital tablets, because the C-Bean doesn't interact with us or want to teach us things like it used to. Instead it keeps going through loads of information about what's been happening for the last hundred years since 2018. I watched it all at first, but it's too much to take in. I don't want to sound depressing, but the future doesn't really look that good - everything that's still on dry land seems to have been used up or ruined, and everything else is basically flooded. I mean, the sea has risen loads and, from all the satellite images of Earth the C-Bean has been going through, countries like Holland and Denmark and Bangladesh are completely underwater now. I have no idea what that means for St Kilda - the one place it hasn't given us any information about is where we actually are. At least, that's where we think we are but, until Charlie comes back, we don't even know that for sure.

I can tell the boys and Hannah are feeling homesick, and I've tried to get the C-Bean to cheer them up by requesting some nice things to eat, or something to watch, like their favourite cartoon, but it just won't take any notice of me. It's as if I'm no longer the one in charge. And then, to make matters worse, half an hour ago, the person with the German accent who sounds spookily like Karla announced that I'm next to be interrogated. I should have expected it since I'm the next oldest, but Edie is really worried about how she's going to cope with the three younger ones by herself.

I know it sounds awful but I just want to get out of here - the others will be fine without me. I don't care what happens to me - I just want to know where we are, why we're here, and what they've done with Charlie.

A lice was ready when they came for her. She had her trainers on and had taken the precaution of putting her dressing gown on over her red tartan pyjamas, in the hope that when the red droid fired the dart it would not be able to penetrate her skin as it had with Charlie. When the droid came to collect her, it swivelled its head and eyed her coldly with its flashing eyes – but for some reason did not attempt to inject her. The moment the walls started to become humid and misty, she stood waiting. Alice was glad of her dressing gown since it was so cold outside the confines of the C-Bean that she could see her breath. The droid made an abrupt noise as if instructing her to follow, then moved off down the corridor. Alice kept her distance, listening to her own footsteps echo off the stainless-steel floor. It sounded like more than one pair of feet. Alice turned to look behind her and, to her relief but also her dismay, saw that Spex was trotting after her, also keeping a safe distance from the droid.

The chilled corridor curved continuously round to the right, lined with smooth silvery-white panels, and was brightly, almost blindingly lit from above. Alice couldn't tell if it was daylight or artificial light. To her left at regular intervals there were pale green doors with circular vision panels that she hardly dared to look into. But she was anxious to know what they'd done with Charlie – what if he was imprisoned in one of the rooms? After she'd passed two or three, she slowed down a little and risked a quick sideways glance into the next one. It looked like an operating theatre, with trolleys of instruments and two people with green masks over their mouths. They were standing opposite each other, bending over a table and opening up what looked like a human head, except inside there was just a load of complicated circuitry. Somewhat unnerved by this, Alice turned to face the other way. To the right there were no doors whatsoever. She passed a thermometer on the wall that indicated it was minus ten degrees centigrade. Alice could already feel the moisture in her nose and eyes frosting over. The droid continued. Alice noticed that it moved by hovering slightly above the ground, making no contact with the floor at all. She could hear that Spex had stopped to sniff something and half turned around, just in time to witness a door slide open and an arm grab the dog. Spex yelped with fright and the door slid shut. Alice hesitated, and immediately a voice intoned from nowhere:

ALICE, LEAVE THE DOG. HE WILL BE TAKEN CARE OF. MOVE ON.

Alice gulped and realised she was breathing more quickly now. She continued along the corridor. She passed a laboratory containing what appeared to be another C-Bean. Several people with white coats and clipboards were standing around testing its invisibility function – Alice momentarily saw the black cube disappear and then reappear. What was this place? Was she inside the factory where they made C-Beans? She felt very anxious all of a sudden. It was as if Spix was squawking inside her head: *Muito mau, perigroso!* Her lips silently translated over and over again: 'Very bad, dangerous!' But this was no time to get upset, Alice realised. She knew she needed to get a grip of herself, so she gritted her teeth and began silently counting her footsteps in order to focus her mind.

A little further down the corridor she almost tripped over the droid, which had pulled up sharply in front of a pair of black-and-gold doors to their right. It was the first time there had been a feature of any kind on the right-hand side of the curving corridor. Alice examined the doors more carefully – the black was darker than the blackest bits of outer space, and across the centre of the doors there was a golden globe protruding from the black. As she moved closer to the door, the globe started spinning rapidly on its axis and it appeared to be lit from within. A whirling stream of letters and numbers like an ancient formula passed across the surface. Alice was just trying to make out what they said when the doors slid apart.

She peered into the dimly lit interior. It was an enormous circular chamber lined with spikes of blue foam projecting from the walls and ceiling. Alice realised she must have been skirting around the outside of this chamber ever since she left the C-Bean. The droid behind her squeaked 'SHOES OFF'.

Alice bent down to remove her trainers, placing them neatly to one side of the entrance, and stepped into the chamber. The floor gave way slightly and she realised that, like the walls, it too was spongy. The droid withdrew and the doors slid shut behind her. Alice was suddenly aware that she could hear nothing. Not a sound. The room was so absolutely quiet that the only thing that made any sound was her own breath. In a strange way it was peaceful after the clattering noise of the metallic corridor, like being inside an enormous soft blue cloud. It was also, she noticed untying her dressing gown, very warm.

Alice padded across the floor through the inky gloom towards the middle of the chamber, where she could just make out a dark looming shape. As she got closer, she could tell it was a C-Bean, and for one moment she felt as if she had somehow been led full circle back to her starting point, until she noticed that this cube was slightly different. The surface looked like it was crawling with tiny insects, all roving over each other in an endless swirling motion, as if the surface material itself was moving around, or was made of countless particles that were constantly rearranging themselves. She reached out to touch it, but her arm passed right through, just like the first time it had passed through the C-Bean's wall when she wrote the coordinates in pen and it transported itself accidentally to Village Bay. But now it was somehow happening in reverse. That time she emerged out of the C-Bean. This time, in a split second, the C-Bean device had managed to envelop her inside itself. The next thing she knew, she was standing in a small room. Except that it wasn't just any old room,

Alice realised with a shock – it was her own bedroom.

Alice sat nervously on the edge of her bed, her feet on the orange shaggy rug, looking up in disbelief at the stars glowing softly on the ceiling. Beside her stood the luminous globe on her bedside table. It was spinning on its axis, ever so slowly, just like the hologram on the C-Bean's cardkey and like the globe on the doors she'd just passed through. Alice closed her eyes and shook her head. Maybe she was dreaming all this? But when she opened them again, she was still there. It was a peculiar sensation to be here in her own room – it made her feel both scared and comforted at the same time.

Had the C-Bean conjured up this virtual version of her room from its memory banks? And, if so, how much detail had it recorded? She smoothed her hand over the duvet cover with its printed pattern of grey pebbles. The texture of the cotton felt exactly as she remembered. Alice found herself wondering at what point in time this replica of her room had been made. She slowly knelt down to look under the bed and there in the shadows was the shoebox she'd used as a temporary time capsule. Her heart was beating fast as she pulled it out. There was nothing written on the lid, and it just contained the same junk as it had before – toys, old birthday cards and dead batteries. So the record of this room must have been generated at a time before 1st September 2018, but how long before?

Shaking with nervous anticipation, Alice reached forward and very slowly slid open the drawer of her bedside table to see what was inside. She had butterflies in her stomach, knowing somehow what she would find there. And there it was – James' old brown notebook, together with the rubbery black Mark 4 cardkey, just where they had been before the fire broke out. She reached into the drawer to grab hold of the precious notebook, but her fingers seemed to move past it and just graze the bottom of the drawer, as if it wasn't really there. Disappointed, she felt around inside the drawer, her fingers apparently moving in and out of the book and the cardkey but not touching them, when suddenly the wall opposite her bed sprang to life with a huge projected version of James' brown notebook, whose scanned pages were slowly turning by themselves.

A shiver passed down Alice's spine. She pulled the duvet off the bed, wrapped it round herself and slumped down onto the shaggy rug beside her bed to watch in awe as James' designs, diagrams and calculations for different C-Bean inventions became animated and three dimensional, emerging out of the screen in front of her as shimmering, mutating forms. Somehow she thought she could hear the sea shanty that she'd sung to her own C-Bean to get it working again. But it was playing so softly that she wondered if she was just imagining it. Luminous green words started appearing alongside a series of 3D design models, explaining the C-Bean's process of invention and organising them into some sort of annotated visual timeline. There was a primitive Mark 1 version with the date '2057–' floating beside it, then a Mark 2 version labelled '2077–' and then she recognised their own Mark 3 version with its illuminated digital keypad and the slot for the hologrammed cardkey. The sequence ended with the Mark 4 version theirs had become. Alice noticed that it had the trademark 'Øbsidon*' floating in space next to it.

Lulled by the music of the sea shanty, she was awash now with weak, untidy memories that had built up inside her like a tidal wave. Immersed in all this information, Alice closed her eyes, struggling to retrieve what she'd once read about Øbsidon in James' notes. She vaguely recalled something about a patent for a material that was being manufactured in China, but frustratingly her mind went blank. She opened her eyes to find that the music and images had vanished. Out of the silence a male voice started speaking in a slow whisper.

'Alice, welcome home. My team has gone to a lot of trouble creating this experience for you. I hope you like it. Make yourself comfortable – climb into your bed if you like – because we need to talk now. It's so nice to see you again. My official name is Commander Hadron, but you know me as someone else.'

The girl woke in a hot, sticky sweat. She had difficulty remembering anything that had happened before she fell asleep, and felt drowsy and sluggish. In fact she was having difficulty simply breathing. She had a dim recollection of a dream about looking for something in her bedroom, and for some reason half expected to find herself there. Maybe she was there – it was too dark to see properly, but she was aware she had her duvet wrapped around her. She struggled to wake properly, and found that she was actually lying on the ground, not in her bed. The ground felt spongy, her hair and clothes were damp with sweat and her arm had gone numb where she'd been lying on it instead of a pillow. It was so hot and airless that she could hardly breathe. Near where she had been lying was a cylinder with straps and a mask attached to it. She thought the label on it said 'XYCEN'. The girl realised she was breathing in short stabs. None of her thoughts would connect together, and the only thoughts that made any sense were about her physical condition – hot, damp, hungry, breathless. Then, above the urgent feeling of hunger, was the realisation that her throat was sore, really sore.

She staggered to her feet, licking her lips and straightening her crumpled limbs. She put on her trainers. A dry, desert wind was whistling through the enclosure, stinging her skin. Despite these external sensations, inside there was still just an empty blank feeling – she had absolutely no idea who she was supposed to be or where. At the same time, she had a nagging sense that she should know these things. A strange orange light was coming from somewhere outside and seemed to be getting brighter. She could read the label on the cylinder clearly now – OXYGEN – and wondered if breathing the oxygen would ease her sore throat. She tentatively put the mask to her face, turned the key on the top of the cylinder as the picture on the mask showed, closed her eyes and breathed in. She had an image that kept flitting through her consciousness of a seething mass of moving particles, none of which she could get hold of. She felt that she needed to latch onto something, anything, to jolt her into remembering. Like this wind – it must be coming from somewhere.

The girl lifted the oxygen cylinder onto her back and slipped her arms through the straps. She turned round until the wind was blowing into her face, inhaled slowly and then walked forwards. After a few steps she banged her forehead on a rough stone lodged in the wall at head height. She reached out and felt the stone, and the one next to it, in fact a whole collection of rough, misshapen rocks that made up the wall through which the wind was blowing. Her eyes were adjusting in the half-light now and, as far as she could tell, the stones went all the way round and over her head. She walked round the perimeter of the stone enclosure, counting her footsteps. The ground was uneven in places. On the fourth or fifth time round, she tripped and half cried out. The sound she'd made tugged at something in her brain – a memory of someone crying in this place. She focused her mind very carefully on the sound of weeping, sniffing – she could picture someone wearing glasses, someone sullen, pale and skinny… and a name: Karla! For a few seconds she simply clung to the recollection of the name alone because, even though she had a partial image of the person it belonged to, she had no idea who 'Karla' was.

'Why is this so hard?' she rasped out loud, her throat laced with pain. 'Am I Karla? I should know who I am!'

She felt her face, but there were no glasses. She felt around on the ground, thinking she could have dropped them, but could not find them anywhere. In all the times she had walked round the stone enclosure she had not looked to see if there was a way out, but she now had an urgent desire to flee from this hot, confined space. Didn't Karla get claustrophobia? Just as this thought surfaced in her mind, another name came to her that seemed in some way associated with this confined and draughty enclosure – Lady Grange.

'Am I Lady Grange?' the girl asked herself, more bewildered than ever. She felt sure she wouldn't be wearing a scruffy old pair of pyjamas if she had such a grand name. She felt in the pocket of her dressing gown for a clue – anything that might remind her of who she was – and found a black felt-tip pen along with a piece of paper on which was written 'HADRON BURN IN HELL'. It was only then that everything fell into place, and she pulled the mask away from her face.

'I am not Karla Ingermann or Lady Grange!' the girl croaked, finally finding the way out of the stone enclosure and shoving the wooden door open with her shoulder.

'My name is Alice, I am eleven years old and I live on a really small island called St Kilda!'

A hot, dry blast of air whipped up to greet her, almost knocking her over. But it was nowhere near as dramatic as the scene that confronted her.

It took Alice a long while to realise that she was looking down into Village Bay. She held the duvet over her head to shield herself from the unbearable heat and drew heavily on the breathing mask. From where she was standing, the whole lower part of the Village was under water. The waves in the bay were rougher and fiercer than she'd ever seen before and, when a wave receded, she briefly caught a glimpse of twigs and sticks protruding from the surface of the seawater. The extent of the flooding was shocking. But it was nothing compared to the raging tempest overhead – the sky was alive with strange sulphurous yellow and orange clouds and billowing flashes of green lightning that made Alice wince.

Things were slowly coming back to her. She felt sure this was some kind of punishment – the term 'Solitary Deconfinement' drifted into her mind, along with the threat of 'SK Zone 1'. In her recollection, there was something dark and ominous attached to both of them, even a hint of death.

With the thought of death uppermost in her mind, Alice

remembered St Kilda's little oval graveyard with its crooked old headstones. She looked around and could see the curved stone wall encircling the graveyard in the distance. She headed to where she knew the old entrance gate was. When she reached it, Alice stopped short – gone were the random assortment of gravestones dating from before 1930, each with its name half-obscured by lichen and moss. In their place stood five or six neat rows of translucent blocks, which reminded her of objects she'd once seen sculpted out of ice. She entered the oval graveyard and approached the nearest block, expecting it to feel cool and wet. But, when Alice touched it, she was surprised to find that it wasn't cold at all – in fact it seemed to come to life, showing first an image of the person whose grave it was, and then scrolling through details of their life. As she moved among the rows, each block sprang to life in turn, sensing her presence. At the end of the third row, Alice gasped. The picture on the grave in front of her was a face she recognised instantly – it was her own mother.

Her throat closed up and tears filled her eyes as she read about an event that, as far as Alice was concerned, had not yet happened: Jennifer Robertson, died in Glasgow Hospital in October 2029, leaving two daughters aged 26 and 22 and a son aged 11. Alice was not sure what she felt most upset about – being confronted with the fact of her mother's death, or that there was no mention whatsoever of her dad. Whatever happened in their lives running up to 2029 meant that their family would no longer be together.

Alice couldn't bear to look anymore. She ran out of the graveyard down the hill towards the school, sweat and tears rolling down her face. The grass was boggy and water quickly soaked her trainers and the bottoms of her pyjamas, but she carried on regardless, not even thinking about where she was going or why. She was dimly aware of passing the derelict remains of the old stone houses and seeing strange igloo-like shelters in some of the gaps between the houses. She could hear the wind howling and whimpering in amongst these ruined dwellings, amplifying the hurt inside her. It sounded almost human, this whimpering. Alice had a stitch and stopped for a moment, clutching her side. The whimpering was coming from the house to her left. She stepped inside the doorway to shelter from the fierce wind and crouched down, suddenly exhausted. A voice croaked from the shadows in the far corner of the dwelling.

'Who is there?'

Alice kept very still, afraid that she was so tired she was starting to imagine things. Someone was breathing in short, panicky gasps. There was a pause.

'Alice …' the voice croaked again. It was vaguely familiar. And whoever it was also knew her. Then something seemed to click in her brain.

'Charlie? Is that you?' Alice burbled through the mask, forgetting for a moment she had it on. She rushed over to the corner, where she could see a figure slumped on the ground.

'Oh my God, Charlie! What happened to you?'

Charlie's eyes were rolling in his head, and his lips were dry and crusty and caked in mud. It looked as if he'd been trying to eat soil. Alice noticed his fingernails were black and broken and the ground beside him had scrape marks in it. An oxygen cylinder identical to hers had been tossed aside, presumably because it was now empty. Alice stroked his hair and tried to wipe around his mouth with a corner of her duvet. Then she pressed her oxygen mask to his face and told him to breathe. Charlie's eyes closed and he looked for a moment as if he had passed out, but then he spluttered and sat forwards. The effort of coughing made him open his eyes again – two narrow slits, the whites red and with dark circles on the skin around them. He shivered but managed a limp smile as Alice cuddled up next to him, wrapping her duvet around him.

'Thank goodness I found you! I think we're still on St Kilda, but it's totally different. It's like the climate has changed completely because the village is half under water and the sky is doing weird things. And Charlie, in the graveyard ...' Alice bit her lip and failed to finish her sentence.

Charlie tried to lick his lips to speak: 'W –' When he realised he couldn't speak, he made an action that looked like someone drinking.

'Yes, you're right. We desperately need to find water. And food. And more oxygen.'

But neither of them moved. They leaned against each other and in a few moments they had both fallen asleep.

Alice woke for the second time that morning. This time, despite her extreme thirst and hunger and her difficulty breathing, at least she could remember who she was and who she was with. She nudged Charlie awake and helped him to his feet. They were taking turns to breathe the remaining oxygen in the cylinder. A warning light had come on, indicating that there was less than ten minutes' worth remaining.

Without saying a word to each other, Alice led Charlie downhill in the direction of the old wireless station, thinking that there was a slim chance it might contain supplies. But there were bolts and metal shutters on all the doors and windows. They pressed on towards the chapel and the schoolhouse. Alice felt a wave of homesickness wash over her as she stood with her hand on the doorknob to her old classroom. It was unlocked.

The room smelled of mildew and there were strange plants and fungi growing out of what remained of the wooden parquet floor. There were no desks left, but the fireplace was still there, the grate covered in what looked like half a century of dust. Covering one wall, in place of the old maps Alice remembered from Dora's classroom in 1918 and their own project work about the rainforest and Antarctica that adorned the walls in 2018, was some kind of translucent surface similar to the gravestones and the interior walls of the C-Bean. It flickered into life and started showing a presentation entitled 'Two Centuries of Climate Change and Species Extinction'. The images were of Victorian chimneys belching smoke and gridlocked traffic spewing out exhaust fumes. There were maps of the world and graphs dated 1900, 2000 and 2100 showing animal habitats shrinking and growing numbers of animal and plant species becoming extinct. Alice touched the screen gently and another presentation started.

'Charlie, look at this …' Alice whispered. Charlie turned round. The second one began with battle scenes and bombs exploding, and a title came up: 'World War III, 2027–2035'. Alice and Charlie stared at each other in silent disbelief.

Above the sound of the wind outside they could hear a tap dripping.

'Water!'

They both stumbled across the classroom and into the little broom cupboard where Karla used to work and where Dr Foster used to make himself cups of coffee. There was no kettle, no fridge, not even a desk or sink anymore, but attached to the back wall there was still a tap. Charlie cupped his hands under it while Alice tried to turn it on. It was very stiff and in the end it took both of them to force it open. Finally the water came out in a dirty gush of brown liquid.

'Don't drink it, Charlie!' Alice stammered, but he was too thirsty to care. After a few minutes the water ran clear and Alice gratefully slurped some handfuls. They were both soaking wet by the time they'd quenched their thirst, faces wet and shining.

'Better?' Charlie whispered after taking a quick puff of the remaining oxygen.

Alice nodded, her throat soothed by the cold liquid. Whether triggered by being in their old schoolroom or by the running water, she couldn't say, but it was as if a floodgate had opened in her memory. What stuck out in particular was the image of a sturdy metal container.

'Our time capsule, Charlie – we put food inside it, remember? We need to get inside the chamber!'

They found the hatch to the hollowed-out chamber under the gun had been left open. The two children peered down into the dark cavern below in a state of trepidation – was it a trap?

'You first,' Charlie hissed.

'Thanks,' grunted Alice, her palms sweating as she clung to the top of the ladder. She realised she had nothing to lose and no choice but to descend and confront whatever awaited them.

After the intense heat above ground, the chamber was pleasantly cool. Alice spied some shiny items stacked against the far wall, next to something else large and circular. She worked her way towards them, and found that the circular object was some kind of metal airlock, with a control keypad numbered '01' next to it. It reminded Alice of the ominous cave with the leaking nuclear warheads and spent nuclear fuel rods she and Charlie had found down here back in the 1950s. She sincerely hoped the airlock wasn't concealing more of the same or, for that matter, something much worse.

'Alice, look over here!'

Charlie found a crate of oxygen cylinders marked '48 Hour Rebreathers'. They took two out of the crate and helped each other put them on and start the flow of oxygen. It felt good to breathe freely again. Their eyes were slowly getting used to the gloom. Alice looked around her.

'Can you remember where we left the time capsule, Charlie? The stuff inside might still be edible, you never know.'

Without a torch it was difficult to locate the pile of rocks they'd used to hide the box. In the end both Alice and Charlie were crawling on their hands and knees over the slimy cave floor, moving stones aside and feeling underneath for a smooth metal lid. Alice came across something with machine-sealed cellophane edges. Could it be the packet of rice Charlie had put in the time capsule? She fumbled around the same area and felt a long straight ridge. It was the inside rim of the metal time capsule. The lid had been prised open. Other than the packet she'd already retrieved, there was nothing else inside the box. Whoever had raided it had already taken the rest of their items including James' notebook, her hamburger seabean and the C-Bean Mark 3 cardkey. Alice sighed miserably and stuffed the packet into her dressing-gown pocket.

'What have you got there?' Charlie whispered. 'Did you find the box?'

'Yeah, but it's been broken into. They've taken all our stuff.'

'What, all of it?'

Alice felt around once more and came across one half of Sam's walkie-talkie set, but it felt all crusty where the batteries had leaked at some stage.

'More or less, yep. Just a single packet of something.'

'C'mon then, let's not waste any more time down here – let's go.'

Charlie stumbled back over to the ladder where he'd draped Alice's duvet. He pulled it round his neck like a towel and was halfway back up when they heard a male voice shouting above ground.

'Hey you, boy, stop! That's an order!'

Alice froze. Was the order directed at Charlie? She watched as he waited a few seconds before quickly peeping out of the hatch. He immediately hurried back down the ladder, jumped off the last rung and ran over to Alice.

'Quick. Hide. He's coming!' Charlie whispered.

Sure enough, as they crouched in the shadows under the duvet, the man started descending the ladder. Except that he didn't come down the rungs the normal way; he seemed to make his body go stiff and then, holding onto the metal handrail at the side of the ladder, just slid down until his feet touched the floor. Then he turned and marched steadily towards the airlock, as if he could see in the dark exactly where he was going. When he reached the airlock he placed his index finger on the control pad. A tiny bar of light came on, apparently scanning the man's finger. It shed just enough light for Alice to see that the man had curly white hair. A voice spoke.

'Go ahead, Agent AFOS21XV.'

'Code Red. Rudy has escaped again. Request back-up.'

'Back-up declined, Agent AFOS21XV. Leave all flammable items and return to the lab,' the voice droned from a speaker somewhere in the cavern.

The man twitched slightly, fumbled in his pockets for a moment and dropped something, then pressed the control pad again with his index finger. Alice could hear a sucking sound as the airlock opened and a whoosh of freezing cold air together with a shaft of bright light escaped from the exit tunnel on the other side. The Agent entered the tunnel and resealed the door behind him, leaving Alice and Charlie panting with fear in the darkness.

'Who's Rudy? Was it the boy he shouted at?'

'No idea, but I think we need to get away from the village.'

Alice walked towards the ladder, but Charlie went to the airlock.

'It's this way, Charlie.'

'I want to know what that guy dropped just then.' Charlie was crouching down, feeling the ground around the airlock door. 'Got it,' he said, standing up and brandishing a slim blue cigarette lighter.

'Let's take a couple more oxygen cylinders, just in case,' Alice added.

When they got above ground, Alice examined the packet she'd found in their box. It contained some kind of instant vegetable soup mix. Printed on the cellophane was a use-by date: March 2120. Charlie, meanwhile, was staring in dismay at the flooded expanse in front of him that had once been their village, his shoulders hunched. Alice could hear his stomach rumbling louder than the wind whistling around them. It was hotter than ever.

'My God, Alice – what happened?'

Alice tried to count how many trees there must have been before the flood came. The community said back in 2018 that they were going to plant one tree every year, and it looked like they'd done just that for many years. It was hard to tell exactly how long, because there were gaps here and there where nothing was poking out of the water, but Alice reckoned there were more than 50 rotting away under the sea. She had an image of the submerged forest gradually accumulating in boggy layers of rotting carbon under the sea over millions of years. Like peat.

'I've just thought of a way to light a fire, Charlie – come with me. Let's go back to the broom cupboard, get some water and make some soup.'

'How do we cook it?'

'We light a fire. You've got that lighter thing, remember?'

'But there's nothing to light. All the wood around here is soaked.'

'You'll see.'

They headed off up the village, water lapping their ankles. The tide had now turned and was retreating between the derelict houses, leaving a long line of debris along the middle of Main Street – no seaweed, just a straggly heap of plastic bottles, dead fish, bits of nylon rope, and some empty metal containers. Alice picked up two of them and returned to the tap in the broom cupboard. She rinsed out the containers, filled them with water and took them into the schoolroom, where she stood them beside the old fireplace.

'Right, come with me. I'll need your help.'

Charlie was too weak to protest, and followed meekly behind her, silently breathing into his mask.

Having hunted around for a small rock with a sharp edge, Alice searched inside the cluster of cleitean at the back of the village, well above the tideline. Inside the third cleit she found a patch of peat that was dry and loose, and started to rip small rectangular pieces and hand them to Charlie. They carried back an armful each to the schoolroom, where Alice laid the turfs in the fireplace. At first they struggled to get the fire going with the lighter, using some dry grass as kindling. Eventually, with the containers nestled inside a sort of spongy teepee of burning peat, Alice was happily stirring a brownish vegetable slurry with a twig, waiting for the water to boil.

'Hey, Charlie, do you remember my mum telling us this is how they used to heat our schoolroom in the olden days and how the children took it in turns to bring the peat to school each morning?'

Charlie didn't reply. He was watching the World War III presentation on the wall again and sighing.

'I've been thinking,' Alice continued. 'Assuming it definitely is 2118 and this definitely is St Kilda and we're not stuck in some weird virtual reality computer game, we need to get help. I mean, we need to contact someone on the mainland. I don't think we can trust the people here on St Kilda, since they're the ones who abducted us.'

'How d'you suggest we do that, Alice? Pigeon post? There don't even seem to be any birds left.'

'We'll make a mailboat. Like they did in the olden days. We could use one of the empty oxygen cylinders as the container – I bet they float. We'll put a message inside and seal it up somehow.'

'I s'pose. But didn't they used to take ages to get anywhere? We'll be dead before anyone comes to our rescue.'

'Don't talk like that, Charlie. As long as we stay away from the village and avoid being recaptured, we can concentrate on coming up with a plan to rescue the others and get our C-Bean back. But I reckon we need to make a move before it gets dark – then, if the Agent guy comes looking for that boy who escaped, we won't be around for him to find us.'

'So what's the plan, Alice? I'm too hungry even to think.'

Alice gave the soup a final stir. She tried to pick up one of the containers but it was scalding hot. She thought for a moment and then pulled the tie belt off her dressing gown and, using it like an oven glove, lifted the containers out of the fireplace and handed one to Charlie.

'Here, just eat.'

They both fell silent while the hot broth burned their tongues because they were too hungry to wait for it to cool down.

When their bellies had stopped grumbling, Alice stood up, retied her dressing-gown belt and said, 'Up for a walk now, Charlie?'

'Where are we going?' Charlie asked, following Alice out of the classroom.

'The Amazon's House on the other side of the island in Gleann Mor – if it's still there, that is. We can get some sleep there and then make the mailboat and figure out a plan to rescue the others in the morning,' she puffed as they made their way up to the wall that ran along above the village.

'Who are these "others" you keep talking about?'

Alice turned and looked at Charlie, aghast.

'Well, hello? As in: Edie, Hannah and both Sams. They're still stuck inside the C-Bean where you left us, remember?'

'I don't remember anything ... Oh wait, wasn't there a sleepover?'

'Yes, that's when we were taken. During the night. It's how we landed up in this mess in the first place.' Alice carried on walking.

'It's all so hazy. All I remember is some commander guy with red hair asking me loads of questions.'

Alice stopped in her tracks again and turned to face Charlie. It was his mention of the red hair that finally jogged things back into her memory.

'That guy – the one who calls himself Commander Hadron – when I was taken for questioning, it was all pretty creepy. He knew all about me and, what's more, he'd built a complete replica of my bedroom.'

'Weird. What was all that about?'

'I'm not sure, Charlie, but I've got this funny feeling that Commander Hadron is in some way related to me.'

Next morning, while they were assembling the mailboat inside the Amazon's House, Alice had the impression they were being watched. Once when she came to this place, she'd sensed the presence of the ghostly female warrior breathing right next to her inside the dwelling. But this time it felt more real, more human. She could actually feel someone's eyes on her, and kept glancing over her shoulder to check. Alice was about to write a note to go inside the mailboat using the slip of paper and the black felt-tip pen she had in her dressing-gown pocket. As she crossed out the words 'Hadron burn in hell', she not only realised that she must have written them during her interrogation, but also that they were the same words they'd found written in graffiti on the C-Bean when they returned to Central Park in New York. Who was this Commander Hadron and why was he messing with her head? She angrily tore off a scrap of red tartan fabric from the sleeve of her pyjama top and started to attach it to the cylinder so the mailboat would be spotted more easily when it was floating in the sea.

Suddenly a voice spoke.

'I know better Way.'

Alice jumped.

'Who's that?' she mumbled through the rebreather, relieved that her hunch about someone watching was correct, but alarmed all the same.

A skinny boy rolled out of one of the narrow ledges inside the walls of the dwelling. He must have been there all night, but they hadn't noticed.

'Me,' the boy said, standing up and stretching. He was about 14 or 15, Alice guessed, with dark brown skin and almost no hair in places, and was wearing what looked like a faded, slightly ripped, grey wetsuit onesie and neoprene shoes with toes. When he turned to look at her, she noticed that the whites of his eyes were bright yellow.

He adjusted a small orange box that was strapped to his arm just above his elbow and then reached into the recess where he'd been sleeping to retrieve a drawstring bag.

'Want eat?' he asked, opening up the bag and taking out a handful of pale green speckled eggs and a coil of rope, which he carefully placed on Alice's duvet. Charlie crept into position behind the boy, his feet planted squarely on the ground, ready for any sign of trouble. Alice was silent. She wasn't sure if this was the same kid they knew had escaped yesterday. The boy carried on regardless, reaching into the bag for another item. This time it was a penknife.

'Not so fast, buddy,' Charlie warned when he saw the first glint of metal.

The boy turned quickly and flicked open the knife. To Alice's amazement, trailing from its handle was a long fluorescent yellow shoelace. It looked exactly like the penknife their teacher Dr Foster had used the first morning he arrived. Alice could picture him now, slitting open the prickly seedpod he'd brought to show them, and all the little seabeans falling out. This unexpected turn of events made her more on edge than ever.

'Charlie, don't move. It's some kind of trap – he must have captured Dr Foster too, if he has his knife!' Alice screeched, pulling away her oxygen mask and pointing at the shoelace. Had this boy made Dr Foster and their parrot Spix disappear in Liverpool? Or was she jumping to conclusions too quickly? Could Dr Foster's penknife still be here on St Kilda simply because he lost it somewhere on the island a century ago and this boy just happened to find it? She stared at the shiny blade. In that case, why wasn't it rusty?

As if reading her mind, the boy quickly flicked the knife shut, stuffed it back in his pocket and grinned toothlessly at her.

'You Prisonbird too?'

'Yes. I mean no. Look, who are you?'

'Rudy,' he said, and held up a grubby hand to high-five Alice. On the palm she could see he'd been branded with an eight-digit code: RBOK2104. Alice's stomach lurched. It was the same format as Karla's username.

Alice looked at her own blank palm, suddenly recalling the strange fortune-teller with all those little Kumalak beans that she'd met in the other St Kilda in Australia. The woman had asked her what she wanted to know the answer to. She still didn't have the answer to her question – she still didn't know why. Why were all these things happening to her? What did it all mean? Alice looked into Rudy's sad yellow eyes, wondering if somehow he was the one with the answer.

'I'm Alice. Are you a prisoner here? Did they capture you from 2018, too?'

'Prison yes. Work in Lab to punish. Four Years. Stole Fishboat. Born 2104. Like Hand say,' he pointed to the numbers.

'So the number is your year of birth …' Alice mused.

'What kind of lab, buddy?' Charlie didn't look convinced, and stood rigidly with his arms folded.

'Hadron Lab. Fix Stuff. Now eat,' Rudy said, sitting down cross-legged on the rough ground. He cracked open one of the eggs, poured the contents expertly into one half of the shell and offered it to Alice. She sat down and took the egg, not sure if she could manage to eat it.

'Like dis,' Rudy said, laughing and tipping the contents of a second egg into his mouth and swallowing. Alice removed her rebreather and did the same, feeling the glop as the yolk passed her throat and headed for her stomach. It had a strange fishy aftertaste.

'Did you collect the eggs yourself? From the cliffs?' Alice asked, wondering if the rips on Rudy's wetsuit were caused by climbing for food.

'Yes. Most Bird die. Too hot now. Few Egg still in Nest. Fall many time. Not like Jutland. Easy-flat there.'

'Jutland? Is that where you come from?'

'Jutland no more. All Water.' Rudy looked forlorn. Then he brightened.

'You want send easy-fast Mailboat? Me knowhow.'

Rudy's offer made Charlie relax a little and he stepped forward.

'Yeah, that's right. You wanna help us, buddy?'

The boy nodded.

'Help me, too. Want get-away. Far. In Blackbox. Like try before.'

'Do you think he means the C-Bean?' Alice whispered in Charlie's ear.

'Maybe. At any rate, he knows stuff,' muttered Charlie. 'Hey, so what's this other way we can send a Mailboat around here, Rudy?'

'Come. Go Terra-station, send Mailboat. Get new Sniff too,' Rudy suggested, pointing at the low oxygen level warning light on Alice's breathing equipment. He picked up his drawstring bag and slung it over his shoulder.

'OK, mate. It's worth a try, but don't try anything funny,' Charlie warned.

The ground was dry and dusty and they kept slipping as they climbed up out of the Gleann Mor side of the island towards the top of the mountain. Charlie led the way with grim, silent determination. Alice left him to his own thoughts and tried to make conversation with Rudy. Despite his really limited English, Alice managed to get out of the boy that his family were rice growers from Jutland, but when he was ten, the sea rose dramatically and he got separated from them. After that, he said, he'd had to survive on his own, and one day he got caught stealing a fishing boat in his hometown – somewhere he called the 'City of Smiles'.

'No Smile now,' he added grimly.

The building Rudy referred to as Terra-station turned out to be a replacement for the radar station near the top of Mullach Mor. It looked quite different from when Alice met James Ferguson there back in 1957. In fact, she decided that this hut looked more like an elaborate bird hide, with its green camouflage pattern printed onto the exterior. Pity there are no birds left to observe, Alice thought to herself.

'Wait, I get in,' Rudy told them.

He pulled something out of a pocket in his grey wetsuit and pressed it on the control keypad beside the door. The door slowly opened. As he shoved the item back into his pocket, Alice caught a glimpse of what he had used to open the door, and recoiled in horror. It was the grubby stump of someone's index finger.

Inside there was some brand-new equipment that looked like it had only just been installed because there was a whole load of discarded packaging lying around and its digital operating manual still sealed. Rudy stood with his hands on his hips admiring the new kit and making appreciative noises for a moment or two. It was obviously not the first time he had forced his way in. He flipped the power switch and a large screen instantly flickered on. He grinned when he read the first thing that appeared on the screen:

```
10.45 HOURS 10/09/2118
@HADRONET ISSUED CODE_RED: @RBOK2104
ESCAPED FROM AIRLOCK 01. @AFOS21XV FAILED
TO INTERCEPT. NB @RBOK2104 UNTAGGED.
```

'Look see!' He was pointing at the word 'untagged' and then pointed at Alice and Charlie and gave them a thumbs-up sign. Charlie peered at the screen and read the message:

'Want untag too?' Rudy proposed.

'How do you know we've been tagged?' Charlie asked warily.

'Look see!' Rudy pointed at two other updates on the screen:

```
08.00 HOURS 10/09/2118
@HADRONET DETECTED @AROB2007 AWAKE IN
```

CLEIT85 & @CCHE2006 AWAKE IN HOUSE06

13.30 HOURS 10/09/2118
@HADRONET DETECTED @CCHE2006 & @
AROB2007 LIT FIRE IN SKSCH.

'That was us making soup yesterday, Charlie!' Alice whispered nervously. 'Rudy's right – they not only know exactly who we are and when we were born, but where we are and what we're up to out here.'

'I guess. But how and when did we get tagged?'

'Maybe it was when the C-Bean scanned us the day we got taken here, or when we got taken for our interrogation – let's face it, neither of us can remember much about what happened before we found ourselves out here in SK01.'

Rudy walked over to Charlie, took hold of his arm and started to push up his left sleeve.

'Hey, get off me,' moaned Charlie, pulling his arm away. Rudy shrugged his shoulders and let go.

'You want untag, Alice?' Rudy asked, tapping his upper arm.

Alice removed her dressing gown, pulled up what remained of her left sleeve and stared at her arm in alarm.

'Eurghh, what's that? I didn't even know that was there!'

Embedded in her skin just above the elbow on the outside of her arm was a small flesh-coloured rubbery disk that appeared to be covering something. Rudy gently flipped the disk back and underneath was a tiny switch and a hole that looked like a headphone socket. It had a gold rim and was set into Alice's skin. The area around it was red, as though the procedure to fit it had only recently taken place.

'Press Button, count three Minutes. Untag,' Rudy assured her.

Alice held her thumb over the tiny switch, pressed hard and counted slowly to 180. It was excruciatingly painful at first, but after she got past 100, she could feel the pain ease off.

'What's the other thing for, Rudy – you know, the, er… hole?' Charlie asked, peering over Alice's shoulder.

'Is BioPort. For Sniff,' Rudy explained, pulling away the little orange box that he wore on his arm. They could both see the bioport in his arm, and that the orange box had 'O2' printed on the back of it.

'Charlie do untag, I find new Sniff.'

Charlie slowly rolled up his sleeve to inspect his own bioport.

Rudy searched the drawers and cupboards in the hut until he found a long white box with lettering on it that looked like it might contain medicine. Inside was a row of orange units, each one in a protective transparent casing. Rudy removed the casing from one and peeled a sticker off its back to reveal a gold jack plug.

'Ready?' he asked as Alice finished counting. She nodded and Rudy pressed the metal jack plug on the unit into the bioport on her arm. She felt a quick stab of the most unbelievable cold spread through her veins up and down her arm, and then … nothing.

'It only hurts to begin with,' she reassured Charlie, rolling down her sleeve over the unit and putting her dressing gown back on. 'But it's much easier getting oxygen like this than through those rebreathers, that's for sure.'

Rudy handed Charlie another unit and left him to fit it himself. He put the rest of them in his drawstring bag.

'Now we do Mailboat,' Rudy said as he rooted around in another cupboard and produced a small hand-held device shaped just like a giant hamburger seabean. When he opened it up to reveal two hemispherical compartments, Alice first thought that they would simply put a handwritten message inside and float it out to sea, but it soon became clear that it was actually a communications device that used satellite technology and functioned like a very powerful walkie-talkie.

'Think, Alice. Give Instant Message. Right in Brain,' Rudy explained.

'But how does it work?'

'You Instant Alice. Think,' he said again, showing her the band around the middle, which was in actual fact a screen on which a text message could appear.

Alice closed her eyes and focused. The thought that was uppermost in her mind formed into a silent message:

'My name is Alice. I've been taken to 2118 and I'm trying to reach my parents Jen & Mike Robertson to tell them I'm OK.'

When Alice opened her eyes, she saw that the same message she'd uttered in her head was slowly scrolling around the rim of the device in blue. Rudy nodded, as if satisfied with the message.

'Who for Mailboat?' Rudy wanted to know in order to send it.

Alice had been wondering that herself. Who did she know in 2118 that could help them? There was only one person she knew who might be from the future, but she also knew in her heart she was not to be trusted.

'Erm … Karla?' Alice said tentatively.

'You know Namecode?'

'I think it's KROB2090.'

'Hang on a minute, Alice!' Charlie butted in. 'Are you seriously considering letting Karla know we're here? You must be mad!'

'Well, who else do we know that could help us, Charlie? At least she'll know how to get us back to 2018. We're pretty sure she can control the C-Bean remotely. Plus, she did return the Mark 3 to us, remember?'

'Mark 3?' Rudy repeated, pulling something else out of his drawstring bag.

'Like dis?' He pulled out the Mark 3 cardkey and held it up by the corner with a triumphant expression on his face.

'Hey, gimme that. You shouldn't have taken it. It's not yours.

What else did you steal from our time capsule?' Charlie tried to snatch the cardkey from Rudy, but he was too quick. In an instant he had Charlie gripped around the chest and was pressing Dr Foster's penknife against his neck.

'Rudy want go Blackbox, want be TS100 like you. We go Airlock 01 now. Back to Lab.'

Alice still had no idea what 'TS100' meant, but she understood from his urgent tone that Rudy was in no mood to be messed with – this was not a suggestion but a command.

'OK, Rudy, easy now. Give me the knife. We'll go and find the C-Bean. Together.' Rudy relaxed his grip slightly and Charlie slid from under his arm and dropped to the floor.

'Charlie, are you OK?' Alice asked as she gently took the penknife from Rudy's hand and closed away the blade. Charlie nodded and stood back up. She instinctively started to sing the sea shanty she used to revive the C-Bean, in an attempt to calm things down. Rudy and Charlie were scowling at each other.

'Rudy, do you know how to make the airlock door open? The one in the underground chamber by the gun?'

Rudy nodded. 'With Deadman Finger' he said matter-of-factly, patting the pocket where he kept it.

'Good, that's settled then. We'll go there now.'

The sky was an angry, seething mass of reds and oranges that afternoon as the three children walked headlong into a fierce hot wind, making their way back down into Village Bay.

'How long has the sky been like this, Rudy?' Alice asked.

'Many Solar-storm. Since few Year. Sometimes 60 degrees C. Many Deadmen. Rudy lucky. Got Solarsuit,' he said stroking the sleeve of his faded grey onesie.

'I see.'

As they approached the gun emplacement, Charlie took the Mark 3 cardkey out of his pocket.

'Hey, look at this, Alice!'

The globe on the cardkey was turning very slowly. As they got closer to the gun, the rotations appeared to be getting faster.

'Hmm. Maybe we will be able to summon it without opening the airlock,' Alice wondered aloud, taking the cardkey from Charlie. 'But let's not do it above ground – we might be seen.'

Rudy was the last to climb down the ladder. He stood in the patch of daylight at the bottom and appeared to hesitate for a moment. Then he took Sam J's torch out of his drawstring bag, handed it back to Charlie and said in a quiet voice 'Rudy sorry. Took Light. Took Rice too. And Chopsticks. Was like Home. Taste nice.'

'That's OK, Rudy, we understand. You were hungry,' Alice said. They all were. She raised her eyebrows at Charlie for support.

'Yeah, no worries, buddy,' Charlie said, but there was not much warmth in his voice.

Alice closed her eyes. She had to get the cardkey to work. She pictured the other children still trapped inside, hungry and frightened. The globe was spinning fast. Charlie flashed Sam's torch beam across the room and Alice thought she could see a flicker of black forming.

'Keep going, Alice.'

She held her breath and concentrated on an image of the black cube, but she couldn't seem to make it appear fully – there was just a fleeting glimpse of it, and then it would disappear. She sang, hummed and talked in a coaxing voice to the C-Bean, but still nothing happened.

'It's not working. The walls of the lab must be too thick for the cardkey to summon it from in there,' Alice muttered finally, disappointed.

Charlie growled with frustration.

'Use Mailboat?' Rudy suggested, getting the device out of his bag.

'Genius. To do what, exactly?' Charlie said sarcastically.

Alice was thinking.

'Wait a minute, Charlie. Karla's laptop is inside the C-Bean.'

'Yes, but it's no good to us there, is it?'

'Can you stop being snotty for one minute and just listen? What if we try to access it remotely using Rudy's Mailboat device? Maybe we could log into it and use it to summon the C-Bean like Karla did.'

'Sounds complicated.' Charlie scuffed his shoe along the ground, kicking rocks. The sound echoed off the ceiling like a clap of thunder.

'Alright,' he muttered eventually.

Rudy handed Alice the Mailboat device and she silently transmitted Karla's namecode into it: 'login KROB2090.'

The reply arrived in her brain almost instantaneously: 'Enter Password'.

'What do you think Karla's password is, Charlie?'

'No idea, Alice. We tried everything already, remember? I'm not a mind-reader.'

Alice rolled her eyes.

Then it came to her. She held her breath and telepathised the words: 'Plan B'.

The band around the Mailboat device said, 'Please wait, processing…'

Then a status query appeared: 'Allow remote access?'

It was only a matter of seconds before Alice found herself consulting her watch, and entering the location of the chamber and the exact date and time for Karla's laptop to command the C-Bean to travel: 11/09/2118 12.35GMT.

It was only when Charlie suddenly leaped aside, wincing and hopping on one leg, that Alice realised the C-Bean had not only materialised but had almost crushed his foot.

The first to emerge from the C-Bean was Edie. Her face was pale and gaunt and she was shaking slightly. Behind her, Alice could see Hannah, rubbing her eyes and squinting.

'Edie, Hannah!' Alice said and rushed forwards to give them both a hug.

But they stood limply like rag-dolls and said nothing.

'Where are the Sams? Where's Spex?' Charlie enquired. They still didn't speak.

'Hey, don't worry, it's really us, silly – and you're outside the lab, so you can talk now!' Alice assured them, and it suddenly came back to her that she had been too afraid to speak to Commander Hadron when she was being interrogated in the replica of her bedroom. Somehow he must have got her to speak eventually, because she could now remember roaring as loud as she could, over and over, 'LET ME OUT OF HERE PLEEEEEEASE!' She still couldn't remember what he had said to make her act that way, but she knew now it was the reason she had such a terrible sore throat when she woke up in the cleit …

Edie peered suspiciously through her glasses. She looked long and hard at Rudy before turning to examine Alice's face, as if she was looking for any anomalies that would confirm she was not who she appeared to be.

'It's really me, Edie, honest,' said Alice, and then added a piece of information that she thought would help convince her friend she was genuine: 'Spex was taken when I went to be interrogated. He's somewhere in the lab. We'll get him back too, don't worry.'

Edie still looked nervous and only half convinced. She hesitated for a moment, then rolled up her sleeve and wordlessly showed Alice the bioport on her arm.

'They did it to me too, Edie,' said Alice, patting the unit on her own arm. 'Here, let me untag you.' Alice pressed the button and held it down, counting under her breath. Edie winced with pain and tried to pull her arm away.

'I know it hurts, Edie, but once it's done they won't be able to detect where you are anymore.'

Edie's expression was more confused and frightened than ever.

'Rudy, can I have two more of the "sniff" things for my friends? They're going to need oxygen now, too.'

Finally it was Hannah who spoke.

'Who's Rudy?'

Rudy stepped forward with a big smile on his face, holding out two orange packages. Alice started to unwrap them and explain what they were to the girls, but they both looked terrified and ran back inside the C-Bean. Edie was shaking with fear.

'Edie's completely traumatised, isn't she?' Alice sighed.

'She must have gone through the same thing we did. I bet that's where the Sams are right now – that's why they're not in the C-Bean,' Charlie said as he inserted the Mark 3 cardkey into the slot in the C-Bean's access panel. Rudy was watching him intently, his yellow eyes bright with curiosity.

'That means they won't have interrogated Hannah yet, since she's the youngest,' Alice surmised.

'Or tagged her. I bet she doesn't have an oxygen port fitted. She'll have to use a cylinder.'

Charlie took another rebreather out of the crate beside the airlock door and they both stepped inside the C-Bean. Edie and

Hannah were cowering in the corner. It smelt of unwashed bodies and stale air. But almost as soon as Alice noticed this, a newer, fresher smell swept through the pod. Without being prompted, the C-Bean produced several sets of clean clothes, all folded neatly in their own recess in the wall. A bowl of clean water appeared in a recess on the opposite wall, together with fluffy towels, a soap dispenser, a tube of toothpaste and five new toothbrushes. She realised the C-Bean must be back to its old cooperative self if this was happening.

'Time for a wash and brush up, guys! My teeth sure do feel furry,' said Charlie, peeling off his pyjama top.

'Who's the fifth one for?' Hannah asked in a raspy whisper.

Alice counted the faces in the pod. Then she stuck her head outside the door. Rudy was standing guard outside.

'Why are you out here, Rudy?'

'Keep Eye open,' he explained, 'Not want AFOS21XV find Blackbox.'

'Is that the namecode of the guard who was after you?'

Rudy nodded and pointed at the airlock door.

'He Cyborg. Can come back. Stop Blackbox.'

'Don't worry, Rudy. You'll be safe inside the C-Bean. I mean, the Blackbox seems to be working normally again now.'

Rudy stepped tentatively into the pod. Alice held her breath, waiting to see if her hunch was correct. Sure enough, the C-Bean didn't scan Rudy in that same unfriendly way it had scanned them upon arrival, and she decided it was therefore no longer under Hadron's command now that it was outside his compound.

As if to prove it was no longer their enemy, once the children had washed and changed into the clean clothes and were busy brushing their teeth, the C-Bean produced a huge picnic hamper, even bigger than the one Alice had left for the starving St Kildans back in 1851. Charlie and Rudy lifted the hamper down and Alice opened the lid to find that it was full of delicious food for them: perfectly ripe bananas, sticky buns, warm sausage rolls, little tangerines, cherry tomatoes, fat juicy grapes and chocolate biscuits. Alice picked up a biscuit and demolished it in one mouthful. It tasted just like the one she had imagined the first time she ever went inside the C-Bean.

Hannah crept out of the corner and stole a grape.

'Edie, it's real food!' she said, savouring it slowly.

Edie shot a look at Alice, then darted forward and grabbed a banana from the hamper. Rudy was watching her, utterly fascinated, as she peeled back the skin in strips and started eating.

'Would you like a banana too, Rudy?' Alice asked.

'What is Bana-na?'

'It's a fruit. It grows in bunches on a tree,' explained Alice, gesturing with her hand. 'Have you never seen one before?'

'No. Never see Banana. Never eat Fruit. No Fruit now. Grandpa show Picture. When Boy, he eat Fruit.'

In the end, the children devoured everything in sight and at the end of the meal the C-Bean produced a large jug of water and a set of paper cups.

'I want to go home,' Hannah announced tearfully when they had all finished. She started to cry.

'We can't go home just yet, Hannah, not until we figure out a way to get the Sams back. We can't go back to 2018 without them, can we?' Alice coaxed, stroking Hannah's hair.

Charlie had a very particular look on his face, like he'd just had an idea.

'Look, the Sams must be somewhere inside Hadron's lab right? So let's just open the airlock exit where Rudy escaped – maybe they'll figure it out and come running.'

'Problem. Rudy open Airlock. Buzz Buzz. AFOS21XV come.' Rudy put his hands over his ears to show them just how loud the alarm would sound.

'Well, I can't think how else we're going to rescue them,' said

Charlie in a resigned tone.

'OK, let's give it a try,' Alice agreed. 'Edie, Hannah and I will stay inside while you boys go and open the airlock, but they'd better be quick or we'll all be caught.'

Alice stood blocking the entrance after the two boys stepped out, because she didn't want the girls to see Rudy use the dead finger. She watched as Charlie shone Sam's torch on the airlock while Rudy pressed its fingerprint against the keypad to be scanned. When she heard the airlock seal open, she braced herself for the alarm going off, but none of them could have imagined just how loud it would be. Charlie dropped the torch and slammed his fingers in his ears. Rudy just winced and they both ran back to the C-Bean. Alice could hear something else amidst the alarm, another sound. Something unmistakably familiar. A bark. Just as Alice was closing the C-Bean door, a wet black nose appeared out of the darkness and pushed his way through the gap, tail wagging.

'Spex!'

The dog rushed around the pod, licking everyone hello, including Rudy. Charlie shut the door and the sound of the alarm halved in volume. Hannah was cuddling Spex and laughing until Edie pointed to one side of his body where all his fur had been shaved off and there was a ragged row of stitches.

'What have they done to you, Spex, your poor little mutt?' Alice cried. 'Oh, I wish the Sams would hurry up, so we can get out of here.' She noticed Spex was making quite a fuss of Rudy. 'Have you met our dog before, Rudy?'

'Yes. Know Bork. Meet inside Lab. Sleep by Rudy Cell. Give him Food. Cry in Night. Scar hurting.'

'He's not really called Bork, you know.' Alice tickled the dog's tummy and saw that Spex was still wearing the black-and-gold disk that said 'Børk'. 'Someone else put that thing round his neck.'

She still hadn't worked out how or why Spex came back that day in Liverpool. Was it some kind of side-effect of resetting the C-Bean a day into the future – had they opened up a tiny glitch in time and he'd fallen through from 1960? Or had someone engineered an exchange remotely, taking their parrot Spix hostage in exchange for Spex? She remembered how faithfully Spex had stayed beside the injured Donald in 1944, keeping him company in that lonely valley until help came. It was nice to think that Rudy had done the same thing for the wounded Spex.

'Can't we just go home now?' Hannah pleaded, bringing Alice out of her reverie.

'Yes, TS100 now,' urged Rudy.

'I've got another idea: Rudy, pass me the Mailboat, quickly!'

Alice held the device and mentally entered what she assumed would be the two Sams' namecodes: SFIT2011 and SJAC2011. Their replies came almost in unison, a string of blue letters racing around the perimeter of the device: 'Alice, is that you? It says AROB2007. We're inside this weird round room with spongy blue spikes. Where are you?'

Alice thought quickly.

'Boys, you need to get out of there. The rest of us are all here in the C-Bean waiting for you. We've opened Airlock 01 – that's why the alarm's gone off – so you haven't got long before Hadron's people work out what's happened. We've brought the C-Bean up to the chamber beneath the gun, just the other side of the airlock exit. With any luck when you get here it'll be invisible. Come immediately!'

More blue letters from both of them, this time saying 'OK. Roger that!'

Alice put the Mailboat down and muttered the invisible command to the C-Bean, and they all waited.

And waited.

The alarm outside suddenly cut out.

Silence.

Out of the corner of her eye, Alice noticed another message scrolling around the Mailboat device. She was just about to pick it up and read it when the C-Bean broke the silence. The walls suddenly started pulsing with light, and a robotic voice said over and over:

INITIATING EMERGENCY INTERVENTION PROTOCOL.
COMMENCING REMOTE OVERRIDE AND RESTRICTED ACCESS.
PROCESS CANNOT BE INTERRUPTED.

Alice barked 'Manual override!' but the C-Bean did not respond.

Quick as a flash, Charlie grabbed Karla's laptop and tried to perform a remote override with her username. It allowed him system access, but the laptop screen displayed exactly the same status message as they were hearing over the C-Bean's audio channel:

REMOTE OVERRIDE COMPLETE. RESTRICTED ACCESS IN
OPERATION.
ONLY PRE-PROGRAMMED DESTINATIONS AVAILABLE.
SELECT ONE OF THE FOLLOWING OPTIONS:
1) TEST SITE 01: E.D.
2) TEST SITE 02: Ø.F.
3) TEST SITE 03: H.S.

The last option was greyed out – Alice then realised that H.S. must stand for Hadron Services – and was therefore greyed out because they were already at that location. A cursor blinked on and off, waiting for a command. None of the children spoke, afraid this was another trick. After a minute or so, a system prompt came up:

YOU HAVE 30 SECONDS REMAINING TO MAKE YOUR SELECTION.
FAILURE TO SELECT WILL RESULT IN PERMANENT SHUT DOWN
OF THIS C-BEAN MARK 4.

'OK, guys, we have to do something,' Charlie urged.

'Yes, but which one?'

'I vote we go for Test Site One, E.D. Get it? "Edie"! What could go wrong with that?' Charlie joked, rolling his eyes at Edie, but Alice knew that in reality he was feeling terrified.

She cleared her throat.

'Test Site 01. Now.'

The emergency intervention had obviously made the C-Bean Mark 4 very unstable. The system would run for a while, then, without any warning, crash and reboot. Alice couldn't tell whether they had actually departed for Test Site 01 or not. Meanwhile, the C-Bean kept trying to show them an information briefing, but it had stopped and started so many times that Alice wasn't sure if she had understood things correctly. From what she could make out, Test Site 01 seemed to be some sort of gold recovery and production centre, located somewhere in the Amazon Basin, judging by the glimpse of a map of Brazil they were shown.

On all four walls around them, the C-Bean now displayed various snippets of old video footage of gold being mined at this location in the 21st century. There had evidently been some kind of gold rush there. Alice saw clips of trees being felled, gold being panned and men in suits shaking hands about some deal that had been struck. It was when she saw footage of a bulldozer digging the claggy yellow earth to make a new building that Alice started to wonder if it was the same place where they'd found the gold nugget. A date flashed up quickly – 2025 – and the voiceover explained how the world changed from using paper money that year and went back to using gold as the main global currency. It appeared that countries without gold to mine seized all the gold belonging to their people instead – there were images of men and women standing in long queues, forced to hand over wedding rings, watches and jewellery – and then a bit of a documentary showing how all of this was melted down and turned into rectangular ingots or tokens that were the new money system. Alice saw piles of the tokens glinting in vaults, each one stamped with a number. Then the walls went blank again as the C-Bean's system went down for the fifth time.

'There's something spookily familiar about all this, Charlie. Do you think it's the same place we found the gold nugget in 2018?' Alice asked slowly.

'Yeah, maybe we were sent there on purpose back in January – maybe the gold nugget was put there for us to find.'

'And Spix too.' Edie spoke for the first time.

'But why?' Alice half whispered.

The C-Bean's system came back up again before anyone could reply. It was as if it was trying to answer her question – apparently shortages of real gold meant that people started to experiment with making gold out of other metals, mercury in particular, whose chemical structure was not that different from gold. They found that if they changed the mercury particles using a nuclear process, they could fabricate gold quite easily. But the problem was not only that this was a very expensive thing to do, but also that the resulting gold was radioactive. However, it was still circulated on the black market, which meant that many people got sick from handling it and died.

All Alice could think about were the globules of mercury spilled on the forest floor, the mercury they'd accidentally spilled into the sea when they'd crashed the C-Bean on the rocks coming back from Australia, and the nuclear leak they'd discovered in the hollowed-out chamber on St Kilda that had given their fathers radiation sickness …

The C-Bean continued with its little lecture. Since 2060, improvements had been made to the synthetic production of gold. Scientists came up with the idea of using a giant particle accelerator 100 km in diameter to produce a non-radioactive version. Then, in 2089, a group of 'TS50 engineers' who had been working for CERN in Switzerland in 2039 on the new Hadron Antimatter Collider, defected to Brazil to build the giant accelerator at a top-secret facility, El Dorado.

Upon hearing the words Hadron and El Dorado in the same sentence, Alice's jaw dropped open. Edie and Charlie were also gawping at each other, speechless.

'So that's what E.D. really stands for – El Dorado,' Charlie said finally in a low voice. 'And yes, Alice, in answer to your question we have been here before.'

None of it meant anything to Rudy, of course, who had no idea the others had come here by accident one day back in January. While Charlie, Edie and Alice were still trying to figure out why they might have been brought here again, Rudy was busy staring at the walls because they looked like they were about to disintegrate.

'But what do they mean by "TS50 engineers", Charlie? Didn't Rudy say something about TS100? Rudy?' Alice's voice trailed away as she realised that Spex had scampered off through the porous remains of the C-Bean's walls into the space beyond, with Rudy following.

Alice and Charlie looked at each other. Edie grabbed Hannah's hand and started to walk off after them.

'Get the cardkey, Charlie – let's go.'

The part of the rainforest they'd arrived in looked dull, dusty and a lot less dense than Alice remembered. The overall impression was of masses of tall grey tree trunks against a gloomy grey sky. Up ahead were a high perimeter fence and a set of security gates with that familiar green-and-yellow El Dorado logo fixed to them, beside a post bristling with surveillance cameras. It was eerily quiet. Alice remembered the roar of insects and animals, the lush vegetation and the din of a waterfall the last time the C-Bean brought them here. This time there was no greenery – in fact no sign of any wildlife at all. Nor could she hear the waterfall. She ran to catch up with Rudy and Spex.

Rudy turned and pointed to a metal grille in the base of one of the trees, just where its roots spread into the ground. He put his finger to his lips for them to keep quiet. Alice noticed that all the trees had something similar, and from one or two of the grilles she saw a puff of steamy air emerging. Rudy seemed to be leading them away from the gates and into a part of the forest where there was a gap in the trees. He stopped and turned to face Alice with a distraught look on his face.

'What's the matter, Rudy?' Alice whispered.

'Is not good. All Trees here 3DPOs.'

'What does that mean?'

'I think he's saying they're fake,' Edie said bluntly. 'Some of them back there had loudspeakers in them.' She tapped one of the trunks and, sure enough, there was a resounding hollow sound. Rudy nodded vigorously. Alice bent down to examine a leaf that appeared to have fallen from one of the trees. It looked real enough but, when she handled it, it crumbled away into a fine green dust in her hand.

'They print Trees. Make look real 3D. No real Forest left now. Make animals too. Not like Bork. He real Dog.'

They walked a bit further. It was ferociously hot.

'So, no insects either? Is that why it's so quiet?'

'Tried print Bees. Not work. That why no Fruit,' Rudy explained, shaking his head.

Alice looked down at her feet. The ground felt real enough – it was still the same claggy yellow soil she remembered from last time. And the gold nugget must have been real, too, if Lori got so much money for it in Glasgow. But Alice now realised it was not something that had been dug out of the ground. For all she knew, it was a man-made lump of radioactive gold.

'Look out!'

A green-and-yellow flatbed truck came into view carrying wooden crates of some kind. They all ducked behind a tree as it sped past. Spex had picked up an invisible scent trail and seemed to know where he was going. He ran after the truck, and the children followed him. Ahead there were several discarded broken crates lying on the ground. Spex started sniffing the crates and wagging his tail. Alice gasped when she got close enough to read the label on one of them. It said:

LIVE SPECIES COURTESY OPERATION
SEABEAN DELIVERY DATE: 13 JUNE 2114

Charlie pointed for them to follow the truck, which was heading slowly towards a building just inside the security gates. As the gates started to slide open, Rudy leapt forwards, grabbed hold of the handle on the tailgate and jumped on the back of the truck, beckoning to the others to do the same. Edie and Hannah hung back but Alice and Charlie managed to leap up. Alice could see the back of the driver's head in the cab, wearing a green-and-yellow baseball cap. The dog trotted along behind the truck and, just before the gates slid shut, he ducked inside too, leaving Edie and Hannah watching forlornly from outside the El Dorado compound. Alice signalled for them to stay there, and Edie nodded gravely.

The truck drove into the delivery bay of the first building. Inside it was much cooler and quite dark. Alice could see row upon row of storage racking, ten metres high or more, and decided it was a vast warehouse. Spex suddenly darted off to the left down one of the aisles of racking marked 'M' and stopped to investigate one particular crate that had been deposited there. Rudy jumped down and followed him and, by the time Charlie and Alice did the same, the dog had ripped the whole side off. Suddenly a flurry of green, blue and yellow feathers surged into the air, almost in slow motion, the colours appearing to change from blue to green and back again. A label on the piece of crate by Alice's feet said 'Macaw Clones, derived from 2014 sample type SP045'. Once they started squawking, Alice realised they were all parrots. Then all at once from amongst the squawking came a lone cry, like a small, lost child:

Muito mau, perigroso!'

Alice rapidly scanned the seething mass of parrots – could it be? Or was she just imagining things? But who should rise up into the air and descend onto Alice's shoulder but an old friend, bobbing his head and tugging a strand of her hair with his beak.

'Spix! However did you get here?' Alice whispered incredulously. The bird moved from side to side along her shoulder, swaying to and fro as if he couldn't quite account for his whereabouts either. Spex started barking excitedly and jumping up to say hello to the parrot.

There were voices coming from the warehouse entrance and a torch beam suddenly flashed into the aisle. Alice glanced behind her and could see the silhouette of the truck driver walking towards them, scanning the aisle with his torch. Rudy quickly pulled Charlie and Alice behind the crate and they hid in the shadows. Charlie held Spex's muzzle to stop him from barking. Through the gaps in the crate they could see the parrots flapping around the truck driver, who was batting them away with his arms as he struggled to get something out of his pocket. He muttered something and then there was a single phut! like a shot from a gun with a silencer. All the parrots immediately stopped making a noise and dropped to the ground simultaneously, apart from Spix. Alice stared in horror at the carpet of blue-and-green birds, unable to fathom how the man had killed all of them with one shot. The truck driver grunted, then cleared a path between the creatures with his feet and walked off.

When he'd gone, Charlie picked up one of the inert parrots. There was no sign of any blood or injury and his eyes were still open.

'Is it dead?' Alice breathed, stroking the feathers.

'I don't think so, it's like he's been … switched off,' replied Charlie with a puzzled look on his face.

'They not real Bird. They cyborg too,' Rudy remarked, turning the creature over and showing them a panel under its tail bearing a printed 'UAT' serial number and the words 'CHICO® Colour-Changing Artificial Macaw. Made in Brazil'. Rudy then flicked a tiny switch on the side of the bird's beak and it began to ruffle its feathers and come alive again. It flew out of Charlie's hands to join Spix, who had perched on the edge of the storage racking.

'*Olá!*' Spix said cheerily to his cloned double, checking him out.

'Ooaa!' replied his cybernetic friend.

'Hmmm. Looks like there's room for improvement with Chico's mimic function,' joked Charlie.

Just then, a deafening announcement in Portuguese came over the audio system:

AVISO: GUARDA PROTEÇÃO A CORREDOR "M". INTRUSO!

'Come on – I think that means we need to get out of here,' Charlie hissed.

They ran to the end of the aisle and back into the delivery bay where the truck was parked. A security guard had just arrived with an enormous wolf-like creature straining on a leash. Spex slunk behind Alice, sensing he was no match for it. Rudy jumped up inside the cab of the truck and pressed a button that made the security gates start to open.

'Run!' Rudy shouted to Charlie and Alice, pointing to the gates.

Then he turned, strode towards the security guard, grabbed the wolf's collar with one hand, and then swung his other arm back in one fluid motion, landing a massive punch on the security guard's chin. Alice ran past just as the man's limbs crumpled under him and he fell to the ground. She watched Rudy feel inside one of the wolf's ears to find the switch and immobilise the cybernetic animal.

'*Vamos, vamos!*' fretted Spix, hovering nervously over the entire scene. Alice started running again.

Edie and Hannah appeared from behind some fake bushes opposite the gates and they all sprinted as fast as they could between the fake trees, back towards the spot where they'd arrived. Sweat was dripping into Alice's eyes. She wiped her face on her sleeve and looked up ahead. She could see Spex bounding along beside Rudy,

Edie and Hannah clinging to each other as they ran, Spix whirling around in circles over their heads, and Charlie out in front staring hard at the C-Bean's cardkey, willing the globe to spin and show him the way. Would their Mark 3 key still work? The C-Bean somehow didn't seem to be in a stable state. But that was nothing compared to the state of the world in 2118, where it appeared everything was, well… ruined. She had never felt so homesick in her whole life – she desperately wanted to get back home to St Kilda in 2018, back to where there was a real tree, real birds and real air, where the sky wasn't a crazy colour and where the village wasn't half under water – and, most of all, to where her family was all still in one piece.

The C-Bean Mark 4 presented them with only one pre-programmed option this time – they had no choice but to select 'Test Site 03: H.S.' and return to St Kilda, 2118.

'What if we arrive back inside the lab?' asked Edie. 'I can't bear the thought of going back inside there.'

Alice tried to input the coordinates she remembered for their schoolyard and even tried to request a different date, but the C-Bean responded with a pre-recorded announcement, similar to the one they'd heard when they were first abducted:

ANY ACTS INVOLVING MALICIOUS DAMAGE TO THE NATURAL COURSE OF EVENTS AND WILFUL MANIPULATION OF STATUTORY TIME ARE STRICTLY FORBIDDEN AND UNDER PRESENT LAW IF CONVICTED CARRY THE HARSHEST PENALTY: TS100.

'What on earth does that mean?' Charlie asked of no one in particular.

'It mean bad News.' Rudy looked glum.

'Rudy, can you please explain all this TS business? I don't understand,' Alice said impatiently.

'TS mean timeshift. People come from Before. Like You. You TS100 – I see Namecode 2018. Jump 100 Year. Most TS50. Bring for Knowhow.'

'Like those TS50 engineers, you mean? The ones they recruited from CERN to work on the El Dorado project?'

Rudy nodded.

'So does this TS100 penalty mean that the punishment for messing around with time is to send you another 100 years into the future – like to 2218?'

Another nod.

Judging by the terrible state of things in 2118, Alice couldn't begin to imagine what kind of worse fate awaited the poor person who received that kind of punishment.

'Is time travel illegal?' Edie enquired hopefully.

'Not allowed go Backwards, only Forwards. But still do. Black Market. People want go back whole Century, minus 100. Want swap for better Life. Want real Food. Want free Sniff. Want no War. Make People from Before come here. Swap. Timeshift in Blackbox. Costs much Gold.'

Alice allowed this new information to sink in, and it triggered a whole new set of questions in her head: Who had brought them to 2118, and why? Was it because someone wanted their knowhow? But what could a bunch of schoolkids know? Or had there been some case of mistaken identity? Was that why Dr Foster appeared in Liverpool, to warn her they were about to be abducted – is that why he said there was something wrong with the C-Bean? Or had they been kidnapped by Hadron Services in order that some people from 2118 could swap places with them? Were they simply here because someone had paid a fortune for the privilege of being taken back to 2018, to take their places and be able to live a better life? Did that mean Alice and her classmates were the unwitting victims of this illegal black-market time-travel operation? And, if so, were they now stranded in 2118 for ever? Rudy was their only way to get answers.

'Is that what Hadron Services do, Rudy? Help people timeshift?'

'Yes. Fix Blackbox for Timeshift.'

'Have you ever met Commander Hadron, Rudy?'

'He bad Man. Many Enemy. This his Finger,' Rudy informed her proudly, patting his pocket.

Alice grimaced and decided she would rather not know how he had come by Commander Hadron's index finger. The very thought of it made her feel sick. Without realising it, she had been pacing around the C-Bean with Spex and Spix following her, while Charlie, Rudy, Edie and Hannah lay in the middle on a pile of sleeping bags.

'What does he want with us?' she murmured. 'It doesn't make any sense.'

There was an abrupt judder, and the C-Bean seemed to bounce slightly. Alice felt a sharp pain in her lower stomach. She clutched her belly and saw that the others were doing the same. The C-Bean went into another shut-down cycle and then started to reboot. Lines of computer code scrolled up the walls and then they heard a further announcement:

WELCOME TO 2118. MY NAME IS COMMANDER HADRON. AS EXCLUSIVE AND VALUED MEMBERS OF OUR REVOLUTIONARY TS100 PROGRAMME, YOU WILL NOW UNDERGO A COMPREHENSIVE INDUCTION SESSION WITH ONE OF HADRON SERVICES' AGENTS. YOU HAVE BEEN ASSIGNED AGENT AFOS21XV.

Hearing this made Rudy's yellow eyes go wide with fear and he scrambled to his feet. It was the same namecode of the guard who had pursued him when he'd escaped.

'Rudy take Agent,' he said, asserting himself. Everyone was startled by Rudy's sudden change of mood. Alice watched as he increased the flow rate on his oxygen unit, flipped open the silver penknife, rolled back his shoulders and then stood in front of the exit door, poised and ready to spring into action as soon as it opened.

A voice queried: 'Passenger verification' and the C-Bean responded by supplying an alphabetical arrival list of its five passengers:

AROB2007
CCHE2006
EBUR2007
HBUR2010
RBOK2104

The voice confirmed this information – 'Verification complete' – and the door to the C-Bean opened.

Standing outside the meet them was a man with white curly hair, wearing sneakers and a grey duffle coat. It was none other than Dr Foster. He smiled at the children and stepped forward.

'Welcome. I am your agent, AFOS21XV, but you can call me Dr Foster. I hope you had a pleasant journey,' he said in a flat monotone. 'Rudy, may I have my knife back, please?'

In one move, Rudy leapt towards him and rugby-tackled him to the ground. He seemed to be struggling to take something off Dr Foster's wrist. Alice could see that her teacher was still wearing some kind of identity bracelet. Dr Foster's limbs were flailing around uselessly.

'Charlie, help! Need neutralise Cyborg.'

'Don't worry Rudy, that man's not a cyborg – he's our old teacher, Dr Foster,' Hannah assured him, looking relieved to see a familiar face at last. Spex was not so sure, and started barking.

Alice tried to step forward to stop Rudy from hurting Dr Foster, but Spix started making a fuss.

'*Muito mau, muito mau!*' the parrot warned, strangely agitated by the sight of the agent.

'Hannah, Alice, stay back! Rudy might be right – maybe he's fake too,' Edie said, looking horrified at the three bodies grappling in front of them.

Dr Foster's face seemed to be going through a whole collection of different expressions, as if rehearsing a palette of emoticons. When Charlie finally managed to remove the bracelet, Alice watched in astonishment as Dr Foster's head twitched a little and then rotated a full 360 degrees before coming back to its original position with the eyes shut.

'Safe now,' panted Rudy. 'Quick, we go.'

Alice had been so shocked by the bizarre reappearance of Dr

Foster and the realisation that he was clearly not who she thought, that she hadn't even noticed where they had arrived. But, judging by the look on Edie's face, it was exactly as she'd feared – they were in one of Hadron's laboratories. Surrounding the C-Bean were trolleys with stainless steel instruments laid out, and on a desk in the corner Alice saw a laptop just like Karla's that had been partially dismantled. Alice walked across the room to take a closer look.

'C'mon Alice, we haven't got time to look around,' urged Charlie. 'I've got the cardkey – now let's just go!'

Alice turned to look at the C-Bean. She was worried that if they left it here in the lab with these instruments, the people in the green gowns with masks might take their C-Bean apart too – like they did to Spex, judging by his scars – and then they would never be able to get back to 2018.

She suddenly felt exhausted and overwhelmed by everything that had happened. The C-Bean was their only link to home in this cruel future world. A small tear welled up in the corner of her eye but, just as it began to roll down her cheek, the C-Bean wobbled in sympathy and obediently disappeared. Alice let out a sigh of relief.

'Alice, come!' Rudy had opened the pale green door with the circular vision panel and was leading everyone out and back into the long curving corridor. It was icy cold compared to the fake forest in Brazil, and her breath was forming in a cloud in front of her face. Spix suddenly landed on her shoulder and gripped tight. Rudy was heading for the airlock, the others running along behind him in single file and Spex weaving in between their legs. When they reached the airlock, Rudy touched the control pad with the severed finger and quickly ushered the children through, just as the deafening alarm flared up.

Rudy slammed the airlock door shut and the alarm stopped. They all stood panting in the dark chamber beneath the gun emplacement, ears ringing and hearts pumping, reeling from the events of the past ten minutes. It was only after they'd got their breath back, and Charlie found he had Sam's wind-up torch in his pocket, that they realised the hatch at the top of the ladder was securely closed up.

'We're trapped!' cried Alice in dismay, feeling just like she imagined Karla did when she was claustrophobic.

'Great! So let me get this right – we manage to get away from the fake jungle, out of the C-Bean, away from that weirdo version of Dr Foster, then escape from Hadron's lab, only to find we're on St Kilda but it's still 2118 and we're in a worse mess than ever,' groaned Edie.

Hannah started to cry. 'Poor Dr Foster,' she sobbed. Spex went up to her and licked her hand in sympathy.

Rudy climbed up the ladder to inspect the underside of the hatch, but there was obviously no way of rotating the gun to open it from the inside. He pummelled it angrily with his fists and grumbled some words in a language that Alice didn't understand. The wind-up torch clicked off and they were plunged into darkness again. She heard Rudy climb back down the ladder and rummage in his bag for something. Alice could see the blue light of the Mailboat device receiving a message. Rudy frowned and looked like he was about to reply, but suddenly changed his mind and hurled it against the roof of the chamber in a frustrated outburst.

The Mailboat clanged off the rock and landed somewhere near Edie's feet. She knelt down to look for it.

'Hey, steady on, mate. No need to lose the plot just yet,' said Charlie reproachfully.

'Is more Trouble now – we all get TS100,' Rudy snorted and kicked a loose rock but said nothing about what he had just learned. Alice realised the message he'd received must have been to inform him that they all faced the punishment of being shipped to 2218.

'Charlie, can I have the torch please?' Alice asked quietly.

Charlie wound it up again and flashed it on, pointing it to where she was kneeling. The Mailboat lay in pieces on the ground next to their time capsule.

'It's broken, isn't it?' sobbed Hannah.

'Now what do we do?' Edie shrieked, glaring at Rudy, who stared helplessly back at her. 'Rudy, that was really stupid. For a start you could have really hurt someone. And now we don't have any means of communicating with anyone outside this cave!' she added petulantly.

Edie's tone of voice reminded Alice of the time her sister Lori was having a go at her and, in that same moment, Alice realised she was so homesick she was even missing Lori. She bent down to gather up the broken pieces and, as she opened the lid of the time capsule to clear the broken Mailboat away, her hand brushed past something that hadn't been there before. The torch switched off.

'Charlie, the torch – quick, wind it up again!' she said in an urgent whisper.

'What is it?'

'Someone's left a note inside the time capsule.'

Alice's Blog

Wednesday 12th September 2018

Just as I was reading out the note from Sam F saying they had escaped and were going to hide out in the old schoolroom and wait for us, we heard voices above ground. There was a lot of grinding and scraping as someone tried to get the hatch open. We didn't realise then, but it was the Sams. They'd found a metal pole and bit by bit managed to get the rusty hatch to budge. Suddenly they flipped it open, Spix flew up into the sky and we all climbed out. They were a bit surprised to see this tall black kid with us, but Rudy had calmed down by then and even managed a friendly grin.

As it was raining hard when we got above ground, we ran round to the chapel to take cover. The Sams told us breathlessly how they were chased by 'some guy who looked just like Dr Foster' but that he tripped over and they got away and hid in a cleit. We told them he was there to meet us when we arrived back in the C-Bean and when Rudy added 'He Cyborg. He Hadron guard' the two Sams gawped at each other going 'No way!' To be honest, the rest of us are still trying to get our heads around the fact that our teacher was an imposter.

Then, just as Rudy was about to untag the boys' bioports and get them sorted with oxygen units, who should walk into the chapel but Reverend Sinclair! 'Ah, children, thank God, you've come back! We have all been praying so hard for your safe return. Hallelujah!' The vicar was so overjoyed to see us again he didn't even notice Rudy. Instead he ran out of the chapel, proclaiming 'a miracle has befallen the good people of St Kilda'.

We all just stood there in a daze. Rudy asked in a quiet voice, 'We timeshift? TS100? This your Time?' I went over to the window to check. I could just about make out through the dreary rain that the tide was out, our white sandy beach was right where it should be, and both the sea and the sky seemed to be back to normal. No flooding in the Bay, no weird colours in the sky, just some nice plain old Scottish rain. I had never felt so happy in my entire life! I ran outside and the others followed and we all pranced round the schoolyard, seven children, a dog and a parrot all doing a silly little dance, singing songs and getting soaking wet. But we didn't care.

I still haven't worked out what happened yesterday – it was as if the C-Bean's powers had seeped out into that underground chamber and let us time travel back to 2018 without the pod itself actually being there, just like when I found myself back in the present with Lady Grange. Perhaps it was because Charlie still had the Mark 3 cardkey in his pocket. When he gave it back to me, the black cube loomed into view in the middle of where we were dancing. The door opened as if to say 'hi' and Rudy walked inside. He was laughing and crying at the same time. He stood in the middle of the pod and said triumphantly, 'I Timeshift! Rudy now City of Smiles. First time since little Boy.' Hearing him say that, the C-Bean produced a steaming bowl of rice and some chopsticks, and then started displaying pictures of Jutland on all its walls, like it was trying to make him feel really at home. Rudy grinned from ear to ear, ate the rice and chatted to us about the places he recognised. Then he curled up on the floor inside the pod like a baby and fell asleep with Spex by his side.

We left the two of them there to rest and walked off up Main Street, six tired, wet, happy children. Our parents came running out of our houses to meet us, and a lot more tears were shed.

When I tried to tell Mum and Dad everything that had happened since we went to sleep inside the C-Bean the night of our sleepover, at first they were really angry that we'd gone against their instructions. But I kept telling them we didn't do it on purpose – we were abducted - the C-Bean just got taken to 2118. Of course, it all sounded pretty crazy, so in the end they decided I was imagining things and needed to rest. It was when I started telling them about Commander Hadron's secret underground lab in 2118, and about Dr Foster being a cyborg, and about how we went to El Dorado with its fake trees, and that there are no birds or animals or fruit or bees in 2118, they just said 'Poor Alice, whatever's the matter with you?' The only thing Dad took any notice of was when I said 'You know, Dad, in the future everywhere is flooded. Even St Kilda. The sea was right up to Main Street. I saw it with my own eyes.' He looked at me, and said in a solemn voice, 'I'm sure you're right, Alice. The marine biologists who are coming over on Sunday just sent me an email with the latest report saying sea rise is unstoppable - our glaciers and ice caps will have melted away completely by then'.

Thursday 13th September 2018

Something awful happened this morning. While I was still in bed asleep, some people arrived in a helicopter to confiscate the C-Bean like they said they would, which is bad enough, but of course it means they also took it with stowaways inside – Rudy and Spex! When Mum and Mr McLintock went down to school at nine o'clock to sign for it to be taken away, they didn't think to check inside, and so the two pilots just attached the C-Bean to the helicopter and flew off.

Now my parents think I really have gone mad because when they told me the news at lunchtime I kept saying 'But what about Rudy and Spex? They were inside the C-Bean!' Mum sat by my bed and stroked my hair for ages saying there was nothing to worry about, I was home safe and sound. Poor Rudy, I hope he's OK. He's only just arrived in 2018, and now this happens. And Spex – he's been through more than enough already.

Friday 14th September 2018

It gets worse! Mum just got a phone call from the Ministry of Defence at eight o'clock this morning to say someone would be arriving on St Kilda shortly to impound the C-Bean so they could carry out a full investigation into the 'suspicious circumstances' that have been brought to their attention. Mum sounded all confused on the phone. She was trying to explain to the person on the other end that the C-Bean had already been taken away. I could tell by her tone of voice she was starting to think something didn't quite add up.

Just now Mum and Dad were talking in the kitchen trying to figure out what could have happened. They were mentioning some of the things I've been telling them about Rudy and stuff. Mum is really panicking. She said something about checking the paperwork, so Dad's gone back down to school to fetch all the forms Mum signed to have a closer look at them.

PS You'll never believe it, but five minutes ago, Dad burst through the back door yelling 'Jen, did you realise the person who authorised the C-Bean's removal yesterday was Karla Ingermann?'

It was Saturday evening and Alice was at home looking after her baby brother Kit while her parents were round at the Burneys. She was having difficulty coming to terms with the fact that the C-Bean, Spex and Rudy were, more than likely, gone for good. Neither of her parents had been able to get any information about Karla Ingermann, and the two Ministry of Defence officers, who had arrived the previous day to fetch the C-Bean and were obliged to leave empty-handed, accused the people of St Kilda of withholding information and obstructing their investigation. Alice had tried her best to explain to the officers and to her parents what had really happened, but it just seemed to make matters worse.

Alice was expecting Charlie and Edie to arrive at any minute – they were going to watch a DVD together. There was a loud knock on the door. She thought Charlie was messing about, because usually he just walked straight in without knocking – no one ever locked their front door on St Kilda.

'Come in,' Alice yelled, tucking Kit into his cot.

There was a second knock, more urgent this time.

'What are you playing at, Charlie?' Alice frowned and went to the door.

There on her doorstep stood Rudy and a smaller, skinnier person dressed in black jeans with a black hoodie pulled over their face. Whoever it was also had their arms behind their back and Rudy appeared to have a firm grip on them. He pushed the person forwards and the hood fell down, revealing spiky red hair and a pale freckly face.

'Karla!' Alice gasped. She felt a strange frozen wrench in the pit of her stomach.

No one spoke. Alice could hear Kit murmuring in his cot. Her heart was beating fast. Karla was looking at the floor, a muscle twitching in her jaw. Rudy let out a loud sigh and Alice couldn't tell if he was exhausted or just exasperated.

'Rudy, are you OK? I'm so glad to see you! Whatever happened?'

'KROB2090 tell whole Story, Alice,' Rudy assured her, handing Alice the Mark 3 cardkey before leading Karla to the sofa, where he made her sit down.

'I should hope so. There are lots of things I'd like to know. Charlie and Edie will be here any second. You can tell all of us together,' Alice said firmly. The whole situation felt peculiarly formal. Alice realised this would be her chance to conduct her own interrogation. There was an awkward pause.

'Rudy, can I get you anything to eat or drink?'

Rudy shook his head and continued to stand guard behind the sofa in case Karla tried to escape. Finally, Alice heard the door open and Charlie and Edie walked into the living room carrying a bowl of home-made popcorn.

'We did it salty this time, Alice, 'cos we know you prefer it … Oh,' Edie's voice trailed away when she caught sight of the two extra people. Charlie raised his eyebrows.

'You didn't tell us it was going to be a party, Alice. We'd have brought more to eat,' he said wryly.

'I didn't know they were coming,' remarked Alice, wondering how this whole scene was going to play out. 'But apparently Karla can explain everything. So why don't you sit down?'

Karla sneezed loudly and asked for a tissue.

'I'm very allergic,' she said, a little too pitifully.

'Yes, we've noticed. You're always sniffing and sneezing. Why is that?' asked Alice, relieved to find an easy way to start the conversation.

'In 2118, where I come from, there is no real pollen. Every plant and every crop is pollinated artificially. There are no bees or butterflies.' She paused and Alice noticed something creep out from behind the sofa – it was Spex. Karla looked at the dog and rolled her eyes.

'I am also allergic to animal fur,' she continued. 'Where I come from, there are no real animals, either. So my body is not used to dealing with such things.'

'I see,' said Alice, patting Spex, who had lain down beside her. She was thrilled to have him back, but she couldn't afford to show it now, not while she was conducting this interrogation. What Karla was saying seemed to make sense in terms of what Rudy had told her.

'I take it that KROB2090 is your namecode and 2090 is your birthdate,' said Alice, doing a quick sum in her head. 'So you're 28, right?'

Karla nodded.

'But we know for a fact that Karla Ingermann is not your real name. Charlie found your passport. Everyone around here thinks you're an industrial spy working for a rival German company that's trying to steal the C-Bean idea from the people who really invented it. But I did begin to wonder if you were from the future. The label on your laptop says it was last checked on 1 April 2118, for a start. So who in actual fact are you, where do you come from and why did the C-Bean record your laptop as belonging to Karla Robertson?'

'Because my name is Karla Robertson.'

'Let's not play games, Karla. We need to know the truth now,' Alice said, trying not to get cross.

'I am telling the truth, Alice. Ingermann is the name of the suburb where I grew up. But my real name is Robertson. I work for Hadron Services. Commander Hadron owns all the rights to the C-Bean invention now – he inherited them from his old boss. I was originally sent here from 2118 to secure the safe return of Hadron Services' property – the C-Bean Mark 3. I didn't want to go, but Hadron insisted. After the C-Bean broke and the cyborg-supported mission went wrong, he said sending me was the only solution to get things back on track.'

'I don't get it. What mission?' Charlie demanded, glowering at Karla from the other side of the room.

'They realised that sending the cyborg Dr Foster to 2018 wasn't working when they started getting data reports from the C-Bean saying that the cyborg had lost control of the mission, so Hadron pulled him off the job. Then, to make matters worse, before he could send a replacement, you went off to Hong Kong and Australia unsupervised. They sent another cyborg to St Kilda, Melbourne, to try and steer you back on course. Remember the kumalak fortune-teller? That was also a cyborg, Alice …'

'Who are you talking about?' interrupted Charlie.

'I think she means the fake Dr Foster, stupid,' Edie mumbled.

'So wait – let me get this straight. You're telling us that you work for Hadron's company in 2118 and they sent a C-Bean to St Kilda with a cyborg teacher in tow and then, when it didn't go according to plan, they sent you back in time instead to sort things out. But why?' Charlie was pacing up and down impatiently.

'Keep your voice down, Charlie. We don't want to wake Kit,' Alice whispered.

'Shut up, Alice. Who cares about your brother when we've got all this going on?' growled Charlie. 'So come on, Karla, answer me – why?'

'Because of the close match between our DNA,' Karla said quietly, biting her lip. She turned to face Alice. 'Look, I shouldn't be telling you this. But since everything's gone wrong, I might as well.'

'Tell me what?'

'Your brother is part of all this, Alice.'

'What do you mean?'

'Your brother – Kit Robertson – is my Dad.'

Awhole new and unidentified feeling of rage and confusion surged through Alice's body. She stared at Karla unblinkingly.

'That's not possible,' she stuttered, once again doing the mental maths. 'My brother would be a hundred years old in 2118.'

'He timeshifted, Alice,' Karla's voice was softer and more gentle all of a sudden. 'You need to understand that after your dad was called up and then disappeared during World War III, and your mum got sick and died in 2029, your sister Lori had to look after Kit. It was not an easy time for either of them. The minute he left college he agreed to become a TS50 and moved to the future to work on a top-secret project at El Dorado in Brazil.'

Alice's brain was reeling with all this information concerning her family. It felt as if her head was full of those teeming particles, like the outer surface of the replica C-Bean she'd been taken to during her interrogation. She tried to keep her mind on the current situation, but bits and pieces kept flying out. She had this constant edgy feeling that there was no longer any overall stable pattern of events. Nothing could be thought of as having a strict chronological order, and everything seemed to loop round and join up to something else – Dr Foster, Karla, her brother, El Dorado, Hadron. What next?

'So what you're saying is that Kit timeshifted fifty years, met someone … and then you were born in 2090?' Alice asked slowly.

'I know this is awkward for you, Alice. You weren't meant to find out like this. But you didn't cooperate with us during your interrogation like we expected. They must have got your dosage or the psychological profiling wrong. You wouldn't respond. Neither would Charlie. It's a shame because Dad went to such a lot of trouble making your room. When it didn't work, he had no choice but to put both you and Charlie in solitary de-confinement. Except that you escaped. Just like the last time, when you abandoned me in 1918. I was so frightened there. I thought I'd never get home again. It was your fault I got stuck there as a prisoner of war, Alice. But you – it's like you and the C-Bean are one seamless entity, and you can just control it with the power of your own thought! Dad told me everything would be fine, that it would be an easy first job. But it was a lie and I'm still angry. When I finally escaped from Donald's time back to 2118, Dad just said he had no idea you would have so much control over the C-Bean. It took me forever to figure out a way to make the C-Bean come back and fetch me. I don't understand why I have so little influence over it – I passed all the training with top marks!' Karla protested tearfully, the muscles in her jaw tensing up again.

'Hang on a minute!' Alice said, raising her arms as if to protect herself from this latest onslaught. 'Forget Donald and all that 1918 nonsense for a moment. So are you seriously trying to tell me that your Dad – my brother – is Commander Hadron?'

Karla didn't reply. She wouldn't look Alice in the eye. Her breathing sounded strange. She sniffed and then her head flopped forward, the hood falling over her face.

'Karla, speak to me!'

After Karla collapsed and they couldn't seem to rouse her, Charlie and Rudy carried her into Alice's bedroom and laid her on the bed.

'She funny Colour,' Rudy observed.

'But she is still breathing, right?' Edie asked, taking off Karla's hoodie and grabbing her wrist to feel her pulse, like she'd seen her mum do on countless occasions. 'Charlie, get her a glass of water, will you?'

'What are we going to do with her? And Rudy? Where are they going to stay?' Edie was fretting when Charlie returned with the drink.

'Who cares?' said Charlie. 'It's not our problem.'

'Well, in my opinion, it is our problem,' Edie insisted. 'I mean, if it wasn't for us taking off in the C-Bean in the first place, we wouldn't be in this situation. Alice, what do you think?' Edie turned round and realised that Alice had not left the living room.

'Charlie, go and see if Alice is alright. She must be feeling pretty shaken up by everything Karla let out just then.'

Charlie found Alice beside Kit's cot, stroking his downy red hair. There were tears rolling down her face.

'You know, he does kind of look like Karla, when you think about it. They have the same colour hair, and his nose is a bit similar, too,' she said miserably.

'Look, I know this is about as weird as it gets – meeting your brother's kid from the future and finding out about all the crappy things that lie ahead for your parents and everything – but we can't wind back time now to where we didn't know all of this stuff, Alice. So we're just going to have to deal with it, figure it all out, and maybe try to use what we know to make things less bad than they might otherwise be.'

'How do you mean?'

'Well, like we used time travel to make our dads better, get rid of that nuclear dump, save those babies from dying, and rescue Donald so he didn't die, remember? We've already moved mountains, Alice! Think what else we could do with this kind of knowledge about the future.'

Alice shrugged and dried her eyes.

'You're right. I just can't think about it right now. Maybe tomorrow.'

'OK. Hey, I've had an idea – how about Karla stays with Lady Grange this evening?'

'Mmm.'

'She won't ask any questions. We could ask Rudy to keep watch – sleep on the sofa or something – to make sure Karla doesn't run off or do anything stupid.'

'Whatever you think is best,' said Alice absent-mindedly.

Between them, Charlie and Rudy managed to escort Karla back down Main Street to Lady Grange's cottage. The cool autumn breeze seemed to revive her when they went outside and, by the time they knocked on Lady Grange's front door, Karla was able to walk by herself. Lady Grange appeared in a nightgown holding her ornate candlestick. She stared at them with a puzzled expression and seemed a little bit tipsy.

'What is it, Charlie my dear?' she hiccupped.

'Do you have room for two visitors, Lady Grange? They just arrived today. Like you did, erm… from another time. It's all a bit hush-hush, you know. The other grown-ups don't know yet. They just need somewhere to sleep.'

Lady Grange held the candle up to have a better look at Karla.

'You look familiar,' she slurred. 'I've seen those clothes before. Do I know you?'

Karla didn't speak.

'She's Alice's niece, Lady Grange.'

'I see.'

'The other visitor is a poor boy from Jutland who hasn't seen his family for years, like you,' Charlie said, artfully appealing to Lady Grange's sympathies.

At first Lady Grange looked doubtfully at Rudy, who responded with a quick flash of his toothless grin. She pursed her lips for a moment, and then handed Rudy the candlestick.

'You poor child. Ah, how I long to see my lovely babies. So far, far away. Come inside, dear boy. You look famished. I have some nice leftover stew you can eat.'

Alice's Blog

Sunday 16th September 2018, 11am

I hardly know where to start. A lot has happened since Rudy kidnapped Karla and brought her back to St Kilda in the C-Bean. It was very brave of him - but then I'm sure he must have been so angry and disappointed when he arrived back in 2118 it made him determined to get back here somehow. Besides, Hadron's people weren't expecting to find a boy and a dog inside the C-Bean when they summoned it. Apparently Rudy and Spex took them all by surprise, and once Rudy realised Karla was KROB2090 and that she knew how to control the C-Bean, he took her hostage with the penknife, shoved her inside the pod, and made her bring it back here.

Charlie thinks it serves Karla right after she threatened Donald and me in 1918. But strangely enough, I actually feel sorry for her. Charlie says I'm just being soft because I'm related to her. But it's not that. However much what Karla said has upset me, I can't help thinking none of it's her fault. It's my brother's doing really. Karla said herself she didn't want to have anything to do with the C-Bean mission, but he didn't give her a choice.

Last night I fell asleep beside Kit's cot. Mum and Dad said they found me with my arm around the baby when they got back from the Burneys. I don't remember them carrying me back to my bed. This morning Mum asked me who the black hoodie belonged to. I didn't know what she was talking about at first until Charlie came round and I remembered. He told Mum the hoodie was his. Then he whispered in my ear 'Houston, we have a problem'. It turned out that he'd taken Karla and Rudy to Lady Grange's house last night, and she'd agreed to let them stay there, only instead of going to bed, Rudy helped himself to her drinks cabinet in the night and when Charlie went over this morning, he found Rudy in a drunken stupor. Thankfully Lady Grange wasn't up and Karla hadn't escaped, so Charlie took Rudy up to Old Jim's underground house, gave him a banana and left him to sober up.

The team of marine biologists from Portugal are turning up on the ferry in a couple of hours' time, so Mum and Dad left the house bright and early this morning to get a big welcome lunch ready down at Evaw's offices with Charlie's parents. After lunch Dad says they're going to install a proper sea level marker down by the jetty. I told Dad before he left the house that the marker was completely under water in 2118 and he gave me this worried look like he thinks I've gone completely mad. I hope not, because otherwise we'll never work out what to do about Karla and Rudy. And the C-Bean.

To wind Karla up, Charlie told her this morning that unless she 'spills the beans' as he put it, he would have to put her in Jim's mouldy old hovel too tonight. She reacted really weirdly, probably because she gets claustrophobic in confined spaces. Just the idea of it has made Karla keen to tell us the rest of her story - she's agreed to have another meeting today. I'm not sure I am ready to hear any more yet, but I do want to get to the bottom of everything, and more than anything I want to understand why the whole C-Bean thing happened to us in the first place.

It was Charlie's idea to have the meeting in the C-Bean. He escorted Karla from Lady Grange's house, and Alice used the cardkey to make the C-Bean materialise in the schoolyard while Charlie and Edie went to get Rudy from Old Jim's underground house. When Alice and Karla stepped into the C-Bean, Alice realised that the last time they'd been inside it together was when Karla threatened Alice with a knife and Donald had to intervene to stop her. She was glad Spex was there this time to protect her if Karla tried to do something violent.

However, on this occasion Karla seemed quite calm and contrite, and it occurred to Alice that she must have been thinking about the same event because Karla sat down on the floor and suddenly blurted out a little speech about it.

'I'm sorry I was so unfriendly when we were prisoners together, Alice. I didn't know how much I was allowed to tell you – they didn't brief me about that part properly before I was sent to 2018 – so when you said I'd been talking in my sleep and that I'd mentioned something about Plan B, the only thing I could think to do was stop talking to you altogether. I could not understand why Dad wasn't calling me off the project when things were going so much worse than when the cyborg Dr Foster was here.'

'That's OK,' Alice said, quite taken aback. 'But what exactly is Plan B?'

Karla sighed. 'There's a lot more to what Hadron Services does than simply enabling people to timeshift, Alice. It started off as a totally different kind of project, doing something really positive – they were basically using a prototype C-Bean to bring species of plants and animals from the past that were extinct in the future, so they could breed or grow them again and replenish the planet's gene pool. That was Plan A – bringing live samples forward in time. Dad – I mean Kit – used to joke about it being a kind of reverse Noah's Ark, but its official project name was Operation Seabean – named after those seeds that wash up on beaches sometimes. Dad gave me one once. I think it's called a Mary's Bean. Your mum gave it to him. Anyway, he still gives this little speech to all the new H.S. employees about how their role is to operate like a seabean – bringing the possibility of life from one place to another, in the hope that it will germinate there.'

Alice was pacing round the C-Bean, remembering the Mary's Bean she'd found in her Christmas stocking and given to her mother as a good-luck present the night before her brother was born. She wondered if it was the same one that Karla now had. She suddenly felt quite upset and needed to change the subject.

'Why did they call the time-travel device a "C-Bean" with a C, and not "Seabean"?'

'Because the default timeshift period was set to 100 years, so Dad's boss came up with the idea of "C-Bean" – the letter C is the Roman numeral for a hundred – so it's basically a "bean" or pod that can travel 100 years through time.'

'Cool, I like that,' Alice said, wiping her eyes. Then she remembered her original question.

'You still haven't told me what Plan B is, Karla.'

'OK. Here goes … When the public got to know about the new animal species arriving from the past, Dad's boss started getting requests from people who wanted to go backwards in time. But they'd done some research that showed it could be bad for your health, as well as messing around with the time sequence. They ran a load of tests, sending mice back and forth in time, which confirmed the risks but it got them into a whole lot of trouble with the Animal Protection League. A year later the International Senate passed a worldwide law making it illegal to go back in time. That wasn't just because of the health risks, but also because they realised the more people that went back in time, the more it was just going to create problems in the past – I mean in your time.'

'And did that make them stop?'

'Nowhere near – the threat of imprisonment and severe illness was never going to be enough to stop people wanting to timeshift. Once Dad's boss realised he had a huge number of customers willing to pay a hefty price tag to timeshift back to a better time, he cashed in. That was the start of Plan B, and it's when the C-Bean project turned into something much less noble. They have a waiting list of over a hundred thousand people now,' Karla paused.

'And what about the crates we saw in El Dorado, marked "Operation Seabean"? There were loads of fake animals there. Are they that part of Plan B, too?'

'You weren't supposed to go there – to Brazil, I mean. Looking back, I blame El Dorado for everything – Kit was basically a good man and a talented scientist and then he went to work for the wrong guys,' Karla said knowingly, pushing her glasses back up her nose. She paused. Alice was looking at her doubtfully, waiting for more of an explanation.

'People get very desperate and devious when there's not enough to go round, Alice. You've seen for yourself already how much damage has been done to the world's ecological balance in 2118 – the climate has changed massively everywhere. With so many countries flooded, the places that aren't underwater are hopelessly overcrowded. Food is a real issue. People are starving and getting ill …'

'Like St Kilda in the olden days …' said Alice.

'Exactly. It was all over the news when St Kilda was evacuated for the second time, exactly a hundred years later in 2030 during World War III, for the same reasons as in 1930 – because people were starving, getting ill and dying. By 2110, it was happening the world over – and people would do anything just to stay alive – you name it, looting, killing, fighting. There were tribes all over the place smuggling gold, bees, food and water illegally. And, in Dad's case, trafficking animals and humans as well. Kit's done a bit of all of it in his time.'

'You make my brother sound like a pirate.'

'Well, he is. Especially once he started working at Øbsidon.'

Alice's head was starting to reel.

'Øbsidon. OK, slow down, Karla. That's something else you need to fill me in on – Spex has "Øbsidon" engraved on his collar. Look!' Alice bent down and showed Karla the gold-and-black disk.

'Is James Ferguson something to do with Øbsidon?' continued Alice. 'He mentioned it a few times in his notebooks – isn't it some kind of flammable material he once invented? Ever since our house caught fire, I've been wondering if Øbsidon was the black rubbery stuff they put on the back of the C-Bean Mark 4 cardkey and if that's what made the fire start. What do you know about it, Karla? You've got to tell me! Is the C-Bean owned by Øbsidon? Charlie and I read something about a factory in China – is that where Øbsidon is made?' Alice stopped in full flow, breathless and dizzy all of a sudden. Karla paused, studying Alice's face.

'You saw what was in James' notebooks?'

Alice nodded and Karla looked quite shocked.

'Maybe if you want all of this to make sense, we actually need to go there and meet him,' Karla mused out loud.

'Go where? Meet who? My brother?'

'No, Foster.'

Sensing that Alice was starting to feel frantic and perhaps realising that Karla needed a little help in explaining everything, the C-Bean began singing the sea shanty to her, and its white walls became a sort of photo album of images of someone with white curly hair in a lab coat, who looked exactly like their old teacher, smiling into the camera as he posed with various pairs of animals: badgers, crocodiles, eagles, gorillas, leopards, turtles, monkeys, iguanas, penguins, wolves.

'I thought Foster was a cyborg. Is that him in the pictures with animals that have been imported to the future as part of Plan A?' Alice asked, staring at the walls in awe.

'Yes and no.'

'What do you mean?'

'The man in the pictures, who you recognise as Dr Foster, your old teacher – and who does indeed look exactly like the cyborg Hadron Services sent back to 2018 – is actually the real Dr Foster.'

'I still don't get it. Who is he?'

'He's the real person on whom your teacher – the cyborg – was based, or copied from, if you will. The real Dr Foster was Dad's boss and mentor for many years. He's the C-Bean's real designer – not me. He's also the guy in charge of Øbsidon and the person who set up Operation Seabean and subsequently Plan B.'

'I see. So where is the real Dr Foster now?'

'It depends what you mean by "now", Alice. In 2018, of course, he is not yet born. In my now – 2118 – he has been dead for eight years ...' Karla's voice trailed off.

'Listen, Alice – maybe this isn't such a disaster, after all.' Karla stood up and starting cleaning her glasses. 'When Rudy kidnapped me, I thought it couldn't get any worse, but you've just given me an idea. You could put a stop to all this. You could put an end to Plan B for good – confront Dr Foster in person and convince him that what he's doing is wrong. Think about it – if we allow people from the future to go back 100 years, it'll create even more pressure on the earth's limited resources in your time. The sheer impact of that extra burden of human population will make climate change escalate totally out of control. The earth will be completely uninhabitable within just a few decades.' Karla put her glasses back on and blinked at Alice.

'Hang on, Karla. I still don't get the connection between Kit and the real Dr Foster.'

'Foster was an entrepreneur – some say a genius. He developed a time-travel algorithm and built the first C-Bean using a revolutionary material he'd invented called Øbsidon. When he died, he left the formula for it to Dad in his will. Dad refined the formula and brought out the C-Bean Mark 4, using a new isotope of Øbsidon in its construction. It gave the C-Bean more advanced functionality but it also became much more dangerous and unstable. Quite apart from being flammable, as you found out, the discomfort people started experiencing when they were being timeshifted is likely to have disastrous long-term genetic consequences unless they are treated in good time.'

Alice gulped, remembering how she'd allowed their C-Bean Mark 3 to be upgraded to a Mark 4, and the unpleasant feeling of being rearranged she'd experienced when they travelled in it ever since. She didn't even want to consider the consequences it had already had on her own body.

'Right, let me get a few things straight. Does my brother work for El Dorado, Øbsidon or Hadron Services?'

'It's complicated, Alice.'

Karla sat down on the floor again.

'Kit went to work for El Dorado in 2089. About ten years later the real Dr Foster, who was a major shareholder in El Dorado, spotted how talented Dad was and persuaded him to go and work for him at Øbsidon HQ in China. By the time Foster died in 2110, timeshifting had been made illegal, so in order to carry on as a business, Dad set up Hadron Services to continue their work. That's when he relocated the whole operation to St Kilda, to keep his timeshifting work well hidden. He knew that Evaw's underwater research facility was still intact and it didn't take much to overhaul it to run it as a pirate base – a black ops site, if you will.'

'I see,' said Alice slowly, finally discovering the connection between the C-Bean and her island home. She was leaning against one wall and staring at the ceiling.

'I think I get the picture now, but how does James Ferguson fit into it? How come his notebooks were full of stuff about the C-Bean and Øbsidon too?'

'James was working with Foster before Foster recruited Dad. In fact they never actually met – Dad and James, I mean. James was Foster's first business partner – when they started working together, they were separated in time by a century. Basically, Foster was in 2058 sending messages to James in 1958 about his early version of the time-travel algorithm using some elementary messaging technology.'

'The instant mailboat drawer?'

'Yes – that's how they communicated to begin with. Wow, Alice. Do you know about that, too?'

Alice nodded. 'Go on,' she urged.

'Foster sent James his designs for a prototype C-Bean that way and James built one and started sending live samples to Foster in the future. Initially he could only send small stuff like insects, birds' eggs, butterflies, moss, wild flowers – things he'd collected on St Kilda. They knew Plan A was going to be a success when James sent a pair of live puffins to 2059 and they raised a family of chicks in an artificial burrow that Foster set up for them.'

'Then what?'

'After James' dad died in 1960 …'

'You mean Donald Ferguson?'

'Yes, Donald. James decided to risk transporting himself to the future – to 2060 – in order to work on the next phase of Plan A with Foster. They did that right up until 2077 and then, one night, James suddenly vanished. Foster always maintained that James had somehow gone back to his own time, but at that stage the C-Bean Mark 1's timeshift function was not advanced enough to enable any living things to go backwards in time. So it was a real mystery how James got away and where he went. It left Foster without a business partner, and he struggled on by himself for a few years, until he recruited Dad. Dad thinks Foster never told him the whole story about what happened with James, but there was obviously some kind of breakdown in trust between James and Foster.'

'I see,' Alice said, mulling over all the pieces to what felt like a vast jigsaw puzzle. She was running her fingers over the wall of the C-Bean and creating a complex pattern of colours and interlocking lines. When she stopped, the C-Bean seemed to take what she had drawn and turn it into a moving kaleidoscope of music and maths, playing gently in the background and constantly changing. Karla watched for a while as the shapes changed and merged together. She sighed.

'You know, Alice, Dad told me recently that if James hadn't disappeared in 2077, Dad would never have gone to work for Øbsidon. None of this would have happened. I am so angry with him – he knew it wasn't safe for people to go backwards in time, even with the Mark 3. But he went ahead with it anyway. With his own family members! You and me! We're Hadron Services' guinea pigs, Alice! I had no idea what would happen when we did the reset and it sent us back in time by 100 years. Then, next thing I knew, you and Donald insisted on taking us all back to 1851 on some pointless trip to that crystal palace. And now, to top it all, that delinquent kid Rudy made me travel back in time yet again. I'm going to get sick, I know I am!'

At that point, Karla started sobbing uncontrollably, which made Spex start to paw the door to get out of the C-Bean.

'Yes, for God's sake open the door, Alice – I'm feeling so claustrophobic in here!'

Alice opened the C-Bean and Spex ran outside. Charlie and Edie were walking across the schoolyard towards her, trying to control Rudy, who was still rolling drunk.

As they reached the C-Bean, Rudy blurted out, 'I happy boy Rudy today!' and was promptly sick on the grass outside the door.

'I'm pleased to hear it, Rudy. Come inside – you're just in time, guys,' replied Alice.

'In time for what? Rudy's in no fit state for anything,' Edie advised, producing a tissue for him to wipe his mouth. Rudy let out a loud burp. 'See what I mean?'

'OK, but we have some more important things to deal with than Rudy's hangover,' Alice said bluntly.

'Like what?'

'Karla's been filling me in on a few things, and thinks we need to confront the C-Bean's real inventor – the person in fact who invented time travel – the real Dr Foster. He's behind everything – none of this would have happened if it wasn't for him, and Karla says he's about to exploit the power of time travel for all the wrong reasons. It's up to us to stop him before it becomes an utter disaster.'

'Whoever this guy Foster really is, and whatever he's up to, the answer is simple Alice – No way.'

'Edie, I'm begging you!' Karla wailed, 'This is important. He's a very determined scientist. Please let's make him stop what he's doing before it's too late! I'm only asking that you come with me in the C-Bean to visit Dr Foster at Øbsidon HQ before he goes ahead with Plan B.'

'I'm not going anywhere ever again in this thing, and that's a fact,' announced Edie. 'And I'm not falling for your story, Karla – as far as I'm concerned, you've been lying to us right from the start and if you believe a word she's saying, Alice, you're an idiot. It's all just one big wind-up. She doesn't even bother putting on her fake German accent anymore. I was only here for the meeting, so you can let me out right now.' Edie looked defiantly at Karla, who just shrugged and turned away.

The C-Bean's door opened and she stepped out. Alice could see Spix flying around outside. The parrot flew down to perch on Edie's shoulder for a moment, looking at her quizzically.

'Don't look at me like that, Spix. I'm the only one with any sense around here.'

But Spix didn't want to miss out on another adventure, so when

Edie started to walk home, he flew inside the C-Bean and blurted out a loud 'Olá!'

'*Olá, olá, olá, olá!*' hollered a drunken Rudy at the top of his voice, teetering around, his yellow eyes bleary and unfocused.

'Shut up, Rudy,' Charlie said, grabbing his shoulder and making him sit down on the floor of the C-Bean. Spex started licking Rudy's face and making him giggle uncontrollably. Alice started sniggering.

'OK, that's the funny bit over. So what's the real story?' asked Charlie, hands on hips.

'I'm not lying. Not now, anyway,' Karla said quietly.

'Go on,' Charlie urged.

'I had to lie about who I was the first time I was sent back to 2018 or the mission wouldn't have worked at all. You had to think I really was the C-Bean's inventor who'd come over from Germany to help you fix your mobile classroom. You would never have known any different if I hadn't got stuck in 1918 when we reset this stupid thing, and then you found my fake passport. But I'm telling you the truth now, Alice. Honestly.'

Alice nodded. 'So when exactly do we need to arrive in the future to confront Dr Foster?'

'Ideally, just before James Ferguson left in 2077. That's when we'd stand the best chance of convincing Foster,' Karla replied.

Alice remembered from James' notebooks and the internet research she and Charlie had done that James was nominated for a Nobel Peace Prize in 1977, so what Karla was saying made sense – he must have somehow travelled back to his own time around then.

'And where exactly are we going to find him?' Charlie said.

'Øbsidon HQ.'

Alice could hear Edie's voice pestering her in the back of her mind, and had a feeling that maybe Edie was right. Should they all step outside the C-Bean now and just let Karla and Rudy go back to 2118, and then the whole thing would be over with? But Alice was aware of an even stronger feeling that, even if they did that, it would not be over – there would just be further complications.

'OK, Charlie, are you up for this?' Alice asked, a little warily.

'Right now I'm up for anything that will keep Karla, Rudy and the C-Bean from being discovered, because I don't think we could pull off any more bizarre explanations, Alice,' Charlie sighed.

Rudy had fallen asleep in the corner, with Spex curled up beside him.

'In that case, let's do it.'

'Thank you, Alice!' said Karla, her voice full of grateful relief.

'Don't thank me till it's over,' Alice said as she closed the door and instructed the C-Bean to take them to Øbsidon HQ on 18 September 2077. But the C-Bean seemed unable to produce the exact coordinates and instead showed a map of the general area where it presumed it was located, in the south of China. It added one short piece of information: 'Øbsidon Futures® (Ø.F.) registered 2098, CEO Dr Adrian Foster'.

'Where is Øbsidon's HQ, Karla? Why isn't it coming up?' Alice asked.

'Wasn't it listed as one of the test sites before, Alice? Remember, it said "Ø.F.",' offered Charlie.

'It's been blocked now. Hadron must suspect. Look, trust me. I'm going right out on a limb here, and Dad would kill me if he knew I was doing this,' Karla said conspiratorially. 'But I happen to know that although Øbsidon's whereabouts is classified, there is a guide who can get us there.'

In the absence of a precise location for Øbsidon HQ, Alice instructed the C-Bean to use the coordinates for Charlie's grandparents' tower block, Harbourside Tower 6, from their last visit to Hong Kong. Just before they arrived, the C-Bean announced that oxygen levels would be acceptable for human life at their destination, and they promptly landed on the roof of the skyscraper, just like the previous time. But Hong Kong in 2077 was not quite how Alice remembered it. Even before they set foot outside the C-Bean, she could hear a hammering sound on the roof and when they emerged there was a fierce autumn monsoon in progress. As they stepped out, curtains of hot acid rain were plummeting onto the roof of the building and evaporating on contact into swirling clouds of vapour, the wind stirring it all up together with shards of metal and other debris. The rain stung their skin and a piece of debris struck Charlie on his head, which started bleeding. Spix was swept up in a ferocious gust, and for several tense minutes seemed unable to fly out of the maelstrom. Eventually, Rudy was able to hook him down using what remained of a lightning conductor rod that he found lying on the roof near an exit hatch.

'Quick, let's get down below and out of the storm,' Alice shouted, tugging at the hatch.

When they climbed through it and down to the floor below, they could see that the building was abandoned and in a bad state of repair. The only thing working was some emergency lighting, which kept flickering on and off. There was obviously not enough power left in the building to make the lifts work, so they walked down the escape stairs to Charlie's granddad's apartment on the 30th floor. They found the door to the apartment wide open. Spex trotted straight in, following a trail he'd picked up. By the look of the mess, someone had obviously been through the contents and taken anything valuable or edible. Charlie's family's beautiful grey plush carpet and elegant antique furniture were long gone, with bare concrete floors in their place, and vestiges of the last occupants' silk wallpaper still clung to the damp walls in places.

'Looters,' Rudy observed grimly.

'Come on, let's go. There's no point in staying here,' Charlie scoffed, looking round in dismay.

They walked down 30 storeys in silence. Some of the steps were broken and there were gaps where the balustrades and handrails were missing. Alice followed Karla, Rudy and Charlie down, wondering what kind of scene would greet them when they reached the lobby. The storm seemed to have subsided but, as they came to the last flight of stairs, they all stopped. It appeared that the marble steps disappeared into a lake of murky water that filled the last few metres of the emergency stairwell. The dog pushed past them to investigate something he'd spied in the water, but Spix had the opposite reaction and suddenly became quite agitated. He flung himself at the windows, desperately looking for a way out. Alice peered outside through the dirty plate-glass windows. Where the street had once been, with its crowded pavements and tangle of overhead tram wires and telegraph cables, was now a vast canal. It looked like pictures she'd seen of Venice, water flowing between all the buildings.

In the gathering twilight, the only signs of any human activity Alice could see were a couple of boats tethered to lampposts. Charlie waded in chest-deep and started swimming towards one of the boats. He turned and beckoned to the others. Spex launched himself into the water and was paddling over to Charlie. Spix clung to Alice's collarbone until they were out through the door. The water didn't smell too good and there were dark, indeterminate objects floating around in it, but it was cooler than the stifling air temperature, so Alice actually found it quite a relief to have to swim over to the boat.

There was a large fan-like motor at the stern and a solar panel taped onto the front deck. There was also some kind of pole lying in the bottom of its hull.

'We need to get a move on before someone comes back for it,' Karla warned as they hauled themselves aboard.

'Where's Rudy?' Alice asked.

Rudy was standing up to his neck in the water on the other side of the street, looking scared stiff.

Charlie was trying to work out how to connect the starter cable to get the rotary blades working. Suddenly he managed to start the motor and the boat sprang to life.

'Which way?'

'North. But first we need to go down to the old harbour. That's where we'll find a guide,' Karla advised.

The boat drifted towards Rudy, who flung himself across the stern when they got close. Somehow the movement caused by his clambering aboard made the engine shift up a gear and the blades start turning slowly. Once Rudy had settled on a seat, he noticed that there was a taped-up break in the cable that connected the motor to the solar panel. He gripped the join and the blades speeded up immediately.

'Must be a loose connection, but we can't see in the dark well enough to fix it. Keep hold of that cable, buddy,' Charlie muttered to Rudy. 'Alice, you steer. It looks like Spix and Spex are our lookouts.'

It was true – the dog and the parrot were both sitting motionless on the foredeck, eyes trained on the water ahead of them. Alice moved to the back of the boat and manoeuvred the boat to head towards the place she remembered the harbour to be. She steered a course down the very street where last time there had been a night market and, as she rounded the corner at the end of the street, she remembered the spot where she'd bought a large spiky durian fruit from a street seller. It all seemed so long ago, like another world.

The harbour was bigger than Alice remembered, until she realised that the sea now came up higher than the old harbour wall and had flooded the surrounding dockside. Mounted on a pontoon floating on the water was a little wooden cabin with a light in the window. Karla pointed to it.

'That's where we'll find our guide,' she said.

Alice waited in the boat with Rudy and the animals, while Karla and Charlie climbed out onto the pontoon and went inside the cabin to enquire about the guide.

Charlie appeared a few minutes later. 'It's no good,' he said. 'They want payment in gold, and we don't have any.'

'Gold?'

'Yeah, real solid gold. They made it sound as if everyone just walks around with heaps of it in their pockets these days.'

'Maybe people do in 2077 – you heard what they were making in El Dorado.'

Rudy started undoing the collar from around Spex's neck. He detached the gold-and-black 'Øbsidon' disk and handed it to Charlie.

'Here. Is Gold.'

Charlie took the disk, turning it over in his palm. 'You reckon this is real gold, mate?' He chuckled. 'OK. I'll give it a try.'

Moments later, a wizened old woman came out of the cabin. She was dressed in faded dungarees with a headscarf wound around her head and she was sucking on something that had stained her lips and chin dark red.

'Where you get?' she held up the disk and peered at Alice. Alice just shrugged. The woman tutted, and pocketed the disk.

'Øbsidon is bad place, is in DeeZee. Dangerous place,' she grumbled, but was nevertheless clambering into their boat and pointing out which way they should be heading.

'What's DeeZee?' Alice asked Karla. But it was Rudy who replied.

'DeeZee mean Dead Zone. Nothing grow. No life. All dead.'

'And Øbsidon, what exactly is it?'

Karla cleared her throat to speak.

'Øbsidon's a fortress. It's Dr Foster's answer to the Dead Zone. Technically it's an experimental biome. They built it as an artificial habitat so they could breed and nurture all the creatures they imported from the past.'

'So basically it's a giant greenhouse?' Alice asked, remembering the Great Exhibition with its huge glass structures and the elm trees inside that she'd visited with Donald in 1851.

'Yes, something like that – it's a climate-controlled environment that perfectly replicates tropical conditions found on earth a century or more ago. As far as I know, it's the only one of its kind in the world. From what I can remember about Plan A from my training, by 2077 they were just starting to populate the biome with larger species of mammal. Which is fortunate for us, because I reckon the only way we'll get inside Foster's fortress is to offer to trade with him.'

'Trade what? We've given our only piece of gold to this boat woman,' Charlie pointed out.

'We have something they want more than gold, Charlie,' said Karla tentatively.

'Huh?'

'Live specimens.'

'You mean we offer ourselves as trade? Are they populating this biome with live children?' Charlie joked.

'Not us, Charlie. I mean Spix and Spex.'

Alice looked at Karla in horror. Had she been lied to after all?

'I'm not giving our animals up, Karla, no way! Spex has been experimented on enough as it is in Hadron's lab, and who knows what happened to Spix in El Dorado before we found him again there!' she said. Spix had pricked up his ears and edged closer to Alice when he heard his name mentioned. Spix responded by fluffing out his chest feathers and chirping loudly '*Spix-Spex, Spix-Spex*'.

But no one laughed.

'I don't see how we're going to gain admittance into the compound any other way, Alice. It's impossible,' Karla retorted in a high, defiant tone, the muscle in her jaw continuously twitching. Everyone fell silent.

The solar battery only lasted about an hour, long enough to get the boat north of the city before it got dark. They were heading up a narrow channel that led inland through a vast mangrove swamp when the engine cut out. Alice looked around. The trees surrounding them were long since dead and the heat was more intense than ever. Everything was silent apart from a low droning buzz, which they realised was coming from a dense, moving cloud up ahead. As they got closer Alice realised that it was not mist but a swarm of large, long-legged insects feasting on what looked like a dead animal, its bloated belly protruding from the water.

Suddenly the old woman started muttering something under her breath that sounded like 'mung, mung!' She rummaged in the pockets of her dungarees and pulled out some incense sticks. When she lit them and gave one to each of the children, Rudy suddenly seemed to understand what she was saying and went rigid with fear.

'Mung!' he repeated and, without warning, suddenly stood up in the boat, making it rock violently from side to side and veer off course.

'What's the matter, Rudy? What is "mung"?' asked Alice.

'It's Cantonese slang for mosquito,' Karla whispered. 'I've heard they all carry malaria around here. Rudy, sit down and stay still,' Karla urged. Rudy flashed her a look, his yellow eyes glinting with fear in the dark.

'Don't want get sick! Happen before.'

The swarm had detected the scent of fresh human flesh in the boat and was coming towards them. The woman leaned over the side of the boat and used her arms to try to turn it around and move back down the channel, but the insects were in their hair, noses and eyes within seconds.

Alice felt herself drift slowly into unconsciousness, the malarial organisms from copious mosquito bites pulsing through her veins. She lay still in the boat, dimly aware of Spex licking her face, but everything else was foggy. She could sense the others going slack around her, as they too fell victim to the attack. All except the old woman, who somehow pulled the pole out from under them and took charge. With a burning incense stick gripped between her teeth for protection, the woman peered into the darkness, still sucking on the red seeds. As if guided by some inner compass, she let the pole slide into the water until it touched the bottom, pushed off and continued north towards the Øbsidon compound.

When Alice awoke she felt swollen, feverish and itchy. In the pale dawn light, she could see mosquito bites covering her arms and legs, every one a raised red blister the size of a saucer. They were still in the boat, Rudy and Charlie lying awkwardly back-to-back next to each other. Karla was curled up in a ball at the front, her face pallid and her lips blue.

All around the boat, the seawater was grey, inert and polluted with occasional pieces of rotting organic matter floating among degraded plastic containers. The sun's early-morning rays skated across the surface, piercing the translucent objects nearest to the boat, making the detritus look almost beautiful for a moment. So this was the Dead Zone – one vast sterile expanse, ruined forever by humankind. The old woman pulled in the pole and let the boat drift. Shielding her eyes from the low sun, she peered at the islands up ahead. Spex yawned and whined softly in Alice's lap. The parrot, meanwhile, clung to her shoulder and was watching the old woman's every move.

'I'm starving,' Charlie groaned as he woke, obviously forgetting their predicament. He pushed Rudy over onto his front and eased himself up into a sitting position.

'You lucky,' said the old woman. 'Øbsidon only place make own food. Almost there, look!' she said, pointing ahead.

They were approaching an island that appeared to be surrounded by a high fence whose posts stood in the water. Beyond the fence, Alice could see what looked like a giant soap bubble enclosing the whole island, its glassy surface reflecting the pinks and oranges in the sky. Foster's biome.

The old woman had brought the boat to within 20 metres of the line of fence posts when Alice suddenly felt an electrical charge ripple across her skin. She let go of Spix and Spex and clutched her arm in terror.

'The fence. It must be electrified,' Charlie said in a tense whisper.

'Yes. But not water,' the old woman grunted. 'You kids swim rest of way. Keep heads under all way to shore,' she advised, waving her arm to demonstrate that they needed to exit the boat quickly. Rudy was still asleep, so she poked him hard in the ribs with her foot to wake him. He woke with a start, his yellow eyes blazing, ready to confront whoever had kicked him, until he realised it was the old woman.

'C'mon, out now, boys and girls!' she urged. 'Take goods with you. Hurry! Øbsidon watching us. Don't want be seen!' She seemed quite anxious to get going and had untied her headscarf to drape it over her face so she would not be recognised. Charlie pointed out the surveillance cameras mounted on the top of each of the fence posts. In the distance, the Øbsidon biome suddenly looked totally impenetrable.

Alice was the first to slip over the side of the boat and into the warm, dirty water. She had no idea how long she could hold her breath for, and the island still looked quite some distance away. Charlie followed, and as he lowered his torso into the water, Spix took off, wheeling up into the sky and squawking his usual mantra '*Perigroso, perigroso!*' Sensing the bird's panic, Spex barked and splashed in beside Alice, paddling rapidly towards the shore. Alice realised she would have to push the dog's head under when they got in line with the electric fence to avoid him being electrocuted. Meanwhile, Rudy sat in the boat, refusing to move. No matter what the old woman said to him, he just shook his head. Finally he admitted, 'No swim. Not knowhow.'

'Karla, come on – you're going to have to help him,' Alice called, treading water and pushing the rubbish on the surface out of her way. But Karla just shook her head.

'I'm not coming with you.'

'What?' Alice spluttered, nearly swallowing some of the water.

'You have to do this on your own, Alice. I'm allergic to everything inside there.'

'Well, thanks for not telling us earlier, Karla!' Charlie said angrily as he grabbed one side of the boat and somehow managed to manoeuvre Rudy into the water with them. Alice swam across and got hold of Rudy's other arm. The old woman started arguing with Karla when she realised she wasn't getting out of the boat. Karla said something in Cantonese, pulled up her hood and the woman turned the boat round and started heading back the way they'd come.

Alice was trying her best not to panic. It was taking all her effort to make sure none of the dirty water got into her nose or mouth, and she still had to keep Rudy afloat. She could feel her legs tiring before they were even halfway to the shore. Spex had swum on ahead, out of reach. Alice grabbed something that was floating on the water and threw it to Spex, shouting 'Fetch'. Thankfully the item plunged under the surface and Spex dived after it, reappearing on the other side of the line of electrified fencing. Alice could feel the charge on her skin again and knew it was time for her to go under, too. She closed her eyes, took a deep breath and sank down into the filthy grey water, dragging Rudy with her and trying to judge how many strokes she needed to make before she was clear of the fence above. She could feel Rudy's legs instinctively kicking against her as he struggled to reach the surface. She held his arm tightly and uttered a silent and fervent wish that they would all make it safely to dry land. It was only when they resurfaced on the inside of the perimeter fence that Alice noticed that Rudy was now swimming by himself without realising it. She let go of his arm and watched as he splashed towards the shore.

'Rudy, we made it – you can do it!' He beamed at her and kept up his frantic paddle until the water was shallow enough to stand up.

Spix was waiting for them, perched on a rock that looked like it was streaked with veins of melted plastic the same colour as his blue feathers. He eyed the humans nervously as they squeezed out their clothes. Spex shook himself dry, barked and bounded off, following a vivid scent trail that led off the beach and into a scrubland of black thorny bushes. It looked as if there had been a fire – the bushes were in fact not black but burned, and the ground was scorched and cracked. The children followed the dog in single file, unsure where the trail was leading. Up ahead, the glass biome loomed over them, and Alice could now see a dense jungle inside reaching right up to the top of the dome, hundreds of different kinds of trees, flowers and creepers all competing for sunlight.

Spex brought them to a place where the scorched terrain had been dug away to form a cutting that led deep into the ground beneath the biome. At the bottom of the cutting there was a kind of cage surrounding entrance gates. There was a sign beside the gates stating 'Goods Inwards', next to an entry keypad similar to the one for the airlock on St Kilda in 2118. Alice began to wonder if Rudy's dead finger would work here too. She looked at him.

'The finger, Rudy?'

Rudy nodded and produced the gruesome item from his pocket, placing it on the keypad.

No response.

Then they heard a click and a voice said, 'Enter UAT to enable us to identify your goods.'

'What's a UAT?' asked Charlie. 'Some kind of password?'

'It's that serial number the cloned parrots in El Dorado had under their tails, remember. I don't think either Spex or Spix have one ...' Alice sighed with disappointment.

She thought for a moment, trying to remember the inscription on the gold disk. When Spex had reappeared with it around his neck, she assumed it was because someone had given him a new name – but what if it was, in fact, a code?

'Wait, I've got it.'

She wiped the sweat off her forehead and slowly typed the letters 'B-0-R-K' into the keypad.

The gate clicked open so faintly that Alice thought at first she had imagined it. She picked up Spex and tucked him under her arm before walking through the cage and into the biome. The atmosphere inside was pleasantly warm and steamy. Spix flew off high above them, swooping and squawking in sheer delight as he discovered his favourite nut hanging from one of the tropical trees. It was obviously a close approximation of his native environment. Alice could hear a stream trickling through the undergrowth and, as she got closer to it, she noticed something floating in the crystal-clear water. It was a seabean. She bent down and fished it out of the stream, holding it dripping wet in her palm. She felt sure it was a sign that she was getting closer to finding out the truth.

'Look, Alice – there are durians growing in here!' Charlie was staring up at the spiky fruit hanging overhead. Alice gazed in awe at this lush and verdant scene and saw that it was alive with butterflies, dragonflies, grasshoppers and tree frogs.

'Look – Bee too,' said Rudy, smiling as he watched a small swarm flying in and out of a hive hanging from a branch above his head.

'Come on, guys – this isn't a nature lesson,' Charlie urged them as he scratched his mosquito bites.

'But that's exactly what this is!' a voice said, seemingly from nowhere. 'Welcome, my friends, step this way.'

Alice looked up and noticed a high-level walkway, suspended in the treetops and running around the perimeter of the biome. A man with curly white hair wearing a lab coat appeared to be waiting for them there. She knew straight away they were in the presence of the real Dr Foster.

D r Foster led them to a large wooden villa with deep overhanging eaves in the middle of the biome. At the entrance, he asked them to remove their shoes, and then ushered them into a beautiful room lined with bamboo panels overlooking a garden. The floor was covered in soft woven matting and strewn with silk cushions. Alice and Charlie sat on the cushions and waited while Dr Foster stepped out of the room for a moment. Alice realised that she felt nervous. She was worrying about where Spix and Spex were, and her bites were driving her crazy, but she didn't dare scratch them. The only things to ease her sense of discomfort were the fans blowing cool air over their damp clothes. Rudy kept walking restlessly around the room, opening and shutting various glass cabinets displaying a collection of black rocks. It reminded Alice of the display cases she'd seen in the American Museum of Natural History in New York.

'Rudy, don't touch anything,' Alice hissed.

'I see you like my little museum,' Dr Foster observed when he returned.

'Sorry, Dr Foster. He doesn't mean to be rude. What are all those rocks, exactly?' enquired Alice politely.

'It is my father's collection. They are more than just rocks; they're meteorites – fragments from a very old, very large meteor that crashed into the Earth in northern Russia in 2042. Father discovered that they had the strangest properties. I think you will find them most interesting. Watch this.'

Dr Foster opened one cabinet and took out a particularly uninteresting lump of black rock and gave it to Charlie. As he handled it, the whole rock changed colour and became a vivid sky blue.

'Son, the specimen you are holding came from Outer Space. It has time-travelled many hundreds of thousands of light years. All the energy from its time travel is encoded in its chemistry at a subatomic level. It's what I used to derive Øbsidon. You see, Øbsidon is not just the name of my company, but also the name I gave to my most important invention to date – a powerful patented material that exploits the same molecular structure as this meteorite. Without it, Operation Seabean could not exist because, you see, it is the very thing that enables my C-Bean device to time travel.'

Charlie handed the rock to Rudy, whereupon it changed colour again, becoming a fiery reddish-orange. When it was completely orange, Rudy suddenly dropped it.

'Burn Hands. Very hot!' he exclaimed.

'Ah yes, in the wrong hands, its thermopower is also activated. We are working on a fix for that right now.' Dr Foster bent down and picked up the rock and beckoned to Alice. 'You have a try, my dear.'

Alice reluctantly took the rock, holding it with her fingers wide apart, ready to let go should it become scalding hot again. But instead the rock turned a deep translucent green and then became virtually invisible. Charlie and Rudy watched, transfixed. Alice noticed that even Dr Foster looked dumbstruck.

'How very interesting, my friend. You appear to have a unique power over this little rock.' He stared quizzically at Alice for a moment. She felt embarrassed, so she placed the invisible rock back inside the cabinet beside its identification card, marked 'Øbsidon Mark 3'. As she closed the cabinet door, she could that see the rock was already reappearing, just like the C-Bean had reappeared when they were at the Great Exhibition in 1851.

A door slid open behind them and a dark-haired girl about ten years old, who Dr Foster addressed as Rachel, brought in a pot of jasmine tea and some delicate porcelain cups and set them down on a low black table. Dr Foster proceeded to pour the tea with great care. Alice watched him carefully and studied his face – he looked exactly like their old teacher, but his movements as he handed out the cups seemed to be more smooth and natural. Then she saw that, when he picked up the teapot, the heat left a blue circular mark on the table. Her own cup did the same.

'Is the table made of Øbsidon too, Dr Foster?

'Yes, naturally. Now, please, try the tea. I am very proud. It has been made with our first flush of jasmine, pollinated by real insects. So it is, technically, the first real tea that has been produced in over fifty years. I hope you like it.'

Alice noticed that his voice, with its gentle Asian inflections, also sounded more natural and authentic than the cyborg Dr Foster's American drawl. She took a sip of the tea. The others did likewise. The warm aromatic liquid tasted exquisite. There was a long pause, during which Alice felt a sense of calm descend. She was so relaxed that, before she realised what she was doing, she found herself making a direct proposal to their host.

'Dr Foster, I can see that your Operation Seabean is a great success. We have recently arrived in Hong Kong and would like to offer something we hope will add to your project – an, um, unusual breed of dog from New York and a rare Spix's Macaw that we rescued from a recent trip to the Amazon.'

'Is that so? But please, we will talk business in due course, my dear. For now, I suggest you rest and recuperate from your travels. Later I would like to show you more of our work before we enter negotiations. You must all be tired. Rachel will show you to your lodgings. You can bathe, change your clothes, relax. Leave your specimens with me – their value to us will be assessed in due course.'

Dr Foster pressed a bell to summon someone. Alice stared helplessly when a lab technician appeared with Spex and Spix in two cardboard boxes. The technician showed them briefly to Dr Foster and said something to him in Cantonese before carrying them off. Charlie gave Alice a sharp dig in the shin but all she could do was stare after them.

'So, it is agreed. We will meet at sundown for dinner in the Great

Hall when we will be joined by my business partner, Rachel's father, and we shall be delighted to hear your proposal then.'

Rachel took them down a wide passageway and into a side wing of the villa, where several rooms opened off a central courtyard. In the middle of the courtyard was a beautiful water sculpture made of Øbsidon that changed by itself from black to gold to invisible and back again as the water ran in rivulets over its smooth surface. Rachel led them around the edge of the courtyard and slid back a paper screen to reveal the main room. There were beds unrolled on the floor for each of them and lying on top of each bed was a quilt, a folded silk robe and a pair of silk slippers.

'Papa made all the silk himself – with imported silkworms,' Rachel informed them, smiling shyly.

'It's beautiful,' Alice said, kneeling down to touch the soft fabric. 'I'm Alice. Do you live here, Rachel?'

'Yes, with my papa, James Ferguson. You will meet him later.'

'Of course,' said Alice with a sharp intake of breath, realising that, in the past few months, she had met not only this girl's father but also her grandfather, Donald, and her great-grandmother, Dora.

'I look forward to meeting him,' she said lamely, at a loss as to what else to say.

'The bathrooms are through that way.' Rachel was pointing to another doorway to the left of a large bookcase.

'Will our animals be well treated? I am quite concerned,' Alice questioned her further.

'All our animals are well cared for. Would you like to see our newest arrivals before dinner? They came yesterday – we have two baby pandas. Papa gave them to me as a gift for my birthday. I'm their keeper,' Rachel said with a certain amount of pride.

'Pandas?' Charlie asked, incredulous.

'Yes. I will come back for you in an hour, to show you.' And with that, Rachel bowed politely and withdrew. Charlie waited until she had gone before he laid into Alice with a volley of criticisms.

'Brilliant performance back there with Foster, Alice – absolutely priceless. What did you want to go and offer him our animals for? I thought you said you didn't want to trade them? Have you thought any of this out, and if so, would you mind filling Rudy and me in on your Grand Plan?'

'Calm down, Charlie. I haven't got a plan as such, but we'll figure something out, don't worry.'

'I got Knife,' Rudy advised them, solemnly patting his pocket. Alice winked at him.

'Yes, but let's hope we won't need to use it, Rudy.'

'Anyway, who's Rachel?' Charlie mumbled.

'Don't you get it? She's Old Jim's daughter,' whispered Alice.

Rachel picked up the smaller of the two giant pandas from its playpen and cuddled him in her arms.

'Papa just had them sent from a zoo that was closing down in 2028. He gets a lot of the animals from the time during World War III, because most zoos around the world were having to close then. Some of the animals arrive in very bad condition, but these two came from Edinburgh Zoo and were well cared for.' She put the panda down and he crawled back to his mate, who was munching bamboo.

'We must go now. Dr Foster doesn't like anyone to be late for dinner,' said Rachel, looking at her watch. Alice noticed for the first time that the whites of Rachel's eyes were yellow, like Rudy's. They followed her back into the main part of the villa, up a flight of steps and into the Great Hall, where a long table had been lavishly laid. A maid was lighting some kind of crystal candelabra in the middle of the table, while two others carried in bowls overflowing with tropical fruit.

'Good evening, everyone. I trust you are well rested. Rachel tells me you have met our newest recruits,' said a beaming Dr Foster as he showed them each to their seats. As he came to help Rudy to his place at the table, he said consolingly, 'I can tell by your eyes that you too have suffered from malaria like Rachel. I am sorry you had to endure the mosquitoes on your journey here today. They are a mutant strain that escaped from the biome. It is my fault entirely. A careless lapse in our containment protocols. However, I trust you all found some relief from your stings. The medicine we serve in our jasmine tea will prevent any malaria from developing. It's one of my most lucrative product lines.'

Alice gulped. Had they been exposed to the swarm on purpose? What had they been drugged with? She suddenly felt a little uneasy.

A gong sounded six times.

'Now, where is James? We need to eat.'

But James failed to appear. Dr Foster looked very displeased and growled at a maid, who was dispatched to look for him. The meal proceeded in silence without him. Course after course of strange, exotic food, elaborately piled on enormous platters, were set before them, and Alice noticed that both she and Charlie were struggling to eat any of it. She longed for something simple like the spaghetti with tomato sauce her Dad cooked. Rudy, meanwhile, was noisily tucking into everything, including some craggy-looking things that Dr Foster said were oysters. Alice watched as Rudy hacked one open and slurped the contents into his mouth, just like she'd watched him eat the bird's egg on St Kilda. But the taste of the oyster was obviously not to Rudy's liking, because he immediately spat it out and pushed his plate away, wiping a trail of saliva from his mouth with the back of his hand. The plate caught the edge of the crystal candelabra, which shattered into hundreds of pieces, showering sparkling smithereens all over the table. The maids rushed in to clear up the mess and Alice started apologising and trying to help, when she suddenly realised that Rudy was having some kind of fit. His eyes were rolling and his body was jerking violently.

Dr Foster got up from the table and calmly walked over to a chest of drawers in the corner. He took out a syringe, filled it with a green liquid and proceeded to inject Rudy in the leg. Rudy slumped forward in his chair and passed out.

Alice and Charlie stared in horror, not sure what to say or do, but Dr Foster just snapped his fingers and two maids reappeared with a huge silver tureen.

'And now, the crowning glory of tonight's feast – bird's nest soup!'

Alice shot Charlie a look, remembering the expression on Sam J's face when Charlie had pointed out a bird's nest for sale in the Hong Kong night market for $5,000. Rudy was starting to come round. He looked worse than the morning after he'd helped himself to Lady Grange's drinks cabinet.

Just as they were eating a dessert of stewed grey lychees, which to Alice looked like eyeballs and tasted of perfume, James walked into the room. He was older than she remembered, with grey strands in amongst his brown hair and beard, and he now walked with a limp. But he still had the same speedy determination.

'Foster, I demand an answer right now or this whole project is over!' he bellowed as he strode right up to his business partner. Rudy jumped and almost fell off his chair.

'Not now, James. Can't you see we have company?' Dr Foster replied sweetly, his hand gesturing in a circular flourish to indicate the others round the table.

James sighed and ran his hands through his hair. He seemed to have something very troubling on his mind as he sat down heavily in the last remaining chair at the table, opposite Alice, with his head in his hands. Alice wanted to attract his attention, but he was so preoccupied that he hadn't even noticed who his guests were. She stretched out her leg under the table and kicked him on the shin.

James looked up with a start and stared at her.

There was a very odd moment when their eyes met, and Alice saw the flicker of recognition pass across James' face. His lips moved briefly, as if he was mouthing her name, and then he shot a quick sideways glance at Dr Foster. There was no doubt in Alice's mind that he knew exactly who she was, but it was also obvious that, in the present circumstances, he could not afford to let his business partner see that he knew her.

From that moment, James' mood seemed to change dramatically. He turned to his business partner and said politely, 'Dr Foster, aren't you going to introduce me to everyone?'

'My dear James, of course,' said Foster, faltering slightly. 'But forgive me, my memory is very poor these days. Would you good people mind introducing yourselves to James and say why you are here? You see, James, they have some new animals to offer us.'

Alice was back in their quarters and almost asleep when she heard the paper screen slide back and in the semi-darkness she could see a man creep into their room. He moved quickly between Charlie and Rudy's sleeping bodies as if he was looking for something or someone. She half closed her eyes and pretended to be asleep when suddenly he tapped her on the shoulder.

'What on earth are you doing here Alice?' he hissed, 'I nearly had a heart attack when I realised it was you at dinner!'

It was James.

'We came to stop Dr Foster going ahead with Plan B,' she whispered.

'However do you know about Plan B? It's classified information.'

Alice didn't know what to say without breaking her own time traveller rules, so she remained silent.

'Never mind, the thing is, now that you're here, it occurs to me you could help me out. I take it you arrived in the C-Bean Mark 3?'

'Mark 4, actually,' Alice confirmed. She had no idea where the conversation was leading.

'I see. Listen, can we go somewhere a bit more private. I don't want to others to hear what I've got to tell you.'

Alice slid out of bed and slipped on her silk slippers. They padded silently out of the room and sat in the courtyard beside the water sculpture, in what Alice thought was a patch of moonlight, until she realised it was an artificial moon mounted on the glass roof of the biome.

'I need a way out. Foster has become impossible to work with. I don't know how much you know about it, but he's started exploiting our Operation Seabean project in ways I could never have imagined, to the extent he's now talking about making money on the side from smuggling people back in time. Last month I had to stop him from sending a secret pilot consignment of twenty people from Hong Kong back to 2027, but the list of names got out. Øbsidon's been constantly in the news ever since and vigilante gangs have sprung up all over the DZ. Like you, they're hell bent on stopping Plan B from going ahead, But Foster doesn't seem to care – he just calls it 'bad publicity' and says it doesn't matter as long as no one knows where Øbsidon's HQ is. His mind is set. He wants to 'assist' all the people who are basically unhappy with their lot in 2077 and want out. It was bad enough when he started to produce and sell infertile clones of all the plant and animal species I was importing from the past. But now this … As far as I'm concerned it's all gone far enough. And to top it all, his latest plans for developing the C-Bean further involve using a very unstable isotope of Øbsidon – something I can't possibly agree to.'

'So what are you going to do?' Alice asked, curious.

'I hadn't got the foggiest idea until you turned up this evening, Alice. Once again, your timing is impeccable! I desperately need to borrow your C-Bean to get away from here – back to my own time – and take Rachel with me. I should have done it when she was a baby after her mother died, but I couldn't be sure the C-Bean Mark 1 that I built to Foster's design was safe enough to go backwards through time, and we are still having development issues with the Mark 2. From the maths I've done, it looks as if there could be some pretty nasty genetic side effects.'

Alice wondered if he meant that peculiar feeling of being rearranged that she'd noticed when they first travelled in the C-Bean Mark 4.

'So I've developed a chemical antidote – Foster doesn't know I've been working on it – so far I've manufactured only a very small amount of it – about half a dozen doses, using, would you believe it, three parts durian juice mixed with one part artificial gold and some other ingredients. I'd made enough for Rachel and me to be protected from the side effects of going back in the C-Bean Mark 2

– but now you're here too, we'll have to split it. I hope there's enough. How many of you in total have gone backwards in time so far?'

Alice stopped to think.

'Four, I think. The others have only gone forwards in time up til now. But if you mean how many of us need to get back to 2018, it's 8 in total. Oh, and Lori went backwards once too. So nine.'

James frowned and tugged his beard for a moment.

'Who's Lori?'

'My sister.'

'Is everyone more or less the same weight as you?'

'Yes, except Rudy, he's the heaviest.'

'Should be fine then – I have six adult doses but more if I split them into kids' doses. Now, where exactly did you leave the C-Bean?'

'On the roof of Charlie's granddad's old apartment building back in Hong Kong. Are you serious about this James? The Mark 4 does makes you feel a bit weird – even Charlie and I have noticed that.'

'It's a risk we'll have to take. There isn't any alternative! Here's the plan: you go back in there and wake the others. I will get Rachel and pack our things. I'll book a personal Maglev to take us back to Hong Kong quickly tonight, before Foster realises what's going on.'

'Personal Maglev?'

'Magnetic Levitator. It's a sort of high speed taxi that works by magnetism – they laid the guideway track over the lagoon in the 2040s – it's old hat now, but still, a great invention, just a shame it can't teleport through time too!'

'OK, but I can't leave without our pets Spex and Spix – Dr Foster took them both away from us before dinner. He said he would offer us a price in the morning. But I don't really want to sell them to him at all – it was the only way we could get inside the biome without causing suspicion.'

'Rachel will know where they are, come on, there's not much time. Meet you back here in twenty minutes.' And with that, James disappeared through a door in the corner of the courtyard.

Rachel arrived with two animal carry cages when they returned. Her face was white with nerves and Alice could tell she had no idea why they were all stealing away from the biome, from her home, in the dead of night.

'Here you are, Alice,' she said, 'I wanted to bring the pandas too, but Papa said I couldn't. I don't know why.' A tear rolled down Rachel's face.

'I'm sorry, Rachel darling, but it's for the best,' James said consolingly, 'Now everyone, this way, quickly.'

James led them out through a back entrance to the waiting Maglev, which turned out to be a long, sleek, silver, bullet-shaped pod. He loaded two large bags into the back of the hovering vehicle, and when all five of them plus the two animals were safely inside, the Maglev sped off, skimming rapidly above the surface of the vast inland lagoon back to Hong Kong.

A few minutes into the journey, James unzipped one of the bags and pulled out a neat insulated case. When he opened it, Alice saw it was lined with rows of compartments, most of them containing a small phial of liquid. Tucked into a pocket in the side of the case was another of his leather notebooks. When they were a safe distance from the biome he spoke.

'These are the time travel antidote doses, Alice.' James checked the labels on each of the phials, and then showed her the notebook.

'I'm giving you this too. Everything is in here – all the work I've been doing at Øbsidon, the whole of Plan B, including the formula for Øbsidon itself. It's all in my head too, of course. Thanks to you arriving when you did, we're already more than halfway to stopping Foster from going any further with Plan B. I managed to wipe all our research files from the computer servers before I left the biome as well as taking my share of the gold from the vault, so with any luck Foster and his minions wont be able to continue with his evil project because he will have neither the computer code nor the investment funds to proceed. He'll have to stick to developing the habitat like we discussed. The world in 2077 needs to restore biodiversity, so there's nothing wrong with Plan A as a legitimate and constructive use of time travel, but as for all this human trafficking racket, I want nothing to do with it. I think I've dealt with everything. Now, let's find your C-Bean and get back to 1977.'

They arrived at the base of Harbourside Tower 6 just as it was getting light. Alice and Charlie each took a carry cage, leaving Rudy and James to carry the bags up thirty-two flights of stairs. Halfway up they heard noises on one of the landings and James muttered something about it most likely being a gang of vigilantes.

'We waiting for you,' the gang leader announced in a gruff voice when they reached the next floor. He stood barring their way on the broken concrete landing, an immense bare-chested Chinese guy covered with elaborate tattoos and multiple scars. 'Girl here tell us you coming back,' he added, dragging someone from behind him. She was gagged and blindfolded and wearing a black hoodie. Alice suddenly realised it was Karla.

James spoke back to him in Cantonese and took the gang leader by surprise, which gave Rudy enough time to flick open his penknife. He lunged towards the gang leader, while James swung a bag at two of the others, clipping them on the head and knocking them out cold against the stair balustrade. It gave Rachel enough time to slip past them and up another flight, but the gang leader had by then produced a handgun from the holster and was pressing it to Rudy's head, taunting him in a loud voice.

'Come on, Mr Yellow Eyes. Better tell us where Øbsidon is or I shoot girl!'

Alice could see Rudy was getting angry and upset. He twisted round and grabbed the gang leader's wrist to free Karla from his grip.

They both edged closer to a gap in the stair balustrade.

'You making me angry, Yellow Eyes!' the gang leader muttered ominously.

The gang leader cocked the trigger on his gun in readiness to shoot. Another gang member was creeping closer. Rudy managed to kick him sideways and the man stumbled. Karla stood in their midst, shaking with fear. Her head hung down and her hands were tied behind her back with a dirty rag. Rudy lunged towards the end of the rag and tugged it loose but just at that moment the gang leader pulled the trigger and shot Rudy in the arm.

Alice gasped. She realised Karla couldn't see what was happening.

'Karla move away!' she blurted out.

Karla's head lifted slightly as if she'd just realised Alice was there. She shuffled back a step or two.

'No Karla, the other way!' Alice yelled as Karla lost her footing on the broken edge of a step. She lost her footing and fell between the gap in the balustrade, plummeting down the stairwell. James jumped forward and reached out to try and grab her, but it was too late. There was a thud as her body landed on the marble floor fifteen stories below.

Alice shrieked and Rudy peered over the edge of the landing.

'She dead!' he growled, angrily turning on the gang leader with raised fists. There was a scuffle as he tried to wrestle the gang leader to the ground.

'Rudy, be careful!' yelled Alice.

She looked up the stairwell and saw that Charlie had blocked the way using with the two animal cages to protect Rachel, who was crying on the landing above them. Both animals had somehow escaped from their cages. Spix was flying frantically around in the stairwell squawking *Muito Mau, Muito Mau*, while Spex rushed up and down the broken steps barking. Suddenly James threw an emergency flare into their midst. A massive cloud of red smoke billowed around them, making it impossible for anyone to see each other. Someone let off a round of bullets and the gang members dispersed, shouting to one another in Cantonese. Alice heard one say the word 'police' and from the echoing voices it sounded like they ran off into an empty apartment.

Her eyes streaming with tears and smoke, Alice managed to find the handrail and started climbing the stairs. Charlie was calling down to her and she could hear James' footsteps up ahead, but she couldn't see a thing. Eventually they emerged on the roof, coughing and spluttering in the morning air, including Spix and Spex. As Alice regained her sight, the first thing she noticed was that the gang had obviously discovered the C-Bean, because across its black surface in graffiti were the words 'ØBSIDON: BURN IN HELL!'. She commanded the door to open and everyone stepped into the C-Bean. Everyone, that is, except Rudy.

Alice's Blog

Friday 21st September 2018

I can't stop thinking about what happened in Hong Kong. It was bad enough what happened to Karla, but then it got even worse. After we'd escaped back to the C-Bean on the roof, we huddled together inside until we were sure the coast was clear. James and I left Rachel with Charlie and went with Spex to look for Rudy.

We found him lying face down on the landing. James turned him over. Blood was seeping out of his side and his yellow eyes were rolling. We tried to pick him up, but he groaned with pain. Spex ran round in circles whining in sympathy. James gave him something to ease the pain. All I could do was hold Rudy's hand. He made me cry when he said to me 'It OK Alice. Going to see family. Little sister, Mama, Papa, all together now.' Then he took the severed finger out of his pocket and gave it to me, like it was a precious gift. He smiled and said 'Might need Deadman Finger'.

Torches started flashing from the lobby below and just as James whispered it was the military police, Rudy started having a seizure. There was this horrific moment when his body just seemed to go limp. James checked his heart to find it wasn't beating any more and told me Rudy was dead. My own heart almost stopped beating too when I heard that. James had to carry me back to the C-Bean. As he lay me down on the floor, I realised I was covered in blood.

I asked him, 'Am I bleeding, James?'

'No, it's Rudy's,' he told me grimly. 'Now let's just take the antidote and go home.' I have no idea how we managed to get Rachel and James back to 1977, but Charlie tells me we managed somehow and then got ourselves home.

You can imagine the scene when we arrived back on St Kilda in 2018: Our parents were beside themselves – although they were overjoyed that Charlie and I had reappeared, it was two whole days since we'd vanished and we were in a terrible state – dehydrated, dirty, wearing some strange oriental clothing, and covered in someone else's blood. And on top of that, none of what we said made any sense to them. I was crying about someone called Rudy, and Charlie was trying to explain to them that Rudy had kidnapped Karla Ingermann but that she'd died in an unfortunate accident. As far as they were concerned, we'd both gone missing the day the marine biologists arrived, and the last person to see us was Edie. She'd told them we must have done something stupid, but she didn't know what. I could kill her for saying that. At least she didn't mention anything about the C-Bean.

Needless to say, I am not allowed out of the house now. Charlie is grounded too. This morning he texted me 'Sorry about Spex'. It's been so bad I hadn't even noticed he didn't come back with us – apparently the poor dog wouldn't leave Rudy's side when he died, so James had to leave him there. Now Spix won't leave my side. He keeps saying over and over in a demented high-pitched sing-song 'Spix-Spex Spix-Spex'. It's driving me mad but I can't make him stop. Mum says someone is coming over from the Outer Hebrides mental health team to talk to me on Monday. But there's nothing they can do to help. Unless they can explain to me why it's always got to be like this! I mean, why it is that every time we manage to make something good happen, something terrible has to happen as well.

Monday 24th September 2018

Edie came to see me after school today. She apologised for getting us into trouble. I was a bit grumpy towards her at first, but eventually I told her everything that happened to Charlie and me, and now she feels really bad that she didn't come with us.

I'm supposed to be going back to school tomorrow, but I just don't feel up to it. And I have this awful tummy ache all the time; it feels like when you get a stitch. Mum says that she can't let me go on the trip to our new school in Glasgow unless I show some signs of improvement soon and I do really want to go, so I guess I'll have to force myself to show up at school. Charlie went back to school last Friday, even though he says he's got stomachache too. It's my heart that hurts more. It's so hard feeling sad about losing two people that no one here even knows, and worse than that, that they think you're making it all up.

Friday 28th September 2018

School was actually quite fun this week. I'm going to make a real effort from now on with my schoolwork, because I've realised it's the best way to get over everything that's happened. There are lots of things to look forward to - like the Armistice Day Centenary Celebrations on November 11th - apparently some of the people whose families used to live here and whose relatives from St Kilda served in the war are coming over that day to mark the occasion. Mum has got us all working on a project about the First World War and why it happened and how they managed to end it on Armistice Day. I can't help wondering about World War III and how that will start and what will make it end. I don't think war achieves anything. It just seems to mess everything up and make things worse. I said in class today that it would be far better if instead of going to war, we could think of a way to stop the sea from rising and all the animals from becoming extinct. But Mum just said it was 'besides the point' and that we would be doing a project about climate change and the environment next term. Why don't adults realise they are all connected? It's like they're pretending it's not really happening because it's just too difficult to deal with.

Monday 1st October 2018, St Kilda

Mum says she's booked for Edie and me to go by ferry to the mainland on Friday morning. When we get there, we have to get the train by ourselves from Oban to Glasgow, and someone from Lori's school will be there to meet us. Edie's really nervous but I can't wait.

Friday 5th October 2018, Glasgow

We arrived at 7 o'clock this evening. There are girls here from twenty-two other schools around Scotland. I sat next to a few of them at dinner and they seem nice but a bit talkative – they've all seen the latest films and know lots more about pop music than Edie and me. Some of the girls had been to some really exotic places on holiday this summer like Turkey, Disneyland and the Maldives. When it was our turn to introduce ourselves, I really wanted to say that I'd been all over the world, that I'd been to London once in 1851, that I'd visited a real rainforest in 2118, and that I'd cuddled pandas in Hong Kong in 2077, but of course I couldn't, so I just said 'My name is Alice, I come from St Kilda, the furthest-away islands in Scotland, and I have a pet parrot called Spix'.

After dinner, we were allowed to buy sweets in the tuck shop and then we were taken back to our dorms. I saw Lori in the corridor, but she more or less ignored me. I was probably wearing something she didn't approve of. The other girls all arrived in school uniform but as we don't have uniform at our school, I wanted to wear jeans and my flowery wellies like I usually do, but Mum said we needed to look a bit smart, so I ended up wearing my stripy rainbow fleece with a boring brown skirt, socks and trainers.

I'm sharing a room with Edie and this other girl called Lucy. She's from Edinburgh. I asked her if there were pandas at Edinburgh Zoo these days. I was going to ask her something else but Edie gave me this look that said 'don't say anything weird or I'll kill you', so I changed the subject.

The really cool thing is, we are having an English lesson tomorrow and it's going to be about *The Time Machine* by H.G. Wells – the teachers gave us each a very scruffy copy of the book after dinner and said we had to read up to chapter three before tomorrow morning. I wish Donald was here too – that's his favourite book!

Saturday 6th October 2018, Glasgow

It feels funny being at school at a weekend. Instead of wandering down to the beach after breakfast with Spex like I often do on a Saturday, I had to sit in a massive classroom and answer mental maths questions. After that the English teacher took us for a lesson. She got us to read bits of *The Time Machine* out loud in turn. My bit had this sentence:

'I am afraid I cannot convey the peculiar sensations of time travelling, they are excessively unpleasant.'

It made me wonder if H.G. Wells had been inside a C-Bean Mark 4. The teacher talked about other writers who have written books about time travel and then she told us we had to write a short story about what we thought it would feel like. I thought to myself, that shouldn't be too hard! But the thing is, I didn't have enough time to finish my story because there was so much to say. The teacher picked me to read mine out because she'd noticed I'd written quite a lot, and the other girls all stared when I started describing the Dead Zone, the Biome, and especially all the stuff about how the C-Bean works. Edie went bright red when I was reading, probably because she was petrified I was going to bring her into the story at any moment.

After lunch we had some free time and some of the prefects took us into the centre of Glasgow on the bus. Edie and I were put in Lori's group, which I wasn't too keen on, mainly because she acts so weird when her friends are there. But she did let us do some fun things, like have a milkshake in an Italian café a bit like the one we went to in New York with Dr Foster. She also let us look round a funny little curio shop that was all dark inside and sold a lot of musty old things like stuffed birds and animals in glass domes, collections of coins and medals and bits of rock.

Lori whispered in my ear 'See that creepy guy over there – that's who bought the gold nugget Alice.' I got a bit of a shock when I realised the person she was talking about looked exactly like Dr Foster. Seeing his face brought back the sharp pains in my stomach, but I managed to duck behind a bookcase before he saw me. It was probably another of Hadron's cyborgs, but unless I got up close enough to see if he was wearing an identity bracelet, I couldn't be sure. Then it suddenly occurred to me it could be the real Dr Foster and that he'd come looking for James, not realising he died in July. All I knew was that I had to get out of the shop.

Alice and Edie were getting ready for bed in their dormitory. Their roommate Lucy was in the bathroom and Alice sat on her bed holding her toothbrush and towel, waiting her turn. Her stomachache had got a lot worse.

'It's been quite fun, but I'll be glad to get back to St Kilda,' Edie said as she folded her clothes and put them in her suitcase.

'Me too. I don't know what I've eaten today but I feel really ill,' Alice admitted.

By the time the prefects came round to tell them it was lights out, Alice was doubled up in agony on the bathroom floor. Someone went to fetch Lori, who stood over her sister with her hands on her hips, saying 'Come on Alice, pull yourself together.'

But Alice just writhed with pain. In the end, they called the night Warden and she sent for an ambulance.

Lori and Mrs Blythe, the Warden went with her to the hospital, and while Alice was being admitted to the children's ward Lori used Mrs Blythe's mobile phone to call her parents.

As soon as a doctor examined her, Alice was taken into the operating theatre. One of the nurses told Lori to wait outside and that her sister was being treated for suspected appendicitis. Lori frowned and wondered if she should say anything to Mrs Blythe. Something didn't add up: her parents said on the phone that Charlie was also ill, doubled up with stomach pain, and when they asked Lori to describe Alice's symptoms, they decided to tell the Cheungs to call for an air ambulance to send Charlie to Glasgow Hospital too. Her parents had said Charlie and Alice had both been up to something, something to do with that C-Bean again. Whatever it was, Lori knew there was no way they could both have simultaneously developed appendicitis. It just didn't seem possible.

When Alice came round, she found herself lying in a hospital bed surrounded by her parents, her sister and her baby brother and Charlie was in the next bed with his parents.

'What's going on?' she asked restlessly.

'Just relax, darling. We're right here – Dad and I are staying overnight with Kit in a hotel near the hospital. The doctors say it's not appendicitis after all, but they're working hard to try to work out what's the matter with you both,' Alice's mother replied, her face drawn and pale.

'They found traces of something unusual in your blood, Alice. They wanted to know if you'd been travelling somewhere exotic recently,' whispered her father, adding in an even quieter voice, 'whatever it is, Charlie's blood tests showed up the same thing. You also both have something very strange on your arms, some kind of metal insert. Is there something you haven't told us Alice?'

Alice sighed wearily, lay back on her pillow and closed her eyes. She thought of all the exotic places they'd been to recently that her parents had no idea about and all the things they'd eaten and drunk: the weird banquet at Øbsidon HQ in Hong Kong in 2077, not to mention the disgusting food rations, dirty tap water and soup they'd had on St Kilda in 2118. Any one of them could have given them some deadly virus, and judging by the weather they'd encountered in the future, even the air they'd breathed could have caused their mystery illness. They could easily have been infected by the water in the Dead Zone, or when their bioports were fitted, or poisoned by the swarm of mutant mosquitoes or, for that matter, by the drug Dr Foster had put in their tea to stop them getting malaria. Then Alice remembered James' antidote to combat the effects of travelling back in time. Could it have been that? But before she could even begin to answer her own questions, Alice fell asleep.

She seemed to be drifting along an endless corridor. All the doors had windows and were labeled with different dates and there were people inside each room. She peered through the windows one by one as she went past and saw Lady Grange reunited with her family, Dora Ferguson with Donald, Elsa and baby James in her arms, Karla as a little red-haired girl playing a game with Kit, and Rudy with his mother and father and little sister sitting round a table eating bowls of rice. She tried to get inside the rooms but the doors were all locked. In the last room she saw a family gathered round a hospital bed. When she turned the handle, she found this door was not locked and she went inside the room. The little boy and his older sister turned to see who it was as she entered. She opened her mouth to speak but no words came out. 'Come and say goodbye to Mum, Alice,' Lori said to her and the boy pulled her towards the figure lying in the bed. 'Is that Alice, Kit? Is she here now?' The mother said softly. The little boy nodded. 'Have you got a seabean to give to Alice too?' he asked.

Someone was gripping Alice's arm. She opened her eyes. It was dark in the ward and he was standing over her, his face sweaty and his body shaking. At first she thought she was the mother lying in the hospital bed. She was sure she was in a hospital. But the boy leaning over her was not Kit. It was Charlie.

'Alice, listen, I've looked at our notes – you know the clipboard at the end of our beds – it says we've got acute blood poisoning from unknown contaminants. It doesn't look good. We have to do something tonight or I think we're going to die!' his voice sounded strange and high-pitched.

'Charlie, relax, the doctors are doing what they can, my parents said so,' Alice assured him, but she could feel a rising tide of panic inside her as the pain in her stomach started to return. The dream had disturbed her and the painkillers she'd been given at bedtime must have worn off.

'Look, I brought the C-Bean's cardkey with me just in case. I think we should use it. If we go back in time to the day before we time-travelled to Liverpool in the C-Bean, whatever it was that's made us ill won't have happened.'

'Nor will a lot of other important things, Charlie. Let's not react too quickly. I need to think about this.' She paused. They were both breathing a short, shallow gasps.

Alice cast her mind back to the start of term, the day they got back to St Kilda and she'd decided to make the time capsule. It was, she realised with a shock, only six weeks ago. So much had happened since then. It seemed so ironic that they had been the ones who found the time capsule a hundred years later, not some archaeologist like Charlie thought. If Donald had left a time capsule in the same cave under the gun a hundred years ago back in 1918, Alice realised they might have found that one too in 2018 when the Sams discovered the cave. Even Lady Grange herself was a sort of time capsule, imprisoned on the island in the eighteenth century until Alice found her and brought her back to 2018. Looking back, the first aid kit they'd left on St Kilda for the dying babies and the food hamper for the starving villagers in 1851 were a kind of reverse time capsule, left in the past by people from the future, to help solve their problems or the unforeseen outcomes they were causing.

But how could they go back in time and solve their own problems? What should they leave in the past to help things turn out right? If, as Charlie suggested, they used the C-Bean to go back to a time before the sleepover, they would avoid being abducted to 2118. Better still, if they used the C-Bean to go back to the morning of Alice's birthday in January, when the black cube first arrived on the beach, and then just ignored it altogether, they wouldn't get into any of the difficulties they'd experienced.

But Alice had this nagging feeling in the back of her mind. The very thought of rewinding events like that made her realise the experiences she'd had because of the C-Bean were more important to her than anything else. Even the really awful tragic things they'd had to deal with because of meeting Karla, Donald, James, Dr Foster and Rudy, were part of her own life now.

'Remember what you said to me the night Karla told us that Kit was her dad, Charlie?'

'What did I say?'

'You said we should use what we know about the future to make things less bad.'

'Sort of, why?'

'Well I'm ready to do something about it now,' Alice said slowly.

'Good. Let's go back to St Kilda the day we were due to leave for Liverpool, and actually go on the ferry this time.'

'That's the thing, Charlie. I'm not ready to wipe everything that's happened from our existence – I mean from our memories – by going right back to before any of it happened. That would make us cowards.'

'OK. So what *do* we do?' Charlie demanded.

'Let's at least try to pinpoint what's made us sick. If Edie and Hannah are OK it can't have been something we were exposed to in Brazil, or when we were imprisoned in the C-Bean in Hadron's compound. So it must have been after that.'

'Reckon it was the dodgy tap water? Or that packet of soup mix you cooked? Our bioports?'

'Edie has one too, remember?'

'What about James' antidote – do you think it could have been that?'

'The antidote … you've just given me an idea, Charlie.'

Lost in thought, Alice climbed out of bed and stood up, panting and grimacing with pain. Her legs felt weak and jelly-like, but her mind was made up.

'Charlie, where's the C-Bean's cardkey? I know the answer.'

The two children crept out of the ward and into the day room at the end, where they pulled the curtains across so that no one could see them from the nurse's station. Alice shoved a couple of armchairs out of the way, to clear a space in the middle of the room that was big enough for the C-Bean to fit into. It left her feeling dizzier and more wobbly than ever. She sat down on the one of the chairs to get her breath back before summoning the black cube, and when it appeared it only just fitted – the top of it was practically touching the suspended ceiling. They stepped inside, once again wearing their pyjamas, and Charlie looked quizzically at Alice.

'OK, so what's the plan?' he asked.

'Remember in May when Karla and I did a factory reset on the C-Bean and we accidentally went back to 1918?'

'Yep.'

'Well, I don't think I ever told you but we went on a little school trip with Dora and Donald to the Great Exhibition in 1851.'

'You did what?'

'It was Donald's idea – he just wanted to time travel somewhere for real and that's what they'd just been learning about in history.'

'And?'

'We arrived in this massive glass building in the middle of Hyde Park in London. I remember wondering what the Victorians would make of our futuristic C-Bean, but I used the invisible command for the first time, so until it started wearing off, no one could actually see it.'

'Alice, can you please get to the point – we haven't got time for a long-winded story!'

'OK, be patient, I'm getting to it. What if we go back there now, but this time with a whole bunch of things that are visible? Whatever we take with us, the Victorians will assume they're amazing modern inventions from somewhere or other – the whole place was full of them. But in actual fact, our C-Bean would be a sort of time capsule, delivering on a plate to people in 1851 all the knowhow from the future that would mean they never have to burn fossil fuels to make their factories and their vehicles run, because they would have the technology to get all the energy they need from the wind or the waves or the sun. Think about it, Charlie – it'd be the best antidote ever!' Alice's face was flushed with excitement.

'Maybe your parents are right after all – you have gone bonkers!'

'I'm not bonkers Charlie. This is the way we can use what we know about the future, just like you said. This is how we can change everything. If we give the Victorians enough information – show them what our dads already know – that it's cheaper and cleaner to use things like wave power instead of burning coal and oil – the ice won't melt, the sea won't rise, the animals won't die, get the picture? There'll be no need for either Plan A or Plan B – that'll mean no need for Operation Seabean whatsoever!'

Alice paused for breath, her eyes shining.

'I suppose it could work,' Charlie admitted.

'It *will* work – all the damage to the earth's atmosphere was done after 1851, Dad told me. You never know, it might even prevent wars from happening.'

Charlie sighed and slumped onto the floor.

'But what can the two of us do in the state we're in?'

'You're right, we need help. Let me think …'

Alice appeared to be lost in thought. But the C-Bean produced a map showing the layout of the Great Exhibition indicating a suitable space to set up their exhibit in 1851 without obstructing the red carpet walkway. It said the whole exhibition was due to close on the 11th October, but one or two of the Russian exhibitors had already vacated their spaces, so it chose one of their empty stands. Then it produced detailed 3D scale models of the latest solar panels, wave energy machines and wind turbines in large recesses around its walls. Alice clapped her hands with delight at these miniature worlds: there was a wind farm installed on a mountainside, a hydro-electric plant like a mini Niagara falls, a solar energy farm in a desert, and of course, a model of the Evaw wave energy device their own fathers had built in the sea west of St Kilda. Before long they could hardly move in the C-Bean because it was so full of exhibits. Alice looked at her watch – it was four o'clock in the morning. She was aching all over with the effort of it all and her stomach ache felt like a knife slicing through her.

'Nice work, Alice, but how ever are we going to get all of this stuff to London? I'm really not feeling great.'

'Me neither, Charlie,' Alice said weakly.

'Maybe we should just call it quits.'

'Wait, I know who could help us: Kit.'

'What? Where on earth are we going to find him? There's no way I'm going back to Øbsidon.'

'We don't have to go there. He's right here in this hospital by my mother's bedside, in 2029.'

The C-Bean didn't seem to need any further instruction. The models all shunted slightly from side to side and then came to a standstill. They appeared to have timeshifted.

'Wait here, Charlie, I'll be back.'

Alice stepped out of the C-Bean into the day room. She peeped round the curtain and saw the children's ward was still in darkness. As she passed her bed, she could see there was another child asleep there. So far, so good. The nurses' station was in a different place and there were no staff working there except for a strange white robot filing paperwork. She managed to avoid attracting the robot's attention and slipped out of the ward into the main corridor. A little unsteady on her feet, Alice walked back to the reception desk and asked the night porter if he could look something up on the computer system for her.

The night porter scratched his head, peered at Alice and frowned.

'What are you doing down here young lady? It's the middle of the night.'

'I know, but I sleepwalk and now I can't remember where my bed or my ward is. Please help me – my name's Jennifer Robertson.'

He chuckled to himself and tapped in the name on his keyboard.

'Ward sixteen, first floor, bed nine. Down the corridor, take the lift up one floor, turn right.'

'By the way, what's tomorrow's date?'

'Sixth of October 2029, now off you go.'

'Thank you,' Alice called, hurrying back along the main corridor.

When she reached Ward 16, there was a row of seats outside the double doors. Her stomachache was really starting to trouble her now, and she sat down to rest for a moment in one of the seats. Just as she was about to gather her strength and enter the ward to look for her family, the double doors swung open and a boy with red hair and freckles came out.

'Kit?'

The boy glanced in her direction with a sorrowful expression on his face. He was clutching something in his hand.

'Who are you?'

'May I see the seabean?'

The boy looked surprised, and opened his palm to reveal a shiny round seed.

'Did your Mum just give it to you?' He nodded, welling up.

'She's very sick isn't she?'

He nodded again.

'What would you say if I told you I know a way to help her survive?'

'It's too late, the doctors said.'

'Kit, it's not too late, come with me,' Alice urged, taking his hand. He was exactly the same size as her.

'But Lori told me to wait here.'

'It won't take long, I promise. But I need your help.'

'OK.'

And with that, the two eleven-year-old children walked in silence back to the ward where Alice had left the C-Bean.

Alice's Blog

7th October 2018

When we got back to the day room, I told Kit to stand in front of the curtain. But before I pulled it aside, he turned to me with a very solemn look on his freckly face and whispered 'You're my sister right? You came in the C-Bean, didn't you? Is that what's behind the curtain Alice?' I was completely dumbstruck. Kit had somehow worked out who I was and how I'd got there.

'You don't have to explain. You used to tell me stories about the C-Bean all the time when I was little. You told me I had to keep them a secret because no one else knew about it. Mum just used to laugh and said you had a very vivid imagination, but I knew somehow it was all true. I just never thought I'd get to see it with my own eyes,' he said simply.

I pulled back the curtain then, and Kit walked round and round the C-Bean, just like I did when I first found it on the beach. He left a trail of little blue handprints all over the black exterior until finally he found the door.

'Make it open, Alice,' he whispered, holding his breath.

Moments later me, my brother and my best friend, stepped out of the C-Bean into the Great Exhibition in Hyde Park. As soon as I caught sight of the huge glass roof and the elm trees, I knew we were in the right place, even though it was the middle of the night and the whole place was completely deserted.

I asked the C-Bean for three torches but it went one better and produced the kind of torches you wear on your head like a miner. We pulled the stretchy bands around our heads and adjusted the beam of light so that they shone out in front of us. Then we started to carry or drag all the exhibits out of the C-Bean and arrange them on the empty stand left by the Russians. I found a ladder leaning against one of the iron columns and Kit climbed up, took down their old sign and put ours up instead. It read:

'ENERGY OF THE FUTURE:
COME AND SEE HOW WIND, SUN, WAVES AND WATER
CAN PROVIDE ALL THE POWER WE WILL EVER NEED'

It didn't take Kit long to realise that Charlie and I were very ill. He ended up doing most of the work, poor boy, lugging the models into place. Once everything was arranged just how I'd imagined it, the C-Bean seemed to take over and add some finishing touches of its own. We all watched in amazement as a vivid stream of holograms started to flow out of the C-Bean and, one by one, brought all the 3D models to life. I think the C-Bean wanted to make sure the Victorian visitors understood exactly how each invention worked. It transformed our modest exhibition with real clouds, rainstorms, waterfalls and ocean waves. There was even a miniature sun above it all casting warm golden rays on the models below. It was definitely the C-Bean's finest moment!

The effort of producing these special effects seemed to have exhausted the C-Bean too, because its outer surface started pulsating with weird patterns, then it started flipping from black to gold and back again. A strange countdown sequence started, and the C-Bean remained golden, shimmering and luminous as if it was lit from within.

That was the moment I panicked, because I remembered the last time it did that - just after we arrived in Liverpool - the C-Bean vanished! I shouted to Kit and Charlie to get back inside but I don't remember anything after that. I must have blacked out.

I still have no idea how my brother managed to control the C-Bean. He must have somehow issued a command to take him back to 2029, and then send Charlie and me to the same hospital but in 2018. Maybe the C-Bean realised he was my brother and that I was too ill to control it myself any more. Anyway, it doesn't matter, I'm just happy that Kit is going to grow up with the memory of what we did that night.

When Alice woke she found herself lying in her bed in the dormitory. She sat up quickly and looked over at Edie and Lucy still asleep in the beds next to her. She felt very confused. Why wasn't she still in hospital with Charlie next to her? Had she somehow recovered overnight and been brought back to the school? She was relieved to discover her stomach ache had gone. She rolled up her sleeve. The bioport had gone too. In fact it looked like it had never been there.

Alice had a tiny feeling of dread when she reached under her pillow for the notebook where she'd been drafting her blog entries. It was still there. She sat up in bed, turned on her bedside light and started to flick through the pages. She'd written in it the evening before, but had said nothing about being rushed to hospital, nothing about going back to 1851 in the C-Bean with Kit and Charlie. She turned back a few pages to read the earlier entries, only to find there was no mention of James Ferguson or Rachel and their escape from the biome, and nothing at all about Commander Hadron or Dr Foster. She was even more shocked to find she hadn't said a single thing about Karla or Rudy and their terrible deaths. But most importantly, she seemed to have written nothing whatsoever about the C-Bean.

Alice flicked all the way back to the start of the book, which was dated 1st August, expecting to find an account of the house fire and their trip to Liverpool at least, maybe even something about her plans to bury a time capsule. But instead, the notebook contained one long, boring account of everything they'd been doing at school since the start of term. About three pages in she'd commented how she still felt sad about Old Jim passing away in July, and on another about how she longed for a dog. Apart from that, even though she knew it was her own handwriting, Alice could hardly recognise her own life as depicted in the notebook.

It was hard to take it all in. Why was there nothing recorded there about all the hundreds of things she could remember as having happened when the events were all still so vivid in her mind, especially of last night? Could it be that the only thing that hadn't disappeared were her own memories? Alice gulped. This feeling of having your head messed with was worse than the feeling of your insides being rearranged in the C-Bean Mark 4. What if she was the only one that could remember anything now about the C-Bean?

'Morning,' Edie said sleepily from the next bed, 'are you still reading that rubbish Time Machine book Alice?'

'So we did at least do that ...' Alice murmured slowly, turning to look at her friend. 'Edie did I read out a story yesterday in class about a time travel device called a C-Bean?'

'No, why?'

'Nothing.'

*E*verything was different. Or back to normal, depending how Alice looked at it. Either way, life had taken some getting used to when she returned to St Kilda after her trip to Glasgow. Her parents had commented that she seemed more thoughtful and mature afterwards, and decided the experience had obviously been good for her. But Alice simply had a lot on her mind.

Her parents were still the same people, and she still had a little brother called Kit and a big sister called Lori, there were still six children in her class and her mum was still their teacher. But that's about where the similarities to her other life ended. As far as everyone on the island was concerned, no one, not even Charlie or Edie, had ever heard of something called a C-Bean, they'd never met Lady Grange, Dr Foster or Karla Ingermann, and they couldn't recall there ever being a dog called Spex or a parrot called Spix on St Kilda. Even the reason the Robertsons were living there was different – Alice's dad was in charge of renewable energy across the whole of Scotland, and managed a hundred different solar, wave, wind and hydro-electric power plants by satellite from his office.

Every now and again, especially on misty days, Alice felt sure she caught a glimpse of the black edges of the C-Bean appearing in the distance. But whenever she ran towards it, there was nothing there. One day she found what she thought was Dr Foster's fluorescent string from his penknife. She showed it to Charlie but it meant nothing to him. She must have asked Charlie a hundred times where he put the Mark 3 cardkey but he always said, 'Alice I keep telling you: I don't know what you're talking about.'

Over the years Alice stopped asking questions, and even her memories of the C-Bean and everything that had happened seemed to fade.

One sunny December morning just after Christmas in 2030, Alice was walking along the beach on St Kilda with her family. Kit and her dad were up ahead scouring the tideline beside the crystal clear water for interesting shells and rocks, while Alice and Lori walked arm in arm with their mother.

Alice saw Kit pick something up, show it to his father and then come running towards them, his red hair blowing across his face in the wind.

'Look what I've found Alice, it's just like one of your stories!' In his palm was a thin, flat, black rectangle of metal the size of a credit card.

Alice's heart skipped a beat as she turned it over. On the reverse were the familiar raised letters and the spinning globe logo. She smiled and gave it back to her brother.

'You keep it, Kit. You never know, one day you might need it.' The twelve year old boy tucked the cardkey in his pocket and ran back to his father. Alice sighed and stared out into Village Bay, watching the sunlight sparkling off the sea.

'Mum, do you remember the Christmas I got a seabean in my stocking?' Alice asked.

'Yes, I do. In fact I still have it: didn't you give it to me as a good luck present just before Kit was born? I've no idea what you were so worried about – he turned out just fine!'

They walked back home through the little group of Scots pines on the foreshore. Someone had dug a deep round hole at the edge of the path.

'That must be where we're planting the next tree on New Year's Day,' Lori remarked.

'I forget how beautiful St Kilda is when I'm working in Edinburgh. Why did we come to live here, Mum? Alice asked casually.

'Years before you were born Alice, your Dad read about this amazing place, a world heritage site on a beautiful island with a unique sustainable community that was miles and miles from anywhere. It sounded wonderful. Then, when Lori was about four and you were still a baby, your Dad heard that one of the cottages here had come available. When we arrived, we were greeted by this kind old man who turned out to be Old Jim. Before we'd even introduced ourselves, he took you in his arms and said 'Welcome home, little Alice' and that's the moment I knew it was the right thing to do – coming to live here. It was as if Jim had met you before in another life and remembered you.'

10102118

Would the defendant please stand.

KROB2018, your status as aTS50 does not affect your statutory rights. You are under oath.

Let the record state that you are charged with three counts: with perverting the statutory course of time and conspiring to interfere in third dimensional reality using the C-Bean's emergent fifth dimensional technology; with colluding with your co-defendant, to traffic animal, vegetable and human species from the past in order to populate the illegally-built Øbsidon biome and thereby profit from product lines which you sought to reverse engineer from the samples you had abducted as part of your 'Plan B'; and thirdly, illegally tampering with the DNA of many subjects, ultimately leading to the manslaughter of your own daughter KROB2090 and of the individual referred to in the casenotes as 'Rudy'.

You are required by law to answer to each of these charges in turn and to account for your actions.

In response to the charges brought against me, I wish to provide the court with a full account of the events leading up to the planned arrival of the C-Bean Mark 3 and the field agent known as Dr Foster, at the remote location referred to in the evidence as the island of St Kilda, on 18/01/2018.

I am aware that what I am about to set out in this deposition will only make matters worse, but given what has transpired since the start of Plan B, not least the death of a valued member of my staff, it is paramount that I now divulge the truth. I am in any case, as you state, under oath.

Firstly, I will confirm that it was my decision to deploy the C-Bean Mark 3 when we did, as well as to perform the later upgrade to the C-Bean Mark 4, even though I was aware of the issues regarding the legality of time travel protocols. Circumstances meant that I had no other choice.

Everything was arranged in minute detail to ensure good integration with the prevailing 3D reality in 2018. The choice of the obscure location of St Kilda was important to its success. But more important was the involvement of the minor AROB2007 known as Alice Robertson, aged 11 on the day of its arrival, who had been covertly vetted over a period of two years prior to the mission to verify that she had the best genetic, cognitive and personality profile to serve as the C-Bean Mark 3's system administrator. Thus it was a unanimous decision to make her the first to encounter the device upon its arrival on St Kilda.

We planned that AROB2007 would find the C-Bean Mark 3 on the beach unaided, and, in a natural and intuitive manner, would gradually learn how to access, interact with and gain control over the device.

Under the guise of being an experimental new teaching resource for the children of St Kilda, the mission was devised to appear to the islanders to have been provided by an anonymous donor, and as such we were able to minimise any suspicion that the C-Bean Mark 3 was some kind of surveillance technology. We worked hard to ensure that neither parents nor educators would have any cause for concern, since its memory would be well-stocked with age-appropriate, engagingly dynamic and responsive educational media. In particular, any data gathering that the C-Bean was programmed to carry out would run in the background, with virtually no threat of user awareness or interference.

The insertion of the cyborg AFOS21XV, whom we characterised as a suitably qualified middle-grade teacher from New York for the benefit of the Hebridean School Board responsible for hiring a temporary replacement for Alice's mother, Jen Robertson, was timed to coincide with the arrival of the device, but not in such a way that the two could be in any way connected. The cyborg was programmed to give a surprised reaction to the arrival of the C-Bean Mark 3, and to display a gradual 'discovery' of its latent capabilities, as part of the deliberate deception. The cyborg's role was simply to facilitate and assist during the early stages of the mission. A premise was then to be introduced that would bring about its withdrawal from the scene.

Whilst things went almost seamlessly up to that point, the events that unfolded afterwards were most unfortunate, and you must understand that we had no choice but to intervene in order to bring the mission back on track. Any psychological trauma or bodily harm caused to the children as a result of their experiences in the C-Bean Mark 3 were minimised by the scene-setting and coding protocols we put in place during its development phase. The C-Bean Mark 3 is more than a time travel device: it is more accurately classified as a tesseract which operates within a complex five dimensional space-time paradigm, unknown to – or at least poorly understood by – human beings in 2018. Its true potential could therefore only be partially recognised by its system administrator, and as you will see from the blog posts which Alice wrote and uploaded voluntarily during the course of 2018, there is very little to suggest that she was adversely affected or manipulated by her early interactions with the device. In fact quite the opposite; she appeared to enjoy her initial engagement with it very much. I take great pride in this particular indicator of success, as indeed I do with the success my sister and I were able to achieve at the Great Exhibition in wiping out the use of fossil fuels in the twentieth century, and with the consequent emergence of free energy in that timeline …

I apologise, sir, I digress. It was only as the mission progressed that certain unforeseen consequences arose, due to the system administrator deviating from her 'script', and that was when, despite several attempts to intervene and rectify the situation, things started to go badly off track. Nevertheless, I still maintain that the research and development period for the C-Bean Mark 3 was conducted thoroughly and to rigorous standards, even though its upgrade from the Mark 2 was considered fringe technology. My boss and mentor, Dr Foster, incorporated many special features into its operational and material specification, while simultaneously trying to minimise their detection by conventional means in 2018. As such, the device is thermochromic, resistant to water, self-organising, exerts a strong electro-magnetic field of its own, and, most importantly, is coated in Øbsidon, a nano-meteoritic cloaking technology that means it cannot be located or tracked by sonar, radar or GPS, which were the main navigational systems in use in 2018. Whilst this might seem impressive, it was in fact merely harnessing breakthrough technologies derived from my research work conducted at CERN over a century ago. The reason Foster wanted me to work for him after I left the El Dorado facility was to gain access to this technology.

Owing to a non-disclosure agreement I signed when I first began working on the C-Bean project, I am not at liberty to divulge the patented material used in its construction, namely the extra-terrestrial coating material Øbsidon, but I want to make it clear that despite being exo-terrestrial in design, it too conformed to current safety standards at the time of its initial deployment.

I should also add, for the record, that at the time of his death, Foster was a determined 'catastrophist', that is to say he was firmly of the opinion that climate change on our planet has only been exacerbated by the actions of its resident population over the last hundred years, and that the real impetus for the huge increase in atmospheric and oceanic temperature, in flooding and hurricanes, volcanoes and earthquakes that began to be noticed by scientists towards the end of the twentieth century, is primarily due to forces external to our solar system, most likely highly-charged plasma, proton streams and cosmic rays emanating from the galactic centre. But I digress again ...

To get back to the counts brought against me, I admit that implementing the reverse time travel protocol was at the time illegal.

That said, for reasons that will become clear, whilst some timelines were admittedly affected, no life was endangered in the initial phase of Plan B, particularly since our first field agent, AFOS21XV, was a cyborg specially adapted for the purpose of travelling back in time. It was only when the mission went into Abort mode that we were forced to deploy a human agent, KROB2090. Whilst ideally suited genetically, sadly as a result of my actions, she subsequently died (along with Rudy) in Hong Kong at the hands of a rogue gang who had intercepted that particular timeline. This is regrettable, and I will suffer the loss of my daughter Karla and the consequences of my decision for the rest of my life …

PAUSES

Sir, could I please have a glass of water?

You may. Let the record state that the Defendant KROB2018, who calls himself Commander Hadron, made an initial Statement lasting 5 minutes. Court adjourned until tomorrow morning.